DARK MAN

THE DARK DREAMS

by Peter Lancett

illustrated by Jan Pedroietta

SADDLEBACK
EDUCATIONAL PUBLISHING

DARK MAN

Danger in the Dark
The Dark Dreams
The Dark Glass
The Dark Side of Magic
The Dark Waters of Time
The Shadow in the Dark

© Ransom Publishing Ltd. 2007

Texts © Peter Lancett 2007

Illustrations © Jan Pedroietta 2007

David Strachan, The Old Man and The Shadow Masters appear
by kind permission of Peter Lancett

This edition is published by arrangement with Ransom Publishing Ltd.

SADDLEBACK
EDUCATIONAL PUBLISHING
www.sdlback.com

© 2010 by Saddleback Educational Publishing

ISBN-13: 978-1-61651-017-6
ISBN-10: 1-61651-017-X

Printed in Guangzhou, China
1110/11-03-10

15 14 13 12 11 2 3 4 5 6 7

Chapter One:
The Old Man's Home

The Dark Man is in the good part of the city.

He is at the home of the Old Man.

The Dark Man is weary and sits back in a chair.

"How long must I live like this?" the Dark Man asks.

The Old Man thinks before he speaks.

"The Shadow Masters will never stop," he says.

Chapter Two:
The Dark Man's Question

"What if they did find the Golden Cup?"
the Dark Man asks.

"Would it be so bad?"

"Close your eyes," the Old Man says softly.

"Sleep."

The Old Man's words have power, so the
Dark Man sleeps.

As he sleeps, he is visited by dreams.

Chapter Three:
The Dark Dreams

He sees the bad part of the city and it is
in flames.

Men and women are crying out.

Some are lying dead in the streets as others burn.

Demons force others to drag a huge wagon.

On the wagon is a vast, stone, evil god.

In dark corners, looking at this world they have made, are Shadow Masters.

Then the Dark Man sees that this is not the bad part of the city.

It is the good part!

Chapter Four:
The Dark Man's Destiny

He wakes with a scream.

The Old Man has gone.

He lets himself out onto the street.

It is night as he heads back to the bad part of the city.

Now he knows why he cannot ever rest.

THE AUTHOR

photograph: Rachel Ottewill

Peter Lancett used to work in the movies. Then he worked in the city. Now he writes horror stories for a living. "It beats having a proper job," he says.

MICHAEL DRAYTON
AND HIS CIRCLE

LOCKET WITH A MINIATURE OF MICHAEL DRAYTON
ATTRIBUTED TO PETER OLIVER
In the collection of the Duke of Portland at Welbeck Abbey

Below: SIGNATURE OF MICHAEL DRAYTON

Frontispiece

MICHAEL DRAYTON

AND HIS CIRCLE

By BERNARD H. NEWDIGATE

M   D

OXFORD
PUBLISHED FOR THE SHAKESPEARE
HEAD PRESS BY BASIL BLACKWELL
M CM LXI

KATHARINAE TILLOTSON
TAM MICHAELIS NOSTRI
QVAM MVSARVM ANGLICARVM
CVLTRICI ERVDITISSIMAE
NECNON IN STVDIIS DRAITONIANIS
COADIVTRICI INDEFESSAE
DICAVIT
B. H. N.

THE PREFACE

THE PREFACE of a book is like a shop-window, at which the author is free to display some of the goods and especially some of the novelties that are on offer within. Let me draw attention here, therefore, to some of the episodes and aspects of Drayton's life about which I have written in these pages. Although there have been many stimulating studies of his poetry, notably by Arthur Henry Bullen, Harold Child, Cyril Brett and Oliver Elton, little has hitherto been known about his life beyond its barest outlines. I have here filled in some of the detail out of all that the late Professor Hebel, Mrs Tillotson and I have found while working on the Shakespeare Head edition of Drayton's poems, to which this book is supplementary.

Take Drayton's early years. It was known that he was born about the year 1563 at the village of Hartshill, near Atherstone in Warwickshire, probably of yeoman stock; that he studied under a tutor, and that when no more than

> a proper goodly page
> . . . scarce ten years of age

he already felt a call to the service of the Muses:

> O my deare Master, cannot you (quoth I)
> Make me a poet?

that for many years he was in the service of the Gooderes of Polesworth; that Anne, the younger daughter of that house, was the 'Idea' of his early verse. We have been able to add a good deal to these known facts. Research in parish registers and among the wills at Somerset House and in the Lichfield register, unhappily interrupted and left incomplete by the war, has brought to light many names and entries about members of the Drayton family. My chapter on Drayton's schooling, indeed, rests chiefly, but not wholly, on conjecture. From an interesting bit of evidence given by Drayton himself in the course of protracted legal proceedings for the succession to Polesworth, we learn that besides being

the servant of Sir Henry Goodere he was for a while in
the service of Thomas Goodere, Sir Henry's younger
brother, also.[1] Concerning Anne Goodere I have found
little beyond what Drayton wrote about her; but in a
passage hitherto overlooked Shakespeare's son-in-law,
John Hall, the Stratford physician, pays a charming
tribute to her character and attainments. I have tried to
trace the course of our poet's life-long devotion to her as
shown first in the allusions to Idea found in *The Shepheards Garland* and *Ideas Mirrour* and lastly in the verses
which 'weare made by Michaell Drayton Esquier Poett
Laureate the night before hee dyed.'

We know from Drayton himself how a little while
before Sir Henry Goodere's death his old master 'bequeath'd' him to the service of Lucy Harington, then no
more than thirteen years old; how Lucy, married to the
Earl of Bedford, rained her 'sweet golden showers'
upon the poet, who dedicated to her one new poem after
another between 1594 and 1598. Then the dedications
to her suddenly cease. When *Mortimeriados*, dedicated to
Lucy in 1596, was rewritten as *The Barons Wars* in
1602, all allusion to her was removed and the poem was
dedicated to a new patron, the youthful Walter Aston.
In my fifth chapter I enquire how that brilliant lady,
who was Ben Jonson's

> Lucy the bright,
> Than which a nobler heaven itself knows not;

of whom Donne wrote even more profanely—

> Gods masterpiece, . . . divinity—that's you,

calling her also

---

[1] See pp. 33-5. The interrogatories and the answers made to
them by the several witnesses were found at the Record Office by
Professor C. J. Sisson, who kindly allowed Mrs Tillotson and
myself to use them. The interrogatories and Drayton's replies are
printed in full, with a commentary, in K. Tillotson's *Drayton and
the Gooderes*, MLR XXXV, 341-9 (July 1940).

the first good Angell
That ever did in womans shape appear,

came to be cursed by Drayton as 'Selena' in his Eighth
Eglog of 1606:

Let age sit soone and ugly on her brow,
No sheepheards praises living let her have . . .
Nere be her name remembred more in rime.

In another chapter, pointing out the curiously
parallel lines followed by the lives of Drayton and
Shakespeare through a great part of their careers, I
nevertheless question whether there was really such
close friendship between the two Warwickshire poets as
is generally assumed. Without conviction one way or the
other I consider the claim made for Drayton that he may
be the 'Rival poet.' If he be so, then his young patron,
Walter Aston, the grandson of Sir Thomas Lucy of
Charlecote, where he was born, the heir to great pos-
sessions, must be the 'lovely boy' to whom Shakespeare
addressed the greater number of his Sonnets. The case
for Aston is as strong, I think, as for either Southampton
or William Herbert, but that is not saying much. It may
at least stand on record as a wholesome *caveat* against
other more or less plausible conjectures too readily
made on such scanty evidence as we have.

I have also reviewed Drayton's supposed friendship
with Ben Jonson in the conflicting light of Ben's 'conversations' with William Drummond of Hawthornden
and of his 'Vision . . . on the Muses of his Friend.' The
letters that passed between Drayton and Hawthornden
are printed in their order and in full for the first time.[1]

Drayton's circle of friends was wide. It embraced the
chief scholars and antiquaries of his day as well as his
fellow-poets. I have touched on Drayton's relations

[1] I have to thank the Librarian of the National Library of
Scotland and Mr William Park, Assistant Keeper of MSS., for
answers to my enquiries about Drummond's letters and for
permission to have them photographed.

with some of them as disclosed in his own writings and
in the allusions made to him by his contemporaries. Hebel had collected and transcribed a great number of
these and many by later writers.[1] More about some of
Drayton's friends will be found in Mrs Tillotson's
notes in the fifth volume of the Shakespeare Head
edition.

Details of Drayton's work as a playwright in the team
of poets employed by Philip Henslowe for the Admiral's
Company are well-known to us from Henslowe's *Diary*,
so admirably edited by Dr Walter Greg, who has allowed
me to borrow from it freely. Drayton's share in the ill-
starred adventure of the Whitefriars playhouse, however, has hitherto been overlooked by his biographers. I
give an account of it here for the first time.

I have said that this account of Drayton is supplementary to Professor Hebel's edition of Drayton's
Works, the completion of which was interrupted by his
untimely death in February 1934, after the four volumes
containing the text had come from the press. It was
written as an integral part of the fifth volume, which
was planned to contain the poet's Life, as well as introductions, notes, the variant readings, a bibliography
and indexes. The task of writing or editing these fell to
Mrs Tillotson and myself, to whom Mrs Hebel sent the
material which Hebel had gathered. The largest and
perhaps the most valuable part of that material was the
collection of variant readings, which with resolute and
astounding industry he had made from a collation of
the many successive editions of Drayton's work. Since
in his revisions Drayton would change, cancel, rewrite
and add long passages to much of his work, these
variants assume a quite unusual importance; for they
make available a mass of verse not found in Drayton's
definitive text and hitherto quite inaccessible to the

[1] Some that he had overlooked have been transcribed by Russell
Noyes in his unpublished thesis on the *Influence and Reputation of
Michael Drayton*, which he has generously allowed us to use.

student. In the sum they bulk so largely that of themselves they would fill as many pages as the average volume of the Shakespeare Head edition. The significance of these numerous revisions is considered in Mrs Tillotson's introductions and notes, which also embrace a study of Drayton's work in its sources and in relation to Elizabethan poetry as a whole, and an explanation of many of his allusions. When these were added to the variants, the fifth volume threatened to assume proportions far beyond the space allotted to it. It was therefore judged better to print Drayton's life separately than to cut down the valuable material which the three editors had got together. From this separate publication it is hoped that a greater number of readers may become interested in Drayton and his work, and so be drawn to the fuller study of his poetry. My book is meant to be used as a companion to the collected Drayton and should be read with frequent reference to the introductions and notes of the fifth volume as well as to the text of the poems, on which it is a biographical commentary; for the chief material for Drayton's life is to be found in his own works, and in the allusions to it and to the poet himself made by so many of his contemporaries.

The list of those who have furnished or supplemented information conveyed in these pages is a long one. Thanks are due above all others to my colleague, Mrs Tillotson. In the course of our work we have exchanged whatever material bearing upon Drayton or his writings has come the way of either of us. Her many suggestions and her occasional corrections have been of the greatest help and value; but it would be unfair to associate her with some of the conjectures which are submitted in these pages.

Much of the help for which acknowledgment is made in the preface to the fifth volume has been of use in writing this book too, and the thanks there offered by name to those who gave it are here tendered to them anew. Those whose information bears more directly on Drayton's life include representatives of many of the families with which Drayton himself was associated. The late Mr Edward T. Goodyear furnished Hebel and myself with copies or abstracts of many of the documents on which my accounts of the Gooderes are based, and since his death Mrs Goodyear has allowed me to search among the records of his family which he had collected. The late Duke of Bedford and Miss Gladys Scott Thomson answered enquiries which I put to them on events in the life of Lucy, Countess of Bedford, as did Lord Lowther on the kinship of the Lowthers and the Gooderes. Major Cecil Chichester-Constable, M.C.,[1] prepared for me lengthy genealogical notes on the Aston and Sadleir families, and an account of his ancestor, Walter Aston, which I have used in writing my chapter on Drayton's friend and bountiful patron. Lord Bagot allowed me to search among his papers for letters of Sir Edward Aston. Sir Henry Fairfax-Lucy gave me information from the Lucy pedigree, and the Rev. B. Hyland, Vicar of Charlecote, transcribed for me the Lucy-Aston entries in his parish register, which he allowed me to consult. Mrs Rees-Mogg, Lord of the Manor of Clifford Chambers, lent me her copy of the Clifford registers. She gave me much information concerning Anne Rainsford's home after her marriage as well as the photograph, taken before its destruction by fire in March 1918, from which the drawing that faces page 46 has been made. Mrs Clifton, of Clifton Hall, Notts, the home of Lady Penelope Clifton, gave me notes about Clifton Grove, where Drayton saw Lady Penelope in 1613, 'not three months before she died.' I am indebted to the Duke of Portland and Mr Francis Needham, the librarian at Welbeck, for photographs of the Welbeck miniature of Michael Drayton and for per-

---

[1] Major Chichester-Constable rejoined his old regiment, the Royal Warwicks, on the outbreak of the War. After the retreat to Dunkirk he was missing, and it is feared that he was killed.

mission to reproduce it as the frontispiece to this book. Miss M. A. Trye of Hartshill, the late Miss Mary Dormer-Harris, my friend Mr F. C. Smith, the Town Clerk of Coventry, and the Rev. A. T. Corfield, Vicar of Polesworth, have answered enquiries which I put to them about the Drayton and Goodere families and their homes at Hartshill and Polesworth. The Rector of Witherley, the Rev. Canon J. A. Wood, transcribed for me the Drayton entries in his parish register, and the Rev. G. G. Hall, Vicar of Mancetter, allowed me to search for those in the register of that parish, to which both Hartshill and Mancetter used to belong. Mr N. Tayler, the headmaster of Atherstone School, kindly gave me notes on the early history of that school. I have also to thank Dr Ruth Hughey, Dr R. W. Short, Dr R. E. Bennett, Mr I. A. Shapiro, Mr Geoffrey Tillotson, and Mr Percy Simpson for information that they gave me bearing severally on Drayton's relations with Sir Henry Goodere, Lucy Bedford, John Donne, William Browne and Ben Jonson. Mr F. C. Wellstood kindly answered a number of enquiries which I addressed to him at Shakespeare's Birthplace.[1] For Drayton's newly found sonnets to John Weever and the translator of *The Redemption of Time* grateful acknowledgment is made on pages 98–9, 135, where they are printed in a modern book for the first time. My sister Miss Katherine Newdigate transcribed for me some of the Aston papers at the British Museum. She also made the index to this volume. Lastly, I must express my special gratitude to the *doyen* of Draytonians, Professor Oliver Elton, author of *Michael Drayton: A Critical Study*, who has given me constant help and encouragement ever since I first began to study Drayton's life and poetry nearly twenty years ago.

B.H.N.

[1] I must add the names of Miss H. L. E. Garbett, of the William Salt Library, Stafford, who gave me information relating to Staffordshire and the Astons, and the late Mr A. P. H. Wykeham-George, who helped me in some of my research.

THE CONTENTS

THE PREFACE   *page* v
Chap. I. Drayton's Birth and Parentage   1
II. Drayton's Education and Reading   16
III. The Gooderes of Polesworth   25
IV. Anne Goodere   40
V. Lucy Countess of Bedford   56
VI. Early Friends and Patrons   70
VII. Literary Friends 1591–1603   87
VIII. Drayton and the Theatre   101
    I. The Admiral's Company   101
    II. The Whitefriars Playhouse   112
IX. Drayton and King James   124
X. Drayton, Ben Jonson and Shakespeare   136
XI. Walter Aston   146
XII. *Poly-Olbion*   158
XIII. Drummond of Hawthornden   173
XIV. Drayton's Literary Circle 1603–1631   191
XV. Drayton's Later Years   210
XVI. Drayton's Death and Funeral   219
ADDENDA ET CORRIGENDA   225
APPENDIX:
    Conjectural Family Tree of Michael Drayton   226
    Pedigree of Goodere of Polesworth   227
INDEX OF DRAYTON'S POEMS   228
INDEX OF NAMES   229

THE ILLUSTRATIONS

Locket containing a Miniature of Michael Drayton, attributed to Peter Oliver, in the possession of the Duke of Portland   *Frontispiece*
'The Chapel,' Hartshill   *page* 1
The Gateway, Polesworth Abbey   16
Clifford Manor before its Destruction by Fire, March 1918   *to face page* 46
John Hall's Treatment of Michael Drayton, from his *Curationum Libellus* (BM, MS. Egerton 2065)   50

Inscription on the Monument to Sir Henry Rains-
ford   53
John Hall's Treatment of Lady Rainsford, from
his *Curationum Libellus*   54
Receipt by Michael Drayton in Henslowe's Diary
                                            *to face p.*106
Drayton's and Shakespeare's Arms in trick (BM,
MS. Harl. 6140)   151
The Gate-House, Tixall   156
Inscription by Michael Drayton in a Copy of *The
Battaile of Agincourt* presented to Sir Hugh
Willoughby, now in the Victoria and Albert
Museum   207

For a key to the abbreviated titles of Drayton's Poems see the Index of the Poems on page 228. The following abbreviated references also are used in the footnotes:

BH: Camden's Britannia, translated by
   Philemon Holland, 1610
BM: British Museum
Bodl: Bodleian Library
Chambers *ES*: Sir E. K. Chambers,
   Elizabethan Stage
Hist. MSS. Comm.: Historical MSS.
   Commission.
MLN: Modern Language Notes
MLR: Modern Language Review

*PMLA: Proceedings of the Modern
   Language Association of America*
PRO: Public Record Office
RES: Review of English Studies
*SP, SPD, Cal SPD: State Papers,
   SP Domestic, Calendar of SPD*
*STC: Short-Title Catalogue of English
   Books . . . to 1640*
TLS: Times Literary Supplement
VCH: Victoria County History

'THE CHAPEL,' HARTSHILL. DEMOLISHED 1939

CHAPTER I

DRAYTON'S BIRTH AND PARENTAGE

Drayton in the Hundred of *Sparkenhoe*, and in some Deeds cal'd
Fenny Drayton, standing neere *Warwickshire* upon *Watlingstreet*,
. . . gave the name to the Progenitors of that ingenious Poet
Michael Drayton Esquire, my neere Countriman and olde acquaintance; who, though those *Transalpines* account us *Tramontani*, rudè
and barbarous, holding our braines so frozen, dull, and barren,
that they can affoord no invention or conceits; yet may compare
either with their olde *Dante*, *Petrarch*, or *Boccace*, or their *Neoter-
icke Marinella*, *Pignatello*, or *Stigliano*; but why should I goe about
to commend him, whose owne workes and worthinesse have
sufficiently extold to the world.

WILLIAM BURTON, *The Description of Leicester Shire*, 1622.

A GLANCE at the map shows how at one part of
Watling Street the straight course of that ancient
highway forms the boundary line between North-East
Warwickshire and South-West Leicestershire. Burton's
home at Lindley lay a mile or so south-east of Fenny
Drayton; and we must respect the testimony of so good
an antiquary regarding the stock from which Michael
Drayton sprang. But Michael himself was born not in

B

Leicestershire, but in Warwickshire across the border.

My native Country then, which so brave spirits hast bred,
If there be vertue yet remaining in thy earth,
Or any good of thine thou breathd'st into my birth,
    Accept it as thine owne whilst now I sing of thee;
    Of all thy later Brood th'unworthiest though I bee.[1]

On the Warwickshire side of Watling Street, high up on the plateau which flanks the river Anker, stands the little village of Hartshill. It is situated three miles south of the market-town of Atherstone, of which Dugdale writes inaccurately that it 'gave birth to one of our late famous Poets, *scil. Michaell Draiton.*' That Hartshill was Drayton's birthplace we learn from the portrait of our poet engraved by William Hole in 1613, but first used in the folio edition of his collected Poems in 1619.[2] The inscription round the oval is our authority also for the year of Drayton's birth: EFFIGIES MICHAELIS DRAYTON ARMIGERI, POETÆ CLARISS. ÆTAT. SVÆ L. A. CHR. CIↃ.DC.XIII. The Latin quatrain at the foot reveals the name of the hamlet, until then shrouded in obscurity, wherein the author of *The Barons Warres, Englands Heroicall Epistles* and *Poly-Olbion* first saw the light:

Lux Hareshulla tibi (Warwici villa, tenebris,
    Ante tuas Cunas, obsita) Prima fuit.
Arma, Viros, Veneres, Patriam modulamine dixti;
    Te Patriæ resonant Arma, Viri, Veneres.

These lines 'in the vein of Ariosto' are englished as follows in the Life of Drayton which Oldys contributed to *Biographia Britannica:*

HARSHULL, small town, where first your breath you drew,
Till by your birth renown'd was known to few:
Albion, Arms, Legends, Love with fame you crown'd:
Albion, Arms, Legends, Love, your Fame resound.

If Drayton was in his fiftieth year in 1613, he must

---

[1] *Poly-Olbion* XIII, 8–12.
[2] It is shown as the frontispiece to Vol. II.

have been born at some date between 26 March 1563
and 25 March 1564. But on 16 August 1597, in his
depositions in the case *Englebert v. Saunders* quoted
later in this book, his age is said to be 'xxxv yeres or
thereaboutes.'[1] Setting the two records together, we may
put the date of his birth early rather than late in 1563.[2]

In his day Hartshill was in the parish of Mancetter,
which has its historian in Benjamin Bartlett. In his
History of Manceter, published in 1791, he thus describes Hartshill and its site:

> The village is built on the North end of [a] hilly
> plain, forming a rustic square, near the centre of
> which stands an old building (now a cottage) called
> the chapel, which name I find it bore in the reign of
> James I; but when it was used for any religious
> purpose does not appear. . . . From the village the
> grounds fall gently to the river Ankor, which runs
> pleasantly through this manor, directing its course
> from South East to North West. . . . On the further
> or North-east side of the river the grounds gently
> rise again, until the bounds are determined by the
> Watling Street. The hilly part or plain is one large
> and very deep rock, breaking when dug into small
> and very irregular pieces, more fit for the repair of
> the highways than buildings, very great quantities
> having been carried away for some years past for
> that purpose. . . . From this hilly plain is seen a
> most beautiful and fruitful landscape, interspersed
> with a very great number of churches, more than
> forty of which may be seen with the unarmed eye.

Since Bartlett wrote, the Hartshill quarrymen have
bitten even deeper, scarring and searing the great
quartzite mass which the hamlet crowns and which
gave our poet his chosen pastoral name of 'Rowland of

[1] Below, page 33.
[2] The year agrees with Drayton's age as stated on the portrait
in the National Gallery, shown as the frontispiece to Vol. 1.

the Rock.' In the village there were till lately three
cottages for each of which some sort of claim has been
made that Drayton was born there. The best-known
was the little half-timbered cottage which used to stand
on an island in the middle of the village, near the
remains of the village stocks. To the villagers as well
as to Bartlett it was known as the Chapel. Bartlett
shows an engraving of it in a very ruinous state with
the thatched roof falling in; but it survived until its
recent demolition to make a parking place for motor-
cars. Bartlett, who writes at some length on Drayton
and his work, makes no mention of his having been
born either at the Chapel or in any other cottage in the
village. Had any particular cottage been known in his
day as Drayton's birthplace, he would certainly have
put it on record. Even though it may never have been
his home, lovers of Drayton must regret the dis-
appearance of such a feature as the Chapel, which was
standing during his lifetime, and perhaps many
centuries before. Of the other two cottages, either of
which, it is said, may have been the birthplace, one is still
standing at the corner of the road to Atherstone at the north
side of the Green; the other, which has been demolished
for road-widening, until lately faced it on the south.[1]

Of Drayton's parentage we have little exact information. 'He was a butcher's sonne,' wrote Aubrey,[2] who
says just the same about Shakespeare. It is certain that,
like Shakespeare, he sprang from Warwickshire yeoman stock and that most of his kinsfolk on his father's
side were farmers, butchers, tanners or shoemakers.
Many of the name are found in a Court Roll of Atherstone of Edward VI's reign,[3] when Henry Grey, 3rd
Marquis of Dorset—he was father to Lady Jane Grey
—was lord of the Manor:

[1] That on the north is at present occupied by Mr Sutton; that
on the south was occupied by Mr Pratt until its demolition.
[2] *Brief Lives*, ed. Clarke, 1898, Vol. 1, pp. 239–40.
[3] Bartlett, *Hist. of Manceter*, p. 152.

Atherstone, a market-town nine miles from Coventry, standeth in the great highway called Watlyng-street, on the border of the Felden joining to the Woodland . . .

Demayn Lands

Christopher Drayton holdeth at the will of the lord five acres of land at 3¹ [*sic*] 6ᵈ and a barn in the market place at 6ˢ 6ᵈ total xˢ

And among the Customary Tenants with their rents are six of the name: John Drayton (13s. 1d.); Christopher (5s. 11d.); William (10s. 3½d); Hugh (1s. 3d.); Thomas (1s. 3d.); and Robert (1s. 1½d).

John Rampton and Christopher Drayton were joint-masters of the Gild of the Blessed Mary of Atherstone in 1542, when they became bound to Nicholas Ripton in £10 insuring him in possession of two messuages in Much Park Street, Coventry.[1]

The will of Christopher Drayton, described as a butcher, was proved in 1556.[2] That of William, tanner of Atherstone, who is likely to be Christopher's son— we will call him William I to distinguish him from his son, grandson and great-grandson, all of the same Christian name—was proved 7 March 1556–7.[3] There is reason to believe that he was the poet's grandfather. He left to

Syssley my wife the third part of all my goods . . . and my house that I dwell in and my part of the lytle more and his parte of Bratyswast untill my son Wyll'm do come to his full age and then he shall injoye . . . this howse and his parte of brattswast and his parte of lytle moore during his mothers life and after her death the said Wyll'm shall injoye all the whole hymselphe . . . Item I bequeath to my son Thomas Drayton my howse that Kysse dwellyth in.

He left the residue to all his children in equal portions.

[1] Coventry Corporation MSS., Drawer 15 (Hen. 8), Bundle 6.
[2] Elton, *Michael Drayton*, p. 3 n.   [3] Lichfield 86 b.

If his wife should have a posthumous child and it should be a son, he was to have

> all my howsys and lands and meddowes and pastures at Wetherley with all that apperteynith thereunto and if fytt [*sic*] be a wench she shall have the house and yard land and meddow with a close that Robt. Kysse of Wetherley hath.

His wife was to be executrix. 'John Drayton my brother' and Hugh Drayton are also named in the will and in the inventory of goods taken after the testator's death. His son, William II, is probably 'my brother-in-law' on whose behalf John Radforde of Atherstone, tanner, left 20 marks in trust to William Drayton the elder tanner and Thomas Drayton shoemaker

> to be employed to the use of William Drayton my brother-in-law and Katherine his wife concerning the redeeming of the house he now dwelleth in from one Thomas George of Grendon.[1]

For reasons given below it seems likely that this William II is our poet's father. John Radforde's wife was named Cicely, and we may suppose her to have been the daughter of William Drayton I and Syssley his wife. But Radforde mentions also in his will 'William Drayton my son-in-law' (III), and yet another son-in-law, Thomas Drayton, to whom is left the reversion of a moiety of the residue of his estate on Cicely's death. The husbands of three other daughters, married respectively to Thomas Bissell, Richard Bissell and — Kempe of Southam, are mentioned in the will; but he seems to have left no son. In a further bequest he shows how highly he esteemed the family of Drayton, which had furnished him with a wife and two of his daughters with husbands. He leaves

> to William Drayton [III] my son-in-law and the said Thomas Drayton to be employde for ever for the use

[1] P.C.C. Leicester 55.

of the schoole of Atherston £5 and to the poore £5 and to their heirs males if they be of age abilitye and wisdome worthie the disposition of the same . . . and in defaulte thereof to be and remaine to fower of the cheefest Draytons inhabitants in Atherstone being of sufficient abilitie and wisdome and in default . . . to other fower cheefest inhabitants.

The residue was left to Cicely. The witnesses were 'Mr. John Drayton the writer,' Christofer Drayton, John Nutt and Thomas Drayton. The testator signed with his mark.

The wills of Draytons of Mancetter, Atherstone, Tamworth and other neighbouring places but not of Hartshill are found again and again in the Lichfield registry, where their descriptions and inventories show most of them to have been butchers, tanners or farmers. Their names are found in greater numbers still among the baptisms, marriages and burials recorded in the Mancetter register and in that of Witherley on the Leicestershire side of Watling Street, which parish adjoins Fenny Drayton. We have seen that William Drayton I owned property there, which he left to his children. Atherstone like Hartshill was at that time in the parish of Mancetter, and the register, which begins in 1576 by recording the baptism of one Elizabeth, daughter of William Drayton, who is probably our William II, records their names only without showing in which part of the parish they lived. Their mutual relationships, therefore, are hard to trace ; but it is clear that the Draytons were a prolific clan. If Edmund Drayton, son of William, baptised at Mancetter in 1579, is the same Edmund who in 1632 administered the estate of his deceased brother Michael, then John Radforde's brother-in-law William II was Michael's father and Katherine, whose maiden name is unknown, his mother. Michael had another brother Walter 'of Atherstone . . . Butcher,' whose will was

proved at Lichfield 23 June 1625. He left twenty
pounds in the hands of his executors

> for the maintenance of my . . . sonne Christopher
> if he go to the Universitie to be a scholler there or
> otherwise to be placed apprentice to any honest and
> lawful trade.[1]

Walter left legacies to his other six children, Elizabeth More, John, Mary, Abigail, Daniel and Dorothy:

> And I do intreate my loving brother Mr Michaell
> Drayton and Mr Abell our minister to be overseers
> to see my will in all things to be performed.

Accompanying the will is a tuition bond providing for
the education of four of the younger children, who, like
Christopher, were still minors. Walter Drayton is
named in 1621 in the will of Amias Mabell as one of the
trustees for a bequest of £20, half the interest on which
was to be spent on coals for the warming of Atherstone
school and half in buying books for poor scholars.
Mabell had built a fireplace for the school at his own
charges.[2]

An inventory of the goods of William Drayton of
Mancetter deceased was taken on 15 June 1616.[3] This
is likely to have been William II, and also Michael's
father, although we cannot be quite sure, for William,
like Christopher, John, Ralph, Hugh and Edward
were favourite names among the numerous Draytons of
Atherstone. The house in which the inventory was
taken must have been a substantial one, for there was a
Hall, a 'Parlor,' a 'High Chamber,' a Buttery, an
'Yeile house' (ale-house), Kitchen and 'another Parlor.'
William owned three acres of barley, three acres
'arrable,' and meadows. His apparel was valued
at 1^1 10^s, his debts and funeral expenses came to

[1] He matriculated at Exeter College, Oxford, 18 February
1626–7, aged 18. (*Al. Oxon.*)

[2] Bartlett, p. 92.   [3] Lichfield 116.

12^1, and the 'somme totall' of his estate to 41^1 3^s 4^d.

The Mancetter register records baptisms of ten children of William Drayton between April 1576—Elizabeth, the earliest entry in the book—and 1589—Richard. But there is no Walter or Michael among them. It is likely that other children, including perhaps Michael and Walter, were born prior to Elizabeth. Moreover, some of those born at the later dates were certainly children of another William (III)—himself perhaps one of the elder children of William II.

The conditions of Radforde's bequest to Atherstone school were observed to the letter as late as 1617, when there were four Draytons on the governing body—Edward, Ralph, Samuel and Christopher,[1] all of whom except the last are recorded in the register as children of William Drayton. In the Visitation of Warwickshire begun by Thomas May and Gregory King in 1682 we find another William Drayton, who married Mary Grey, elder daughter and later co-heir of Richard Grey of the Inner Temple. Mary had a sister Elizabeth, who was married to one James Martin, M.A. In 1630 Martin revised and published Joshua Sylvester's *Panthea: or, Divine Wishes and Meditations*. In the book is a 'Funerall Pyramid' written by him for his deceased wife with the following statement subjoined:

Erected to the Honor of that rare-vertuous Gentle-Woman (now in Glory) Mrs. Elizabeth Grey, *Daughter to* Richard Grey. *Esquire, and sometime Wife to* J. M. *Master of Arts.* (By her Sister Mistris *Mary Drayton;* allyed to the Prince of English Poesie, Michael Drayton, Esquire) *Interred at Atherston: where she departed this life, calling on the Lord Jesus (to the last) Anno* 1614. Aetat. 24.

Mary's husband, William Drayton IV, died in 1642.

[1] From the minute-book of the school, which dates from 1608 I am indebted to the headmaster, Mr N. Tayler, for the information.

He was perhaps the son of our supposed William III and so may be Michael's nephew. His son Harrington Drayton is described in the Visitation as being 'of the City of London merchant, afterwards of Atherston . . . ob. circa 1670 aet. 68.' And Bartlett records that ' in 1662 Harrington Drayton presented [to the living of Mancetter], whose ancestors either by marriage or purchase enjoyed the said advowson.' Dugdale describes him as 'gent.,' but the Visitation notes that 'No arms [were] exhibited.' Bartlett, who died in 1787, wrote that his descendants were then still living at Atherstone.

John Drayton 'the younger' of Atherstone, who is doubtless 'Mr John Drayton the writer,' that drew up and witnessed John Radforde's will, was another of the poet's kinsmen who attained the rank of gentleman. He is so described in his will dated 7 August 1599 and proved on 2 November following.[1] His parents were then living, and he remembers them in his will as an afterthought, for a clause is added to it below his signature and the names of the witnesses:

> Item I gyve unto my father John Drayton 20^s and my rougged gowne. Item I gyve unto my mother Drayton 10^s.

He left £40 pounds a-piece to his children Horton, Jane, Esther, John, Repentance, Unita and Bridgett. To Hester his wife he left all his lands for life, and the sum of £100. She was to be sole executor and to have the government and bringing up of his son John till he came of age.

It is clear from the records, then, that, although Drayton himself was born at Hartshill, the market-town of Atherstone was the home of most of his kindred and the centre of their business and their life. The hamlet and its immediate neighbourhood had associations with many persons, places and events which

[1] P.C.C. 81 Kidd.

are found in Drayton's verse. It stands within the boundaries of what was once part of the great forest of Arden; but in Drayton's time—and Shakespeare's— was known as the Woodland. The Warwickshire Woodland stretches across the county from the neighbourhood of Stratford-upon-Avon in the south-west to the boundaries of Leicestershire in the north-east; but according to Drayton the forest had at one time been much greater in extent:

Muse, first of *Arden* tell, whose foot-steps yet are found
In her rough wood-lands more then any other ground
That mighty *Arden* held even in her height of pride;
Her one hand touching *Trent*, the other, *Severns* side.[1]

A gloss in the margin at that passage makes mention of 'Divers Towns expressing her name: as *Henly* in *Arden*, *Hampton* in *Arden*, etc.' But except in such Warwickshire place-names the name Arden had passed out of general use[2] like the bounds of the forest itself:

For, when the world found out the fitnesse of my soyle
The gripple wretch began immediatly to spoyle
My tall and goodly woods, and did my grounds inclose:
By which, in little time my bounds I came to lose.[3]

No other part of England is so closely linked with Drayton's life and poetry.

Hartshill stands above the river Anker, which is named again and again in Drayton's verse; for lower down its course is Polesworth, the early home of Anne Goodere, his 'Idea':

Cleere *Ankor*, on whose silver-sanded shore,
My soule-shrinde Saint, my faire *Idea* lyes:
O blessed Brooke, whose milk-white Swans adore
That christall streame refined by her eyes. . .

[1] PO[13] 13–6.
[2] 'ARDEN (*id est*, . . . the *Woodland*, which then bore the name of ARDEN).' (Dugdale, p. 1086.)
[3] PO[13] 21–4.

miles west of Hartshill, how Amabil gave to the nuns of Polesworth with her body for sepulture her mill at Kingsbury,[1] two miles further to the north-west.

Merevale, which lies four miles north-west of Hartshill, may also have helped to foster in young Drayton that concern for the ruins of Time and that interest in the material ruins of the abbeys and lesser religious houses which later found repeated expression in his poems.[2] There Sir William Devereux, son of the first Viscount Hereford, had 'patcht up some part of the ruins' of the old Cistercian Abbey, 'and resided thereon.'[3] He had also succeeded to land at Hartshill which had belonged to Merevale Abbey. To his widow, 'the godly and vertuous Lady, the Lady *Jane Devoreux* of *Merivale*,' Drayton dedicated in 1591 his earliest printed book, *The Harmonie of the Church*,

> most unwilling to bee founde ingratefull, either in the behalfe of my Countrie or the place of my byrth: To the one, your godlie life beeing a president of perfect vertue; to the other, your bountifull hospitalitie an exceeding releefe.

We do not know the nature of Lady Devereux's benefactions to Hartshill; but her husband, Sir William, had a share in the endowment of the grammar-school at Atherstone, which within living memory was held in the chancel of the old church of the Austin Friars in that town. There is a vague local tradition that Michael Drayton was a scholar at that school,[4] in which, as we have seen, his kinsmen took such practical interest. Its chief founder seems to have been one Amyas Hill, a 'servant' of King Henry VIII, who in 1538 held on lease most of the land formerly belonging to the Austin

---

[1] Dugdale, p. 1058.
[2] e.g. PO³ 293–312; Cro 697–712, 718–20, 749–60.
[3] Dugdale, p. 1088.
[4] Notes collected for a sketch of the Q. Elizabeth Grammar School, Atherstone, by F. W. Drew (unpublished).

Friars of Atherstone, and in 1546–1547 was bailiff on behalf of the Crown for the property of the dissolved religious houses. We may suppose that at Atherstone, as elsewhere, before the dissolution of their house, the Friars themselves kept school in the chancel of the church. Hill endowed the school by will with a tithe-rent charge of 26s. 8d. from the lands in Warwick. By a charter of Queen Elizabeth, 22 December 1573, twelve 'honest and discreet men of Atherstone' were incorporated as Governors of 'the Free Grammar School of William Devereux, Kt, Thomas Fulner, and Amias Hill.'[1]

[1] *Victoria County History of Warwickshire*, II, p. 106.

THE GATEWAY, POLESWORTH ABBEY

CHAPTER II

DRAYTON'S EDUCATION AND READING

WHEN in 1573 the Grammar School at Atherstone received its charter from Queen Elizabeth,
Drayton was ten years old:

> from my cradle (you must know that) I,
> Was still inclin'd to noble Poesie,
> And when that once *Pueriles*, I had read,
> And newly had my *Cato* construed,
> In my small selfe I greatly marveil'd then,
> Amongst all other, what strange kinde of men
> These Poets were; And pleased with the name,
> To my milde Tutor merrily I came,
> (For I was then a proper goodly page,
> Much like a Pigmy, scarse ten yeares of age)

Clasping my slender armes about his thigh.
O my deare master! cannot you (quoth I)
Make me a Poet, doe it; if you can,
And you shall see, Ile quickly bee a man.
Who me thus answered smiling, boy quoth he,
If you'le not play the wag, but I may see
You ply your learning, I will shortly read
Some Poets to you, *Phæbus* be my speed,
Too't hard went I, when shortly he began,
And first read to me honest *Mantuan*,
Then *Virgils Eglogues*, being entred thus,
Me thought I straight had mounted *Pegasus*,
And in his full Careere could make him stop,
And bound upon *Parnassus* by-clift top.
I scornd your ballet then though it were done
And had for Finis, *William Elderton*.[1]

So wrote Drayton in his lines to Henry Reynolds on 'Poets and Poesie,' printed in 1627. It has generally been assumed that he was a page in the service of Henry Goodere, 'whose I was, whilst he was,' and, as he told the younger Henry Goodere, to whose 'happy and generous family . . . I confess myself to be beholding, for the most part of my education.'[2] If so, it is possible that he attended school in the Abbey Gatehouse at Polesworth, which is still standing, having been spared the fate that befell the Abbey itself and the chancel of the church. Before its suppression in 1539 the nunnery was the resort of 'gentylmens children and sudjournentes . . . to the nombre of xxx^ti and sometime xl^ti and moo';[3] and the late Arthur Gray

[1] El[8].

[2] Dedications to EHE[5], EHE[10]. See below pp. 75, 80.

[3] Letter from the Commissioners to Cromwell; see *A Chapter in the Early Life of W. Shakespeare*, pp. 65–69. But Dr Gray had no good grounds for holding 'that it is more than probable that Shakespeare . . . was a page in Sir Henry Goodere's household: that he received his schooling at Polesworth.'

c

suggested that the nuns kept school there either in the chancel or in the Gatehouse. After the dissolution a school seems to have been maintained by Sir Henry Goodere and his heirs, until the present school was built in 1655 by Sir Francis Nethersole, who had married the daughter and co-heir of the younger Sir Henry Goodere. In the year 1585, as we shall see,[1] the elder Henry sent Drayton to bring an orphan nephew from Nottinghamhire to Polesworth, where the lad was to be kept in his house and 'at schoole where he thought good at the proper charges of the said Sir Henry.'[2] So may Michael himself have been brought up at his patron's charge. If at Polesworth, the vicar of the parish may have taught him,[3] or some tutor in the service of the Goodere family or of one of their neighbours. Raphael Holinshed, for instance, was in the household of Thomas Burdet, Esq., of Bramcote, about a mile distant from Polesworth;[4] and Drayton's studies in the history of his country may have received their first impulse and direction from the great chronicler himself.[5]

Drayton had 'been a witnes . . . ever from your cradle' of the 'excellent education and milde disposition' of Goodere's elder daughter Frances,[6] who cannot have been more than six or seven years younger than he. As a page in the household he and Frances may have learned from the same tutor. A little more substantial than the belief that Drayton attended the Atherstone school, is the evidence that he was at one time at that of Coventry. The Gooderes were living in that city about 1572, and lines written many years later by Abraham

[1] See below, p. 35.

[2] *Victoria County History of Warwickshire*, II, p. 659.

[3] Sir John Atkyns was vicar from 1557–1578, and John Savage from 1578–1584. (Dugdale, p. 1115.) Savage may have been the father of John Savage of the Inner Temple, to whom D wrote an Ode (Vol. I, p. 489 and note).

[4] Died 1591. See p. 204 below.

[5] See p. 93.   [6] See p. 80 below.

Holland, whose father, Philemon Holland,[1] practised medicine at Coventry and was afterwards appointed first an usher and later, at the age of seventy-six, head master at the Grammar School there, suggest that Michael himself had been at that school:

> So may the place wherein wee both were bred
> Bring forth good poets. . . .[2]

The Grammar School at Coventry had been founded by John Hales in the former church of the Whitefriars. At his death in 1572 he left to the school amongst other properties the site of St John's Hospital, at which it was carried on until the present buildings were built to receive it in 1885. Thomas Fuller, writing in the seventeenth century, said of this 'fair Grammar school' that 'herein I have seen more (abate the Three English schools of the first magnitude) and as well learned scholars . . . as in any school in England.'[3]

It has been supposed on rather shadowy authority[4] that shortly before his death Hales appointed Leonard Cox to be master of his school. If that distinguished but now almost forgotten scholar taught at Coventry, he was a link connecting the humanists of the Continent and England with the Warwickshire of Drayton and Shakespeare. He was born at Thame in Oxfordshire—doubtless at some date before the end of the fifteenth century, for he matriculated at Tübingen in 1514 and at Cracow in 1518. He corresponded with Erasmus and claimed Sir Thomas More for his friend. He was master successively at schools in Poland and Hungary before he returned to England, where he was appointed master of

[1] Philemon Holland was living at Coventry in 1579. His son Henry was born there in 1583.

[2] Bodl. MS. Ashm. 36. See below, p. 198.   [3] *Worthies*, p. 130.

[4] See F. L. Colvile, *The Worthies of Warwickshire*, nd, p. 883. The earliest authority I have been able to find is Tanner, who says in his account of Cox (*Bibliotheca Britannico-Hibernica*, 1748), 'Forsan etiam ludimagister fuit Scholae Coventriensis fundatae a Joh. Hales.'

Reading school about the year 1528. He edited a number of classical texts, and in 1540 wrote a lengthy commentary on Lily's Latin treatise on the Eight Parts of Speech. He would have been an old man when Drayton was at school; but if he was ever at Coventry it is possible that Drayton learned under him there. It is pleasant to think that he may even have been 'the milde Tutor ' of whom Drayton writes so affectionately in the Epistle to Henry Reynolds, or the aged Wynken, who reproves 'little Rowland' in the Second Eglog.[1]

Drayton's lines to Henry Reynolds make it clear that for his early education, wherever he may have received it, he went through the ordinary course followed in the grammar schools which in Elizabeth's reign and long after flourished in nearly every important town. Between the ages of six and nine he would first be put through the *Sententiae Pueriles*, a collection of short Latin sentences from various authors, designed as a first introduction to Latin, and next through *Cato's Distichs*, a series of sententious Latin hexameter couplets on rural subjects, compiled in the third or fourth century.[2] His tutor or master would next take him through the Eglogues of the Carmelite poet of the Renaissance, Baptista Spagnuoli, the 'Mantuan' of *Love's Labour's Lost*,[3] and then those of Virgil himself. In some schools both these books were learned by heart. In his writings, too, there is abundant evidence that he, like Shakespeare, was well schooled in the *Metamorphoses* of Ovid, whose *Heroides*, later on, suggested the name and form of his own *Heroicall Epistles*. For the rest of his reading we may take it that he was taught his grammar out of Lily—or, perhaps, from the *Intro-*

[1] The fullest account of Leonard Cox will be found in Frederic Ives Carpenter's edition of Cox's *Arte and Crafte of Rhetoryke* (Chicago, 1899). See also *Opus Epistolarum . . . Erasmi*, edited by P. S. Allen (Vol. VI, Oxford, 1928, p. 2), who has traced Cox's scholastic career in Poland and Hungary.

[2] J. Howard Brown, *Eliz. Schooldays*, p. 73.

[3] D also alludes to Mantuan in EHE[9b] 50, O 649-652 n.

ductiones ad Grammaticam, which, according to Anthony Wood, John Hales wrote for the Free Grammar School which he set up at Coventry. It was the aim of the grammar-schools to teach Latin as a language to be spoken,[1] and Cicero and Terence were used as sources for Latin phrase-books, such as that translated by Nicholas Udall in 1560, or that drawn out of Tully's *Offices* by Thomas Ashton for use at Shrewsbury School.[2]

There is no reliable evidence that Drayton ever studied at either Oxford or Cambridge; Sir Aston Cokaine, indeed, writes of Oxford,

> our other academy:
> Here smooth-tongu'd Drayton was inspired by
> Mnemosynes's [*sic*] manifold progeny;[3]

but Drayton's name is not found in the University lists, neither does Anthony Wood claim him for his *Athenae Oxonienses*. In *Poly-Olbion* Drayton writes of Oxford without any such expression of personal knowledge or special affection as we might expect of him had he been a member of that University. He writes of Cambridge with much greater warmth as the chosen home of poetry, and implores the muses to rain their dews upon her;[4] but there is no evidence that he ever studied there. He is named with 'Master Davis of L[incoln's] I[nn]' and other contemporary poets by William Covell in a marginal gloss to his pamphlet, *A Letter from England to her three Daughters, Cambridge, Oxford, Innes of Court*,[5] which seems to indicate that he studied at one of the Inns. Covell confirms the evidence, abundant from other sources, that the Inns of Court ranked with the

---

[1] Cf. *English Grammar Schools to 1660: their Curriculum and Practice*, by Foster Watson, M.A. (Cambridge, 1908), p. xix.

[2] Ibid., p. 333, quoting G. W. Fisher, *Annals of Shrewsbury School* (1899), p. 43.

[3] See below, pp. 203–4.   [4] PO[21] 211–217.

[5] In *Polimanteia*, 1595. But John Davies was at the Middle Temple.

Universities as schools of humane learning and that they were nurseries of poetry as well as of the law. While it is probable that Drayton as well as Shakespeare frequented them, there is no evidence that either of them ever studied law at any Inn of Court or of Chancery.

We do not know how much of Drayton's education was comprised in that 'most part' of it for which he so gratefully acknowledged his indebtedness to Sir Henry Goodere. Whatever its nature, and whosoever the masters from whom he received it, the bent which it gave to his studies and the tastes which it fostered in him are conspicuous throughout his poetry. His reading was both wide and deep. Leaving out of count the writings of his contemporaries, we find evidence in his poems that among the earlier English poets he knew intimately the works of Chaucer, Langland and Gower; perhaps less intimately those of Skelton, Alexander Barclay, Wyatt, Surrey, Bryan, Southern and Gascoigne. In the mediaeval legends of Arthur, Bevis of Hampton, Robin Hood and Guy of Warwick he found food both for his poetry and for his love for England. Among the French poets, whom he had read in the original, and from whom he sometimes borrowed, we find Ronsard, Pontoux, Desportes and du Bartas. He alludes to Dante once only. He recognizes Petrarch as 'the great master of Italian rymes.' He mentions also Ariosto and Tasso. He knew the *Novelle* of Bandello, Rabelais's *Pantagruel* and *Don Quixote*. From the notes on his poems, too, we may gather how much he owed to the Greek and Latin classics.[1] To him they were not as dead authors: some of them suggested patterns for his prosody or were sources of inspiration for his verse. He names Homer, Anacreon, Pindar, Musaeus and Theocritus amongst the epic, lyric and pastoral poets of Greece, and Sophocles and Euripides among the tragedians. Among the Greek moralists and philosophers he knew Pythagoras, Arche-

[1] See the Introductions and Notes in Vol. v, *passim*.

laus, Democritus, Plato, Epicurus, Zeno and Plutarch.
Of the Latins not only did he know intimately Virgil,
Horace, Ovid, Martial, Juvenal, who in Drayton's time
and almost down to our own day formed the staple of
every liberal education: he is also able to quote the authority of Lucan, Tibullus, Silius Italicus and Claudian.
He knew the comedies of Plautus, the Senecan tragedies
as well as Seneca's Stoic philosophy, Cicero's and
Pliny's Letters and Pliny's Natural History. He alludes
to passages in Caesar's Commentaries and in the *Agricola*
of Tacitus. In *The Man in the Moone* he borrows repeatedly from Macrobius.

His reading in the old chronicles was immense. They
were his principal sources for his Legends, *The Barons
Warres*, *The Battaile of Agincourt*, and for large tracts of
Poly-Olbion. So far from taking his history at second
hand from Holinshed, Stow or Camden, he went to the
authors from whom Holinshed himself had drawn:
Gildas; Bede; Giraldus Cambrensis; Geoffrey of Monmouth; Hoveden; Higden; Nicholas Upton; Hauteville; Froissart; Philip de Commines; Polydore Vergil;
Buchanan, and many more. He has knowledge of the
Christian philosophy of Boethius, of the magical sys-
tems of Cornelius Agrippa and Paracelsus, and of the
divinity of Wicliffe, Luther and Erasmus. The Bible is,
of course, the only source for *The Harmonie of the Church*,
with which his poetical career began, and his chief
source for the three Divine Poems with which it closed;
but his knowledge of Scripture may be traced also in
other parts of his work: in *Poly-Olbion* especially, in
his satires and many of his Elegies.

His reading was not confined to printed books.
Twice in *Poly-Olbion* we find references to manuscript
records which he consulted in search of topographical
detail. It is likely that the archives of his friends and
patrons found in him a diligent student. When writing
Peirs Gaveston he had access to the collections of John
Stow; and there is reason to believe that he was able to

consult the libraries of Camden, Selden and Cotton.

Of Drayton's character in his early years we have no evidence but his own. In two passages of his works he alludes to them with compunction. In his first Eglog he prays to the 'shepheards soveraigne':

> Let smokie sighes be pledges of contrition,
> For follies past to make my soules submission.[1]

In the Second Eglog the aged Wynken, who may stand for one that had been his tutor,[2] quotes 'Rowlands harmes' as a warning to Motto's 'unbrideled youth,' and he says of him:

> Even such a wanton, an unruly swayne,
>   Was little Rowland, when of yore as he,
> Upon the Beechen tree on yonder playne,
>   Carved this rime of loves Idolatrie.[3]

And in dedicating the Heroicall Epistles of Queen Isabel and Richard II to the Earl of Bedford, he writes gratefully of Sir Henry Goodere, 'whose patience pleased to beare with the imperfections of my heedlesse and un-staied youth.'[4] We need not suppose such passages to be more than the self-reproaches of a tender conscience.

[1] SG[1] 47–8.   [2] SG[2] Arg. n.
[3] SG[2] 66–9.   [4] See p. 75 below.

CHAPTER III

THE GOODERES OF POLESWORTH

TO the Gooderes of Polesworth Drayton owed much besides his early upbringing and education. His life was so closely linked with theirs to the third generation by bonds of loyal service, tenderest affection and devoted and enduring friendship that some account of them and of their home must be given here. The family had a measure of affluence even before the dissolution of the religious houses under Henry VIII. When the suppression came, its members shared handsomely in the spoils. In 1545 Francis Goodere, a successful lawyer of Gray's Inn, purchased from the Crown the castle and manor of Baginton, which had belonged to the Dean and Chapter of the dissolved College of St Mary's, Warwick. Baginton may have been the home of his forbears, for there were Gooderes at that place at least as early as the beginning of the sixteenth century. Francis had bought also in 1544[1] the site of the dissolved Abbey of Benedictine nuns at Polesworth, with the lordship and demesne lands thereof, the manor and town of Polesworth, and the grange of Radway, near Edge Hill; for all of which, with Baginton, he paid the sum of £1422 8s. 8d. Francis Goodere married Ursula, daughter and co-heir of Sir Ralph Rowlett, of St Albans, Herts, and Theddingworth in Leicestershire. Rowlett's wife was Margaret, daughter of Sir Anthony Cooke of Gidea Hall, Essex, and therefore sister-in-law to William Cecil, Lord Burleigh, and to Sir Nicholas Bacon. When Francis Goodere died in 1547,[2] his estates at Polesworth and elsewhere passed to his eldest son, Henry, then a boy of thirteen, to

[1] *VCH Warw.*, II, p. 64; Pat. 36 Hen. VIII, 26.
[2] Particulars of Grants, Augmentation Office, 36 Hen. 8, No. 499.

whom Nicholas Bacon was appointed guardian. Henry Goodere built himself a mansion on the ruins of the ancient nunnery of Polesworth, which, according to the legend recorded by Dugdale[1] from a MS. which Drayton may have seen, had been founded by King Egbert for his daughter St Editha. Goodere made it his principal seat. Little now remains of the house. The present Vicarage is built on its site, and in the drawing-room is an old stone fireplace in the spandrels of which is carved the Goodere device, a partridge carrying in its bill an ear of wheat. Henry had married Frances, daughter of Hugh Lowther, of Lowther, Westmorland, by Dorothy, daughter of Henry, 14th Lord Clifford, 'the Shepherd Lord,' by his second wife Florence Pudsey. She became a widow thrice over, for she after-wards married Thomas Talbot, and, after his death, Lord Richard Grey, a younger son of Thomas, 1st Marquis of Dorset. She may have kept the name and rank of her first husband. If so, she is probably the Lady Clifford to whom Polesworth was let about the year 1568.[2] Goodere had a house at Coventry also, where his younger daughter Anne was born, probably in 1571[3].

That was an eventful year in Goodere's career. He had become a man of consequence within his own county and even in London. In January he was arbitrator with Sir Fulke Greville, Sir Thomas Lucy and Clement Throckmorton in a dispute between the Corporation of Stratford-upon-Avon and one Robert Perrott, a burgess of the town, who had sought to evade the honour of serving in the office of Bailiff, to which he had been elected.[4] In the same year Goodere

---

[1] Dugdale, p. 1107; 'ex veteri MS. penes Joh. Ferrers de Tamworth Castro ar.'

[2] Ex inform. nuperi T. Edw. Goodyear.

[3] See page 41 below.

[4] Dugdale Society, *Minutes and Accounts of Stratford-upon-Avon Corporation*, Vol. II, pp. 40–42.

was returned member of Parliament for Coventry.[1] In
September he was committed to the Tower for 'unlaw-
full dealing touchinge the Q. of Scoots.'[2] The nature of
his offence was told many years later in a letter from Sir
Thomas Stanhope to Robert Cecil. From it we learn
that Goodere was in Westmorland with his brother-in-
law, Richard Lowther, in May 1568, when the
Queen of Scots first came out of Scotland to Carlisle.
Lowther and Goodere repaired to her, and Goodere
devised a cipher for the Queen's use in writing to
such as she trusted: 'the which afterwards being dis-
covered Goodyere was committed to the Tower,
where after some time he was delivered, but never
recovered the good opinion of the late Queen.'[3]
Queen Mary had been moved to Coventry in November 1569, and was held there till the January following.
'About the tyme the Quene of Scotts dyd lie at Coven-
trie,' declared Banester, the Duke of Norfolk's servant,
in answer to the interrogatories, 'or verie shortlie after,
Mr Goodyier sent to London by a Boye of his, a Letter
from the Quene of Scotts to Gerarde Lowther, who
then did lie at London, to be delivered to my Lord in
the Tower.' He declared also that 'at the tyme of his
flyeng' Gerard Lowther visited 'his Brother Goodyers
howse in Warwykeshyre.'[4] The Gooderes may then
have been living at Coventry, where their younger
daughter Anne was born, probably on 4 August 1571;
and Lowther's grandmother, Lady Clifford, was perhaps still at Polesworth.

From prison Goodere wrote verses to excuse himself
for his action. They begin with a pun on his own name:

---

[1] Dugdale, p. 1148. He seems to have been unseated the same or
the following year.

[2] BM Lansdowne MS. 73, No. 16.

[3] Hist. MSS. Comm. *Salisbury Papers*, XVII, p. 120 (1605).

[4] Murdin, *State Papers . . . Q. Elizabeth*, 1759, pp. 144, 147; see
also ibid. pp. 85, 113–5, 117, 159, 161, 222–4.

two sets of verses which were laid upon his hearse:

To the honour of Sir *Henry Goodyer* of *Polesworth*,
a knight memorable for his vertues: an affectionate
friend of his, framed this *Tetrastich*:

An yll yeare of a Goodyer *us bereft,*
Who gon to God, much lacke of him heere left:
Full of good gifts, of body and of minde,
Wise, comely, learned, eloquent, and kinde.[1]

And Henry Goodere's brother, William, of Monk's
Kirby, is the author of the following:[2]

Funerall Verses set on the hearse ⎱ of Polesworth
of Henrye Goodere knyghte; late ⎰

Esteemed knyghte, take tryumphe over deathe;
And over tyme, by the aeternall fame
Of natures woorkes, whyle God did lende the breathe;
Adornde wyth wytt, and skyll to rule the same:
And what avaylde, thy giftes in sutche degree;
Synce fortune frownde, and worlde had spyte at thee.
Heaven be thy reste, on earthe thy lott was toyle,
Thy pryvate losse, went to thy Countryes gayne.
Bredde greyfe of mynde, whych in thy brest dyd boyle
Consumynge cares, the Skarres wherof remayne.
Enjoye thy deathe, sutch passage into lyfe,
As frees the quyte, from thoughtes of worldlye stryfe.

W^am: Goodere

We may now enquire into Drayton's relations with
Henry Goodere and his family. If, as has been generally
conjectured with some degree of probability, he was in
Goodere's service as 'a proper goodly page . . . scarce
ten yeares of age,' that would have been about the year
1573. In dedicating the *Heroicall Epistles* of Lady Jane
Gray and Lord Gilford Dudley to Frances, the elder of
Sir Henry's daughters, he uses words which give support to the belief that he was a mere stripling when
he first came into intimacy with the family:[3] 'My selfe

[1] Camden's *Remaines . . . concerning Britain*, 1605, p. 55.
[2] BM Add. 23229, f. 90.　　[3] Below, page 80; Vol. v, p. 134.

having been a witnes of your excellent education, and
milde disposition (as I may say) ever from your Cradle,
dedicate this Epistle of this vertuous and good Lady to
your selfe: so like her in all perfections both of wisedome
and learning.' He remained in the Gooderes' service till
near the end of Sir Henry's life, when his old master
'bequeathed him' to the service of Lucy Harington.[1]
We find, however, that at some period between the
years 1580, or a little earlier, and 1585 he was servant
to Henry's younger brother, Thomas, who about the
year 1574 or 1575 had married Margaret, the elder
daughter of Sir Thomas Saunders, of Charlwood,
Surrey, and widow of Francis Mering, gentleman, son of
Francis Mering, Esq., of Mering Hall, Notts. Thomas
Goodere made Collingham his home, and his eldest son,
Henry, was born there in 1578. About that time the
elder Henry, lying dangerously sick of the stone in
London, had settled Polesworth on Thomas, who,
however, died in January 1585. After Thomas's death
Henry revoked the settlement of Polesworth on his
brother, and settled his property instead on his
daughters Frances and Anne. Nevertheless after Sir
Henry's death in 1595 Thomas's widow Margaret,
now the widow of John Price, her third husband, and
the wife of a fourth, one Lawrence Englebert, claimed
Polesworth on behalf of her son Henry against her
nephew Henry, the son of William Goodere and the
husband of Sir Henry's daughter Frances, to whom Sir
Henry conveyed Polesworth on their marriage. Litigation for the possession of Polesworth and in support of
other claims made by Margaret lasted nearly ten years.
In the first of two actions for the succession, *Englebert
v. Saunders*,[2] one Nicholas Moon, who had been Thomas
Goodere's clerk, describing the scene at Thomas's sick-
bed, deposes how when he was in the room Thomas
said to his wife,

[1] Below, p. 75; Vol. v, p. 112.
[2] PRO C 24/262/28.

D

wyef thou art here A straunger I know thou has no
kinred her but this man meaning this deponent and
therefore sd he call for some more of those that be
thy frendes that thou best lykest of and they shalt
heare and be wytnes what I say unto thee, where-
uppon . . . Margaret called . . . Richard Lee and
Michaell Drayton.

Drayton himself therefore was called as a witness.
'Mychaell Drayton of London gent of the age of .xxxv.
yeres or thereaboutes' deposed that he,

being servant unto . . . Mr Thomas Goodyere at the
time of his deathe was at one tyme in the tyme of the
sd mr Goodyeres sycknes whereof he dyed called
into the Chamber where he laye syck in the presence
of one Mr Mone to geve some attendance to the sd
mr Goodyere At which tyme this dept well remem-
breth that his said master mr Tho: Goodyere thoughe
very syck yet being in good and perfect memory to
this deponentes then Judgment (for he sayth he was
but young at that tyme) dyd utter thes or the verye
like wordes in effect to his wief calling hir as he was
wont to do by the name of Gyrle vidz Gyrle Concerning my lease of Collingham which is in my
brother William Goodyeres handes I knowe that he
will delyver yt thee bak agayne safe for the good of
thee & my sonne of whome I knowe he will have a
speciall Care for I dowte not but thou shalt fynd him a
verye Just & honest gentleman. . .
    That He well remembreth that uppon a tyme
while this dept attended uppon the sd m^r Tho:
Goodyere Sir Henrye Goodyere knight . . . chanced
to be at m^r Tho. Goodyeres howse at Collingham
and in a morning the said Sir Henry and this deponent walking and discoursing together in the great
chamber of that house of matters as yt pleased him
often to doe whersoever this deponent chanced to
mete wth him little henr Goodyere the Sunne of the

said Mr Tho: Goodyere came running into & playing in the said Chamber and the said Sir Henrye
Goodyere then beholding the said Child uttered . . .
thes or like wordes in effect (vide) Michell this is a
goodlye Child and the heire of my house and yf yt
please good [*sic*] that he and I lyve I will deale well
by him. . .[1]

After Thomas's death Michael returned to the
service of the elder Henry Goodere, as we learn from
the answers to the interrogatories made by young
Henry's mother, Margaret, by then the widow of her
fourth husband, Lawrence Englebert, in a later action
for the possession of Polesworth, taken by her son Henry:

> Within a short time of the death of the said
> Thomas, Sir Henry sent two of his servants, whose
> names (as this deponent was told, for she lay then at
> Islington near unto London,) were Michael Drayton
> and one Wylles, to fetch the complainant from
> Collingham in Nottinghamshire, where the com-
> plainant then was, unto Pawlesworth in Warwick-
> shire. And thereupon Sir Henry kept the complain-
> ant in his own house and at school, where he thought
> good, at the proper charges of the said Sir Henry.[2]

In his War poems Drayton describes the clash and
tumult of battle with so much spirit and with such
wealth of lively detail as to suggest that, like Jonson and
Chapman, he at some time served as a soldier.[3] Perhaps
he served under his master's command—'whose I was,
whilest he was'—among the Warwickshire men in the

[1] See *MLR*, July 1940.
[2] Goodier *v*. Goodier; PRO 4 Jas. Chancery: Town Depositions, Bundle 313; abstract made by the late T. E. Goodyear.
[3] In his copy of *The Muses Elizium*, now in the Victoria and
Albert Museum, Alexander Dyce notes Drayton's description of
the Spanish Armada in *Moses A Map of His Miracles*, printed in
1604, as evidence that the poet had witnessed the great sea-fight
from the cliffs of Dover. See MBM 61–72.

army of defence in 1588, if not also in the campaigns
in the Low Countries a few years before.

As we have seen, Drayton would sometimes accompany his master when business brought him to London.
Both were there in February 1590–1; for on the 10th of
that month Drayton dated thence the dedication of his
Harmonie of the Church to Lady Devereux; and on the
11th Sir Henry wrote to Serjeant Puckering 'from my
lodginge: in the Strande,' using his good offices to
prevent a quarrel that was brewing between the
Serjeant and his Warwickshire neighbour, Thomas
Dabridgecourt.[1] In the autumn and winter of 1593–4
the plague was rife in London. From an allusion which
Drayton makes to the plague-stricken people in *Mortimeriados*,[2] it seems probable that he was present and that
he is describing what he had then witnessed. So also ten
years later, when there was a fresh outburst, in writing
of the Tenth Plague of Egypt, Drayton expressly refers
to his own harrowing experience in

Afflicted London *in sixe hundred three.*[3]

It is possible that his master's business sometimes
took Drayton farther afield. An allusion to 'snow-topd'
Skiddaw's 'frostie cleeves' in *Mortimeriados*[4] reminds us
that Lowther, the seat of Sir Henry's brother-in-law,
lies in the neighbourhood of that mountain; and
Drayton may have journeyed thither in Goodere's
company or on his behalf. Later we shall find reasons
for believing that at some time he made his way into
Scotland.[5] Drayton must have been in London when
he was writing *Peirs Gaveston*. That poem was printed
in 1593; and he tells us in the note at the end that he
had ' recourse to some especiall collections, gathered
by the industrious labours of *John Stow*,' who lived in
London. Hebel suggests, however, that he was away
from London when 'by a sinister dealing of some

[1] BM Harl. 6995, f. 31.   [2] Mo 1597–603.   [3] MBM² 625–36.
[4] Mo 2556–60 n.   [5] Pp. 96, 106.

unskilfull Printer,' a surreptitious edition of *Peirs Gaveston* was lately 'put forth contrary to my will, with as manie faults as there be lynes in the same.'[1] The only known copy of this edition is at the British Museum. Its title-page is missing, and the printer's name and the date are unknown. But it must have been printed between 1593, the date of the first edition, and that of the third, 1596.

At the beginning of 1595 Drayton rendered the last service to his old master of which we have any record, when he witnessed Sir Henry's will. It is dated 26 January 1594–5, and was proved 7 May 1595. A copy of it is preserved at Somerset House.[2] Goodere named as his executors his brother William, his younger daughter Anne, his friend Richard Lee, and his friend and kinsman, Thomas Goodiere, of Newgate Street, Herts. He made provision for a sum of £1500 for and towards Anne's 'preferment in marriage advauncement livelyhood and mayntenance.' He appointed as his overseers Sir John Harington of Combe, Sir Henry Cocke of Broxbourne, Sir Thomas Lucy the younger of Charlecote, and Robert Burgoine of Wroxall. He leaves the funeral arrangements to the executors, trusting that they will do 'nothing pompous and unnecessarye.' His estate was heavily encumbered, and, as we have seen, was the subject of a protracted lawsuit between his two nephews, Henry, who was also his son-in-law, and Henry, the son of his deceased brother Thomas, and so heir male, who is not mentioned in the will. The disposition of his estates is told by Anne herself in her depositions in the suit *Goodier v. Goodier* from which we have already quoted. Here is an abstract of her evidence:

Dame Anne Raynsforde, wife of Sir Henry Rainsforde, Kt, aged 35 or thereabouts, was daughter

[1] See *The Library* 1923–4, Vol. IV, pp. 151–155; *The Tragicall Legend of Robert* 1596, To the Reader, Vol. I, p. 251.
[2] 29–30 Scott.

unto the deceased Sir Henry Goodier; she believes that, many years before his death, he made a conveyance of the most part of his lands to Thomas Goodier his brother with power of revocation. A little before his going into the Low Countries with the late Right Honourable Robert, Earl of Leicester, he devised all his lands by a will in writing to this deponent and her sister Francis Goodier; and, in consideration of a marriage between the said Francis, his eldest daughter, and Sir Henry Goodyere, one of the now defendants, son to his youngest brother Sir William Goodyere, he did by deed in writing convey all his lands to the said Sir Henry and Francis. More she cannot recollect, but has some remembrance of some deed of revocation made long before the last recited conveyance, which he made a little before his decease. She cannot recollect anyone reading or viewing any deeds or evidences made by her father to assure or convey his lands, at the house of Sir William Goodyer within the county of Warwick, called Monckes Kyrby. She never heard that her father, when he lay sick of a dangerous fit of the stone, or a little before his going over seas into the Low Countries, made any other devise or conveyance than as above. He gave his manor of Powlesworth, co. Warwick, to her sister Francis, and his manor of Baggington to this deponent.

Anne Rainsforde.

We may close this chapter with a more intimate picture, drawn from the depositions in the same case, of Sir Henry's relations towards the nephew whom he afterwards disinherited and towards his own daughters. One of the witnesses was Rafe Cope, yeoman, aged about 60, who deposed that he had been servant to Sir Henry for some seven or eight years:

He remembers that, when the complainant was a

child of two or three, Sir Henry did hang in a string certain pieces of gold, in which he punched holes with his dagger, about the child's neck, and then asked this deponent, (being then present attending) how he liked the child. Whereunto he answered that he had a right Goodyer's face, and was liker to Sir Henry himself than to his own father. Whereupon Sir Henry took the complainant in his arms, and kissing him said: I tell thee, Cope, this is the heir of my land, this is he that must be thy landlord one day, if he live.

On the other hand, Sir Henry Cocke, of Broxbourne, Herts, Knight, a cousin of Sir Henry's, said in his deposition that he thought there was a 'provision' in the deed of conveyance of lands to Thomas Goodere, presumably in favour of his daughters:

The which he doth the rather beleeve because Sir Henrie Goodyer was then a verie lustie gentleman scarce fortie yeers old, and besides he did as lovinglie affecte his daughters as any father could his children.

CHAPTER IV
ANNE GOODERE

TO understand the honourable position held by
poetry during the period of the English renaissance,
we must trace its part in the lives of those for whom, or
to whom, it was written. More study, however, has
been given to the printers and printing of Elizabethan
poetry than to the literary tastes and habits of those
who passed it from hand to hand in the author's manuscript, or copied it into their commonplace books; who
foregathered to hear it read, or sung to the harp or
virginals, or who themselves took part in singing it at
sight to the madrigal music of Morley or of Byrd.
That spacious age was an age of cultivated leisure also,
at least for those of the noble and gentle families whose
numbers had increased and whose wealth had grown
beyond precedent at the cost of the despoiled religious
houses. Much of that leisure was occupied in reading,
and especially in reading poetry. The gatherings of
shepherds and shepherdesses who met for song and
dance on Cotswold, on the banks of the Trent or Anker,
or on the Elizian plains, were not just poetical fictions
of Drayton's pastoral muse, or echoes from Theocritus
or Mantuan. They had their counterpart in the great
and lesser houses of the land. At some of them poets
held office as privileged servants—secretaries, tutors
to the sons and daughters of the house; and the great
ladies who lived there are living for us still in the verse
of Jonson and Chapman, Daniel, Drayton, and Donne.

Polesworth in Arden, on the river Anker, was one of
those houses where poetry was held in special honour:

Ankor tryumph, upon whose blessed shore,
The sacred Muses solemnize thy name:
Where the *Arcadian* Swaines with rytes adore
Pandoras poesy, and her living fame.[1]

[1] 'Gorbo il fidele,' IM, Vol. 1, p. 97. He is perhaps the Gorbo
of SG[4], SG[6] and SG[8].

The dying Sidney, in his last will, had claimed Sir Henry Goodere for 'my good cousin and Friend'; and it was perhaps due to his influence and that of his sister Mary—Pandora, 'the Muse of Britanye,'[1]—that the tender plant of poetry first took root on the banks of the Anker. It is as Elphin the poet, and not as the chivalrous and heroic knight of Zutphen, that Sidney is mourned in Rowland's 'tears of the greene Hawthorne tree';[2] and in the Sixth Eglog Perkin tells of Pandora:

> The flood of *Helicon*, forspent and drie,
> Her sourse decayd with foule oblivion,
> The fountaine flows againe in thee alone,
> Where Muses now their thirst may satisfie.[3]

Sir Henry Goodere's younger daughter, Anne, was born, not at Polesworth, but in Much Park Street, Coventry in 1570 or, more probably, 1571. The place and day of the month are told us by Drayton himself:

> Happy *Mich-Parke* ev'ry yeere,
> On the fourth of *August* there,
> Let thy Maides from FLORA's bowers. . .
> Decke Thee up. . .[4]

The year may be calculated from her signed depositions in the lawsuit between the two Henry Gooderes, dated 1 August 1606, in which she is described as 'aged 35 yeares or thereabouts.'[5] It is shown approximately in the record of her successful treatment for stone about the year 1632 by Shakespeare's son-in-law, John Hall, the physician of Stratford-upon-Avon, who says that she had then passed her 62nd year.[6]

Drayton was older than Anne by about eight years. He must have seen her grow up almost from her birth through childhood and youth to womanhood. We have

---

[1] SG[6] Arg.   [2] SG[4].
[3] SG[6] 73–76. See notes on these passages, on IM[51], and Pa[8].
[4] Od[17] 43–7.   [5] See above, p. 37.
[6] See p. 54.

seen that he had been a 'witness' of the education of her elder sister Frances; and it is not rash to conjecture that the sisters may have been in part educated by him.

Her wandring sheepe full safely have I kept,[1]

he wrote of Anne in lines perhaps reminiscent of Sidney's,

My sheepe are thoughts, which I both guide and serve.

The character and course of his early love for Anne may be gathered from the Sonnets which in 1594 he printed under the title of *Ideas Mirrour*. In dedicating that volume to Anthony Cooke he tells us that his 'rude unpolished rhymes' had 'long slept in sable night,' and they bear their own evidence that they were written at intervals some years before they were printed. These early Sonnets have Anne Goodere, Drayton's Idea, alone for their subject.[2] They were hammered out in the white heat of a love pure and passionate:

My hart the Anvile where my thoughts doe beate,
My words the hammers, fashioning my desires,
My breast the forge, including all the heate,
Love is the fuell which maintaines the fire.[3]

Though grouped together round a common theme, they have no logical sequence, but are written with all the incoherence of a distracted lover's moods. It is true that Drayton carried in his scrip the current coin—the small change, if you will—scattered lavishly by contemporary sonneteers—those knights errant of the

[1] SG⁹ 53.

[2] There is no reason whatever for supposing with Courthope (*Hist. of Eng. Poetry*, III, pp. 24–6) that the Idea of Drayton's earlier verse was, not Anne Goodere, but Lucy Harington, who was not born till late in 1580. See Elton, pp. 21–3, for an answer to Courthope, who is wrong in saying that Combe Abbey, the Warwickshire seat of the Haringtons, is situated on the river Anker. That Anne is the Idea of *Ideas Mirrour* was known to Bartlett, who quotes Amour 13 and says that Drayton is 'addressing his mistress, Anne Goodyer of Coventry.' (*Manceter*, p. 48.)

[3] IM⁴⁴ 1–4.

quill, whose antics in the service of their Delias and
Astraeas were as fantastic as the deeds of the paladins
and palmerins satirized so tenderly by the author of *Don
Quixote*. There was even a strain of Quixotry in Drayton. His Dulcinea was not a country wench of Castile,
but the daughter of a Warwickshire knight. If, however, we write off all that was merely fantastic in these
sonnets, all that was a mere following of a poetical
fashion of the day, there remains the clear impression of
the genuineness and intensity of Drayton's devout love
for Anne. Without probing too deeply we may follow
its course and learn its true nature in *The Shepheards
Garland* and in *Ideas Mirrour*. There is a note of
Platonism, echoed perhaps from St Augustine, in
Drayton's account of its first beginning. His 'deerest
Love' was the

> Rare of-spring of my thoughts, . . .
> Begot by fancy, on sweet hope exhortive;[1]

and in Amour 16 of *Ideas Mirrour* he writes:

> Vertues *Idea* in virginitie,
> By inspiration, came conceav'd with thought:
> The time is come delivered she must be,
> Where first my Love into the world was brought.

Bereaved of its parentage in the mind, it passed to the
wardship of 'my soveraignes eye.' But Anne's eyes were
pitiless, and his love was

> hunger-starven, wanting lookes to live,
> Still empty gorg'd, with cares consumption pynde.[2]

It was Anne's eyes, again, which

> taught mee the Alphabet of love.[3]

That memory seems to find expression forty years later
in the 'verses made by Michaell Drayton . . . the night
before he dyed':

[1] IM[41] 1–2.   [2] IM[16] 1–4; 13–14.   [3] IM[11] 1.

The seeds of Love first by thy eyes weare throwne
Into a grownd untild, a harte unknowne
To beare such fruitt, tyll by thy handes twas sowen.[1]

Amour 19 tells of Anne's wholesome influence on others:

Whose lyfe doth save a thousand soules from hell;[2]

and Amour 12 the power of its cleansing virtue upon himself:

Blind were mine eyes, till they were seene of thine,
      And mine eares deafe, by thy fame healed be,
      My vices cur'd, by vertues sprung from thee,
      My hopes reviv'd which long in grave had lyne.
All uncleane thoughts, foule spirits cast out in mee,
By thy great power, and by strong fayth in thee.[3]

Drayton had tendered to Anne the

. . . chaste and pure devotion of my youth,
      [The] glorie of my Aprill-springing yeeres,
      Unfained love, in naked simple truth,
      A thousand vowes, a thousand sighes and teares.[4]

But we do not know at what period of his life his love for her began: perhaps he himself could not have told us. We may suppose that fondness for the child grew unperceived into love for the woman. None of the Sonnets in *Ideas Mirrour* give any clue to their date; but in 1600 Drayton printed for the first time his Sonnet 'To Lunacie,' in which, in apology for his 'Bedlam fit,' he says of his own 'distraction,'

Tis nine yeeres now since first I lost my Wit.[5]

We may therefore date back *Ideas Mirrour* to the year 1590 or 1591. Anne would then have been about twenty years old, and Drayton twenty-seven or twenty-eight.

[1] Bodl. Ashm. MS. 38, f. 77. See p. 223 below.
[2] IM[19] 12.   [3] IM[12] 9–14.
[4] IM[38] 1–4.   [5] Id[9] 11.

In none of the Sonnets, with all their changing moods
of lyrical rapture, praise, worship and despair, is there
any hint that Anne returned her poet's love. The first of
the Amours begins with lines reminiscent of Daniel:

Reade heere (sweet Mayd) the story of my wo,
   The drery abstracts of my endles cares:
With my lives sorow enterlyned so;
Smok'd with my sighes, and blotted with my
   teares.[1]

With the rest of the sonnet they give the keynote, not
only to the Amours, but to all those passages in *Idea
The Shepheards Garland* which allude to Rowland's love
for his mistress. Idea, says Motto to Rowland,

      sees not shepheard, no, she will not see,
  Her rarest vertues blazon'd by thy quill,
Nor knowes the effect the same hath wrought in thee.[2]

And in the Ninth Rowland himself bemoans her dis-
dain:

Oh fayr'st that lives, yet most unkindest mayd, . . .[3]

After singing Idea's praises in his Fifth Eglog
Drayton had sworn with Ovid,

Te Dominam nobis tempus in omne fore.

To the end of his life he remained faithful to his pledge.
His devotion to Anne, recorded in poem after poem, in
season and out of season, does not weaken as he and she
advance in years. But it changes its character. He soon
ceases to be the distraught or moody lover; his lines no
longer register his unrequited love. Henceforth he sings
lyrically and triumphantly of Idea's excellence and perfection, hailing her as the special darling of the muses.
Even the ghost of Piers Gaveston at the end of his long
Legend, before returning to the gloomy shades whence
he came,

[1] IM[1] 1–4. Cf. *Delia* XXIV.   [2] SG[5] 167–169.   [3] SG[9] 31.

> . . . to *Ankor* shall repayre,
> And unto chaste *Idea* tell my care . . .
> In whose sweet bosome all the Muses rest.[1]

And the spirit of Matilda the Fair, who had sealed her chastity by death, before it departs hence, prays to be let see

> the Muses owne delight: . . .
> O let mee once behold her blessed eyes,
> Those two sweet Sunnes which make eternall spring,
> Which banish drouping Night out of the skies,
> In whose sweet bosome quiers of Angels sing. . .[2]

Read, too, the closing lines of *Endimion and Phœbe*, where Drayton is addressing Anne:

> Thou purest spark of *Vesta's* kindled fire,
> Sweet Nymph of *Ankor*, crowne of my desire,
> The plot which for their pleasure heaven devis'd,
> Where all the Muses be imparadis'd . . .[3]

Anne was still living with her father at Polesworth in 1595, when Sir Henry Goodere died. In the same year, being then about twenty-four years old, she married Henry Rainsford, a young Gloucestershire squire, some five years her junior, who was seated at Clifford Chambers, a pretty and secluded hamlet, which was then in Gloucestershire but is now in Warwickshire. It lies on the river Stour near its fall into the Avon less than two miles above Stratford. The manor had formerly belonged to the monks of Gloucester.[4]

It is pleasant to find from Drayton's later poems how his love for Anne became fixed in strong and lasting friendship, which ended only with his life. Idea is still the theme of many of them, but when he printed

---

[1] PG[a] 1717–22.   [2] Ma[a] 1114–34.   [3] EP 1011–32.
[4] The old black-and-white half-timbered manor-house remained standing till 27 March 1918, when a great part of it was destroyed by fire. It was rebuilt on the original plan in 1922 at the cost of the lord of the manor, Mrs Rees-Mogg, under the direction of Sir Edwin Lutyens.

CLIFFORD MANOR BEFORE ITS DESTRUCTION BY FIRE 1918

To face page 45

his sonnets in 1599, although he gave the title *Idea* to the collection, not all or nearly all of them were addressed to her. He admitted to the new series only some thirty out of fifty-one Sonnets printed in *Ideas Mirrour*. Amongst those which he discarded are some that we could least have spared. In a succession of new editions he replaced them by some fifty-five more, in none of which is there any mention of Anne or any certain allusion to Idea. Some are addressed to other women: the most famous of all Drayton's poems, the sonnet,

Since ther's no helpe, Come let us kiss and part,[1]

was not printed till 1619, when Lady Rainsford was a matron of near fifty: others are written to patrons, friends, or critics. They are a mere miscellany, with no common theme or purpose. He introduces them with a sonnet which is an apology, begging that his protestations be taken not too seriously or too literally:

Into these Loves, who but for Passion lookes,
At this first sight, here let him lay them by . . .
My Verse is the true image of my Mind,
Ever in motion, still desiring change;
And as thus to Varietie inclin'd,
So in all Humors sportively I range.[2]

There are other poems, however, of Drayton's middle and later periods which show that his friendship and admiration for Anne have not weakened. In the middle of *The Barons Warres*, printed in 1603, he harks back regretfully to his 'virgin unpolluted Rimes' and tells us that, if their course had not been altered,

To sing these bloudie and unnaturall Crimes,
My lays had still beene to *Ideas* Bowre,
Of my deare *Ancor*, or her loved *Stowre*.[3]

In 1606 in the new version of the Sixth Eglog, now the Eighth, Drayton mentions among women especially

[1] Id[61].   [2] Vol. II, p. 310.   [3] BW[2] 545-52 var.

dear to the Muses the two daughters of Sir Henry Goodere—Frances, who in 1593 had married her cousin, Henry Goodere the younger, and Anne, now Lady Rainsford. Frances—'Panape'—is still living at Polesworth, where she is lying sick unto death:

> In shadie *Arden* her deare Flocke that keepes,
> Where mournefull *Ankor* for her sicknesse weepes.

She died there in 1606.[1] But Anne is living at Clifford (near Meon Hill and the Vale of Evesham) on the little River Stour, which until a recent revision of the county boundaries divided Gloucestershire from Warwickshire:

> Driving her Flocks up to the fruitfull *Meene*,
> Which daily lookes upon the lovely *Stowre*,
> Neere to that Vale, which of all Vales is Queene,
> Lastly, forsaking of her former Bowre:
> And of all places holdeth *Cotswold* deere,
> Which now is proud, because shee lives it neere.[2]

The Ninth Eglog of 1606 is new: there is no early version of it in *The Shepheards Garland*. The scene is set at a sheep-shearing on Cotswold, and the 'Shepherds'—the poets with our 'Rowland' as their 'King'—sit down to the rural banquet upon the green. In the cool of the evening they are joined by the Nymphs:

> Here might you many a Shepheardesse have seene,
> Of which no place, as *Cotswold*, such doth yeeld,
> Some of it native, some for love I weene,
> Thither were come from many a fertill Field.[3]

One of them was Spenser's Rosalind, whose identity, like that of the other fair ladies in the throng, remains untraced:

> There was the Widdowes Daughter of the *Glen*,
> Deare ROSALYND, that scarsly brook'd compare,

1 See p. 83.   2 Pa[8] 109–126.   3 Pa[9] 57–60.

The *Moreland*-Mayden, so admir'd of Men,
Bright GOLDY-LOCKS, and PHILLIDA the faire.[1]

Then at command of the Shepherds' King the poets
sing their roundelays—Batte and Gorbo in praise of
Daffodil, and Motto and Perkin of the Moreland
maiden, Sylvia. It is a pity that we do not know for
whom Daffodil or Sylvia stand, for these songs are
amongst the gems of English pastoral poetry.

Lastly, it is the turn of the 'Clownish King,' Rowland himself, 'his Roundelay to sing,'

When shee (whom then, they little did expect,
The fayrest Nymph that ever kept in field)
IDEA, did her sober pace direct
Towards them, with joy that every one beheld.
And whereas other drave their carefull keepe,

Hers did her follow, duely at her will,
For, through her patience shee had learnt her Sheepe,
Where ere shee went, to wait upon her still . . . .[2]

In the beautiful Roundelay that follows, Rowland and
the chorus sing once more of the 'Shepheards Queene,'
who is not only the patient keeper of her own sheep—
her thoughts—but of her poet's also:

ROWLAND. *When shee hath watch'd my Flocks by night,*
CHORUS.   *O happy Flocks that shee did keepe,*
ROWLAND. *They never needed* CYNTHIA'*s light,*
CHORUS.   *That soon gave place,*
            Amazed with her grace,
            That did attend thy Sheepe.[3]

The Tenth Eglog of 1606 is the Ninth of *The Shepheards Garland*, re-written in the same sad strain. But
whereas in the original version Drayton sings of his
unrequited love for Idea, in the later there is no mention
of Idea nor any allusion to her. Its theme is Rowland's

[1] Pa⁹ 61–4 n.   [2] Pa⁹ 173–92.   [3] Pa⁹ 223–228.

E

own vanished hopes, the loss of his influence amongst his fellow-poets, the flattering promises made on his behalf but not kept, his disgrace. But we know from other passages in Drayton's writings that he was still true to his old friendship with Anne. To the end of his life he was a frequent guest at Clifford. In the XIV Song of *Poly-Olbion*, printed in 1612, in which he writes of the Vale of Evesham and the Cotswolds, we have one of those autobiographical allusions which are scattered over the poem:

> deere *Cliffords* seat (the place of health and sport)
> Which many a time hath been the Muses quiet Port.[1]

And on 14 July 1631, the year of Drayton's death, he dated a letter to William Drummond from Clifford, 'a Knight's house in *Glocestershire*, to which Place I Yearly use to come, in the Summer Time, to recreate my self, and to spend Two or Three Months in the Country.'[2] We may assume that he was a guest at Clifford when he was treated not less poetically than medically with syrup of violets by Shakespeare's son-in-law, John Hall, who thus records his prescription and his patient's cure:

JOHN HALL'S TREATMENT OF MICHAEL DRAYTON

---

[1] PO[14] 161–162.   [2] See p. 187.
[3] 'R̸ p. ch. j oʒ. sy. violor' [sic] coch. s. tam ore quam alvo recte purgatus & curatus.' BM Egerton 2065, 18. J. Hall's own title is: *Sanitas a Domino | Curationum Historicarum | Empyricarum in certis | locis et notis personis | expertarum et proba-/tarum libellus.* It was bought in 1644 from Hall's widow at New Place by James Cooke, a Warwick physician, who issued a translation of it in 1657 under the title *Select Observations on English Bodies, in Cures both Empiricall and Historicall performed in very eminent persons in desperate cases.*

In the Thirteenth Song of *Poly-Olbion* Drayton is writing of his native Warwickshire. When the poem was published, Anne was more than forty years old; yet the mention of the river Anker and of Coventry her birthplace evokes a rhapsody of panegyric more extravagantly fantastic than anything that Drayton had yet written. The fame of Coventry and of Polesworth in legend and in history—Ursula and the eleven thousand virgins; St Editha and her nuns at Polesworth Abbey; Godiva riding naked through the city—all these were but a prefiguring and a preparation for the glory that was to be hers when Anne should be born within her walls—Anne Goodere, whose christened title Anne '*doth* Ancor *lively spell*'; and the first part of whose surname

> . . . Godiva *doth forereed,*
> . . . *and* Goodere *halfe doth sound.*[1]

In a noble passage in Drayton's *Hymne to His Ladies Birth-Place*, first printed in his folio of 1619, he once more makes Godiva the antetype of Anne Goodere:

> That Princesse, to whom thou do'st owe
> Thy Freedome, whose Cleere blushing snow,
> The envious Sunne saw, when as she
> Naked rode to make Thee free,
> Was but her Type, as to foretell,
> Thou should'st bring forth one, should excell
> Her Bounty, by whom thou should'st have
> More Honour, then she Freedome gave.[2]

Cooke, being interested chiefly in the medical aspect of the cases, omits many of Hall's personal notes about the character of his patients and some of the expressions of his piety. He renders Drayton's treatment very freely: 'Mr *Drayton an excellent Poet,* labouring of a Tertian, was cured by the following. R/ *The Emetick infusion* j *oz. syrup of violets a spoonfull, mix them*; this given wrought very well both upwards and downwards.' (*Select Observations,* p. 26.) For Hall's treatment of Anne see p. 54. Sir Henry Rainsford was also his patient (BM Egerton 2065, 72), as well as his daughter-in-law, the younger Lady Rainsford (132). Hall understates Sir Henry's age as thirty-five in 1618.

[1] PO[13] 280–1.   [2] Od[17] 29–36.

He drops into the lowest bathos when he writes that
Queen Elizabeth had been set on the throne by Provi-
dence so that

A Maide should raigne, when she was borne.[1]

Anne's husband, Sir Henry Rainsford—he had been
knighted with many hundreds of the like rank and
station by James I at his coronation—died at Clifford in
January 1621–2 in his 46th year. For all its egotistic
note few of Drayton's elegies are finer than that

UPON THE DEATH OF HIS INCOMPARABLE FRIEND . . .

Past all degrees that was so deare to me . . .
This more then mine owne selfe; that who had seene
His care of me where ever I have beene . . .
He would have sworne that to no other end
He had been borne: but onely for my friend.[2]

Henry and Anne are seen kneeling face to face in the
monument on the North wall of the chancel of Clifford
church. It is inscribed with the tribute to his virtues and
to his services to his country, written in Latin by Henry
Goodere the younger, which is printed on the next
page.[3] At the foot are the figures of their three children,
one of them in swaddling clothes, for William had died
in infancy. Henry the heir was Drayton's host in 1631.
He is the author of lines printed before George
Sandys's *Paraphrase of Job* in 1638. He became a
strong Royalist, and Clifford and his other estates were
sequestered in the Civil War.

[1] Od[17] 40.
[2] El[9].
[3] The monument is shown at p. 232 of Vol. III.

Henrico (heu charu: caput) Herculis Fi. Rainsfordi
Eq: Aur: huiusqu' dum
vixit villae Dni: Ingentis animi viri, nec ideo prudentis
aut mitis minus:
Ad honesta quaecunq' nato, ad meliora regresso, fratri
charissimo et (quod pulchrius) amico
Cum lectissima et luctuosissima coniuge eius eorumq;
duobus filiis patrizantibus
Henricus Guliel: Fi. Gooderus tanti vix
damni et doloris superstes, dum suis et suorum
lachrymis indulget,
merentissimè
moerentissimus P.L.
Nec minus exultat in memoria et exemplo

Tantae ⎰ Charitatis
⎱ Industriae
⎱ Pietatis

cuius ⎰ Uxor familia, amicorum consensus
testis ⎱ Patria, patriaeque colonia Virginia
DEUS
Nec sibi exoptat aliud monumentum, aut meliorem
famam, quam quod tantarum virtutum testis sit
HENRICUS GOODERUS

Sir Henry Rainsford of Clifford in the County of
Glocᵉ. Knight (Sonne of Hercules Rainsford, Esq;)
Died the 27ᵗʰ of January 1622 in the yeare of his Age
46: He married Ann Daughter and Co-Heire of Sʳ
Henry Goodere of Polesworth in the County of War:
Kni. wᵗʰ whom he lived 27 yeares and had issue 3 sons.
Williaᵐ Died: Henry married Elianor Daughter and
Co Heire of Robert Boswell of Combe in the County of
Southamp' Esq. & Francis.

INSCRIPTION ON THE MONUMENT TO SIR
HENRY RAINSFORD IN CLIFFORD CHURCH

JOHN HALL'S TREATMENT OF LADY RAINSFORD

It seems likely that Anne continued to live at Clifford or in its neighbourhood during the years of her widowhood. We have seen that Drayton used to go there every summer, and that he wrote to Drummond from there 14 July 1631. A few months later, when he was dying in London, he seems to have recalled and reviewed the whole course of his life-long worship of his Idea with intense and concentrated fervour in the verses which he made the night before he died:

> Soe well I love thee, as without thee I
> Love Nothing: yf I might Chuse, I'de rather dye
> Then bee on[e] day debarde thy Companye. . . .

Soe all my Thoughts are peyces but of you
Whiche put together make a Glass soe true
As I therin noe others face but yours can veiwe.[1]

Anne's eldest son, the younger Sir Henry Rainsford,
writing from Clifford to his uncle, Sir Francis Nethersole, at Polesworth in July 1632, adds a postscript:
'My mother remembers her very kindly to your self and
Lady.'[2] About the year 1633 she was a patient of John
Hall, who in recording his treatment of her for the
stone pays a charming tribute to her character and her
attainments:

> Domina Rainsforde calculo cruciata fe[bri] siti
> circa ætatis annum 62 sequentem curata ita ut nunc
> valet vidua modesta pia benigna et de omnibus bene
> merita, sacrorum librarum [sic] lectioni addictissima,
> linguæ Gallicæ et Itallecæ experta.[2]

We do not know when or where she died. The space
left after her name on the monument in Clifford church
was never filled with the date of her death, neither does
the register record her burial. For lovers of English
poetry her memory lives only but lives for ever in
Drayton's verse.

EXTRACT FROM THE WILL OF JOHN COMBE OF OLD
STRATFORD (d. 1614)

... I do nominate and appoint Sir Edward Blunt
knight, Sir Henry Rainsford knight, Sir Francis Smith
knight, and John Palmer of Compton Esquire, to be
overseers of this my will unto whom I give five pounds
apiece, or unto every one of them a silver salt worth
five pounds. Item, I give Mrs Barnes fourty shillings
to buy her a ring, and to the Lady Rainsford fourty
shillings to buy her a ring.
In the same will he gives:
    To Mr William Shackspere five pounds.[4]

---

[1] See below, p. 223; Vol. 1, p. 507.
[2] SPD, Charles I 16, Vol. 22, no. 49.   [3] BM Egerton 2065, 82.
[4] A Life of William Shakespeare, by J. O. Halliwell, 1848, pp.
234-240.

CHAPTER V

LUCY COUNTESS OF BEDFORD

DRAYTON tells us that he had been 'bequeathed' to the service of Lucy Harington by Sir Henry Goodere himself, '(not long since deceased) . . . the first cherisher of my Muse, which had been by his death left a poore Orphane to the worlde, had hee not before bequeathed it to that Lady whom he so deerly loved.'[1] She was the elder daughter of John Harington, esquire, of Exton and Burley in Rutlandshire, who by his marriage with Anne Kelway, a wealthy heiress, had also come into possession of Combe Abbey, near Coventry in Warwickshire. She was baptized at Stepney 26 January 1580–1. When she was only three years old, Claude Desainliens (better known by his name Anglicized as Holyband), who then kept school at Greenwich, dedicated to her his *Campo di fior or else the flourie Field of Foure Languages, for the Furtherance of the Learners of the Latine, French, English, but chieflie of the Italian tongue.* It was the earliest of a long series of tributes accorded to her by writers of her day. Possibly Holyband, who in 1580 had dedicated to Lucy's mother his *Treatise for declining of [French] Verbes,* and there alluded to the good offices of his patroness on behalf of his *Dictionarie, French and English,* had a hand in Lucy's education. It may also have been part of Drayton's service to her to act as her tutor.

She was little more than thirteen years old when in 1594 Drayton dedicated to her his *Matilda,*[2] 'your selfe beeing in full measure, adorned with like excellent gifts, both of bodie and minde.' On 12 December in the same year she was married at Stepney to Edward Russell, the young Earl of Bedford, who was then twenty-one years

---

[1] Dedication of EHE[5] to the Earl of Bedford; see p. 75 below, and Vol. v, p. 112.

[2] Vol. I, p. 210.

old. The year before Lady Bridget Manners, to whom he and his friend Southampton had been suggested as eligible candidates for her hand, had spoken disdainfully of them both, 'for they be so younge, and fantasticall, and would be so caryed awaye.'[1] It is 'To the excellent and most accomplish't Ladie: Lucie Countesse of Bedford' that Drayton dedicates his *Endimion and Phœbe* in 1595.[2] His tone has already become a little deferential to this 'Great Ladie, essence of my cheefest good,' who rained upon him her 'sweet golden showers.' He professes that:

> but thy selfe no subject will I aske,
> Upon whose prayse my soule shall spend her powers,

and it has been suggested that the allegory was written on the occasion of Lucy's marriage. It is, however, in no sense an epithalamium. Its second title, *Ideas Latmus*, the verses by E. P.[3] and S. G. which introduce it, and Drayton's own fervid lines to the sweet 'Nymph of Ankor' which bring it to a close, all show that Anne Goodere is the subject of the poem. It was dedicated to Lucy out of compliment to Drayton's young patroness and Bedford's bride. Nevertheless, the high-pitched language in which these and Drayton's other dedications to Lucy are written, suggests that at that time he had for her an affectionate admiration only less than the love he bore to Anne. In 1596 he inscribes to her the volume containing the first version of *Robert, Duke of Normandy*, with amended versions of *Matilda* and *Piers Gaveston;* and there is a second dedication to Lucy's mother, Lady Harington. In *Mortimeriados*, in the same year, he addressed the longest of all his dedications in verse to Lucy as the

[1] C. M. Stopes, *Third Earl of Southampton*, p. 66; Belvoir MSS. in Hist. MSS. Comm. Rep. xii, i, 321.

[2] Vol. I, p. 126.

[3] Perhaps Edward Purefoy, Drayton's near neighbour at Fenny Drayton. See Vol. v, p. 20.

> Rarest of Ladies, all, of all I have,
> Anchor of my poore Tempest-beaten state.[1]

Mindful of Lucy's kinship with Sir Philip Sidney,[2] the poet proclaims her the heir of his virtues as the world of his fame. Twice over he breaks off the long story of Mortimer to invoke her who is the inspiration and life of his Muse:

> Renowned *Lucie*, vertues truest frend,
> Which doest a spyrit into my spyrit infuse,
> And from thy beames the light I have dost lend. . .

And later:

> True vertuous Lady, now of mirth I sing,
> To sharpen thy sweet spirit with some delight.[3]

When in 1597 he first published his *Englands Heroicall Epistles*, he inscribed the Epistles of Rosamond and Henry II to the Countess of Bedford, who had not yet reached her eighteenth year; those of Queen Isabel and Mortimer to her mother, Lady Harington; and those of Isabel and Richard the Second to her husband, the Earl of Bedford:[4]

> Thrice noble and my gracious Lord, the love I have ever borne to the illustrious house of Bedford, and to the honourable familie of the Harringtons, to the which by marriage your Lordship is happily united, hath long since devoted my true and zealous affection to your honourable service, and my Poems to the protection of my noble Lady, your Countesse. . .

[1] Vol. 1, p. 306.

[2] Lucy was Philip Sidney's first cousin once removed. Her grandmother was Lucy, daughter of Sir William Sidney (1482?–1554), to whom Penshurst was granted in 1552. She married Sir James Harington, father of John Harington, afterwards 1st Lord Harington of Exton, Lucy's father. Philip Sidney was the grandson of Sir William.

[3] Mo 260–6; 2080–3.

[4] These dedications are printed below, pp. 72–4.

These and some of the earlier dedications to Lucy were reprinted in successive editions of Drayton's poems; thenceforth, however, none of his new work was dedicated to her. When in 1602 he re-cast *Mortimeriados* and printed it as *The Barrons Wars*, the new version was inscribed to a new patron, Walter Aston, and every allusion to the Bedfords was suppressed. Four years later, Drayton printed in his *Poemes Lyrick and Pastorall* a new version of the Eglogs which in 1593 he had published under the title *Idea The Shepheards Garland*. In the main the version of 1606 is that printed later in 1619. But the Eighth Eglog contains a significant and bitter passage, which, one may suppose with satisfaction, Drayton afterwards regretted, for he suppressed it in the later version:

> So once *Selena* seemed to reguard,
> that faithfull *Rowland* her so highly praysed,
> and did his travell for a while reward,
> As his estate she purpos'd to have raysed,
> > But soone she fled him and the swaine defyes,
> > Ill is he sted that on such faith relies.

> And to deceitefull *Cerberon* she cleaves
> that beastly clowne to vile of to be spoken,
> and that good shepheard wilfully she leaves
> and falsly al her promises hath broken,
> > and al those beautyes whilom that her graced
> > with vulgar breath perpetually defaced.

> what dainty flower yet ever was there found
> whose smell or beauty mighte the sence delight
> wherewith *Eliza* when she lived was crown'd
> in goodly chapplets he for her not dighte
> > which became withered soon as ere shee ware them
> > So ill agreeing with the brow that bare them.

> Let age sit soone and ugly on her brow,
> no sheepheards praises living let her have

> to her last end noe creature pay one vow
> nor flower be strew'd on her forgotten grave.
> And to the last of all devouring tyme
> nere be her name remembred more in rime.

In classical mythology Lucina and Selene are sometimes identified alike with Diana or Artemis. There are other and stronger reasons for believing that Selena, who has withdrawn her patronage from Rowland, is Lucy Countess of Bedford. But if so, why did Drayton, hitherto so fulsome in his adulation, now pour scorn and curses on his former patroness? And who is the utterly vile and deceitful Cerberon who has supplanted Rowland in Selena's favour? Before we can suggest an answer, let us review Lady Bedford's social position and influence at this period, and take account of some of those who were prominent in the circle in which she moved.

Her father's namesake and cousin, John Harington of Kelston, whose ingenious invention set forth in *The Metamorphosis of Ajax* entitles him to a niche in the temple of Fame as the father of modern sanitary science, pays him this humorous tribute in the *Apologie* which he wrote for that book:

> John Harington of Exton, in the County of Rutland Knight, *alias* John Har: of Burleygh, in the Countie aforesaide, *alias* of Combe in the Countie of Warwicke, *alias* of Ooston in the Countie of Leceister, come into the Court, or else. &c. Hath he freeholde? Yea he is a prittie free-holder in all these shires; Moreover . . . . though he be a free-holder, yet he hath maried his daughter to one, that for a grandfather, for a father, for two uncles, and three or foure aunts, may compare with most men in England. Lastly, . . . and foure hundred confirme it, . . . hee relieves manye poore and sets them to woorke, he builds not onely his owne houses, but Colledges, and Hospitalls.

Harington also had an estate and residence at Stepney.

Lucy had been baptized there, and she was married there in 1594. Her younger sister Frances was also christened there 6 October 1587, and her brother John, afterwards the 2nd Lord Harington of Exton, 3 May 1592.

The rank and wealth of the Earl of Bedford, the influence of Lady Bedford's mother, Lady Harington, at the Court of Elizabeth, and, perhaps above all, her own beauty and charm and her brilliant and lively parts had won for her a distinguished place among the men and women who flocked about the throne. Related by birth to the Sidneys and by marriage to Francis Bacon, she was also a member—perhaps already the centre—of a brilliant literary circle. As early as 1598 Florio dedicated to her his *Worlde of Wordes*, joining her name with those of the Earls of Rutland and Southampton, and paying a compliment to her knowledge of the Italian, French and Spanish tongues. Florio's translation of Montaigne's Essays was entered in the Stationers' Register two years later. In place of the threefold dedication of *A Worlde of Wordes*, it has three separate dedications, each of them addressed to two ladies of rank in language which surpasses in its euphuism anything in *Euphues* itself. The Countess of Bedford and her mother, Lady Harington, are the first pair, Elizabeth Countess of Rutland and Penelope Rich the next, and Lady Elizabeth Grey and Lady Mary Neville the third. Florio acknowledges that but for Lady Bedford's encouragement he would not have continued the book beyond the first chapter, which he finished in her house. It was she who introduced him to his future collaborators, Theodore Diodati and Matthew Gwynn.

In 1599 we find her already established at Court, for she is named with Lady Harington her mother, the Dowager Countess of Bedford and the Earl of Bedford amongst the receivers of presents from her Majesty on New Year's day.[1]

[1] J. Nichols, *Progresses of Q. Eliz.*, III, pp. 129, 133, 143, 144, 147.

There survives a lightning sketch of Lucy Bedford in a lampoon written two years later on the occasion of the conspiracy of the Earl of Essex. The Earl of Bedford played a somewhat ambiguous and inglorious part in that rising. According to the account which he gave in his own defence at his trial, at ten o'clock, on Sunday, the 8th of February, the day of the rising, he was at his own house, which stood near the Strand, 'preparing to serve God,' when Lady Rich—Sidney's 'Stella' and sister to Essex—came to the house and desired to speak with him. She said her brother had need of him; so he went with her in her coach to Essex House, where Essex had gathered his followers, and was holding under lock and key the Lord Keeper, the Lord Chief Justice and the others who had been sent to reason with him. Bedford went out with Essex and his followers in his dash for the City. He came away, however, when Lord Burleigh was sent to proclaim Essex a traitor, with a promise of pardon to all who should leave him, and instead got some horsemen together and galloped to Court. The lampoonist, a partisan of Essex, sums up Bedford's share in the episode thus:

> Bedford hee ranne awaie
> when ower men lost the daie
> so 't is assigned
> except his fine dancing Dame
> do their hard hartes tame
> and swear it is a shame
> fooles should bee fined.[1]

He was imprisoned and sentenced to a fine of £20,000, which was afterwards reduced to half that sum through Lady Bedford's influence with Cecil.[2] There are passages in the *Heroicall Epistles* of Richard II and his Queen, dedicated to the Earl of Bedford, and in *The Owle* which suggest that, although Drayton condemned

[1] See *The Third Earl of Southampton*, by C. C. Stopes, p. 236.
[2] *SPD* cclxxix, 91, 102; cclxxxi, 67.

the rising of the Earl of Essex,[1] he was not without sympathy for some of those involved in his fall. If so, Bedford's apparent betrayal of his friend at the moment of danger may have contributed to the estrangement between the poet and his patroness which seems to date from about that time.

It is more likely, however, that the cause of the estrangement was Drayton's jealousy or hostility towards some—writers, perhaps, or others—who enjoyed Lucy's favour. At the head of the writers was Ben Jonson. His first play, *Every Man in His Humour*, had established his reputation when in 1598 it was acted at the Globe Theatre by the Lord Chamberlain's company with Shakespeare in the cast. Two years later he produced his Court play, *Cynthias Revells*, of which a printed copy presented by Ben to Lucy is now at the William Andrews Clark Memorial Library of the University of California. In that copy is inserted on a printed leaf a set of verses headed 'Author ad Librum,' in which he bids it go to 'Cynthias fairest nymph,'

> the bright, and amiable
> LUCY of Bedford.

The gift of the book and the words with which it was presented suggest that Ben was already established on terms of easy familiarity with Lady Bedford. Jonson makes the same playful use of her Christian name and its meaning in two out of the three poems to Lucy which he included among his Epigrams.[2] In his Ode ἐνθουσιαστική, too, he writes of her 'illustrate brightness,' her 'wit as quick and sprightfull | As fire,' 'her judgement (adorned with Learning).' That Ode is part of his contribution to the 'Poeticall Essaies . . . on the Phœnix and Turtle' which are appended as a substantial literary make-weight to Robert Chester's *Loves Martyr*, printed, like *Cynthias Revells*, in 1601. Besides

[1] EHE[5] variants and notes; O 1153 ff. and note.
[2] *Epigg.* lxxvi, xciv.

Jonson's *Epos* and Ode the 'Essaies' include Shakespeare's 'Let the bird of lowdest lay'and its accompanying *Threnos*, and lines by one 'Ignoto' (who may perhaps he Donne), George Chapman, and John Marston, all celebrating the excellence and rarity of the Phoenix. If the Phoenix is indeed Lucy Bedford, these 'Essaies' must be added to the mass of verse which they and their fellow-poets wrote in her praise.[1]

In the new reign Lady Bedford's influence became even greater than before, and yet more poets attached themselves to her train. At the accession of James she was not amongst the ladies deputed by the Council to escort the new Queen out of Scotland. Instead, she and her mother with some other ladies of high rank seem to have stolen a march on them; for 'before the departure of these personages aforesaid [these] Ladies of honour went voluntarily into Scotland to attend her Majestie in her journey into England.'[2] She immediately won a place in the new Queen's affections, which she kept not quite unimpaired till the death of Anne in 1619. Her name is found again and again in the list of performers in the Court masques, lavishly produced at an amazing cost, in which the Queen indulged her extravagant tastes. The first of them was Daniel's *Vision of Twelve Goddesses*, which was produced at Hampton Court at Christmas 1603, and seems to have been the occasion of Ben Jonson's expulsion from the audience for his outspoken criticism and unruly behaviour.[3] Daniel printed it in 1604 with a letter to the Countess of Bedford, in which he explained 'the intent and scope' of the Masque.

---

[1] Jonson's Ode ἐνθουσιαστική is found also without that title in a 17th-century commonplace book which once belonged to someone closely associated with the Harington family. It is now in the Bodleian (Rawl. poet. 31) .The lines are headed 'To : L: C: Off: B :' For the text of the 'Essaies' and for possible reasons for identifying the Phoenix and Turtle with the Bedfords, see *The Phoenix and Turtle*, Shakespeare Head Press, 1936.

[2] Nichols, *Progresses Jas. I.*

[3] See my *Poems of Ben Jonson*, pp. 355, 371–2.

He also printed an Epistle in verse to Lady Bedford with the *Panegyrike Congratulatory* which he had delivered at Burley Hill, in Rutlandshire, the seat of Sir John Harington, when the King visited him there in his progress from Scotland to London. It is uncertain whether Jonson is alluding to Drayton or to Daniel when he writes disparagingly to Sidney's daughter, the Countess of Rutland, that 'Lucy the bright'

> [hath] a better verser got,
> (Or *Poet*, in the court account) then I,
> And who doth me (though I not him) envy.[1]

Daniel, no less than Drayton, had some reason to be jealous of the rising poet who was so soon to supplant him as principal masque-writer at Court.

In December 1600 John Harington the epigrammatist presented his kinswoman, Lady Bedford, with a manuscript copy of Philip and Mary Sidney's translation of the Psalms, to which he had added a selection of his own Epigrams. In a letter which accompanied the gift he shows a deference to her rank that contrasts oddly with the buffoonery which is the dominant note of his character and his writings, and also with the breezy freedom used by Ben the bricklayer in his poems to Lucy.[2]

Tobie Matthew, the friend of Henry Goodere and John Donne and Bacon's *alter ego*, was reputed to be another of the moths that fluttered about Lucy's candle. On 8 August 1606 he wrote to Dudley Carleton from Florence:

> What was the reason that drove La: of Bedford thence [*sc.* from the Court] and particularly how thrives shee, whom they would needes persuade me, I was in love withall?

---

[1] *The Forrest*, xii. See my *Poems of B.J.*, pp. 75, 355. Dr R. W. Short (*RES.*, July 1939) argues plausibly that Drayton, not Daniel, is meant; but see P. Simpson's reply, *RES*, Sept. 1939.

[2] Harington, *Letters and Epigrams*, ed. N. E. Maclure, 1930, p. 87.

F

John Donne is one of Lady Bedford's intimates whose acquaintance with her is likely to have been a matter of concern to Drayton. We have no clue to the date at which Jonson presented to Lucy a MS. copy of 'Mr Donnes Satyres,' accompanied with the set of verses which he printed amongst his Epigrammes in 1616,[1] neither can we say with certainty at what date she became acquainted with Donne himself. Gosse puts it as late as 1607 or 1608, believing that the acquaintance did not begin till Lucy went to live at Twickenham in the house where Bacon had once lived and pursued his philosophical studies and research. Donne was then living at Mitcham. He had long been intimate both with Sir Henry Goodere and with Ben Jonson; and it is difficult to believe that Lady Bedford, the familiar friend of both the knight and the poet, would have remained a stranger to Donne. As early as February 1602, on the occasion of the death of Lucy's only child, Donne had written to Goodere of 'young Bedford's death.' That indeed is not evidence of his personal acquaintance with Lady Bedford; but it is unlikely that the brilliant young poet, who as the Lord-Keeper's secretary must have become well-known at Court, would have been overlooked by the great but still youthful lady who gave her patronage so lavishly to the wits and poets of the day.

After glancing at Lady Bedford's position at Court and at the literary circle with which she was surrounded, we shall perhaps understand better the reasons for the break in her relations with Drayton. If she is the Selena of Drayton's Eighth Eglog of 1606, then the 'deceitefull Cerberon' to whom she cleaves in place of the jilted Rowland may perhaps be sought among the writers named above. Some of them we may eliminate at once. Shakespeare stands far above suspicion. Drayton would never have counted the gentle Daniel or his 'worthy friend,' George Chapman,[2] as 'too vile of to be

---

[1] Ep. xciv; *Poems*, p. 31.
[2] See Unc[12] n, Vol. I, p. 503, for D's lines on Chapman's *Hesiod*.

spoken.' He might have written so of John Marston, though Marston seems to have defended him against attacks made by Joseph Hall.[1] It is possible that, like Davies, Marston is alluding to Drayton as Decius when in *Jack Drum's Entertainment* Brabant Junior and Brabant Senior, who is thought to be Jonson, are discussing some of the 'moderne wits':

> Bra. *Ju.* What thinks you of the Lines of *Decius?*
> Writes he not a goode cordiall sappie still?
> Bra. *Sig.* A surreinde Jaded wit, but a rubbes on.[2]

But we have no evidence that Marston enjoyed any great measure of Lady Bedford's favour. The Rabelaisian author of *The Metamorphosis of Ajax* might well have inspired the austere Drayton with stern disgust. Moreover, in his *Apologie* he had written ungraciously of Drayton's patron, the elder Goodere, echoing Norton's sneer:

> *Hic niger est, hunc tu regina caveto.*[3]

On the other hand, the deferential and apologetic terms of Harington's letter to Lucy suggest that, although a kinsman, he was not on terms of close intimacy with her. As for Tobie Mathew nothing that is known of his life and character is likely to have roused Drayton's jealousy or rancour.

We are left with Florio, Jonson and Donne among the writers, any one of whom at that date might have incurred Drayton's censure whether on moral or literary grounds and his jealousy by the favour which he came to enjoy at Lucy's hands.

Much of Jonson's verse, both for its occasional ribaldry and perhaps for its breaking away from the

[1] See below, pp. 99–100.

[2] Act IV. 'Surreinde' is 'over-reined,' 'over-ridden.' Sir E. K. Chambers thinks that Dekker is meant (*Eliz. Stage*, IV, 21). He believes that this play began the 'Poetomachia' and provoked Jonson's *Poetaster* in reply.

[3] See above, p. 28.

high poetical tradition left by Sidney and Spenser, was likely to win a full share of the reprobation which Drayton again and again in his writings poured upon the work of his contemporaries.[1] That is no less true of Donne's. In his *Songs and Sonnets*, in his *Elegies*, and above all in his *Paradoxes*, which, though never printed in his lifetime, circulated freely in manuscript, there was plenty to offend Drayton's much straiter morality. Donne, too, far more than Jonson was a leader in the revolt from the Petrarchan and Spenserian tradition.

But if Drayton's 'deceitful Cerberon' stands for some writer in Lucy's circle, and not rather for some statesman or other high personage, or again some group —some triumvirate perhaps—that she had gathered about her, John Florio might be more likely than any other. The all-British Drayton would be likely to share in the popular dislike felt for foreigners at that day. And Florio, small of stature and mean in figure, in manner pert, provocative and pushing, in religious outlook a little puritanical, was defiling the purity of the English language by his affected diction and strange idioms. Nevertheless he stood high in the favour of the lady to whom, while she was no more than a child, Drayton had been 'bequeathed'; who had ceased to be Rowland's patroness, and had suffered her own gracious parts to be defaced with the 'vulgar breath' of others. It was Lady Bedford who encouraged Florio to translate Montaigne;[2] and her parents, Sir John and Lady Harington, had received him into their household. He had won his way, perhaps through Lady Bedford's influence, into a lucrative and honoured place at Court. He translated the *Basilikon Doron* of King James, 'the great Olcon,' to

[1] In *RES* April 1940 Dr R. W. Short argues that Cerberon is Jonson. See, however, the replies by Percy Simpson and Mrs Tillotson in *RES* July 1940.

[2] Professor Hebel suggested that in the name Cerberon there might be an allusion to Cerberus, the three-headed guardian of hell, applied to the three-fold dedication of the *Essayes*.

whose praise the shepherd Rowland had drawn 'all the rurall Rout,' to be rewarded only with royal neglect and his own disgrace.[1]

We must not, however, be too ready to assume that Cerberon was a writer. The name may be meant to suggest Cranborne, which was the title taken by Cecil when he was made a viscount in 1604. In a later chapter we shall show reason for believing that Drayton regarded Cecil's character and policy as pernicious. There is a hint of Lucy's influence with him in the lampoon on the Essex rising, confirmed by the remission of a great part of Bedford's fine. At this time, too, her father, Lord Harington, used her as an intermediary with Cecil in suggesting that young John Harington should marry the Secretary's daughter. Cecil tactfully and politely declined the honour of the match.[2]

When the Pastorals were next printed in 1619, the offensive passage on Selena was cancelled. The sonnet in which Drayton had inscribed *Endimion and Phœbe* to the Countess of Bedford was included in the successive editions of his sonnets. The prose dedication to her of the Heroicall Epistles of Rosamond and King John was allowed to remain in repeated editions prior to that of 1619. But no new allusion was made to her, and there is no evidence that Drayton was ever restored to Lucy Bedford's patronage or favour.

[1] See p. 130 below.
[2] *Salisbury Papers*, XVII, pp. 629, 291.

CHAPTER VI

EARLY FRIENDS AND PATRONS

WE have already drawn on some of Drayton's dedications for the evidence which they yield concerning events or periods of his life. Throughout they remain one of our chief sources of information concerning his relations with the men and women whose friendship he shared or whose patronage he enjoyed. The earliest of the dedications are all made to members of families prominent in Warwickshire or the adjoining Midland counties. In 1593 he dedicated his *Shepheards Garland* to young Robert Dudley, the only son of the great Earl of Leicester. Born in 1573, Robert had come into possession of his castle of Kenilworth in 1589 on the death of his uncle, Ambrose Dudley, Earl of Warwick, to whom Leicester had left it for life with remainder to Robert. His title to the earldoms of Leicester and Warwick was unjustly denied him; for Leicester refused to acknowledge the secret marriage which he made in 1573 with Douglas, widow of Lord Sheffield, Robert's mother, and the mother also of the Lord Sheffield whose three sons, drowned in the Humber in 1614, are mourned in Drayton's Elegy.[1] To Robert Dudley Drayton subscribed himself 'Your most affectionate and devoted'; but we have no other clue to the nature of his relations with Leicester's brilliant son, unless, indeed, he is the 'Robin-redbrest' of the Third Eglog.[2] In 1594 Robert, then but twenty-one years old, was sent out by Elizabeth to Trinidad and Paria in command of three ships of war; and the expedition is recorded by Drayton in his *Poly-Olbion*.[3]

Henry Caundish, or Cavendish, the 'time-enobled Gentleman' to whom Drayton dedicated his *Peirs Gaveston* in 1593, was the eldest son of Sir William Cavendish, the first builder of Chatsworth, by the

[1] El⁴.   [2] SG³ and the note thereon.   [3] PO¹⁹ 372–5.

redoubtable Bess of Hardwick. A soldier and a politician, we have Drayton's testimony that he was also '*a kinde Mæcenas to Schollers, and a favourer of learning and Arts.*' He was Member of Parliament for Derbyshire in 1572. In 1585 he held Mary Queen of Scots as his prisoner at Tutbury. He died in 1616. In this dedication Drayton assails his hostile critics for the first time with a bitterness which we find again and again in his later work. He begs his patron's protection

> *against the Art-hating humorists of this malicious time, whose envious thoughts (like Quailes) feed only on poyson, snarling (like doggs) at every thing which never so little disagreeeth from their owne Stoicall[1] dispositions.*[2]

We have seen that from 1579 to 1583 Anthony Cooke, 'the deere chyld of the Muses, and his ever kind Mecænas,' to whom in 1594 Drayton dedicated his *Ideas Mirrour*,

> Which but for you had slept in sable Night,[3]

was lord of the manor of Hartshill, although he may not have lived there.[4] He was knighted by Essex at Cadiz in 1596, and afterwards served under him in Ireland, whence he returned in 1602, 'weake and sickly, but very well able to come to the Queen, who used him very graciously.'[5] Two years later he died, 'killed by butchery for surgeon's practice,'—so his plain-spoken aunt, the Dowager Lady Russell, wrote to Cecil, begging him to take his son into his service.[6]

Englands Heroicall Epistles were first printed in 1597 without any general dedication. Drayton dedicated most of them individually to one or other of his friends or else to some person of consequence whose patronage he hoped to win. Most of these dedications are repeated

---

[1] *Sic*, for Satirical? [2] Vol. I, p. 158.
[3] See Vol. I, p. 96. Variant reading 1599. [4] P. 12.
[5] Letter of Cecil to Sir Geo. Carew, ? Aug. 1602, Camden Soc., ed. J. Maclean, p. 125.
[6] Hist. MSS. Comm., *Salisbury Papers*, XVI, p. 292.

in the several editions of the Epistles down to and including the undated edition, which is believed to have
been printed between 1613 and 1618, but not in the
folio of 1619[1] or in the later editions. Apart from the
autobiographical information which we may draw from
some of them, they have high interest as examples of
Drayton's prose.

The first in order is that of the Epistles of Rosamond
and King Henry the Second, addressed to the Countess
of Bedford. It was printed in the first edition of 1597
and in all others before 1619.[2]

To the excellent Lady Lucie,
Countesse of Bedford.

*Madam, after all the admired wits of this excellent
age, which have laboured in the sad complaintes of faire
and unfortunate* Rosamond, *and by the excellence of
invention, have sounded the depth of her sundry
passions: I present to your Ladiship this Epistle of hers
to King* Henry, *whom I may rather call her lover then
beloved. Heere must your Ladiship behold variablenes in
resolution: woes constantly grounded: laments abruptly
broken off: much confidence, no certainty, wordes beget-
ting teares, teares confounding matter, large complaints
in little papers: and many deformed cares, in one uni-
formed Epistell. I strive not to affect singularity, yet
would faine flie imitation, and prostrate mine owne
wants to other mens perfections. Your judiciall eye must
modell forth what my penne hath layd together: much
would shee say to a King, much would I say to a Countesse, but that the method of my Epistle must conclude the
modestie of hers: which I wish may recommend my ever
vowed service to your honour.*

Michaell Drayton.

The next pair of Epistles—that of King John and
Matilda's reply—is dedicated in the first edition only

[1] Vol. ii of the Shakespeare Head edition.
[2] Vol. v, p. 103.

To his singuler
good Lord, the Lord
Mount-eagle.

*My verie good Lord, let mee not need by tedious
protestation to expostulate the long conceived desire I
have had to honour you: your owne noble inclination can
best conceive, what greater testimonie coulde bee demon-
strate: and I had rather abreviate what I woulde say,
then by saying too much, to give doubtfull construction, of
undoubted well meaning. Let this my Epistles be one
staire or little degree, whereby I may ascend into the
entrance of your good opinion, as one whom I have chose,
amongst the number of mine honourable friends, whose
patronage may give protection to my newe adventured
Poesie. Thus leaving your honour to your hopefull fortunes, and my Muse to your gracious acceptance, I wish
you all happiness.*

Michaell Drayton.

William Parker, 4th Baron Monteagle—he succeeded
to that title during his father's lifetime by right of his
mother, daughter and heir of William Stanley, 3rd
Lord Monteagle, who died 1581—was the eldest son
of Edward Parker, 10th Baron Morley, and was born
in 1575. He suffered imprisonment and was heavily
fined for his part in the Essex rising of 1601. He was a
Catholic, but showed himself unstable both in his
religious and his political loyalties. He is best known as
having disclosed the famous letter which is alleged to
have led to the discovery of the Gunpowder Plot. The
dedication to Monteagle was withdrawn after the first
edition of 1597, and was not replaced by any other.

The Epistles of Queen Isabel and Mortimer are
dedicated to Lucy Bedford's mother:

To the vertuous Lady, the Lady
Anne Harrington: wife to the honourable
Gentleman, Sir John Harrington,
Knight.

My singuler good Lady: your many vertues knowne in generall to all, and your gracious favours to my unworthy selfe, have confirmed that in mee, which before I knew you, I onely sawe by the light of other mens judgements. Honour seated in your breast, findes herselfe adorned as in a rich pallace, making that excellent which makes her admirable: which like the sunne (from thence) begetteth most precious things of this earthly world, onely by the vertue of his rayes, not the nature of the mould. Worth is best discerned by the worthie, dejected mindes want that pure fire which should give vigour to vertue. I refer to your owne great thoughts, (the unpartiall Judges of true affection) the unfained zeale I have ever borne to your honorable service: and so rest your Ladiships humbly at command.   *Michaell Drayton.*

In the sonnet to Lady Harington which was printed with the Legends in 1596 he writes:

Your gracious kindnes (Madam) claimes my hart,
Your bountie bids my hand to make it knowne,
Of me your vertues each do claime a part,
And leave me thus the least part of my owne.[1]

Lady Harington died in 1620 and was buried at Exton, where the Countess of Bedford had raised a sumptuous monument to her grandparents.

The Epistle of Queen Isabel to Richard the Second and the King's answer are dedicated from 1597 onwards

To the Right Honourable and
my very good Lord, *Edward* Earle
of Bedford.

Thrice noble and my gracious Lord, the love I have ever borne to the illustrious house of Bedford, *and to the honourable familie of the* Harringtons, *to the which by marriage your Lordship is happily united, hath long since devoted my true and zealous affection to your honourable service, and my Poems to the protection of*

[1] Vol. I, p. 250.

my noble Lady, your Countesse: to whose service I was first bequeathed, by that learned and accomplished Gentleman, Sir Henry Goodere *(not long since deceased,) whose I was whilst he was: whose patience, pleased to beare with the imperfections of my heedlesse and unstaied youth. That excellent and matchlesse Gentleman, was the first cherisher of my Muse, which had been by his death left a poore Orphane to the worlde, had hee not before bequeathed it to that Lady whom he so deerly loved. Vouchsafe then my deere Lord to accept this Epistle, which I dedicate as zealously, as (I hope) you will patronize willingly, untill some more acceptable service may be witness of my love towards your honour.*

Your Lordships ever,
Michaell Drayton.

The Epistle of Queen Katherine to Owen Tudor and its answer are dedicated to Lord Henry Howard in the edition of 1597; but the dedication was not repeated in any subsequent edition.

To the Right Honourable, the
Lord *Henrie Howard.*

Learned and noble Lord, custome and continuaunce have sealed this priviledge to Poetry, that (sometime) the light subject of a laboured Poem, is graced with the title of a learned and judiciall censor: your Lordship sufficiently knoweth what I but put you in remembrance off, your wisedome and experience know what hath beene most usuall in the course of times: your judgement makes me doubtfull, beeing what I am: your honor gives me some comfort, beeing what you are: Counsell is not ever conversant with severitie, and I know true vertue loveth, what is never so little like herselfe, howe unseasoned so ever my rymes seeme to the worlde: I am pleased if you peruse them with patience. Thus wishing my lines may bee as acceptable as I desire, I leave them to your learned censor.

Michaell Drayton.

Howard (1540–1614), described in *The Dictionary of National Biography* as 'the most learned noble of his day,' was the second son of Henry Howard, Earl of Surrey, the poet. Foxe the martyrologist was his tutor, but was dismissed on the accession of Queen Mary. Howard was a Catholic, but like Monteagle wavered both in his religious profession and in his political allegiance. By 'suppleness and flattery' he won a commanding position at the Court of James I, who made him Earl of Northampton in 1604. He died in 1614. He was the enemy of two poets so remote from one another in outlook and achievement as Ben Jonson and George Wither. Ben told Drummond that 'Northampton was his mortall enimie,' by whom he was accused before the Council 'both of popperie and treason.'[1] Wither, when examined at Whitehall concerning a supposed seditious passage in his book, *Withers Motto* (1621), in which he said that he had seen the downfall of his enemies, explained that by those words he meant the late Earl of Northampton.[2]

From 1605 and afterwards the Epistles of Queen Katherine and Owen Tudor were dedicated

To Sir John Swinerton Knight,
and one of the Aldermen of
the Citie of London.

Worthy Sir, so much mistrust I my owne abilitie, to doe the least right to your vertues, that I could gladly wish any thing that is truely mine, were woorthy to beare your name, so much (reverend Sir) I esteeme you, and so ample interest have you in my love; To some honourable friends have I dedicated these Poemes, (with whom I ranke you: may I escape presumption) Like not this Britaine the worse, though after some former Impressions he be lastly to you consecrated; in this like an honest man that would partlie approove his owne woorth, before he would pre-

---

[1] *Conversations*, l. 325.
[2] *Cal SPD* 1619–23, p. 268. Wither deposed that before printing it he 'did acquaint . . . Mr. Drayton' with it. See below, p. 195.

*sume his friends patronage, with whom you shall ever
commaund my service, and have my best wishes.*
That love you truely,
Mich: Drayton.

John Swinerton, merchant-taylor, was sheriff of London in 1602, in which year he purchased the Marquis
of Winchester's property at Austin Friars. He was
knighted in 1603. He took the oath as Lord Mayor
in 1612, for which occasion Thomas Dekker wrote his
pageant, *London Triumphing.*

The tenderest and most touching of all Drayton's dedications is that of the Epistles of William de la Pole
and Margaret of Anjou, which Drayton inscribes to
Elizabeth Tanfield in all the editions before 1619:

To my honoured Mistres, Mi-
stres *Elizabeth Tanfelde*, the sole Daughter and heire, of that famous and learned
Lawyer, *Lawrence Tanfelde*
Esquire.

*Faire and vertuous Mistresse, since first it was my
good fortune to be a witnes of the many rare perfections
where-with nature and education have adorned you: I
have been forced since that time to attribute more admiration to your sexe, then ever* Petrarch *could before perswade mee to by the prayses of his* Laura. *Sweete is the
French tongue, more sweet the Italian, but most sweet are
they both if spoken by your admired selfe. If Poesie
were prayselesse, your vertues alone were a subject sufficient to make it esteemed, though amongst the barbarous
Getes: by how much the more your tender yeres give
scarcely warrant for your more then womanlike wisedom,
by so much is your judgement, and reading, the more to be
wondred at. The Graces shall have one more Sister by
your selfe, and England by your birth shall add one Muse
more to the Muses: I rest the humbly devoted servant to
my deere and modest Mistresse: to whom I wish, the hap-
piest fortunes I can devise.* Michaell Drayton.

Elizabeth Tanfield was born at Burford Priory, Oxon, probably in the year 1586 or 1587, for she is said to have been no more than fifteen years old when in 1602 she was married to Henry Cary, afterwards 1st Viscount Falkland. If so, she cannot have been more than ten or eleven when Drayton wrote his dedication to her. He addresses her as 'my honoured Mistresse,' and that suggests that he was then in the service of her father, Lawrence Tanfield, a distinguished lawyer, who was knighted and made judge in 1606. Perhaps he was tutor to the child. Her wonderful gift of tongues, to which he bears such charming witness, and her precocious learning are told of her at an age even earlier in the life which is believed to have been written by her children and was edited by Richard Simpson in 1861. A convert to the Catholic faith about 1625, she translated into English some of the controversial writings of Cardinal Duperron. Her translation of the Cardinal's reply to James I, printed in 1630, though containing some 400 large folio pages, is said to have been written within a month. We may believe that the poet Falkland, her famous son, killed at Newbury in 1643, owed the nobility of his character and his brilliant parts in great measure to the training and example of his mother. Her third son, Patrick, was also a poet.

The epistles of Edward the Fourth and Mistress Shore are dedicated in all the editions before 1619

To the Right Worshipfull Sir
Thomas Mounson, Knight.

Sir, amongst many which most deservedly love you, though I the least, yet am loth to be the last, whose endevours may make knowne how highly they esteeme of your noble and kinde disposition: let this Epistle Sir (I beseech you) which unwoorthily weares the Badge of your woorthy name, acknowledge my zeale with the rest, (though much lesse deserving) which for your sake doe honour the house of the Mounsons. I knowe true gener-

ositie accepteth what is zealously offered, though not ever deservingly excellent, yet for love of the Art from whence it receiveth resemblance. The light Phrigian harmony stirreth delight, as well as the melancholy Doricke moveth passion: both have their motion in the spirit, as the lyking of the soule moveth the affection. Your kinde acceptance of my labour, shall give some life to my Muse, which yet hovers in the uncertaintie of the generall censure.

Michaell Drayton.

Thomas Mounson or Monson (1564–1641) was knighted in 1588. In 1593 he succeeded to his father's estates in Lincolnshire and Nottinghamshire, and in 1597 he became M.P. for Lincolnshire. He excelled at falconry, and was made by James his master falconer and, in 1611, a baronet. He was imprisoned for alleged complicity in the murder of Overbury, but afterwards received a free pardon and was restored to the royal favour.

The Epistles of Mary the French Queen and the Duke of Suffolk were dedicated from 1597 onwards to Henry Goodere the younger, the nephew of the elder Sir Henry, whose elder daughter and co-heir, Frances, he had married in 1593. To her are dedicated the Epistles of Lady Jane Gray and Lord Gilford Dudley, which follow next but one in order.

To the Right Worshipfull
Henrie Goodere, of Powlesworth
Esquire.

Sir, this Poeme of mine, which I imparted to you, at my beeing with you at your lodging at London in May last, brought at length to perfection, (emboldened by your wonted favours) I adventure to make you Patron of. Thus Sir you see I have adventred to the worlde, with what like or dislike, I know not, if it please (which I much doubt of) I pray you then be pertaker, of that which I shall esteeme not my least good: if dislike, it shall lessen some part of my griefe, if it please you to alow but of my love: howsoever, I pray you accept it as kindly as I offer

it, which though without many protestations, yet (I assure you) with much desire of your honour. Thus untill such time as I may in some more larger measure make knowne my love to the happy & generous family of the Good-eres, *(to which I confesse my selfe to be beholding to, for the most part of my education) I wish you all happines.*
                                    Michaell Drayton.

To the modest and vertuous
Gentlewoman, Mistris *Frauncis Goodere,*
Daughter to Sir *Henry Goodere* Knight,
and wife to *Henry Goodere*
Esquire.

My very gracious and good Mistres, the love and duty I bare to your Father whilst hee lived, now after his decease is to you hereditary: to whom by the blessing of your birth he left his vertues. Who bequeathed you those which were his, gave you what so ever good is mine, as devoted to his, he being gone, whom I honored so much whilst he lived: which you may justly challenge by al lawes of thankfulnes. My selfe having been a witnes of your excellent education, and milde disposition (as I may say) ever from your Cradle, dedicate this Epistle of this vertuous and goodly Lady to your selfe: so like her in all perfection, both of wisedom and learning: which I pray you accept till time shall enable me to leave you some greater monument of my love.
                                    Michaell Drayton.

Henry was the son of William Goodere, of Monks Kirby near Lutterworth, the youngest brother of Sir Henry Goodere of Polesworth, whose elder daughter and co-heir, Frances, he married in 1593.[1] Through her he succeeded to the Polesworth estates on his father-in-law's death in 1595. More than one letter survives in which he writes of the 'decayed estate' left him by his

[1] The marriage is mentioned in a letter from Sir Henry Goodere the elder to the Mayor of Coventry, 12 Oct. 1593, in the Coventry archives.

uncle in 1595, and begs for the royal favour and bounty in recognition of all that the elder Sir Henry had suffered and spent in the cause of the Queen of Scots.[1]

The younger Sir Henry (he was knighted by Essex in Ireland with fifty-eight more in August 1599) is best known from the large number of letters addressed to him by John Donne. They date from 1601 onwards. Many of them lead us to suspect that his own extravagant living and especially his devotion to sport were a principal cause of the debts which are the constant theme of his correspondence and the subject of many other records concerning him. He was one of the crowd of English suitors who sought the favour of the King of Scots in anticipation of his succession to the English throne. He seems to have waited upon the King in Scotland in furtherance of his suit; for in a letter to Cecil, dated 31 December 1604, he writes:

> What courses I have taken some yeares past to intimate to his Ma; bothe the crosses of my deceased unckle and to make tender of myne owne service, I know his Ma^ty doth well remember; together with his princely promises (bothe before I saw him and many times since my attendance upon him) to consider the poore estate of my decayed house wth effectuall favour.[2]

And in a letter written to Buckingham in 1619 'to beg some lucrative office from which his pressures and wants' might be relieved, he recalls how his Majesty, while yet in Scotland, 'receaved mee before almost all others into his service and care.'[3] It may have been in answer to his appeal that about the year 1605 he was appointed one of the Gentlemen of His Majesty's Privy Chamber. He is so described at the head of the verses, not printed till 1619, but perhaps written much earlier, in which Drayton dedicates his 'Lyrick Pieces' to him

[1] See p. 29 above.   [2] Cecil Papers, Vol. 189, f. 124.
[3] Sackville Papers, 2451.

G

as 'my noble Friend.' Three of the lines give a charming picture of the fireside at Polesworth, by which Goodere and his guests would sit listening to the songs of a Welsh harper. They show also that Drayton meant his Odes to be set to music and sung.

> They may become JOHN HEWES his Lyre,
> Which oft at *Powlsworth* by the fire
> Hath made us gravely merry.[1]

The name John Hewes comes last in a list of some of the ship's company who sailed under Amadas and Barlowe to Virginia in 1584, as told by 'the industrious Hakluyt.'[2] It is tempting to suppose that Drayton drew from John's lips his first inspiration for the Ode to the Virginian Voyage and that the author of *Poly-Olbion* got from him also some of his love for Welsh legend and Welsh song.

Goodere entertained Jonson at Polesworth as well as Donne. In two Epigrams Ben writes of the sport of hawking which he witnessed there and of his host's library of books.[3] Whether or no he is the 'H.G. Esquire' whose sonnet, 'The Vision of Matilda,' was written in commendation of Drayton's *Matilda* in 1594, as a near neighbour of the Haringtons in Warwickshire he must have been the friend of Lucy Harington from childhood.[4] In 1607 he seems to have secured on her behalf the reversion of the lease of the estate at Twickenham which had belonged to Francis Bacon.[5] She went to live there in 1608. Goodere wrote much poetry of no great merit. Among Donne's works may be read the verses to a bride and bridegroom which he and Donne wrote *alternis vicibus* at Polesworth, perhaps for the wedding of

[1] Vol. II, p. 344.
[2] For D's use of this account in his *Ode to the Virginian Voyage* see Od[10]n and J. Q. Adams, 'Drayton and the Voyagers,' *MLN*, Nov. 1918, XXXIII, 405 ff.
[3] *Poems of B.J.*, pp. 26–7.
[4] See Vol. I, p. 212; V, p. 33.
[5] Gosse, *John Donne*, I, p. 210.

one of his daughters. Henry Goodere's wife and cousin, Frances, is the Panape of Drayton's Eighth Eglogue, printed in 1606. When it was written, she was lying ill at Polesworth:

> .... that good *Panape*
> In shadie Arden her deare flocke that keepes,
> Wher mornfull *Ankor* for her sicknes weepes.[1]

She died in that year, as we learn from an epigram written by John Owen to Sir Henry Goodere, in which he hints already that the widowed husband should get him another wife:

> Ad D. Henricum Good-yer
> Equitem, optimâ conjuge
> orbatum. 1606.
> Imperitare viros, *Parere* et *Parere* maritas
> Vult Natura. Uxor fecit utrumque tua.
> *Paruit*, & *Peperit* dulces, pia pignora, Natos,
> sustentant Magnas quae *Duo Fulcra* domos.
> ô ter felicem, quater ô Good-yere beatum,
> Si bona tam sequitur, quam bona prima fuit.[2]

John Donne wrote to Goodere from Pyrford to condole with him on her death.[3]

Goodere lived on terms of intimacy with his sister-in-law, Anne Rainsford, and her husband, Sir Henry, at Clifford. On Rainsford's death in 1623 he wrote the inscription commemorating his public services and private virtues which may still be read in Clifford church.[4]

Goodere himself died in 1627. His friend, Tobie Matthew, whom he and Donne used to visit in the Fleet where in 1606 he was imprisoned as a Catholic recusant, afterwards wrote of him that he

> was ever pleasant and kind, and gave me much of his pleasant conversation; and he would ingenuously confess whensoever in discourse he thought I had the

---

[1] Cf. Pa⁸ 112–114 var.   [2] *Epigram.*, 1607, 74.
[3] Gosse, I, p. 128.   [4] See p. 53.

better reason of the two. But if his constancy had
been as great as his nature was good, he had been
much happier in both worlds.[1]

Goodere lost his only son, John, in 1624. Heleftfour
daughters, of whom the eldest, Lucy, a godchild of
Lady Bedford, married Sir Francis Nethersole, secretary to the Princess Elizabeth when Queen of Bohemia,
and brought him the manor of Polesworth.

The Epistle of the Earl of Surrey to Lady Geraldine
was first printed in 1598, but the answer from Lady
Geraldine did not appear until 1599. In 1598 and after
the dedication is:

> To my most deare friend Mai-
> ster *Henry Lucas*, sonne to *Edward*
> *Lucas*, Esquier.
>
> *Sir, to none have I beene more beholding, then to your*
> *kind parents, far (I must truly confesse) above the meas-*
> *ure of my desarts: many there be in England, of whome*
> *for some particularity I might justly challenge greater*
> *merit, had I not beene borne in so evill an houre, as to be*
> *poisoned with that gaule of ingratitude: to your selfe am I*
> *engaged for many more curtesies then I imagined coulde*
> *ever have beene found in one of so fewe yeares: nothing*
> *doe I more desire then that those hopes of your towarde*
> *and vertuous youth, may prove so pure in the fruit as they*
> *are faire in the bloome: long may you live to their comfort*
> *that love you most; and may I ever wish you the increase*
> *of all good fortune.*
>
> Yours ever,
> *Michaell Drayton.*

The boy to whom Drayton wrote the above dedication
was later on the author of a set of verses 'To his wor-
thily deare friend Master Michael Drayton,' printed
in 1607 in front of *The Legend of Great Cromwell*,[2] which

[1] *A True Historical Relation of the Conversion of Sir Tobie Mat-*
thew, ed. A. H. Mathew, 1904, pp. 85–86.
[2] Vol. v, Cro var.

first appeared in that year. One may conjecture that Henry Lucas also was at one time a pupil of Drayton's.

The Epistles of Elinor Cobham and Duke Humphrey were first printed in 1598 without any dedication. In 1599 and onwards they are dedicated:

To my worthy and deerly esteemed Friend, Maister *James Huish.*

Sir, your owne naturall inclination to vertue, & your love to the Muses, assure mee of your kinde acceptance of my dedication. It is seated by custome (from which wee are now bolde to assume authority) to beare the names of our friendes upon the fronts of our bookes, as Gentlemen use to sette theyr Armes over theyr gates. Some say this use beganne by the Heroes *and brave spirits of the old world, which were desirous to bee thought to patronize learning; and men in requitall honour the names of those brave Princes. But I thinke some after, put the names of great men in theyr bookes, for that men should say there was some thing good; onely because indeede theyr names stoode there; But for mine owne part (not to dissemble) I finde no such vertue in any of their great titles to doe so much for any thing of mine, and so let them passe. Take knowledge by this I love you, and in good fayth, woorthy of all love I thinke you, which I pray you may supply the place of further complement.*

Yours ever,

M. Drayton.

In addressing this untitled commoner Drayton uses words which suggest the reason why the dedications to Monteagle and Lord Henry Howard find no place in any but the first edition of the *Heroicall Epistles.*

The Epistle of Edward the Black Prince and the reply from Alice, Countess of Salisbury, were first printed in 1598 without a dedication. They were first dedicated in 1602:

To my worthy and honoured
friend, Maister *Walter Aston*.

*Sir, though without suspition of flatterie I might in
more ample and freer tearmes, intymate my affection unto
you, yet having so sensible a tast of your generous and
noble disposition, which without this habit of ceremony
can estimate my love: I will rather affect brevitie, though
it shoulde seeme my fault, then by my tedious complement,
to trouble mine owne opinion setled in your judgement and
discretion. I make you the Patron of this Epistle of the*
Black-Prince, *which I pray you accept, till more easier
howers may offer up from me some thing more worthy of
your view, and my travell.*

Yours truly devoted,
Mich: Drayton.

That was the earliest of the long series of dedications to
Walter Aston, Drayton's principal patron in the middle
period of his career. An account of him and of Drayton's
relations with him is the subject of a later chapter.

CHAPTER VII
LITERARY FRIENDS
1591–1603[1]

WHEN in King James's reign the younger Sir
Henry Goodere entertained John Donne or Ben
Jonson at Polesworth Abbey, he was carrying on a
tradition of hospitality to poets which had been established in the lifetime of his uncle and father-in-law, the
elder Sir Henry. We have seen how on the banks of the
Anker the Arcadian swains held in high honour Mary
Sidney and her poetry, and how her brother Philip
claimed kinship as well as friendship with Henry Goodere.[2] The Sidneys were also of near kin to the Haring-
ons. Two lines spoken by Winken in his rebuke to
Rowland in the 6th Eglog of 1606 seem to imply that
Sidney had a friendly regard for young Drayton:

Still let thy Rownds of that good Shepheard tel,
To whom thou hast been evermore so deare.[3]

Drayton expresses again and again the honour in which
he held Philip and his sister,[4] and his debt to Sidney's
muse is traced in the notes on the early poems, printed
in the fifth volume of the *Works*. So is his much greater
debt to Spenser, which he acknowledges in the closing
lines of *Endimion and Phœbe*:

Deare *Collin*, let my Muse excused be,
Which rudely thus presumes to sing by thee,
Although her straines be harsh untun'd and ill,
Nor can attayne to thy divinest skill.

[1] For additional information and references concerning friends
to whom Drayton makes allusion in his poems see in Vol. v
the introductions and notes to the several poems in which they
are found.
[2] Pp. 30, 41.   [3] Pa⁶ 135–6.
[4] See the dedication of Mo to Lady Bedford, 29–35; SG⁶ 55–
162; Pa⁸ 55–72; dedication of IM to Anthony Cooke; El⁸ 85–90.

The latter part of Spenser's life was mostly spent in Ireland, and there is no evidence that Drayton was his friend or even that he knew him. It is possible, however, that Spenser is alluding to him amongst contemporary poets in a much discussed passage of *Colin Clouts Come Home againe*, printed in 1595:

> And there though last not least is *Aetion*,
> A gentler shepheard may no where be found:
> Whose *Muse* full of high thoughts invention,
> Doth like himselfe Heroically sound.[1]

Apart from the assonance of 'Drayton' and 'Aetion,' Drayton's pastoral name, Rowland, already widely known, and his Christian name Michael do both 'Heroically sound.' His Legends of 1593 and 1594 are full of 'high thoughts invention'; and although his *Heroicall Epistles* were not printed till 1597, the Preface 'To the Reader' suggests that some of them at least were written at an earlier date. The 'lovely lasse, hight *Lucida*,' who appeals to Colin a few lines later, is likely to be Lucy Bedford.

Of Drayton's contemporaries Richard Barnfield is the earliest to leave on record his personal friendship with Drayton. In his *Affectionate Shepheard* (1594) he alludes to Drayton's *Idea The Shepheards Garland*, or perhaps the *Amours* of 1594, as well as his *Matilda*, also printed in that year. In his *Cynthia* (1595), too, he couples with '*Colin* chiefe of Sheepheards all,'

> gentle *Rowland*, my professed friend.[2]

The lines of *Endimion and Phœbe* in which Drayton pays affectionate tribute to Thomas Lodge and to his influence on his own earliest verse, suggest an acquaintance dating back to early manhood, at Polesworth per-

---

[1] For reasons for believing that Aetion is Drayton, see Kathleen Tillotson in *TLS* 31 Jan. 1935. For other views concerning the identity of Aetion see letters by Arthur Gray and W. L. Renwick in *TLS* 24 Jan. and 31 Jan. 1935.   [2] Sonnet xx.

haps, or in Nottinghamshire, a county with which
Lodge, like Drayton, had many ties:

> my Goldey which in Sommer dayes,
> Hast feasted us in merry roundelayes,
> And when my Muse scarce able was to flye,
> Didst imp her wings with thy sweete poesie.[1]

Lodge repaid him in kind by inscribing 'To Rowland'
the Third Eclogue in *A Fig for Momus*, which was entered in the same month and the same year—April
1595—as *Endimion*. In his Fifth Epistle in that book he
bids Drayton write sacred poetry:

> be thou a prentize to a blessed Muse,
> Which grace with thy good words will stil infuse.

He praises and enlarges upon 'thy learned nines and
threes,' alluding to the laboured treatise on the mystic
significance of those numbers which Drayton had introduced into his *Endimion and Phœbe*. It was Drayton's
reply to the attack which John Davies had made upon the
8th Amour of *Ideas Mirrour* in his Epigram *In Decium*:

> Audacious Painters have nine worthies made,
> But Poet Decius more audacious farre,
> Making his mistres march with men of warre,
> With title of tenth worthie doth her lade.[2]

As a friend of Lodge, Drayton is likely to have
known also Robert Greene, but there is no record of
their acquaintance, unless he should be the 'Robin-red-
breast sitting on a breere' who in the Third Eglog 'already to his roost is gone.'[3] We cannot doubt that Drayton was well acquainted also with Samuel Daniel, whatever occasion for jealousy he may have found a few years
later in the favour which Daniel received at the hands of
Lady Bedford.[4] His influence on Drayton's early poetry

---

[1] EP 1001–4.

[2] See EP 881–974 n. It is unlikely that the 'Swallow, whose
rare *Idæas*, and invention strange' Davies commends in his
Orchestra (1596), Sig. C8[b], can stand for D.

[3] SG[3] 39–46; but see note thereon. Greene died in 1592.

[4] See p. 64.

was strong.[1] His *Delia* is dedicated to Mary Countess
of Pembroke, to whose son, afterwards the third Earl,
he was tutor at Wilton, and Drayton addresses him in
Endimion and Phœbe:

> .... thou the sweet *Museus* of these times,
> Pardon my rugged and unfiled rymes,
> Whose scarce invention is too meane and base,
> When *Delias* glorious Muse dooth come in place.[2]

It is likely that the names we have in the Eglogs—
Motto, 'the gamesome boy,' Perkin, Gorbo, Batte (perhaps the Battus of Weever's Epigramme 9)—are meant
to stand for poets of Drayton's circle, whether at Polesworth or in town; but not even the ingenious Fleay has
been able to suggest whom for the most part they represent. He thinks that Winken may be William Warner,
the author of *Albions England*, probably a Warwickshire
man like Drayton, who writes of him with affectionate
criticism in his Epistle to Henry Reynolds:

> yet thus let me say;
> For my old friend, some passages there be
> In him, which I protest have taken me,
> With almost wonder, so fine, cleere, and new
> As yet they have bin equalled by few.[3]

Fleay suggests that he may have been the 'mild tutor'
who first introduced Drayton to poetry and the muses,
but he was not many years older than Drayton and was
too young to have been either his tutor or Rowland's and Motto's aged mentor. It appears that there
were Warners living in the neighbourhood of Edge Hill
in South Warwickshire, and he may have belonged to
that family; but there is no evidence that he was ever
teaching in North Warwickshire or anywhere else. Warner's tragic death in 1609 at Amwell, Herts, is described

---

[1] See introductions and notes on IM, PG, Ma, EP 992–1000.
For Drayton's later criticism of Daniel see El[8] 123–8.

[2] EP 997–1000.   [3] El[8] 97–104.

by the Vicar of that parish, Thomas Hassall—perhaps the 'Thomas Hassel *Gent.*' who wrote prefatory verses to *Englands Heroicall Epistles* in 1599.[1] Winken is rather more likely to be Leonard Cox, the master of Coventry School,[2] or else the famous Captain Cox of Coventry, who led the Coventry players at Leicester's princely entertainment at Kenilworth in July 1575. 'And fyrst, Captin Cox,' says Laneham,

> an od man I promiz yoo: by profession a Mason, and that right skilfull, very cunning in fens, and hardy az Gawin; ... great oversight hath he in matters of storie.

His library, catalogued at length by Laneham, includes *Sir Gawyn, Robin Hood, Bevis of Hampton, Clem-a-Clough*, and many more of the legends that find a place in Drayton's Pastorals and his *Poly-Olbion*. He had books of philosophy, too, 'both morall and naturall .... beside poetrie and astronomie, and oother hid sciences.' Imaginative biographers of Shakespeare have pictured the young Stratford lad as being present at Leicester's great pageant and as bringing from it impressions which a score of years later inspired a great passage in *A Midsummer Night's Dream*. The biographer of Drayton may believe that Henry Goodere's young page was there too, perhaps in the company of the Coventry players led by the sturdy soldier, mason and ale-conner in whose collection of works he may have read the English legends and romances that have left so many traces in his work. He may have drawn thence his earliest inspiration for the 'prettie tales' of Dowsabel and Nimphidia. That, however, is no more than pleasant conjecture. All we know is that Winken was a Midlander; and it is clear that Drayton looked upon him as in some sort his master, for in the Sixth Eglog of *Poemes Lyrick and Pastorall* of 1606 he puts into the aged Winken's mouth words of fatherly reproof for Rowland's departure:

[1] See Vol. v, p. 101, Vol. ii, p. 131.   [2] But see p. 19 above.

Unhappy *Rowland* that from me art fled:
And setst ould *Winken* and his words at naught;
And like a gracelesse and untutord lad,
Art now departed from my aged sight,
And needsly to southern fields wilt gad.[1]

The 4th Eglog of *The Shepheards Garland* underwent revision at some date prior to its printing as the 6th in *Poemes Lyrick and Pastorall*. The above passage must have been added to it after Drayton had left Warwickshire for good and gone to London, where he chiefly lived during the latter half of his life. Although, like Shakespeare, he found his vocation in that city, of whose majesty and dignity with her 'Turrets, Fanes and Spyres,' as of her goodly situation he was conscious,[2] his thoughts and tastes were those of the countryman born and bred:

Fooles gaze at painted Courts, to th' countrey let me goe,
To climbe the easie hill, then walke, the valley lowe;
No gold-embossed Roofes, to me are like the woods,
No Bed like to the grasse, nor liquor like the floods:
A Citie's but a sinke, gay houses gawdy graves,
The Muses have free leave, to starve or live in caves.[3]

The fine tribute which Drayton makes to John Stow in the note appended to his *Peirs Gaveston* in 1594[4] shows that he was already intimate with the old chronicler and antiquary, to whose 'especiall collections' he had 'recourse' when trying to reconcile the conflicting evidence for Gaveston's career.[5] We may safely conjec-

---

[1] Pa[6] 127–32 var.   [2] PO[16] 315.
[3] PO[19] 21–6.   [4] Vol. 1, p. 208.
[5] See the examination of D's sources in the Introduction and Notes on PG[a]. Powel, the editor of Humphrey Llwyd's translation of Caradoc's *Historie of Cambria*, a favourite book of Drayton's, gives the following testimony to the character and value of Stow's collection: 'In written hand I had Gildas Sapiens *alias* Nennius, Henrie Huntington, William Malmsbury, Marianus Scotus, Ralph Cogshall, Jo. Eversden, Nicolas Trivet, Florentius Vigorniensis, Simon of Durham. Roger Hoveden, and other

ture that his friendship with Stow was a principal influence on his poetical career, fostering within him his love for antiquity which is the motive of the greater part of his work. But, as we have seen, the first inspiration may have come from Ralph Holinshed, from whose chronicle he draws so freely for his historical poems. Holinshed was steward to Thomas Burdet at Bramcote, a neighbouring manor to Polesworth, when he made his will in 1578; and he died there some two years later.[1]

The friend of Stow could not fail to be also the friend of Camden, who in a folio manuscript book, much torn and worn, used for writing drafts of his letters to friends and scholars in England and abroad, inscribed this delicate tribute to one who was already his 'old friend':

Michaeli Draitono Musis arridentibus
nato virtutibus et amœnioribus literis
excultissimo, amico veteri et spectatissimo
Guil. Camdenus
Rex Armorum Clarenceux [qui amat *scored through*]
ex judicio et amore hoc
ad Jovis Philii aram
ut sit *ΔΕΣΜΟΣ ΦΡΕΝΟΠΛΟΚΟΣ*
Libens merito posuit
LONDINI

Two phrases—the Greek δεσμος φρενοπλοκος and the Latin 'libens merito posuit'—are found in an earlier dedication written by Camden just above the lines to Drayton; it is dated 24 August 1585 and inscribed to Jan Douza the younger, between whom and Camden as well as with the youth's father many letters passed. Camden was not appointed Clarenceux King of Arms until 1597, and he must therefore have scribbled in the

whiche remaine in the custodie of Jo. Stowe citizen of London, who deserveth commendation for getting together the ancient writers of the histories of this land.' (*Historie of Cambria*, 1584, To His Reader.)

[1] See p. 18.

inscription to Drayton after that date. It is perhaps the draft of what he proposed to write in a copy of the *Britannia* of 1607 to be offered as a 'mind-enweaving bond' at the altar of Friendship to the poet who was engaged in writing a metrical counterpart to that book.[1] Drayton was using the *Britannia* as early as 1597. Alluding to Rumney Marsh and Rye in Kent in *Englands Heroicall Epistles*, he notes: '*Hereof the excellent* English *Antiquarie Master* Camden, a*nd Master* Lambert *in his Perambulation*, doe make mention.'[2]

In the circle of Drayton's antiquarian friends at this period we may include also William Lambarde (1536–1601), author of *The Perambulation of Kent*, our earliest county history, to which Drayton acknowledges his indebtedness in the above passage. It was also the principal source for his account of Kent in *Poly-Olbion*.[3] Lambarde was appointed Keeper of the Records at the Rolls Chapel in 1597 and of those at the Tower in 1601.

About this time Drayton must have begun his long friendship with two younger men, who, like himself, were antiquaries and poets as well as friends of Camden's. Edmund Bolton (1576–1636) is almost certainly the 'E.B.' whose lines to the Countess of Bedford follow Drayton's dedication of *Mortimeriados* to that 'excellent and most accomplished Ladie.'[4] In his *Hypercritica* Bolton praises *Englands Heroicall Epistles* as 'well worth reading . . . for the purpose of our subject, which is to furnish an *English* Historian with Choice and Copy of

---

[1] British Museum, MS. Add. 36294, ff. 15ᵛ, 16ᵛ. In 1753 the book was bought for the Tixall library. It was sold with other Tixall books at Sotheby's in 1899. Since the above was written, I have found the following inscription by Camden in the copy of his *Britannia* 1607 which he presented to the Bodleian:

Almæ Matri Oxoniensi
hoc qualecunque ΘΡΕΠΤΗΡΙΟΝ
Guilielmus Camdenus Clarenceux
qui plura debet
L.M.S.

[2] EHE[9b] 34, annot.   [3] PO[18].   [4] See note to Mo, Vol. v, p. 42.

Tongue.'[1] When towards the end of James's reign and
at the beginning of that of Charles I Bolton was formu-
lating his scheme for an 'Academie Roiall' of eminent
scholars and writers, he included Drayton amongst the
eighty-seven whom he suggested for the original members.[2] The scheme had won the support of Buckingham. It lapsed after that statesman's murder in 1628.
Among the eighty-seven are many who were Drayton's friends or acquaintances—Ben Jonson, Sir John
Beaumont, Sir William Alexander, George Chapman,
Selden, Sir Edward Coke, Hugh Holland, and Sir Edmund Scory. There was John Williams, too, to whom in
Poly-Olbion Drayton gratefully acknowledges both his
indebtedness and his friendship.[3]

Drayton was fond of revealing in his poetry his
particular admirations and his special friendships.
Many of the contemporaries to whom he alludes in his
poems are younger men, like Drummond of Hawthornden, the Beaumonts and William Browne, whose relations with Drayton belong for the most part to a later
date and are the subject of later chapters; but his friendship with William Alexander of Menstrie began at
least as early as 1600, for Alexander's Sonnet 'To M.
Michael Drayton' appears for the first time in the edition of *Englands Heroicall Epistles*[4] printed in that year.
In Drayton's Sixth Eglog Winken, addressing Alexander, bids him, as he had bidden Daniel (Melibeus)
and other Sidneyan poets just before:

Forget not *Elphin* . . . thou gentle Swayne,
That dost thy pipe by silver *Doven* sound,
Alexis that dost with thy flocks remaine
Far off within the *Calydonian* grounde . . .[5]

---

[1] MS. Rawl. D.1, p. 13. See Haslewood, *Anc. Critical Essays*, II,
pp. 246–247.
[2] MS. Harl. 6143; *Archæologia*, XXXII, 132–149; *Proc. Brit. Acad.*
1915–16, pp. 189–208.
[3] PO p. vii, n.   [4] Vol. II, p. 131.
[5] Cf. Pa[6] 121–24.

These lines must have been written before 1603, when Alexander left his home at Menstrie near the river Doven in Clackmannanshire, 'a water neere unto the author's house whereupon his Majestie was sometimes wont to hawke.'[1] He came to England as Gentleman of the Bedchamber to Prince Henry, whose tutor he had been in Scotland. We shall see that there is some reason to believe that Drayton visited the Northern Kingdom in 1599; if so, it was perhaps on that occasion that he became acquainted with Alexander. Some of Alexander's sonnets, printed in his *Aurora* in 1604, show traces of Drayton's influence.[2]

Amongst Drayton's London friends must be reckoned the churchman Francis Meres, who in his 'Comparative discourse of our English Poets, with the Greeke, Latine and Italian Poets'—a chapter in his *Palladis Tamia: Wits Treasury* (1598)—gives Drayton and his contemporaries, Sidney, Spenser, Marlowe Daniel, Shakespeare and many more, a place apiece at the side of some of the great poets of antiquity. He shows a special regard for Drayton, whom he mentions again and again, paying an affectionate and noble tribute to his high moral character and reputation:

> As *Aulus Persius Flaccus* is reported among al writers to be of an honest life and upright conversation: so *Michael Drayton (quem toties honoris et amoris causa nomino)* among schollers, souldiours, Poets, and all sorts of people, is helde for a man of vertuous disposition, honest conversation, and wel governed cariage, which is almost miraculous among good wits in these declining and corrupt times, when there is nothing but rogery in villanous man, and when cheating and craftines is counted the cleanest wit, and soundest wisedome.[3]

[1] W. Alexander, *Monarchicke Tragedies*, 1604.
[2] See Introduction to *Idea*, Vol. v, p. 137. Cf. *Aurora*, Sonnets 4, 22, 32, 35, 52, 74.
[3] F. 281.

Just before, Meres had written of *Poly-Olbion*, the plan of which he must have learned from Drayton himself, for the First Part of the great undertaking was not to see the light till fourteen years later:

As *Joan. Honterus* in Latine verse writ 3 Bookes of Cosmography with Geographicall tables: so *Michael Drayton* is now in penning in English verse a Poem called *Polu-olbion* Geographical and Hydrographicall of all the forests, woods, mountaines, fountaines, rivers, lakes, flouds, bathes and springs that be in England.

Another of Drayton's London friends was Nicholas Ling, the stationer, who published most of his work prior to 1607.[1] Ling was no mere middleman between the poet and his readers. He was himself an assiduous compiler and editor. He had a chief share with John Bodenham and Robert Allot in getting together material for such collections as *Wits Commonwealth* (1597), *Politeuphia: Wits Theater* (1599), *Bel-vedere* (1600), *Englands Parnassus*, and, most interesting of all, *Englands Helicon* (1600).[2] To the first of these works Drayton contributed a commendatory sonnet.[3] But it is in *Englands Helicon* that we find the best evidence of the close relationship maintained between the poet and the stationer. That anthology includes five poems by Drayton, of which only one had been printed before. 'Rowland's Song in Praise of the Fairest Beta' had already appeared in *The Shepheards Garland*,[4] but in *Englands Helicon* it bears evidence of Drayton's revision. One of the changes made has more than literary significance,

---

[1] In which year he transferred his copies to John Smethwicke. Ling published D's PG, Ma, Ro, IM (1594–6), EHE (1597–), BW (1603), O (1604), *Poems* (1605–6), *Poems lyrick and Pastorall* (1606).

[2] See J. W. Hebel, 'N. Ling and *Englands Helicon*' in *The Library*, v (1924), pp. 153–160, H. E. Rollins, *Englands Helicon 1600, 1614* (1935), II, pp. 41–63, especially pp. 61–3.

[3] Unc³ n.   [4] SG³.

H

for it seems to mark a change in Drayton's outlook in the religious conflicts of his time.[1] Three more of the poems first printed by Ling in *Englands Helicon* under pastoralized titles which were not Drayton's own—*The Shepheards Daffadill, A Roundelay betweene two Sheepheards*, and *The Sheepheards Antheme*—find their places in the Eglogs in *Poemes lyrick and Pastorall* printed three years later.[2] *Rowlands Madrigall* was printed only in *Englands Helicon*.[3]

In 1600 Ling moved his shop from St Paul's to St Dunstan's Churchyard. From there he issued Christopher Middleton's *The Legend of Humphrey duke of Gloucester*, to which Drayton,[4] John Weever and Robert Allot all contributed commendatory verses. John Weever (1576–1636) was one of the younger men who came within Ling's circle. He had published his *Epigrammes in the oldest cut and newest fashion* in 1599, when he was still at Cambridge. In that book he confesses how that

> I cannot reache up to a *Delians* straine, . . .
> Nor *Draytons* stile, whose hony words are meete
> For these your mouths, far more than hony sweet.

His 23rd Epigram in 'The first weeke' is addressed

Ad Michaelem Drayton.

> The Peeres of heav'n kept a parliament,
> And for Wittes-mirrour *Philip Sidney* sent,
> To keepe another when they doe intend,
> Twentie to one for *Drayton* they will send,
>   Yet bade him leave his learning, so it fled,
>   And vow'd to live with thee since he was dead.

In Weever's *Faunus and Melliflora; or, the Original of our English Satyres* (1601), the following Sonnet,[5] signed

[1] See below, p. 214.
[2] See Pa⁹85–132, Pa⁹145–172, Pa²105–28, and the notes thereon in Vol. v.
[3] Unc⁵ and note in Vol. v.   [4] Unc⁴. See the notes thereon.
[5] See the letter by F. B. Williams in *TLS*, 11 Dec. 1937. The only known copy of Weever's *Faunus* is at the Huntington Library, whose librarian kindly allows the lines to be printed

M.D., is certainly by our poet, although in substance not quite worthy of his muse:

> *Of the Author.*
>
> The Greeke *Comœdian* fitly doth compare
> Poets to Swannes, for both delitious,
> Both in request, both white, both pretious are,
> Both sing alike, and both melodious:
> I but the swanne remaineth dumbe so long,
> (As though her Musike were too good to spend)
> That so at last her soule-enchanting song,
> Is but a funerall dirge to her end.
> *Weever*, herein above the Swanne I praise,
> Which freely spends his sweete melodious dittie,
> Now in the budding of his youthful daies,
> Delightsome, pleasant, full of Art, and wittie,
>   Yet heavens forbid he should be neare his death,
>   Though like the dying Swanne he sweetly breath.

In his *Ancient Funerall Monuments* (1631), which is its author's own great monument, Weever quotes repeatedly from Drayton's *Poly-Olbion* and once also from his *Legend of Cromwell*. He alludes to Drayton as 'my fore remembred friend.'[1]

It is curious to find that in his *Faunus*, notwithstanding Drayton's commendatory sonnet, Weever praises Joseph Hall, who in his *Virgidemiae*, printed in 1597, is supposed by some to allude scornfully to Drayton's *The Shepheards Garland*, his Legends of *Gaveston*, *Matilda* and *Robert* and, in another passage, his *Heroicall Epistles*.[2] In *The Metamorphosis of Pigmalions Image*[3] and in *The*

here. The sonnet may safely be attributed to D on the following grounds: 1. The initials *M.D.* are not used by any other contemporary writer, but D uses them in his commendatory verses to Munday and Ling (Unc[1], Unc[2], Unc[3]). 2. He favours the sonnet as a commendatory form and uses it for Ling, Middleton, Palmer, Davies of Hereford, Murray (Unc[3], Unc[4], Unc[6], Unc[8], Unc[9]), and in *The Redemption of Lost Time* (p. 135 below). He also likes double rhymes.

[1] *Anc. Fun. Mon.*, pp. 501, 510, etc. See also note to Unc[4].
[2] *Virgidemiarum* lib. i, sat. v, and lib. vi, satt. i, ii.   [3] pp. 62–3.

Scourge of Villanie,[1] both printed in 1598, John Marston punishes Hall for his attack on heroic poetry and seems to be defending Drayton from Hall's savage allusions to his verse. It is possible, however, that Hall's shafts are not aimed at Drayton or any other particular poet but rather at certain poetical fashions of the day, which may be recognised in Drayton's work.[2]

[1] Sig. G7ᵛ.
[2] For the question whether Drayton is personally attacked by Hall as Labeo see the Introduction to D's *Idea* in Vol. v, p. 138, and the footnote and references there given.

CHAPTER VIII
DRAYTON AND THE THEATRE

I. The Admiral's Company

BETWEEN December 1597 and January 1599 and at various dates between October 1599 and May 1602 Drayton was engaged in writing plays for the company of players who acted at the Rose Theatre, Southwark, and later on at the Fortune in Shoreditch. Officially they were the servants of Lord Howard of Effingham, Lord High Admiral of England, and were therefore known as the Admiral's players. Edward Alleyn was perhaps the principal sharer and the principal actor of the company. He had married the stepdaughter of Philip Henslowe, who owned both the Rose and the Fortune theatres. A book of miscellaneous accounts and memoranda, generally known as *Henslowe's Diary*, is preserved at Dulwich College, which Alleyn founded between the years 1613 and 1616. The entries there of payments to Drayton and his collaborators for the plays which they wrote are almost our only source of information for this part of Drayton's career. In the following list[1] are shown the titles of the plays in which Drayton collaborated, the dates within which payments were made for each, the total sums recorded as paid for each, the names of the other collaborators, and the folios of the Diary on which they are found. They fall within three main periods with intervals between them.

First Period. *December 1597—January 1599*

Mother Redcap. 22 Dec. 1597 to 5 Jan. 1597–8. (Anthony Munday. £6) ff. 37ᵛ, 43ᵛ, 44.
The Famous Wars of Henry I and the Prince of Wales. 13

---

[1] For which we are chiefly and inevitably indebted to Dr W. W. Greg's edition of *Henslowe's Diary*, 1904–8.

March 1598–9. (Henry Chettle, Thomas Dekker. £6 5s.) f. 45.

Earl Goodwin and his Three Sons. First Part. 25–30 March 1598. (Chettle, Dekker, Robert Wilson. £6) ff. 45ᵛ.

Earl Goodwin and his Three Sons. Second Part. 6 April (May)—10 June 1598. (Chettle, Dekker, Wilson. £4) ff. 46, 46ᵛ, 47.

Pierce of Exton. 30 Mar.—7 April 1598. (Chettle, Dekker, Wilson. £2) f. 45.[1]

Black Bateman of the North. First Part. 2–22 May 1598. (Chettle, Dekker, Wilson, who—but not Drayton— also received payments for the Second Part 26 June —14 July 1598.) £6 or £7. ff. 45ᵛ, 46ᵛ, 47.[2]

The Funeral of Richard Cœur-de-Lion. 13–26 June 1598. (Chettle, Munday, Wilson. £6 5s.) ff. 46, 46ᵛ.

The Madman's Morris. '31 June' (1 July)—10 July 1598. (Dekker, Wilson. £6) ff. 47, 48.

Hannibal and Hermes, or Worse afeared than Hurt. First Part. 14–28 July, 1598 (Dekker £6) ff. 47ᵛ, 48.

Hannibal and Hermes. Second Part. 30 Aug.–4 'Aug.' (Sept.) 1598. (Dekker. £5) ff. 49ᵛ, 50.

Pierce of Winchester.[3] 28 July to 10 Aug. 1598. (Dekker, Wilson. £5 10s.) ff. 48–51.

Chance Medley. 19–24 Aug. 1598. (Chettle or Dekker, Munday, Wilson. £6) ff. 49, 49ᵛ.

[1] 'The position of this entry and the identity of authorship almost force us to suppose that it was the first payment for 2 *Earl Goodwin*. If so, there must be some strange confusion of titles, for Sir Piers Exton was the supposed murderer of Richard II.' (W. W. Greg, *Henslowe's Diary*, II, p. 192.)

[2] It was first suggested by F. E. Schelling (*Elizabethan Drama*, 1908, I, pp. 348–9) that the play called *The Vow-Breaker or The Faire Maid of Clifton* by William Sampson (1636) is 'a making over' of *Black Bateman*. See below, p. 206, also K. Tillotson, 'William Sampson's Vow-Breaker . . .' in *MLR*, July 1940.

[3] 'The title suggests some connection with the mysterious *Pierce of Exton*, but none can be established.' (W. W. Greg, *l.c.* p. 195.)

The Civil Wars of France. First Part. 29 Sept. 1598.
(Dekker. £6) ff. 50ᵛ, 51.

The Civil Wars of France. Second Part. 3 Nov. 1598.
(Dekker. £6) ff. 51ᵛ, 52.

The Civil Wars of France. Third Part. 18 Nov.—30
Dec. 1598. (Dekker. £6) ff. 52, 52ᵛ.

Connan Prince of Cornwall. 16–20 Oct. 1598. (Dekker.
£6) f. 51.

William Longsword. 20–21 Jan. 1598–9. (£2 in part
payment of £6) ff. 31, 52ᵛ.

SECOND PERIOD. *October* 1599—*June* 1600

Sir John Oldcastle. First and Second Parts. 16 Oct.,
19–26 Dec. 1599. (Richard Hathway, Munday,
Wilson. £10 for Part I and in earnest of Part II;
£4 for Part II; 10s. at the 1st performance 'as a
gefte.') ff. 65, 66ᵛ, 68. The play was transferred from
the Admiral's to Worcester's men in 1602, when
Dekker received £2 10s. for additions. ff. 115, 116.

Owen Tudor. 10 Jan. 1599–1600. (Hathway, Munday,
Wilson. £4) f. 67.[1]

Fair Constance of Rome. First Part. 3–14 June 1600.
(Dekker, Hathway, Munday, Wilson.[2] £6) f. 69ᵛ.

Fair Constance of Rome. Second Part. 20 June 1600.
(Dekker, Hathway, Munday. £1) f. 69ᵛ.

THIRD PERIOD. *June* 1601—*May* 1602

The Life and Rising of Cardinal Wolsey. First and
Second Parts. 5 June—9 Nov. 1601. (Chettle,
Munday, Wentworth Smith. £6, £7) ff. 87ᵛ, 91,
91ᵛ, 92ᵛ, 93, 93ᵛ, 94, 94ᵛ, 105ᵛ.

---

[1] On a fragment of the Diary now at Belvoir Castle is a receipt
for the above payment, dated 10 January 1599–60, signed by
Hathway, Wilson and Munday, but not Drayton. (W. W. Greg in
The Library, 4th Ser., xix, pp. 180–4.)

[2] Wilson's name and share are mentioned, not in the Diary,
but in a letter from Robert Shaa to Henslowe. (*Henslowe Papers*,
ed. W. W. Greg, 1907, p. 55.)

Cæsar's Fall, or the Two Shapes. 22–29 May 1602. (Dekker, Thomas Middleton, Munday, John Webster. £8) ff. 105^v, 106.

Of the above twenty-four or twenty-five plays seventeen or eighteen were written within the thirteen months which ended with January 1599. Then comes an interval in the payments to Drayton until that made for the First Part of *Sir John Oldcastle* on 16 October 1599. On 8 July of that year, however, he was one of the witnesses of a loan of 5s. made by Henslowe—for Henslowe was a pawn-broker and money-lender as well as a theatrical manager—to John Pallmer, when he played shovegroat at the Court.[1] Palmer was a Groom of the Queen's Chamber and a frequent borrower. If, as seems likely, Drayton visited Scotland in 1599,[2] it must have been in the first half of the year.

Of all the twenty-four plays only the First Part of *Sir John Oldcastle* has survived. Since the poets who made it received the unusual gift of ten shillings at the first performance,[3] it is clear that it was well received. Moreover, it was the only play of them all to be printed, and that in the year following its production. We have no means of knowing what passages in it are Drayton's or which the work of his collaborators.[4] It was followed immediately by the Second Part, which was performed in the spring of 1600. In the following June the Diary records three new plays in which Drayton had a hand. There follows another interval of a year before payments were resumed. The First and Second Parts of *Cardinal Wolsey* belong to the second half of 1601. In May 1602 Drayton received payment only for *Cæsar's Fall*. Thenceforth his name is found no more in the Diary.

Of the payments made by Henslowe for the plays in which Drayton collaborated it is estimated that his

[1] *Diary*, f. 31^v.   [2] See pp. 95–6, 124.   [3] *Diary*, f. 65.
[4] The play is printed in Vol. 1, pp. 393–468, Introduction and Notes, v, pp. 48–52.

share came to some £35 or £40 for the seventeen or
eighteen plays of the first period, from December 1597
to January 1599. As a rule the sum paid for each play
amounted to £6, shared by the joint-authors, not always in equal portions. In October 1599 £14 was paid
for the two Parts of *Sir John Oldcastle*. In 1601 £13
was shared by four playwrights for the two Parts of
Cardinal Wolsey; and in 1602 £8 by the five authors
of *Cæsar's Fall*, a play with the doubtful second title of
The Two Shapes, which may belong to another play.

It is pleasant to think that, however irksome the
syndicated writing of the plays may have proved to the
poet, the plots of most of them were drawn from such
chronicles or ballads as were the favourite subject of his
study. We meet with Mother Redcap again in *The
Moone-Calfe*, printed in the folio of 1627. Dr Greg finds
it difficult not to suppose that *The Wars of Henry I* had
some connexion with a play called *The Welshman*,
which was performed by the Admiral's men 29 November 1595, or with *The Life and Death of Henry I*, performed as a new play 26 May 1597.[1] He shows reason
also for believing that *The Funeral of Richard Cœur-de-
Lion* was the Second Part of a trilogy on Robin Hood,
for the First and Third Parts of which Munday and
Chettle received payments from Henslowe in February
or March 1598.[2] Earl Goodwin, made Earl of the West
Saxons by King Cnut, was father-in-law of Edward the
Confessor, who afterwards outlawed him with his three
sons Swega, Harold and Tostig, but later restored him
to favour. *Connan, Prince of Cornwall*, should perhaps
be Corineus or Corin, Prince of Cornwall, whose
legendary history, taken out of Geoffrey of Monmouth
or Holinshed, is told at length in the First Song of
Poly-Olbion. The hero of *Owen Tudor* was wooed and
won by Queen Katherine in the Sixth of the *Heroicall
Epistles*.

---

[1] *Diary*, II, p. 192.   [2] *Diary*, f. 49.

On a leaf of Henslowe's Diary Drayton wrote the following acknowledgement for payment made:

> I receved forty shillings of M^r
> Phillip Hinslowe in part of vj^{lb} for
> the playe of Willm̃ Longsword to be
> deliu'd p^{r}sent wth 2 or three dayes
> the xxjth of January/ 1598/
>
> Mi: Drayton.

The like amount appears in Henslowe's accounts as paid to Drayton on 20 January 1598–9;[1] but there the name of the play is written *Longberd*. In 1593 Thomas Lodge wrote an account of *William Longbeard, the most famous and witty English traitor;* and the play, if it was ever written, may have been a chronicle of his exploits. But Drayton is less likely than Henslowe to have miswritten the name of his own play, the hero of which was probably Longespee, the reputed son of the Fair Rosamond Clifford. He became the 3rd Earl of Salisbury. 'The doubt,' writes Dr Walter W. Greg, 'would appear to be decided by two breviats in actions by Sir Henry Herbert,' in which he records among plays 'allowed by Mr Tilney. . . 62 years since . . . Sir William Longsword allowed to be Acted the 24 May 1598.' 'If so, there must be some mistake in the date, since Henslowe's first and only payment was made eight months later. It should perhaps be 24 Mar. 1598–9.'[2] On the other hand, the absence of any further payment suggests that Drayton may never have finished the play.

There comes an interval of nine months in the dates of Henslowe's payments, in the earlier part of which it is possible that Drayton went to Scotland.[3] The next was made in October for *Sir John Oldcastle*, the only play bearing Drayton's name that has survived. The

---

[1] *Diary*, II, pp. 190–1.
[2] See *English Literary Autographs 1550–1650*, by W. W. Greg, who quotes Halliwell-Phillipps, *Collection of Documents respecting the Office of the Master of the Revels.*   [3] See below, page 124.

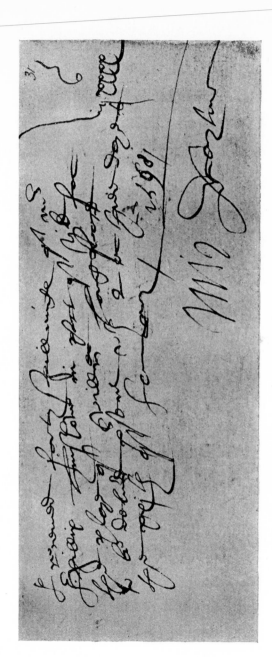

RECEIPT BY MICHAEL DRAYTON IN HENSLOWE'S DIARY

sources for it are discussed elsewhere.[1] In August and September 1602 it was transferred from the Admiral's men to Worcester's, and Henslowe records payments made for additions to it by Dekker for its performance by that company. Of the other plays to which Drayton's name is attached in the Diary nothing is known beyond what their titles may convey. *Constance of Rome*, for instance, was doubtless a play based on the well-known romance which Geoffrey Chaucer had used for his *Man of Law's Tale* and John Gower in his *Confessio Amantis*. From the Diary we learn also that on 9 August 1598 Henslowe advanced to Anthony Munday ten shillings in earnest for an unnamed 'comodey for the corte' and that:

> Mr Drayton hath geven his worde for yt
> the boocke to be done wth in one fortnight.[2]

How did Drayton, who had exalted notions both of the dignity of his calling and of his own eminence as a poet, come to associate himself with the needy band of playwrights, some of them second- or even third-rate men, whom Henslowe paid to turn out plays by the score for the Admiral's company? Were the plays mere potboilers to bring relief at a period of his life when he was suffering from poverty and distress? Or did he turn playwright of his free and deliberate choice, so as to fall in with the literary vogue of the moment? Or, again, was he obeying an impulse to express himself in drama, leaving for a while the rhymed couplets of the *Heroicall Epistles* and the stanza forms of the Legends and *Mortimeriados*?[3]

Drayton was always a poor man. His aspirations for fame were ever in conflict with his fortune:

[1] Vol. v, pp. 45–6.   [2] *Diary*, f. 49.
[3] The Legends and EHE already seem to show a movement towards drama as well as a very close knowledge of contemporary chronicle and revenge plays. See Introductions to EHE in Vol. v, pp. 100 *sqq.*

When graceful *Fame* . . .
Gave me this booke . . .
. . . *Fortune* angry with her foe therefore,
Gave me this gift, that I should still be poore.

That was written at the end of *Robert Duke of Normandy*
in a volume dedicated to Lucy, Countess of Bedford,
and written in 'light . . . borrowed from your beams
. . . under the stamp of your glorious name.' In that
same year, 1596, he dedicates *Mortimeriados* to Lucy as

Rarest of Ladies, all, of all I have,
Anchor of my poore Tempest-beaten state.

A year or so later the epigrammatist Bastard is perhaps
alluding to an impecunious Drayton in company with
Bartholomew Young and Matthew Roydon:

Th'arke-Angell *Michaell* looketh wan and blewe,
More than his predecessor *Bartlemewe*,
More than his neighbour *Mathew*: as men say,
Because he hath so many debts to pay.[1]

Throughout his life he was fortunate in being in the
service or enjoying the patronage of a succession of
friends and patrons of influence and sometimes of great
wealth; and he found shelter for long periods in their
houses. But when their hospitality failed and he lived
in his London lodging—perhaps by the Church of St
Dunstan-in-the-West, where he died more than thirty
years later—he may have had to pick up a living as
best he could. In a later age journalism gave subsistence
to many a good poet in Grub Street. But as yet there
were no journals, and we may conjecture that Drayton
turned to drama as a branch of poetic literature which
seemed to offer a means of livelihood in no way alien to
his genius. His early allusions to the theatre show how
keen was his ambition to take part in the new English
drama which was then entering upon its most brilliant
period and was engaging the talent of the greatest of his

[1] *Chrestoleros*, VII, 27.

fellow-poets. In the Eighth Eglog of 1593 the youthful
Motto wistfully compares the shepherds' 'lowly vaine'
with the vaunting of those who

> strut the stage with reperfumed wordes.

> See how these yonkers rave it out in rime,
>   who make a traffic of their rarest wits,
> And in *Bellonas* buskin tread it fine,
>   like *Bacchus* priests raging in franticke fits.

And Gorbo moralizes:

> My boy, these yonkers reachen after fame,
>   and so done presse into the learned troupe,
> With filed quill to glorifie their name,
>   which otherwise were pend in shamefull coupe.

In his 47th Sonnet, first printed in 1605, Drayton
tells us of the ambitious motive which had first stirred
him to write for the stage and of the applause which he
won there:

> In pride of Wit, when high desire of Fame
> Gave Life and Courage to my lab'ring Pen,
> And first the sound and vertue of my Name
> Wonne grace and credit in the Eares of Men;
> With those the thronged Theaters that presse,
> I in the Circuit for the Lawrell strove:
> Where, the full Prayse I freely must confesse,
> In heat of Bloud, a modest Mind might move.
> With Showts and Claps at ev'ry little pawse,
> When the proud Round on ev'ry side hath rung. . .

All the allusions to the theatre were removed from the
Eighth Eglog when it was rewritten in 1605. When in
1627 Drayton writes of the dramatists in the Epistle to
Henry Reynolds, it is with a touch of scorn. He will not
run

> In quest of these, that them applause have wonne,
> Upon our Stages in these latter dayes,

That are so many, let them have ther bayes
That doe deserve it. . .

Certain students of Elizabethan drama have thought
that traces of Drayton's work may be found in some of
the anonymous plays of the period. Fleay, for instance,
believed that he had a hand in *Sir Thomas More*, the
Second and Third Parts of *King Henry VI*, *Cromwell*,
The London Prodigal, *The Yorkshire Tragedy*, the Induction to *The Taming of the Shrew*, and *The Merry Devil of
Edmonton*.[1] These irresponsible attributions may for the
most part be dismissed, for they are supported by no
serious evidence. Mr H. W. Crundell has suggested
that Drayton was the author of *King Edward III*. That
play, however, dates from 1595 or earlier; and there is
no evidence that Drayton had as yet turned playwright.
Moreover, in his *Heroicall Epistles* he has quite a different version of the wooing of Lady Salisbury from that
found in the play.[2] *King Edward IV* is now generally
attributed to Thomas Heywood; but Sir Edmund
Chambers thinks that the Agincourt song in Act III
of the First Part must be Drayton's. It is almost certainly, however, a ballad of much older date.[3] Dodsley
quotes Coxeter as saying that in an old MS. version of
The Merry Devil of Edmonton (c. 1603) 'he had seen
that play assigned to Michael Drayton.'[4] There is no
other evidence for the attribution; and Coxeter is notor-
iously unreliable.

Indeed, there is no trustworthy evidence either in-
ternal or external that Drayton had a hand in any extant
play except *Sir John Oldcastle*, or in any of the lost plays

---

[1] *Biographical Chronicle of the English Drama*, pp. 119–20. Cf.
EHE[7] n. Vol. v, pp. 119–20.

[2] EHE[4] n, Vol. v, pp. 108–9. See *NQ*, Vol. 176, pp. 258–60,
318–9; also E. K. Chambers, *Eliz. Stage*, IV, 9–10.

[3] Chambers, op. cit., IV, 11; K.T.'s note in *NQ* and Vol. v, p.
147.

[4] Dodsley's *Old Plays*, ed. Isaac Reed, 1780, v, 247.

other than those recorded of him in Henslowe's *Diary*.[1] It was probably for his share in them that later on in 1598 Meres joined him with Marlowe, Peele, Kid, Shakespeare, and other Elizabethan playwrights among the 'Tragicke Poets' whom he named with honour beside those of Greece and Rome.[2]

During the years in which he was working for Henslowe, Drayton was busily engaged also in overhauling and adding to the work by which he had already won his reputation as a poet. There are the new *Heroicall Epistles* in the editions of 1598 and 1599, the new sonnets in *Idea* 1599 and 1600. Between 1596 and 1602 he was recasting and rewriting the long *Mortimeriados*, turning it into the much longer *Barons Warres*. We have seen, too, that he was already 'penning' *Poly-Olbion*.

[1] Lemuel Whitaker, 'M.D. as a Dramatist,' *PMLA*, XVIII, p. 409; Elton, pp. 91–3.
[2] *Palladis Tamia* (ent'd Sept. 1598), f. 283. In an earlier passage, however, Meres says that we may 'truly terme *Michael Drayton Tragœdiographus*, for his passionate penning the downfals of valiant *Robert of Normandy*, chast *Matilda*, and great *Gaveston:*' (Ibid. f. 281.)

II THE WHITEFRIARS PLAYHOUSE

THERE is no evidence that Drayton took any part in the drama between the years 1602 and 1607. In the new reign the Admiral's company, hitherto maintained by Henslowe, became the Prince of Wales's players. In importance they fell far behind their rivals, the Chamberlain's men, who had become the King's men. Drayton seems to have had no hand in any new plays for the Prince's players. From August 1607, however, and perhaps earlier, down to the following summer he was actively engaged with the company known as the Children of the King's Revels. It is not known at what precise date that company was formed. There were entered in the Stationers' Register seven plays whose title-pages announce that they were acted by the King's Children:

Cupid's Whirligig, by E.S., perhaps Edward or Edmund Sharpham. S.R. 29 June. 1607; printed 1607.

The Family of Love (by Thomas Middleton?) S.R. 12 Oct. 1607; 1608.

Humour out of Breath, by John Day. S.R. 12 Apr. 1608; 1608.

The Dumb Knight, by Gervase Markham. S.R. 6 Oct. 1608 ; 1608.

Two Maids of Morclacke, by Robert Armin. 1609.

The Turk, by John Mason, M.A. S.R. 10 Mar. 1609; 1610.

Ram Alley: Or Merry Tricks, by Lo: Barry. S.R. 9 Nov. 1610; 1611.

To these we must add an unknown play called *Torris-Mount*, mentioned in the lawsuit, *Slatyer v. Androwes*, which, as we shall see, is our principal source of information concerning the Whitefriars playhouse and Drayton's part therein. There is some reason for believing also that another play, *Law Tricks*, by John Day, the 1608 quarto of which states that it had been 'divers times acted by the Children of the Revels,' was per-

formed by the King's Children, and not by the Queen's
Children, for whom Day had written *The Isle of Gulls*
in 1606.[1] That so many plays, acted by the Company
within so short a period, most of them by authors of
repute, like Middleton, Day, Markham and Armin,
should have been judged worth printing, seems to show
that at its beginning the Children achieved a consider-
able measure of success. The printing of its plays was
held to be against the interests of the company; and
when in March 1608 an agreement was made with its
new manager, a clause was inserted to forbid it.

It is not known when Drayton first took part as a
sharer in the company. His name and the names of his
fellow-sharers are found again and again in actions
taken before the King's Bench and in other courts in
1609 and many years later. At Easter 1609 Thomas
Woodforde sued for a debt of £120 on a Bond dated
12 August 1607, the endorsement[2] of which reads:

> The Condicion of this obligacion is such that if the
> within bounden lordinge Barrye William Treveele
> Edwarde Sybthorpe & Michaell Drayton or any of
> them theire or any of their executors administrators
> or assignes doe well and trulie pay or cause to be
> payde unto the within named Thomas Woodforde
> his executors or Assignes the somme of three score
> poundes of lawfull money of England on the ffyve
> and Twentieth day of November now next cominge
> att or on the ffirst stone in the Temple Churche neere
> fleetestreet london att one entire payment without
> delay That then this present obligacion to be voyde
> and of none effecte Or els to stande and abide in full
> force and vertue.

It was finally proved that the money was not paid, and
Woodforde was awarded for debt and costs £122.

[1] H. N. Hillebrand, *The Child Actors*, Univ. of Illinois, 1926,
pp. 220–36, 316.

[2] *Coram Rege Rolls*. Easter, 6 Jas. I, m. 483; Hillebrand, p. 229.

At Easter and Trinity 1609 no less than six suits, including the above, were brought against Lordinge Barry for liabilities for which he had bound himself in August and November 1607. In four of them Thomas Woodforde is the plaintiff, and he won them all.[1]

On 29 June 1611 William Trevill of London, tallow chandler, together with divers of his creditors complained against William Methold, William Cooke, Felix Wilson, Thomas Woodforde, George Androwes, Richard Brogden, Richard Jobber, Martin Slatier, John Marks, Michael Drayton, Elizabeth Browne, Richard Black, and Richard Hunter, others of his creditors, to be relieved in equity concerning debts which Trevill owed the said defendants upon bonds and otherwise. The complainants, because Trevill was very poor, and they had pity on him, had consented to remit part of the debt and give long terms of payment. But the defendants would not agree, and, with the exception of John Marks, have gone about to annoy Trevill in common law upon 'diverse bonds and other specialties wherein or in the most whereof the said Trevill is onely suretie for others although there are diverse other more sufficient than hee bound wth him in the same,' and although the most part of the sums due is satisfied, as is alleged. If they persisted, they would ruin Trevill and do the complainants out of any realization of their debts. The case dragged on till 11 November, when for reasons exhibited by the defendants' demurrer it was dismissed in their favour.[2]

So far the cases cited give no information concerning the nature of the business for which Woodforde, Drayton, Trevill and the rest had mutually bound themselves. We learn it from proceedings taken nearly a quarter of a century later, when the unhappy Trevill was still seeking to release himself from the liabilities in which he had become involved. Woodforde sought to recover payment from him under one or other of the bonds, and

[1] Hillebrand, *l.c.*   [2] Hillebrand, pp. 228–9.

Trevill sought relief in equity. The judgement of the court is preceded by a long recapitulation of the case, the following extract from which states how and what consideration was given many years before in the matter of the Whitefriars Playhouse:

> The consideracion wch induced the sd William Trevill to become bound in the sd bonds beinge only for a sixt parte of the Lease of a Playhouse in the Whitefryers whereunto the sd William Trevill was drawne by the perswasion of Sr Anthony Ashley kn^t & one Mr Smith & the Def^t who likewise prevailed wth the sd Trevill (beinge ignorant in the course of sharers in a Playhouse) to become ingaged in severall other bonds & billes to diverse persons for payment of diverse sommes only to make a stocke for supply of the Playehouse And although that the sd Sir Anthony Ashley beinge Landlord of the Playhouse by combinacion with the Def^t uppon pretence that half a yeares Rent for the Playhouse was unpaid entred into the Playhouse & turned the Players out of doors and took the fforfeiture of the Lease whereby the sd William Trevill was frustrated of all benefitt wch he was to have by the s^d Lease . . .[1]

Who are the people whose names in the above proceedings are introduced into a series of actions at law which lasted from the early years of King James down to the Civil War? Thomas Woodforde was the nephew of Drayton's friend, the poet Thomas Lodge. Whether or no he was concerned in the Whitefriars playhouse from the beginning, it is clear that by August 1607 he had acquired a leading interest in it, and that he disposed of some at least of his moiety in shares of one-sixth to other sharers. Lordinge Barry, as we shall see, owned the other moiety. Like Woodforde, he contrived to jettison some of his holding on to others. He was the

---

[1] Trevill v. Woodforde. *Court of Requests (Books)*; *Orders and Decrees*, 17 and 18 Chas. I, fo. 247, in Hillebrand, pp. 227-8.

author of *Ram Alley*, the last in the above list of printed
plays performed by the Children of the King's Revels.
His own adventurous career and the extraordinary
conjectures which the learned have advanced about his
identity are discussed later. We have seen how Trevill,
the City tallow-chandler, who was persuaded by Woodforde and Sir Anthony Ashley to become bound to
Woodforde in return for a sixth part of the lease of the
Whitefriars, and to accept other liabilities, was engaged
more than thirty years later in trying to free himself
from the shackles of debt in which he had become involved. Ashley was secretary to the Privy Council, and
was perhaps acting for the Lord Treasurer, Thomas
Sackville, Earl of Dorset, the landlord of the Whitefriars.

We do not know what was Drayton's part in the
undertaking at this time. It seems likely that the Children of the King's Revels were founded in emulation of
the Queen's Children, who had secured royal protection under patent in 1604.[1] Samuel Daniel was appointed Licenser of Plays to that company, but it does
not appear that Drayton held the same office for the
King's Children. He may already have been their manager. His dramatic work for Henslowe and his reputation
as a poet were qualifications that would make him of
special value in the counsels of the company, though
we may doubt his shrewdness as a business man.

It seems pretty certain that by August 1607 the
company's position was insecure; and it is possible that
on the security of the bond Woodforde furnished
capital to keep it going. By the following February the
position was no better, as we gather from the Bill of
Complaint made about a year later by George Androwes, who sought relief in equity under his liability
as a sharer holding a sixth part, which he had bought
out of Barry's moiety. He was sued by Martin Slatyer,
who by agreement with Barry, Drayton and other

[1] Chambers, ES II, p. 49.

sharers had been appointed manager of the playhouse and the Children. Androwes's complaint and
Slatyer's answers make a very long document. It is
enough to give here an abstract adapted from that
made by Furnivall to accompany the text of the document as printed in full by James Greenstreet in a paper
written for the New Shakespere Society in 1888:

Bill of Complaint by George Androwes.
Nono die ffebruarii, 1608[–9].

I, George Androws, state that about Feb. 1607–8,
Barry had a moiety, first, of the Whitefriars Playhouse, under a lease of March 1607–8 from Lord
Buckhurst to Michael Drayton and Thomas Woodforde for 6 years &c. at £50 a year; secondly, of the
playbooks, dresses, &c. of the Children of the Revels;
that Barry and Martin Slatyer persuaded me to buy
a sixth of Barry's moiety, as the dresses cost £400.
Barry askt me £90, and said I should make £100 a
year by it. So I bought a sixth of Barry's moiety, and
paid him £70 for it. But I was over-reached therein.
The dresses, said to be worth £400, were only worth
£5; the cost of the building and Children fell mainly
on me, and I lost £300 by it all. The lease from Lord
Buckhurst, too, was forfeited before my sixth was
assigned to me. So Barry, Michael Drayton, William
Trevill, William Cooke, Edward Sibthorpe, and
John Mason, of London, gentlemen, being partners
in the Playhouse, &c., signed an agreement with the
said Martin Slatyer on 10 March 1607–8 that he
should be resident and travelling manager of the
theatre and of the Children of the Revels, at one-
sixth of the net receipts, and all the profit on wines,
tobacco, &c., sold, as set forth below:

[*Agreement between Martin Slatyer, Citizen and Iron
monger, and the Other Sharers in the Whitefriars Theatre,
10 March 1607–8*]

    1. For the rest of Lord Buckhurst's Lease of the

Playhouse, Martin Slatyer shall have a sixth of the net profits of all plays, music, &c.

2. The use of all the 13 rooms in the Playhouse, the great Hall, Kitchen, Cellar, &c.

3. The profits on all drinks, tobacco, wood, coal, &c.

4. On the renewal of the licence for playing, Slatyer's name shall be joined to Michael Drayton's, so that when the plague is in London, Slatyer may travel with the Children of the Revels.

5. If any of the company's property worth more than 2s. be surreptitiously sold by any sharer, the offender shall lose his place and profits.

6. Every night, one sixth of the weekly outgoings shall be retained to pay all expenses and keep free of debt.

7. As all the Children are apprenticed to Slatyer for three years, he binds himself in the penalty of £40 not to part with any Child to any persons.

8. All costumes lent shall be called in. No sharer shall print any company play, under a penalty of £40, or the loss of his share, except the play of *Torrismount*, and that not for twelve months.

9. When Slatyer travels with the Children, he shall have one and a half shares.

10. I with Barry, Drayton, Trevill, Cooke, Sibthorpe, and Mason, gave Slatyer a Bond of £200 (dated 10 March 1607–8) to fulfil our said agreement.

But I, Androwes, being ignorant of the law, when I executed the agreement and bond, asked Slatyer whether I rendered myself responsible for default made by any of the parties. Slatyer told me he would hold me bound only for my own acts. So I unadvisedly executed the deeds. But now other obligors have made some slight default, and Slatyer has proceeded against me on the said Bond of £200, has had me arrested, and intends to make me pay, unless your Lordship relieve me therein, as you have done to others in like case. Therefore I pray for a sub-poena to be issued against Slatyer, and that in the interval Slatyer's action may be stayed by the King's process of injunction.

The Answer of Martin Slatyer, Defendant, to the Bill of Complaint of George Androwes, Complainant.

Slatyer answers that though he believes Barry had a moiety in the Whitefriars Playhouse, play-books, dresses, etc., assigned to him by Woodforde, yet he (Slatyer) never persuaded Androwes to take from Barry an assignment of the sixth part in question, and could not have done so, since he was not ac-quainted with either of them until long after the assignment had been fully effected. Slatyer knows nothing of Barry's saying the dresses cost £400, and that Androwes would make £100 a year profit, and thinks that Androwes had bought his sixth before Slatyer knew him or Barry. Slatyer further says that the alleged loss to Androwes of £300 in building was for the erection of structures in no way had in mind until long after the bargain was settled, and he thinks the building was done at the complainant's own direction or with his consent, each of the six sharers being charged with a sixth part of the outlay. Slat-yer says that most of the cost of the Children did not fall on Androwes, who has no right to claim anything from one who has lost more than he has. All the sharers shared alike. Slatyer marvels that Androws should plead ignorance of the law, and denies that either he or the scrivener employed led the com-plainant to believe he was only bound so as to be liable solely for his own acts, as he alleges. Slatyer concludes by averring that in consequence of the litigation he and his family (ten in number) have been ejected from their rooms at the playhouse, and are cast upon the world to seek for their living. He

has had Androwes arrested, and sued him for £200.
Therefore Slatyer prays to be dismissed with reasonable costs.[1]

From Androwes's complaint it appears that in February 1608 the Company was once more in the straits
from which Woodforde had sought to extricate it—or
perhaps himself—in the previous August. By grossly
exaggerating the prospects and resources of the company Barry persuaded Androwes to buy a sixth part of
his moiety, just as Woodforde had done with Trevill
six months before. In each case, too, the lease came to
be forfeited. Possibly the lease to be taken out in Drayton's and Woodforde's names in March, of which
Androwes was to have one-sixth, was granted on the
reconstruction of the company under Slatyer's manage-
ment. Slatyer was a player. He had been one of the
Admiral's men, and his name appears in Henslowe in
the first list of that company 14 December 1594. He
was also a frequent borrower from Henslowe. We find
him selling to the Admiral's men the books of some old
plays of their own. In 1597 he was sued by William
Birde, Thomas Downton and Gabriel Spenser, three of
Henslowe's actors, for dishonestly using the book of a
play which they had lost and Slatyer had found.[2]

William Cooke, whose name we find among the
sharers in Androwes's complaint, was perhaps the son
of Sir Anthony Cooke of Gidea Hall, who purchased
the manor of Hartshill from his nephew Anthony—
Drayton's *Maecenas*—in 1583. When Sir Henry
Goodere 'lay sick of his great sickness'—the stone—at
the sign of the Naked Boy in the Strand near London
about the year 1576, he was removed thence to one Mr
Cooke's house at or near Charing Cross.[3] Cooke had

---

[1] J. Greenstreet, 'The Whitefriars Theatre in the Time of
Shakespere,' Transactions of the New Shakespere Society 1887–
1892, pp. 269–284.   [2] *Diary*, ii, p. 311.
[3] P.R.O. Chancery, 1 Jas. I, Town Depositions, Bundle 313,
Answers by Edward Baskerville.

married Frances, daughter of Lord John Grey and niece of Henry Grey, the ill-fated Duke of Suffolk.

John Mason, who in Slatyer's action is also named among the sharers, was the author of *The Turk*, acted by the Children of the King's Revels, and printed in 1610.

Who was Lordinge Barry? His play, *Ram Alley or The Merry Tricks*, has been playing a merry trick with scholars from the seventeenth century till to-day. The title-page says that it was 'Written by Lo: Barrey.' As early as 1661 Francis Kirkman the bookseller, in his list of all the English plays then printed, interprets 'Lo: Barrey' as standing for 'Lord Barrey' and ascribes it to the ghost of a nobleman of that style. After him, in 1691, Anthony Wood, correcting a false attribution of *Ram Alley* to Massinger, says that

> As to this last, there is without doubt a mistake, for all readers of plays cannot but know that *Ram Alley or Merry Tricks* was pen'd by the Lord Barry an Irish man.[1]

In the same year, 1691, in which Wood wrote, however, Langbaine took 'Lo:' to stand for 'Lodowick,'and Barry will be found in *The Dictionary of National Biography* so re-christened. In 1912 Mr Joseph Quincy Adams and in 1917 Mr W. J. Lawrence arrived quite independently at the opinion that Lo: Barrey must be the Lording Barry whose name is mentioned conspicuously but not honourably in the suit, Slatyer *versus* Androwes, which has furnished us so with much information concerning the fortunes of the Whitefriars playhouse. Lawrence, however, supposed that Lordinge could not be a font name, but must be a courtesy title for the son of a lord. He searched the Irish peerage and found that David, son and heir apparent of David Barry, 9th Viscount Buttevant, was in England during the closing years of Elizabeth and that Cecil put him in the charge of Gabriel Goodman, head of Westminster

[1] *Athen. Oxon.*, ed. Bliss, p. 655.

School, to educate and wean from popery. There was no other Barry in the peerage whose date would admit of his having written *Ram Alley*. David, therefore (he supposed), must be the author.[1]

A pennyweight of recorded fact may overbalance a ton of the weightiest scholarship. It is furnished in *Notes and Queries*[2] by Mr C. L'Estrange Ewen, who finds from the Register of St Laurence Pountney that Lording Barry was christened there 17 April 1580, being the seventh son, not of an Irish Viscount, but of Nicholas Barry, citizen and fishmonger, and a principal taxpayer in his parish, by his second wife, Anne, daughter of George Lording, merchant taylor, whose maiden name was given to the child at the font. In June 1608 or thereabouts, some two months after Barry, Drayton and their fellow-sharers had appointed Martin Slatyer to manage the Whitefriars playhouse, Lordinge was a prisoner in the Marshalsea. Obtaining bail, he absconded. Then in company with one John Thomas of Falmouth he engaged in piracy, first off the Reculvers, and a little later off the south-west coast of Ireland. There they were captured. Thomas was taken to London and hanged at Execution Dock, after confessing that all his robberies had been committed in company with 'Lawding Barry.' But Barry was released. Notwithstanding his narrow escape, he seems to have continued in his piratical adventures for some six years more. Then in 1616, as Captain Barry, he took part in Sir Walter Raleigh's disastrous expedition to the Orinoco. He afterwards became master and part owner of the ship *Edward* of London. He died there in 1629.

We do not know how the various suits in which Drayton and his fellow-sharers were involved by the

[1] Chambers, *ES*, and W. W. Greg, *Bibliography of the English Printed Drama*, Vol. 1, 1939, have 'Lord Barry,' and *STC* 'David Barry,' as the author.

[2] *NQ*, Feb. 1938, 'Lording Barry, Dramatist,' by C. L'Estrange Ewen.

failure of their unhappy venture were eventually
settled. The Whitefriars was closed about the middle
of 1608, and a new company of the Children of the
Queen's Revels was in possession of it in 1609. Drayton
and his colleagues had no part therein.[1]

In two places besides his 47th Sonnet Drayton gives
us a glimpse at an Elizabethan audience. The lines in
which Jane Shore complains to the King of the tight
hand by which husbands sought to restrain their wan-
ton wives suggest also the moral stigma which attached
to the presence of women at stage-plays:[2]

> Blame you our Husbands then, if you they denie
> Our publique Walking, our loose Libertie?
> If with exception still they us debarre
> The Circuit of the publique Theater;
> To heare the Poet in a Comick straine,
> Able t'infect with his lascivious Scene;
> And the young wanton Wits, when they applaud
> The slie perswasion of some subtill Bawd;
> Or passionate Tragedian, in his rage
> Acting a Love-sick Passion on the Stage.

In his 'Ode to Apollo' he is not more flattering to the
audience; but he admits playwrights whether of comedy or tragedy to the poetical priesthood. He counsels
them wisely:

> Let Art and Nature goe
> One with the other;
> Yet so, that Art may show
> Nature her Mother;
> The thick-brayn'd Audience lively to awake
> Till with shrill claps the Theater doe shake.[3]

[1] For further details of the later legal proceedings see M. J.
Dickson, 'William Trevell and the Whitefriars Theatre,' *RES*
July 1930, pp. 309–12, and Margaret Dowling, 'Further Notes on
William Trevell,' *RES* Oct. 1930.

[2] EHE[9b] 133–42 and D's Annotation.   [3] Od[6] 49–56.

CHAPTER IX

DRAYTON AND KING JAMES

IN the closing years of Elizabeth's reign the eyes of men were turned in expectation towards the North. There was much intriguing, much passing to and fro across the border, by principals and their servants in the interest of men like Sir Henry Goodere, as well as those of higher station, who hoped to raise their condition and better their fortunes under a new sovereign. It seems likely that Drayton was in Scotland—perhaps in Goodere's company—in 1599, at some part of the period between January and July in which his name is absent from Henslowe's Diary. In the little volume of *Englands Heroicall Epistles* and *Idea* which was printed in 1600, there appeared William Alexander's lines to Drayton, which, as we have seen,[1] offer evidence of an early acquaintance with the Scottish poet at his home at Menstrie. In the same volume we find rather unexpectedly in company with Drayton's other sonnets that addressed *To the high and mighty Prince, James, King of Scots*.[2] Its closing couplet hints plainly at the favours that poets might look for from one who was

Of Kings a Poet, and the Poets King . . .
But with thy Laurell, thou doo'st crowne thy Crowne;
That they whose pens, (even) life to Kings doe give,
In thee a King, shall seeke them selves to live.

A passage in his Elegy to George Sandys, written about 1622, seems to imply that, before James came in, Drayton had undertaken some perilous adventure on his behalf. Whatever the service may have been, it

[1] See pp. 95–6, 104.
[2] Another English poet—one John Ferrour—visited James in his Scottish capital in the year 1599–1600. A poem which he wrote in James's honour on that occasion is preserved in MS. Royal 18. A. f. 24 at the British Museum. He went there again three years later as a messenger for James's agent in London.

received neither reward nor recognition from the King. Moreover, the 'Paeans' with which Drayton was the first of the poets to acclaim the new sovereign, gave offence and brought disgrace upon him instead of the laureate honours to which he aspired:

> It was my hap before all other men
> To suffer shipwrack by my forward pen:
> When King JAMES entred; at which joyfull time
> I taught his title to this Ile in rime:
> And to my part did all the Muses win,
> With high-pitch *Pæans* to applaud him in:
> When cowardise had tyed up every tongue,
> And all stood silent, yet for him I sung;
> And when before by danger I was dar'd,
> I kick'd her from me, nor a jot I spar'd.
> Yet had not my cleere spirit in Fortunes scorne,
> Me above earth and her afflictions borne;
> He next my God on whom I built my trust,
> Had left me troden lower then the dust.[1]

Drayton's protestation that his too 'forward pen' was the reason for what he regarded as his downfall, however inadequate it may seem to those who study his verses to-day, has the support of Henry Chettle, who, in his *Englands Mourning Garment: worne here by plaine Shepheardes: in memorie of their Mistresse Elizabeth* (1603), printed just before the Queen's funeral, gently reproves 'Rowland' for his silence about the death of Elizabeth:

[1] El² 19–32. In the introduction to the 1748 folio of Drayton's Works the editor, Charles Coffey, associates Drayton's services on benalf of James with Roger Aston, who was James's intermediary with Elizabeth over a long period of years, and was also in the pay of Cecil. Roger Aston's alleged interest in Drayton, however, is more likely to.be a mere conjecture, based upon the poet's relations with Walter Aston, whom Coffey quite wrongly calls 'a near Relative of this Gentleman'; for Roger was of the Cheshire Astons, a stock which for some centuries had been distinct from the Astons of Staffordshire, whose head was Walter Aston.

Make some amends I know thou lovdst her well,
Thinke twas a fault to have thy verses seene
Praising the King, ere they had mournd the Queen.

Elizabeth had died on 24 March, and she was not buried
until 28 April. Drayton's 'gratulatorie poem' *To the
Majestie of King James* must have come hot from the
press within a few days of her death. For all its allusions
to the season of spring and the month of March, in
which the new reign so auspiciously began, it is impossible to believe that the poem, like the 'well-
prepared pollicie' of the Council which Drayton commends, had not been framed and in great part written
in anticipation of the Crown's demise. It was a timely
bit of propaganda, for the pedigree which accompanies
it shows James Stuart's title to the throne by descent
from Henry VII both through Mary Queen of Scots
and through her husband Darnley. But the stern ad-
monition in its closing lines that James should banish
from his Court

Those silken, laced, and perfumed hinds,
That have rich bodies, but poore wretched minds. . .
The foole, the Pandar and the Parasite,[1]

too well warranted by subsequent history, was not
likely to endear Drayton to the fortune-hunters and
sycophants who were ever pressing about the throne.
Even as he wrote it, Drayton was conscious of the hostility to which he was exposed. He perhaps counted
himself amongst

such as rightly propheci'd thy raigne,

and might therefore:

Deride those Ideots held their words for vaine,[2]

although none of his extant writings contain or allude to
such a prophecy. He seems to have meant the poem as a

[1] Maj. 165–68.   [2] Maj. 149–50.

triumphant ending to the labours which he had under-
gone and the perils which he had faced in James's
cause—an answer to the 'envies spite' that they had
brought upon his head. It is a call to the King to give
due honour to poetry in the person of the poet himself:

And know great Prince, that Muse thy glory sings,
(What ere detraction snarle) was made for Kings.

Instead, as we have seen, he found that the emolu-
ments to which he aspired were given to other men,
while his own claims on the royal favour were—so it
seemed to him—shamefully passed over.   Apart from
his 'too forward' poem *To the Majestie of King James*
and his *Pæan Triumphall* 'congratulating his Highnes
magnificent entring the Citie' (on 15 March 1604),
which Drayton wrote for the Goldsmiths' Company,
(perhaps at the instance of his Welsh friend, John
Williams, the Court Goldsmith), his pen contributed
nothing to the festive celebrations which became fashionable in the new reign. When James was entertained
in his progress towards London at Burley Hill in
April 1603 by Lucy Bedford's father, Sir John Harington, it was Samuel Daniel, and not he, who wrote the
Panegyrike Congratulatorie for the occasion; and Daniel
wrote the first of the great masques which presently
became the fashionable entertainment at Court. It was
Ben Jonson, and not Drayton or Daniel, who in July
1603 provided the entertainment at Althorpe, when the
Queen with Lucy Bedford in her train stayed there on
her way south from Edinburgh.

In his Preface to *Poly-Olbion*, printed in 1612,
Drayton shows how strong was his consciousness that
the new reign had brought him dishonour and how long
and how bitterly the thought of it rankled. He tells the
general reader how

that many times I had determined with my selfe, to
have left it off, and have neglected my papers sometimes two yeeres together, finding the times since his

Majesties happy comming in, to fall so heavily upon my distressed fortunes, after my zealous soule had labored so long in that, which with the general happinesse of the kingdom, seem'd not then impossible somewhat also to have advanced me. But I instantly saw all my long nourisht hopes even buried alive before my face: so uncertaine (in this world) be the ends of our cleerest endevors.[1]

James himself took but an indolent interest in contemporary writers and their works. We may therefore suppose that Drayton's loss of the royal favour meant rather that he no longer enjoyed the favour of those about the Court. For that we must seek some reason stronger than his impetuous zeal in acclaiming the new reign, or his want of tact in saying nothing about the Queen's death, or even the boastful and sometimes truculent tone of his lines 'To the Majestie of King James.'

Lady Bedford's influence was now great, and, as we have seen, she was at the centre of a brilliant literary circle. We may perhaps associate Drayton's sense of neglect and rebuff with the withdrawal of her patronage from himself or with her extension of it to the sprightlier set of men like Florio, Edward Herbert, Donne and Jonson, whose spirit and outlook were far removed from his.

A stronger reason for the rebuff, however, is likely to have been Drayton's outspoken hostility to some in high places. Study of the text of some of Drayton's writings suggests that even before the death of Elizabeth he may have both feared and incurred loss of favour with the Council. The Queen's touchiness with regard to the career of King Richard II and to parallels that the disaffected might draw between his reign with its tragic ending and her own is well known. In deference to her susceptibility the deposition scene in

[1] Vol. IV, p. vi*. He is alluding to his work on PO.

Shakespeare's *Richard II* was discreetly suppressed in the early quartos of that play. On the like grounds the Preface of Sir John Hayward's book, *The First Part of the Raigne of Henry IIII*, dedicated to the Earl of Essex, was removed by order of the Archbishop of Canterbury, the entire second edition was seized and burnt, and for writing the book Hayward himself was committed to the Tower and tried for treason.[1] Drayton seems to have feared that his own Heroical Epistles of Richard II and Queen Isabel might incur censure for the same reason. From the new edition of 1599 he cut out more than forty lines, and he changed others which might also be suspected of a treasonable tendency.[2] In *The Barrons Wars*, entered 8 October 1602, however, he moralizes in a sense that seems to relate to Elizabeth and her ministers even more plainly than to Edward II and those who brought him to his fall:

> That State whereon the strength of Princes leanes
> Whose hie ascent we trembling doe behold,
> From whence by coynesse of their chast disdaines,
> Subjection is imperiously controld,
> Their earthly weaknes evermore explaines,
> Exalting whom they please not whom they should,
>> When their owne fall (showes how they fondly
>> er'd,)
> Procur'd by those, unworthily prefer'd.

> Merit goes unregarded, and ungrac'd,
> When by his fauters ignorance held in,
> And Parasites in wisemens roomes are plac'd,
> Onely to sooth the great ones in their sin,
> From such whose gifts, and knowledge is debac'd
> There's many strange enormities begin,

[1] M. Dowling, 'Sir John Hayward's Troubles over his Life of Henry IIII,' in *The Library*, Sept. 1930.

[2] K. Tillotson, 'Drayton and Richard II, 1597–1600,' *RES* April 1939.

K

> Forging great wits into most factious tooles,
> When mightiest men oft prove the mightiest
>   fooles.[1]

That Drayton had already incurred some measure of disgrace seems implied in the lines *To the Majestie of King James*:

> Had not my soule beene proofe gainst envies spite
> I had not breath'd thy memory to write.

In his dedication of *The Owle* to Sir Walter Aston Drayton gives expression to his jealousy of other poets —Jonson, doubtless, and perhaps Daniel—who have been preferred before him:

> The Wreathe is *Ivie* that ingirts our browes, . . .
> We dare not look at other crowning Boughes,
> But leave the *Lawrell* unto them that may.[2]

Those lines date from 1604, when the satire was printed; but it was mostly written before Elizabeth's death. In the course of it Drayton lashes at Cecil and other great men about the throne under the figure of birds of prey.[3] The Owl, the bird of wisdom, who in vague outline perhaps stands for the satirist himself, complains to the Eagle—the sovereign—how that

>   for my freedome that I us'd of late,
> To lanch th'infection of a poysoned state,
> Wherein my free and uncorrupted Tongue,
> Lightly gave taste of their injurious wrong,
> The *Kyte*, the *Crow*, and all the Birds of prey,
> That thy Liege people havocke Night and Day;
> Rushing upon me, with most foule despight,
> Thus have they drest me in this pityous plight.[4]

---

[1] BW[4] 489–504 var.   [2] Vol. II, p. 478.

[3] For its fuller interpretation see the introduction and notes to the poem in Vol. v.

[4] O 309–316.

He goes on to describe the wrongs from which the people is suffering. The allegory is obscure; but there are allusions to certain notorious abuses, sometimes plain, sometimes veiled—monopolies, the sale of benefices, the rapacity of landlords and usurers, the corruption of justice, the penal laws against Catholics, oppression of the poor and of widows and orphans, rack-renting and enclosures, the 'broaching' of treasons and the entrapping of innocent victims therein by Cecil's intelligencers. Many of the birds stand for public men, who may have been suspected or recognized by their contemporaries. To us their identity must be a matter of conjecture, but we are on safe ground in taking the Vulture for Cecil, even without the initial *C* glossed against the passage in the British Museum copy in a seventeenth-century hand.[1] The Vulture conspires with his intelligencer, the Parrot, and the Bat, who is perhaps Bacon,[2] to enrich himself by contriving the ruin of wealthy victims whom he entraps in framed treasons. Adulation, he says in a later passage, has

> His daily Mansion, his most usuall Trade,
> . . . in the Monarchs Court, in Princes Hals, . . .[3]

He has a characteristic fling at those who do dishonour to pure poetry. The 'Carion Jay,' for instance, whose identity, were it known, might throw a flood of light on this part of Drayton's career,

> approching to the Spring,
> Where the sweet *Muses* wont to sit and sing,
> With filthy Ordure so the same defil'd,
> And they from thence are utterly exil'd.

And then follows a noble passage on the poet's calling:

---

[1] Another gloss, faintly written in pencil by a later hand, seems to read, '*Cecill secret. reg/is/*.'
[2] Cf. Baxter's lines, quoted below.
[3] O 655–6.

from whose Sacred Rage,
Flowes the full Glorie of each plenteous Age. . .[1]

Two allusions to *The Owle* made by contemporary
writers show that the satire won wide notoriety. In *Sir
Philip Sidney's Ourania*, printed in 1606, Nathaniel
Baxter says that:

everie Stationer hath now to sale,
Pappe with a Hatchet, and Madge-Howlets tale. . .[2]

And later on, in lines as enigmatic as *The Owle* itself:

Learned *Drayton* hath told Madge-howlets tale,
In covert verse of sweetest Madrigale.
She whoops at all the World in frostie night,
Blazing the sinnes wherein it takes delight.
The Bat and she doth take their recreation,
If *Phœbus* be in declination.
The Owle, banquets with Chickens at her feast,
The Bat delights herselfe with Bacon best.
If you will see as cleare by night as day,
Annoynt your eyes with blood of Bats they say.
And daunce not thou after *Albertus* Fiddle,
Till thou canst better understand this Riddle:
For of this poynt Shepheards warne thee before,
Eyes so annoynted shall never see more.[3]

In Beaumont and Fletcher's *The Scornful Lady*, printed
in 1616, Sir Roger the Curate, finding that the elderly
Abigail Younglove, whom he has long wooed, is trying
to win the favour of young Welford, in giving vent to
his distress makes this double allusion to Drayton's
verse:

Did I for this . . . woo her in *Heroycall Epistles*: Did I
expound the Owle . . .[4]

Drayton's discontent at failing to receive due recognition for his poetry simmers through all his work except

[1] O 663-84.   [2] A2ᵛ.   [3] H2.   [4] Act I, 2.

the last. His sense of frustration is expressed as early as
the First Eglog of *The Shepheards Garland;* but there
he ascribes it to his own shortcomings. After the accession of James he becomes less subjective and more
vehement. In the passage as re-written in 1606 he ascribes his want of preferment to the malice of others:

> My hopes are fruiteles, and my fayth is vaine,
> and but meere showes disposed me to mock ;
> such are exalted basely that can faine
> and none regards just *Rowland of the rock.*
> To those fat pastures others helthfull keepe;
> malice denyes mee entrance with my sheepe.[1]

In the Fourth Eglog, rewritten as the Sixth, he shows
from what quarter blew the wind which had brought a
blight upon poetry with the new reign:

> The groves, the mountains, and the pleasant heath
> that wonted were with Roundelaies to ring
> Are blasted now with the cold northern breath
> that not a sheephard takes delight to sing.

And he pictures Philip Sidney

> singing with Angells in the gorgeous sky,
> laughing even Kings, and their delights to skorn
> and all those sotts them idly deify.[2]

In the Eighth Eglog we find Drayton seething with
indignation at his abandonment by Selena,[3] who, as we
have seen, must be identified with Lady Bedford.[4] He
then turns to Olcon: he can be no other than the King,
to whom as '*the high and mighty Prince,* James, *King of
Scots,*' Drayton had addressed a Sonnet in 1600, and to
whom after his accession he wrote a 'gratulatorie Poem'
and his *Pæan Triumphall:*[5]

---

[1] Pa[1] var. 49–54.   [2] Pa[6] var. 85–88, 98–100.
[3] Pa[8] var.   [4] Above, pp. 59–60.
[5] Pa[8] 91–102.

So did great OLCON, which a PHŒBUS seem'd,
Whom all good Shepheards gladly flock'd about,
And as a God of ROWLAND was esteem'd,
Which to his prayse drew all the rurall Rout:
  For, after ROWLAND, as it had beene PAN,
  Onely to OLCON every Shepheard ran.

But he forsakes the Heard-groome and his Flocks,
Nor of his Bag-pipes takes at all no keepe,
But to the sterne Wolfe and deceitfull Fox,
Leaves the poore Shepheard and his harmelesse Sheepe,
  And all those Rimes that he of OLCON sung,
  The Swayne disgrac'd, participate his wrong.

In changes made in *The Legend of Robert, Duke of Normandie*, as printed in 1619 he puts two significant lines into the mouth of Fame:

The power of Kings I utterlie defie,
Nor am I aw'd by all their Tyrannie.[1]

He makes his last allusion to King James in *The Shepheards Sirena*,[2] not printed till 1627 but perhaps written at a much earlier date. There Olcon is shown as having grown jealous of his own fallen reputation as a poet, and as encouraging the 'Rougish Swinheards,' the 'beastly Clownes,' who are hostile to the Muses and with their swine uproot the poets' pastures:

Angry OLCON sets them on,
And against us part doth take,
Ever since he was out-gone
Offring Rymes with us to make.

Drayton retained his Sonnet 'To the high and mighty Prince, James, King of Scots' in successive editions of *Idea*, in which it was reprinted without change and with no allusion to James's succession to the Crown of England. But it is found neither in the folio of 1619 nor

[1] Ro[b] 342–3. [2] SS 350–375. See note in Vol. v, p. 209, also Mrs Tillotson's letter on 'Drayton, Browne and Wither' in *TLS*, 27 Nov. 1937.

in the subsequent editions. In the XVIIth Song of *Poly-Olbion* the river Thames recites a catalogue of English sovereigns from the Norman Conquest downwards. Precedent and propriety surely demanded that it should reach its climax with the reign of the monarch whose title and virtues had been proclaimed in *The Majestie of King James* and *A Pæan Triumphall*. Instead it ends significantly and abruptly with that of Elizabeth:

> Here suddainly he staid: ...

In a sonnet which has only come to light since these pages were put in type Drayton once more alludes with bitterness to the envy and spite which had robbed him of the honours that he held to be his due. It is written in commendation of a Spanish ascetical book, englished as *The Redemption of Lost Time*,[1] and printed in 1608:

> The *Past*, the *Present*, and the *Time to be*
> Could a man tell, or were there mortall wight
> So farre above earth, raised to that hight
> That heavens dimensions he could clearly see;
> Better that man were to report from thee
> The Benefites, mortallity might raise
> From thy just labours, then th'uncertaine praise
> Attending books, which not their worth can free
> From the Taxation which foule *Envie* laies
> On *Vertues* faire-selfe, and with hellish spight
> Is ever blasting the deserved Bayes,
> That should adorne her: But receive this right
> From TIME it selfe that must thy fortresse be,
> Whose perfect use is only taught by thee.
>
> M. Drayton.

[1] STC 20825. The reader is indebted to Dr Elkin C. Wilson, of Cornell University, who has lately found it in the only known copy of *The Redemption*, now at the Folger Library, Washington. Dr J. Q. Adams, the Director of the Library, kindly allows it to be printed here. The translator 'D. Powel' may have been David Powel (1552?–1598), the Welsh divine and antiquary, whose editions of *The Historie of Cambria* and Giraldus Cambrensis were D's sources for the Welsh part of *PO*, or his son Daniel.

CHAPTER X

DRAYTON, BEN JONSON & SHAKESPEARE

IT has been generally but too readily assumed by biographers of Jonson and Shakespeare that Drayton was on terms of friendship and even of close intimacy with both those his fellow-poets. That Jonson had many friends in common with Drayton is certain. The literary circle in Elizabethan London was a narrow one; and there are many books to which both alike contributed commendatory verses, showing that the authors were friends of them both.[1] Yet we know from Jonson himself that some of their contemporaries doubted whether he and Drayton were really friends:

> It hath beene question'd, MICHAEL, if I bee
> A Friend at all: or, if at all, to thee.[2]

That was printed in 1627, towards the end of Drayton's life, when Ben, too, we may hope, was enjoying a short Indian summer in the autumn of his turbulent career. He proceeds to catalogue Drayton's poems in language too fulsome to be taken seriously. Most of the *Vision* reads like a bit of good-tempered leg-pulling, in which Ben burlesques with deliberate and luxuriously exaggerated pompousness the common run of commendatory verses. The tone suggests that advancing age and the misfortunes, broken hopes and frustrated ambitions which they suffered alike had softened the mutual asperity and jealousy of their earlier years. We can be more nearly sure that Jonson was saying what he felt when in 1619 he told Drummond of Hawthornden that 'Drayton feared him, and he esteemed not of him.'[3]

---

[1] E.g., by Palmer, Coryate, William Browne, Chapman, Sir John Beaumont; also in *Annalia Dubrensia*.

[2] *The Vision of Ben. Jonson* in Vol. III, p. 3. For evidence that Ben had seen the MS. or an early copy of the BA volume before he wrote his *Vision*, see Vol. V, p. 192, and Bibliography.

[3] Conversations with Drummond, l. 153. See Herford and Simpson's *Ben Jonson*, Vol. I, pp. 128–151.

He shows consciousness of Drayton's dislike of him in his remark to Drummond that 'Sir W. Alexander was not halfe kinde unto him & neglected him because a friend to Drayton.'[1] He finds fault with the alexandrines of *Poly-Olbion* and hints that therein Drayton had failed to achieve what he had set himself to write:

> that Michael Draytons Polya[l]bion (if [he] had performed what he promised to writte the deads of all ye Worthies) had been excellent his Long Verses pleased him not.[2]

With a long memory he recalls how twenty years before Drayton had been attacked for using the possessive case in the title of his *Mortimeriados*, a poem of a single book, and quotes John Davies's sneer at his Eighth Amour, printed as far back as 1594:

> That Drayton was chalenged for intitling one book Mortimuriados
> That S. J. Davies played in ane Epigrame on Drayton, who in a Sonnet concluded his Mistriss might been the ninth worthy & said he used a phrase like Dametas in Arcadia, who said for wit his mistresse might be a Gyant.[3]

In his lines to Henry Reynolds Drayton, on his part, pays tribute to Jonson's learning, to his inspiration as a poet, and to his eminence as a playwright in comedy and tragedy; but his language shows no warmth of affection and no personal esteem.

> Next these, learn'd *Johnson*, in this List I bring,
> Who had drunke deepe of the *Pierian* spring,
> Whose knowledge did him worthily prefer,
> And long was Lord here of the Theater,
> Who in opinion made our learn'st to sticke,
> Whether in Poems rightly dramatique,

[1] ll. 161–2.   [2] ll. 25–8.   [3] ll. 188–95. See p. 89 above.

Strong *Seneca* or *Plautus*, he or they,
Should beare the Buskin, or the Socke away.[1]

Jonson was perhaps the 'Jocund Throstle' of Drayton's
The Owle, printed in 1604, who,

> for his varying Note,
> Clad by the *Eagle* in a speckled Cote;
> Because his voyce had Judgement for the Palme,
> Suppos'd himselfe sole Patrone of our Calme.
> All say, for singing he had never Peere:
> But there were some that did his Vertue feare.[2]

Drayton, disappointed in his hope of royal recognition,
had some reason to be jealous of Jonson's brilliant
career at Court, his introduction to which Ben perhaps
owed to the powerful interest of Lady Bedford. In a
less exalted sphere we may suppose that the two poets
often met—at merry meetings held at the Mermaid or
the Tun, for instance; for Michael could be a boon
companion on occasion, and he would find there the
Beaumonts and many more of his friends. Moreover,
his Ode, 'The Sacrifice to Apollo,'[3] was surely written
for the famous Apollo room at the Devil Tavern in
Fleet Street; or, if that was not established till a date
later than 1619, in which year the Ode was printed in
Drayton's folio, then for an earlier club dedicated to the
same deity.[4] In many of its lines Drayton either echoes
or anticipates in austerer language Jonson's *Leges Con-*

[1] El[8] 129–136.
[2] O 1259–64. But the date is a little early to fit Jonson. See also
the note to this passage.
[3] Od[6].
[4] In *MLR* xxxiv (July 1939) Mr Percy Simpson assigns
Jonson's lines to the year 1624. If so, the debt is Jonson's to
Drayton, and Drayton's lines must refer to some other and an
earlier Apollo. On 19 June 1624 Chamberlain sent to Sir Dudley
Carleton a copy of the 'Convivial Laws of Ben Jonson, laid
down for a chamber in the inn of the Devil and St. Dunstan,
by Temple Bar.' (*Cal SPD* 1623–5, p. 278; Jonson, *Poems*,
pp. 304–5, 373.)

vivales, 'engraven in marble over the Chimney in the Apollo of the Old Devil Tavern.' We read of Drayton's drinking in company with Jonson at the Devil Tavern in a story told severally of Thomas Randolph and of Drummond of Hawthornden, which may have a slender basis of fact, although the variations and inconsistencies with known facts which the two versions present, make it more prudent to reject it altogether. As told by Winstanley,

> *Tho.* Randolph the wit of *Cambridge* coming to *London,* had a great mind to see Master *Johnson,* who was then drinking at the Devil-Tavern near *Temple-bar,* with Master *Drayton,* Master *Daniel,* and Master *Silvester,* three eminent poets of that age; he being loath to intrude into their company, and yet willing to be called, peeped in several times at the door, insomuch that Master *Johnson* at last took notice of him, and said, Come in *John Bo-peep.* Master *Randolph* was not so gallant in cloathes as they, however he sat down amongst them; at last when the reckoning came to be paid, which was five shillings, it was agreed, that he who made the best extempore verse should go Scot-free, the other four to pay it all: whereupon every one of them put out their verses; at last it come to Master *Randolph's* turn, whose lines were these:

> > *I John Bo-peep, to you four sheep,*
> > *With each one his good fleece:*
> > *If you are willing to pay your five shilling,*
> > *'Tis fifteen pence apiece.*[1]

In the story as told by Bishop Sage,[2] who acknowledges that it is 'by some ascribed to others,' Drummond of

[1] William Winstanley, *Poor Robins Jests* (1667), p. 78; Thorn Drury, *Poems of T. Randolph,* p. xiii. For other versions of the same story, which omit the names of Jonson's companion poets, see Winstanley, *Lives of the Poets,* 1687, pp. 143–4.

[2] Life of William Drummond in his *Works,* 1711, p. ix.

Hawthornden takes Randolph's place, William Alexander and Robert Carr are mentioned instead of Sylvester (who had died in 1618, when Randolph was a lad of thirteen) and Daniel. Drummond, however, never met Drayton, so in that version at least the story is false.[1] In weighing the likely significance of these and other stories of Drayton's drinking, we must keep in mind the character ascribed to him by Ingenioso in *The Return from Parnassus*:

> he wants one true note of a Poet of our times, and that is this, hee cannot swagger it well in a Taverne, nor dominere in a hothouse.

He who, as Fuller describes him, was 'very temperate in his life, slow of speech, and inoffensive in company,' is likely to have been ill at ease at the boisterous gatherings of Ben and his 'Sons.'

The common belief that Drayton and Shakespeare were friends also rests on doubtful assumption rather than any solid ground. Imaginative biographers have taken their friendship for granted and have even assumed a close intimacy between them. The notion is a tempting one, for the stories of the two men present remarkable points of contact both in the places in which they lived and in the circumstances of their lives. Drayton and Shakespeare were born in the same county of Warwick within a year or so of one another. They both came of yeoman stock. If William II of our conjectural tree was indeed Michael's father, then he like John Shakespeare was at one time oppressed by debt and like him had occasion to mortgage part of his estate. It is likely that both Drayton and Shakespeare were educated at the grammar-school in the town or neighbourhood in which each was living: it is unlikely that either went to a university. Both men found their way to London, where they wrote poetry and plays. Both enjoyed the patronage and friendship of men of a

[1] See p. 189 below.

high station. Both rose to the rank of gentleman—
Drayton indeed to that of esquire; and each became
entitled to a coat of arms. Drayton, too, had many links
with Stratford-upon-Avon. The Corporation records
show that Henry Goodere used to go there on public
business, and it is likely that sometimes Drayton would
accompany his master. Goodere had close and friendly
relations with Sir Thomas Lucy of Charlecote, where,
moreover, young Walter Aston, Lucy's grandson and
Drayton's future patron, was born and reared. Drayton
had his 'Muses quiet port' at Clifford manor, but a mile
outside Stratford. Lastly, there is the tragic event noted
by John Ward, vicar of Stratford, in his common-place
book about the year 1662:[1]

> Shakespear, Drayton and Ben Jonson had a merry
> meeting and itt seems drank too hard, for Shakespear
> died of a feaver there contracted.

That story may be true in part at least, for when John
Ward went to Stratford in 1662 some of Shakespeare's
contemporaries were still living there. His daughter
Judith died that very year. His nephew Thomas Hart
was living at the house in Henley Street where Shakespeare is believed to have been born.

We may be sure, at any rate, that Shakespeare and
Drayton were known to each other. Indeed, the career
of the tanner's son of Atherstone ran so nearly parallel
with that of the glover's son of Stratford as to show how
weak is the major premiss advanced by those who argue
that the son of John Shakespeare could never have
written the plays that bear his name. But there is no sure
evidence that the two were friends. Stratford, like
Hartshill and Polesworth, is in the Warwickshire
Woodland, but it lies in the south-west corner of the
county, while Drayton's country is in the extreme
north-east. Shakespeare was a mere stripling when

[1] Now in the Folger Library, Washington. There is a photo-
graphic copy at the Birthplace, Stratford-upon-Avon.

public business or private friendship first brought
Goodere to Stratford or its neighbourhood. Even if the
stories of Shakespeare's encounters with Sir Thomas
Lucy are not wholly apocryphal, they afford no reason
for believing that the two poets ever met at Charlecote.
On the occasion of Goodere's later visits to South-West
Warwickshire Shakespeare would generally have been
in London or on tour with his company. There is no
evidence that he was intimate with the Rainsfords. The
story of the drinking bout with its tragic end, first
recorded forty-six years after his death, may be nothing
more than the invention of local gossip. Drayton only
mentions Shakespeare once by name, and that with
rather faint praise:

> *Shakespeare* thou hadst as smooth a Comicke vaine,
> Fitting the socke, and in thy naturall braine,
> As strong conception, and as Cleere a rage,
> As any one that trafiqu'd with the stage.

How cold the appreciation compared with the glowing
terms in which Drayton writes of his particular friends,
Alexander of Menstrie, Drummond of Hawthornden,
the two Beaumonts and William Browne![1]
    On such scanty evidence as we have, then, we must
not assume that Drayton was in any sense the friend of
Shakespeare. Is there any ground for believing that he
was Shakespeare's rival? Can he be the so-called 'rival
poet' of Shakespeare's Sonnets? Sir Edmund Chambers
is not satisfied that either Southampton or Pembroke is
the youth to whom the greater part of the Sonnets were
addressed: 'I am not clear that the conditions might not
be satisfied by some young man of good birth and
breeding, but of less degree than an earl. . . The Rival
Poet, from whom we should desire light, only adds to
the obscurity. The 'precious phrase by all the Muses
filed' (Sonnet 85) . . . ought to mean Spenser, or failing

[1] El[8] 119–23; 163-81. For traces of Shakespeare's influence on
D's verse see the Introductions to EP, the Legends and Id.

him Daniel or perhaps Drayton.'[1] George Wyndham, while submitting that 'the one poet singled out cannot be confidently identified,' acknowledges that 'if compelled to select one of Shakespeare's contemporaries, for the Rival Poet, I should select Drayton.'[2] By judiciously selecting passages from Drayton and putting them side by side with some of Shakespeare's allusions to the Rival Poet, it might not be difficult to make out a case for Drayton's identification with him as plausible as that advanced for any of his contemporaries. With no wish to strain the evidence in support of such a case it is interesting to compare Shakespeare's 21st Sonnet with an early sonnet of Drayton's, which he presently discarded:

> So is it not with me as with that Muse,
> Stird by a painted beauty to his verse,
> Who heaven it selfe for ornament doth use,
> And every faire with his faire doth reherse,
> Making a coopelment of proud compare
> With Sunne and Moone, with earth and seas rich gems:
> With Aprills first borne flowers and all things rare,
> That heavens ayre in this hugh rondure hems. . . .

Compare with this Amour 25 in Drayton's *Ideas Mirrour*:

> The glorious sunne went blushing to his bed,
> When my soules sunne from her fayre Cabynet,
> > Her golden beames had now discovered,
> > Lightning the world, eclipsed by his set.

> Some muz'd to see the earth envy the ayre,
> > Which from her lyps exhald refined sweet,
> A world to see, yet how he joyd to heare
> > The dainty grass make musicke with her feete.

> But my most mervaile was when from the skyes,
> > So Comet-like each starre advaunc'd her lyght,

---

[1] *William Shakespeare*, I, p. 568.
[2] *Poems of Shakespeare*, pp. 252–259.

As though the heaven had now awak'd her eyes,
And summond Angels to thys blessed sight.
No clowde was seene, but christaline the ayre,
Laughing for joy upon my lovely fayre.

The Rival, or Rivals—for the 78th Sonnet says that

every alien pen hath got my use—

were learned men, as Drayton was,[1] and the chief of
them dedicated his written work to the youth to whom
Shakespeare is addressing his own Sonnets.[2] His spirit
was

by spirits taught to write.[3]

In Drayton's *Robert Duke of Normandy* the narrators are
the spirits of Fame and Fortune; in *Matilda the Faire* it
is that of Matilda herself; and it has been suggested that
Peirs Gaveston, who comes

From gloomy shaddowe of eternall night,
Where cole-black darknes keeps his lothsome cel, . . .
With black-fac'd furies from the graves attended,[4]

might well be

that affable familiar ghost
Which nightly gulls him with intellegence.[5]

Drayton might have found many a 'whining Sonnet'[6]
amongst those which were going the round of Shake-

---

[1] For D's reputation for learning cf. Weever's Epigramme 25,
p. 98 above.

[2] Sonnet 82.

[3] Sonnet 86. The device of a ghost or vision was a common
convention, used by many of D's contemporaries, especially by
Daniel in his *Complaint of Rosamond*. See the Introductions to
PG^a, Ma^a, Ro^a.

[4] See PG^a 1–2, 11, also 25–30, 1687–92, 1717–28.

[5] Sonnet 86. See letters in *TLS*, 12 Oct. 1933, by Francis
Needham, and by Sir Charles Strachey and myself, Nov. 9, 16.
The allusions to Hades, whence Gaveston's ghost returned to
visit Drayton, are only found in the first version of the Legend.

[6] Id, 'To the Reader. . . .'

speare's private friends; and he might reprobate as a libertine the player that even then was singing fantastically about a boy whose future marriage was a matter of intrigue amongst the matchmakers of Elizabeth's Court.

To read Drayton's lines to the Reader of his *Idea* in that sense would be, I think, to strain their meaning in a direction not in the poet's mind. Nevertheless, a study of Drayton's work, especially in the earlier versions, seems to offer *prima facie* some kind of a case, not indeed more, that he may be the Rival Poet of Shakespeare's Sonnets. To pursue the enquiry further would involve a detailed study of those Sonnets such as would lie far beyond the scope of the present book and bring us no nearer to a solution. Whoever the chief Rival may have been, he was friendly to a boy of good social standing, who was reluctant to marry, to whom, like Shakespeare, he wrote poems, and to whom he and perhaps other poets[1] dedicated books. The only youth whom we can find to fill these conditions among Drayton's young friends is Walter Aston, a 'young man of good breeding, of less degree than an earl,' born and nurtured in Warwickshire, the heir to great estates, who, moreover, while yet a minor, broke off the match which had been arranged for him in favour of a bride of his own choosing.

Quite apart from any notion that he may have been the 'lovely boy' whose unwillingness to marry is the motive of so many of Shakespeare's Sonnets, Aston was so closely linked with Drayton's life and work that he is entitled to extended notice here.

[1] Cf. Shakespeare's Sonnet 82.

L

aggrieved; for Degge gives a long list of Aston's manors and estates in Staffordshire, Derbyshire, Warwickshire and Leicestershire: 'These lands are now above 10,000^l a yeare, as I can make it appeare.' Long before Degge wrote, however, a great part were sold to meet the debts which Aston incurred while serving as ambassador in Spain. Degge continues:

> ffor his person it was very comely his [*erasure*] stature not altogether soe tall as yor Lord'p but went very upright and straite: his skin very pure, all but his face, which was of a browne rudy complexion, with a little wen up^n one cheeke his hayre a yellow red his beard a little sadde he had something a high nose & a rough voyce but would have spoken very well noe drinker noe swearer of an affable courteous behaviour free from all desease but a stone of wch I thinke he was once cut subject to noe passions a very temperate & virtuous worthy good man for ought that I ever saw or knew to the contrary.

If Walter Aston fell in love with Gertrude Sadleir at the time of his knighthood, as Degge tells us, and was married 'before he was of age,' his marriage must have taken place between 25 July 1603 and 9 July 1604; for on that date he had livery of his lands on reaching the age of twenty-one.

In 1602 Drayton wrote the first of a long series of dedications to his future patron in the edition of *Englands Heroicall Epistles* printed in that year. Hitherto the Epistles of Edward the Black Prince and Alice Countess of Salisbury had had no dedication. In the new edition, as we have seen,[1] they were inscribed, in words which imply friendship already well established:

To my worthy and honoured
friend, Maister *Walter Aston*.
Sir, though without suspition of flatterie I might in

---

[1] See p. 86, where the dedication is printed.

more ample and freer tearmes, intymate my affection unto you, yet having so sensible a tast 'of your generous and noble disposition, which without this habit of ceremony can estimate my love: I will rather affect brevitie, . . .

It is possible that Drayton was tutor to the youth, just as Samuel Daniel had been tutor to William Herbert, and that thus was laid the foundation of that great friendship which lasted into the third decade of the new century.

Early in 1603 Drayton dedicated to Walter his *Barrons Wars*, which in 1596 under its old title of *Mortimeriados* he had inscribed to the Countess of Bedford:

To the worthy and his most honoured friend Ma.

Walter Aston.

I will not strive m'invention to inforce,
With needless words your eyes to entertaine,
T'observe the formall ordinarie course
That every one so vulgarly doth faine
    Our interchanged and deliberate choice,
Is with more firme and true election sorted,
Then stands in censure of the common voyce,
That with light humor fondly is transported.
    Nor take I pattern of anothers praise,
Then what my pen may constantly avow,
Nor walke more publique, nor obscurer waies
Then vertue bids, and judgement will alow.
So shall my love, and best endevours serve you
And still shall studie, still so to deserve you.[1]

At the coronation of James I Walter Aston with

[1] If Aston should be the youth of Shakespeare's Sonnets, this dedication, which was replaced in 1619 by a dedication in prose, might be read as alluding to 'another's praise' of Walter which Drayton reprobated as offensive both to 'vertue' and to good 'judgment.' In 1619 it is printed before the Legends.

some sixty more was made a Knight of the Bath. Drayton was one of the esquires whose attendance on a new knight was required by ancient ceremonial. It was doubtless for their use that Walter borrowed the horses 'from Mr Sadler at Stanmore' with such a happy sequel. Henceforth our poet figures as Michael Drayton, Esquire, on all his title-pages. As esquire he was entitled to bear arms; and we may associate with the occasion the arms shown on his monument at Westminster Abbey. At the College of Arms there is no record of any grant; but they are shown in trick beside Shakespeare's in an early seventeenth-century armorial now in the Harley collection at the British Museum.[1] In the same book are many coats of arms granted by Sir William Segar, who was Garter King-of-Arms at James's coronation, and others, like Shakespeare's, by Sir William Dethick, who supplanted Segar as Garter that same year. Save for the difference of the field, the arms— *Azure guttée d'eau a Pegasus salient argent*—are those of the Inner Temple—*Azure a Pegasus salient argent*; and we may believe that apart from its poetical fitness Drayton chose the coat for the sake of its association with that Inn to which he was attached by so many ties throughout his life and even at his death.[2] Doubtless the crest also, *On a sun in glory or, a cap of Mercury vert winged argent*—was chosen for its poetical significance. Drayton's friend, William Camden, Clarenceux, may have guided him in the choice of his device and in its heraldic treatment.

In the year 1604 Drayton dedicated *The Owle* 'To The Worthy *And my most esteemed Patron*, Sir Walter Aston Knight of the Honourable Order of the Bath.'[3] Later on in the same year he dedicated *Moses in a Map of His Miracles*

---

[1] BM Harl. MS. 6140.
[2] See page 219 below.
[3] The sonnet is printed Vol. II, p. 478.

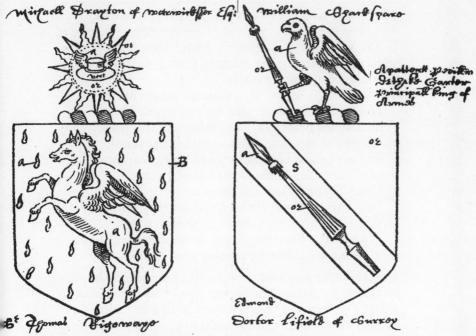

DRAYTON'S AND SHAKESPEARE'S ARMS IN TRICK SIDE BY SIDE
From a 17th-cent. Armorial BM, MS. Harl. 6140 f. 46v.

To my esteemed Patron Sir Walter Aston, Knight of the
Honourable Order of the Bathe.

Although our sundry (yet our sacred) flames,
Worke divers and as contrarie effects:
Yet then your owne, we seeke not other names,
Nor stranger arches our free Muse erects.
Though limmitlesse be (naturally) our love,
We can her powers officiouslie confine:
Who can instruct her orderly to move,
And keepe the compasse wisely we assigne.
To take our faire leave (till that ampler times
Some glorious object strongly may beget)
We make you tender of these hallowed rimes
The vertuous payment of a worthier debt.
　　Till to our names that monument we reare,
　　That steele and marble unto dust shall weare.

In the same book Drayton's friend, Beale Sapperton, addressing Aston in a prefatory poem, writes of Walter's patronage of the poet:

> your noblesse cheeres
> His mounting *Muse*: and with so worthy hand
> Applaudes her flight, as nothing she will leave
> Above the top, whereon she makes her stand,
> So high bright Honour learned Spirits can heave.
> Such lustre lends the Poets pollisht verse
> Unto Nobility, as after-times
> Shall thinke, there Patrons vertues they rehearse,
> When vertuous men they Caracter in rimes.
>   You raise his thoughts, with full desire of fame:
>   Amongst *Heroes* he enroles your name.[1]

Faithful to his promise 'to seek no other name,' Drayton inscribed to Aston his *Poemes Lyrick and Pastorall* in 1606, *The Legend of Great Cromwell* in 1607 and 1609, and his Pastorals in the folio of 1619, besides repeating some of his earlier dedications in the reprints of his collected poems. The monument that was to outwear steel and marble was his *Poly-Olbion*. That 'herculean' task, on which Drayton had been engaged some fifteen years, was dedicated in 1612 to Henry Prince of Wales; but in his letter 'To the Generall Reader' Drayton gratefully acknowledges

> the continuall bounty of my truly Noble friend Sir *Walter Aston*; which hath given me the best of those howres whose leasure hath effected this which I now publish.

And in the Twelfth Song with the emphasis of italic type he prays for heaven's blessing on the family of his patron who had lately been raised to the newly created Order of Baronets:

> ... *Trent* by *Tixall* grac't, *the* Astons *ancient seat*;
> *Which oft the Muse hath found her safe and sweet retreat.*

[1] See MBM var.

The noble Owners now of which beloved place,
Good fortunes them and theirs with honor'd titles grace:
May heaven still blesse that House, till happy Floods you see
Your selves more grac'd by it, then it by you can bee.[1]

In 1619 Drayton dedicated to Sir Walter his care-fully printed folio, containing 'These my few Poemes, the works of that Mayden Reigne, in the Spring of our Acquaintance,' assuring him that 'As it pleased you then to Patronize, as I singly set them forth: so now collected into this small Volume: I make the best Present, that my poore Abilitie is able to render you.'[2]

At least one of Drayton's contemporaries enjoyed a measure of Aston's patronage. Professor Elton tells us that 'if we forget Shakespeare, there is no such store of excellent lyric in any other of the playwrights, or in any two of them taken together, as in John Fletcher's *The Faithfull Shepheardesse.*' That play was, however, ill received at its performance about the year 1609, as Fletcher acknowledges in lines addressed

To that noble and true lover of learning,
Sir WALTER ASTON knight
of the Bath.

SIR I must aske your patience, and be trew.
This play was never liked, unlesse by few
That brought their judgements with um, for of late
First the infection, then the common prate
Of common people, have such customes got
Either to silence plaies, or like them not.
Under the last of which this interlude,
Had falne for ever prest downe by the rude
That like a torrent which the moist south feedes,
Drowne's both before him the ripe corne and
    weedes:
Had not the saving sence of better men
Redeem'd it from corruption: (deere Sir then)

[1] PO[12] 561–8.   [2] Vol. II, p. 2.

Among the better soules, be you the best
In whome, as in a Center I take rest,
And propper being: from whose equall eye
And judgement, nothing growes but puritie:
(Nor do I flatter) for by all those dead,
Great in the Muses, by *Apolloes* head,
He that ads any thing to you; tis done
Like his that lights a candle to the sunne:
Then be as you were ever, your selfe still
Moved by your judgement, not by love, or wiii
And when I sing againe as who can tell
My next devotion to that holy well,
Your goodnesse to the muses shall be all,
Able to make a worke Heroycall.

Given to your service
JOHN FLETCHER.[1]

Aston's career as a courtier and a diplomat belongs rather to the political history of his time than to a study of its literature. He was appointed Groom of the Chamber to King James and, as we have seen, became the companion of the young Prince of Wales. In 1613 he was made a Gentleman of the Privy Chamber—'a testimony of your masters noble remembrance of you,' wrote his friend, the Earl of Pembroke, telling him of the King's decision to appoint him to the vacant place.[2] In 1619 King James wrote to tell him of his intention to send him as ambassador to Spain:

Whereas wee are informed both of y^r integritie, and abilitie, to do us service, by the experience we have had in you in your long attendance on our person as one of the gentlemen in ordinarie of our privie chamber, wee have now thought it fitt to imploye you in our great and more waighty affaires.[3]

[1] *The Faithfull Shepheardesse* (1609–10?). (BM. C. 34, c 33. These lines are not in the Bodleian copy.)
[2] *Tixall Letters*, i, p. 3; BM Add. 36542.
[3] *Tixall Letters*, i, pp. 8–10; BM Add. 36542.

He sailed for Spain early in 1620;[1] and although the 'waighty affaires' with which he was charged, included the whole business of the Spanish match, he won and kept the lasting affection of the Spanish people. When Lady Aston followed him to Madrid in the autumn, Drayton addressed his Elegy to her to wish her god-speed.[2] Some two years later he wrote his Elegy to Aston's chaplain, William Jeffreys,[3] with whom he had promised to exchange letters.

There is no evidence that Drayton resumed his intimacy with Aston and his family when the ambassador was recalled after the death of James in 1625. In that year Aston became member of Parliament for Bridgenorth. He was raised to the peerage of Scotland as Lord Aston Baron of Forfar by Charles in 1627. In 1629 he was made Keeper of the Mulberry Garden, whch had been planted by King James on the site now in part occupied by Buckingham Palace. He made his residence there, receiving a small salary, which must have been poor compensation for the very heavy outlay incurred by him while ambassador and for the official salary which was left unpaid. In 1635, much against his will, for he was broken in health and spirit, he was sent a second time as ambassador to Spain, and was there received with great enthusiasm. During this second embassy he embraced the Catholic religion, which his wife and family had joined while in Spain during his former embassy.[4] He was recalled at his own request in 1638. On 9 December in that year he alludes to his own domestic misfortunes and to his ill-health in a touching letter addressed to Catherine Thimelby on the occasion of her marriage with his son Herbert:

> I cannot promise you success, for I am not master of it; but you may rest confident, my care and utmost endevor shall not be wanting. You come into a family, although united in trew affection one with

[1] SPD Jas. I, 18 Jan. 1619–20.   [2] El⁷.   [3] El¹¹.
[4] Or perhaps soon after their return to England.

THE GATE-HOUSE, TIXALL

another, yet devided in the condition of our fortune;
my wife in one place, my son Aston in another, and
I in a third; and in the worst a poore sutor at court,
with a painfull infirmitie for my companion.[1]

In 1639 he died of the stone. He lies with his fathers in
Stafford Church. Of his great mansion at Tixall only
the gaunt ruin of the Gate-house is still standing.[2]

Walter Aston was himself a writer of verse. In a
letter from his daughter Constantia, wife of Walter
Fowler, Esq., of St Thomas's Priory, Stafford, to her
brother Herbert in Spain, she acknowledges the
receipt from him of 'most admirable verses of my lord's
translating'; and the verses themselves may be seen in
Constantia's common-place book, which is now kept at
the Henry Huntington Library in California:[3]

[1] BM. Addit. 36542; *Tixall Letters*, I, p. 148.
[2] The Gate-house was built about 1580. After her flight from
Chartley in August 1586 Mary Queen of Scots was retaken at
Tixall and was kept in the Gate-house till the end of that month.
[3] HM 904. Walter Aston's Sonnet is printed here by kind permission of the Librarian of the H. E. Huntington Library.

Somtimes by Aprill arrogantly deckt
Th'enameld mountaine shewes her curled head
And somtimes by Novembers rigors check'd
Appeares as naked desolate and dead
Her desert bosome July sets on fire
Which Januaries frosts and snowes doe fill
But though she vary in her state and tire
In her true nature she is mountaine still
Even so my bosome by thy changes tride
still in one state of heavenly Love remaines
though sometimes sadd and somtimes satisfied
For what imports thy favours or disdaines
Love beinge the true essence of my brest
And but exteriur accidents the rest.

Aston seems to have had some reputation as a poet outside his family circle; for there survive two manuscript copies of Donne's *Letter to the Countesse of Huntingdon*, both of which ascribe that poem to 'Sir Walter Ashton.'[1] He was father and father-in-law of a numerous family of poets and readers of poetry. Constantia Fowler's commonplace book has many poems by her brother Herbert Aston. About 1810 Arthur Clifford, to whose elder brother Tixall had passed through his mother, daughter and co-heir of the 5th Lord Aston, found there in an old trunk a mass of poetry written or collected in the course of the seventeenth century by three generations of the Aston family. With it was a quarto manuscript book containing poems written by Aston's daughter Gertrude, who in 1655 after the death of her husband, Henry Thimelby, became a nun at Louvain. From her cloister she wrote 'by command' an elegy on the death of her father, in which we may read the following tribute to his disposition:

So sweet a winning way he had on all
None knew but lov'd him, no desert so small
But he would grace, and still did something say,
That none could goe unsatisfied away.[2]

[1] Grierson, *Poems of John Donne*, 1933, pp. 194–8.
[2] Printed by A. Clifford in *Tixall Poetry*, 1813, p. 93.

CHAPTER XII

POLY-OLBION

DRAYTON meant *Poly-Olbion* to be the great achievement of his career. Professor Hebel has given an account of its writing and publication in his Introduction to the first volume of his edition. But it filled so large a part of Drayton's life in the study and research which it cost him for its preparation and in the sheer labour of writing its 15,000 lines;—it was the object of such high hopes when he set about his task and the cause of such bitter and grievous disappointment when the fruit of some fifteen years labour was received with coldness and neglect;—lastly, it reveals so much of his disposition and tastes and throws so many sidelights on his career, that it calls for more extended notice here.

Hebel notes on the authority of Meres how as early as 1598 Drayton's ambitious plan was already known to his friends.[1] From words used by Drayton in some of the dedications of *Englands Heroicall Epistles* he seems to be tendering them as a kind of payment on account until such time as the much greater work which he already had in mind, and even in hand, might enable him 'in some more larger measure' to show his love and affection for his patrons and friends.[2]

Five years later, as we have seen, Chettle alludes to the great poem on which Drayton was still engaged, bidding him 'forget not' Elizabeth in *Poly-Olbion*. But nine years more were to pass before its First Part came from the printer. Since the last of the *Heroicall Epistles* was finished in 1599, Drayton had produced no major work, although *The Owle*, *Moses* and *Cromwell* and the re-writing of *Mortimeriados* as *The Barrons Wars*, of the

[1] See p. 97.
[2] Dedication to Henry Goodere, p. 80. Cf. also those to Bedford, Frances Goodere and Walter Aston, pp. 74-5, 80, 86, 151.

three *Legends* and of *Englands Heroicall Epistles*, all taken together, make no inconsiderable output. It is reasonable to suppose that he was working upon *Poly-Olbion* during all those years, interrupted first by Henslowe's calls upon him for plays, later by his ill-starred dramatic adventure with the Children of the King's Revels, and most of all by periods of depression, discouragement and disappointment, such as left him for a while without the heart to pursue his vast scheme.[1]

The First Part of *Poly-Olbion* was entered in the Stationers' Register 7 February 1612. Selden dates his Introduction to his Illustrations from the Inner Temple, the 9th day of May in that year. He there excuses himself for any faults by reason of the 'Brevity of *Time* (which was but little more then since the Poem first went to the Presse)' allowed him for compiling his Illustrations; but it is impossible to estimate how long a man of Selden's genius and learning, daily interrupted by 'my other most different *Studies*' and by his legal engagements, would have taken to write them.[2] A remark of his in the Illustrations to Song IV seems to show that he was working on them while the text which he was to 'illustrate' was already at press.[3] He apologises to his 'ingenuous Readers' for his '*faults escaped*': 'Compelled *Absence*, endevor'd *Dispatch*, and want of *Revises* soone bred them.' For all that, these 'Illustrations' ('undertaken at request of my kinde Friend the Author)' are a monument of Selden's sound and conscientious scholarship. After acknowledging his indebtedness to 'that most learned Nourice of Antiquitie ... my instructing friend Mr *Camden Clarenceulx*,' and to Giraldus Cambrensis, he protests withall that he goes to the sources:

May *Mercury* and all the Muses deadly hate mee,

[1] PO, 'To the General Reader,' Vol. IV, p. vi*. See above, pp. 127–8.
[2] Vol. IV, p. xii*.   [3] PO⁹ 445s, and note thereon.

when, in permitting occasion, I professe not by whom I learne! Let them vent judgement on mee which understand: I justifie all, by the selfe Authors cited, crediting no *Transcribers*, but when of Necessitie I must. My thirst compeld mee alwayes seeke the *Fountaines*, and, by that, if meanes grant it, judge the *Rivers* nature.[1]

The book was printed before 6 November 1612, for the Prince of Wales, to whom Drayton dedicated it, died on that day. We may associate with *Poly-Olbion* the grant recorded among the 'anuyties and Pencons' noted by Sir David Murray in the household expenses of the Prince for 1612. After the Prince's death the heads of the Household recommended to the Chancellor of the Exchequer persons

whoe by the comaundement of the late prince without anie graunte in wrytinge were allowed yerely somes by way of Anuyties or Pencons out of the privie purse of the said late prince: viz. Joshua Silvester a poett xx^{li} Mr. Drayton a poett x^{li}. . .[2]

We do not know when the pension began or when it ceased to be paid. But in 1622 Drayton, dedicating the Second Part of *Poly-Olbion* to Prince Charles, recalls his deceased brother's 'princely Bountie, and usage of mee, [which] gave me much encouragement to goe on with this second Part, or Continuance therof; which now as his Successor, I owe to your Highnesse.' Wither's lines on this Second Part,

in Him, *survives*
His brother HENRIE'S *Virtues: and hee lives*
To be that Comfort to thy MUSE, *which* Hee
Had nobly (e're his death) begun to be,

suggest that Charles continued his brother's bounty.[3]

[1] PO xii*, xiii*.
[2] P. Cunningham, *Accounts of Revels*, pp. xvii, xviii.
[3] Vol. IV, p. 395.

The Songs of the Second Part seem to have been finished before November 1618, when Drayton sought the good graces of his new-found friend, William Drummond, as an intermediary with Andro Hart, the Edinburgh stationer and printer, for its publication.[1] Hart had published William Alexander's *Doomes-day* and Drummond's *Poems* and *Forth Feasting*. The First Part of *Poly-Olbion* had been printed by Humphrey Lownes for his brother, Mathew Lownes, John Browne, John Helme, and John Busbie, none of whose names are found in the imprint to the Second Part. Drayton's quarrel with them is indicated in his letter to Drummond of 14 April 1619: '[The Second Part] lies by me; for the booksellers and I are in terms.[2] They are a company of base knaves, whom I both scorne and kick at.'[3] It finds expression later in the petulant address, 'To any that will read it,' which is the Preface to that Part:[4]

> Nay some of the Stationers, that had the Selling of the first part of this Poeme, because it went not so fast away in the Sale, as some of their beastly and abominable Trash, ... have either despightfully left out, at or least carelessely neglected the Epistles to the Readers,[5] and so have cousoned the Buyers with unperfected Bookes; which these that have undertaken the second Part, have beene forced to amend in the first, for the small number that are yet remaining in their hands.

Drayton's negotiations with Hart came to nothing. Perhaps they were brought to an end by Hart's death in December 1621. In the Stationers' Register the Second Part is entered to John Marriott, John Grisman[d], and Thomas Dewe on 6 March 1621–2; and it was printed

---

[1] See below, pp. 181, 184.   [2] i.e. negotiating.
[3] See below, p. 184.   [4] IV, p. 391.
[5] They are wanting from copies at Jesus College, Oxford, and St John's College, Cambridge.

M

for them by Augustine Mathewes in the course of that year. These booksellers and their printer were among the younger men in the trade. Marriott seems to have begun business in 1616. Grismand took up his freedom in the Stationers' Company in that year, Dewe in 1621. Mathewes had taken up his freedom in 1615, but the first book entered to his name was assigned to him in 1619. In the type and lay-out of the pages the Second Part follows the First closely, but Mathewes substituted ornaments from his own stock in place of those used by Lownes. The most notable difference is the absence of Selden's learned Illustrations.

From the first Drayton proposed to continue *Poly-Olbion* so as to embrace the whole island,[1] and he still clung to that plan when the Second Part was published. From the letter, printed below, which Drummond wrote to William Alexander on the occasion of Drayton's death, it is clear that he supposed him to have written 'fragments' of the Scottish portion; but, if so, none have survived.[2]

In Selden's Preface[3] he tells us how his author in 'Passages of *first Inhabitants, Name, State* and *Monarchique succession* in this Isle,' follows Geoffrey of Monmouth, Higden's *Polychronicon*, Matthew of Westminster, 'and such more.' It is well-known also how Drayton found in Camden's *Britannia* a great part of the vast store of information gathered in the thirty Songs of the poem. He was acquainted with that book as early as 1597, for he drew from it at least five times in writing *Englands Heroicall Epistles*, and he refers to it twice in his Annotations thereon.[4] For that he may have used the edition of 1594; but it was the much enlarged edition of 1607, printed in folio and illustrated with maps of all the counties, rendered from Saxton's large Atlas of 1579, that both Drayton and Selden used for

---

[1] Dedications to Prince Henry and Prince Charles.
[2] Pp. 161, 188–9.   [3] Vol. IV, p. viii*.
[4] See Vol. V, p. 128; also Vol. II, pp. 259, 285.

their work on *Poly-Olbion*. In some of the Songs, however, Drayton has details first found in the translation
of *Britannia* which Philemon Holland began about the
year 1606 and finished in 1610.[1]

That Drayton studied local history at the sources
appears from a passage in Selden's Illustrations to *Poly-
Olbion XVI*. Selden there quotes the authority of 'a very
ancient deed of lands' in Warwickshire 'upon the
Authors credit reporting it to me.'[2] Holland was Drayton's countryman, and it is pleasant to think that all
four friends—the poet, the jurist, the antiquary and his
translator—may have been in correspondence or even
in conference about the book while the translation was
in progress. Holland complained later that 'I being
farre absent from the Presse . . . there passed many
grosse and absurd mistakings in my translation.'[3] He
rendered Camden's occasional Latin verse into the six-
foot metre of *Poly-Olbion*; but Holland's alexandrines
are much inferior to those in Drayton's poem.[4]

Although so much of the detail of *Poly-Olbion* was
taken out of *Britannia*, we are likely to exaggerate
Drayton's debt to that book if we do not take account of
his wide reading at early sources both of legend and
history. From Geoffrey of Monmouth he learned the
mythical history of Britain, to which he clung with such
affectionate tenacity, leaving his friend Selden to
examine and refute much of it by the dry light of
scholarship. From Geoffrey, too, and the *Morte*

---

[1] See 'Philemon Holland the Translatour to the Reader,' appended to the second edition of the translation, 1637.

[2] Vol. IV, p. 326.   [3] *BH* 1637, *l.c.*

[4] Drayton had used the twelve-syllable metre of *Poly-Olbion* for
parts of *The Harmonie of the Church*. He used it also for the speeches
in which Silvius the Woodman, Halcius the Fisherman and
Melanthus the Poet praise their several callings in the Sixth
Nimphall of *The Muses Elizium*. The last are so much of a piece
with the Hermit of Arden's speech in Song XIII that we may
suspect that they too were originally drafted as portions of some
Song in *Poly-Olbion*.

D'Arthur and the other Arthurian romances he drew the stories of King Arthur and Merlin. Chiefly from Froissart and Holinshed he took the names of the British and English Kings and the deeds of great soldiers, and from Hakluyt those of the sea-captains and voyagers. Giraldus Cambrensis, Geoffrey of Monmouth and Humphrey Llwyd gave him details of Welsh history, which is the subject of nearly seven of the thirty Songs. His reading of other English chroniclers, from whom he drew freely when writing the *Legends*, *Mortimeriados* and the *Heroicall Epistles*,[1] furnished material for much of *Poly-Olbion* also. Ben Jonson told Drummond that in his great poem Drayton 'promised to writte the deeds of all the Worthies';[2] but Ben's complaint that he had failed in that promise was not quite just, for the poem relates some of the deeds and not the names only of captains, voyagers and kings, and also of British and English saints. He found most of what he writes about the saints in *The English Martyrologe*, written by John Wilson, a Catholic priest, who printed it himself at St Omers in 1608. He seems to have had access also to the lives of British saints written by Nicholas Roscarrock (1548?—1634?), whose manuscript is now in the Cambridge University Library.[3] Roscarrock was the friend of Camden and of William Browne, and is likely to have been a friend of Drayton's also.[4]

For every Song Drayton had at hand the famous series of maps of Great Britain engraved by Christopher Saxton between 1574 and 1579. In Saxton especially he was able to find the names and trace the courses of the rivers which, personified by our poet and given an account of their amours, intrigues and quarrels, are among the more tedious features of *Poly-Olbion*. Saxton also was the principal source for the topographi-

[1] See the Introductions and Notes in Vol. v.
[2] Conversations with Drummond, p. 137 above. Only the first eighteen Songs had as yet been printed.
[3] MS. Camb. Addit. 3041.   [4] See notes to PO[24].

cal detail of the maps, which serve for an entertaining and spirited gloss to the several Songs. But it was perhaps from William Harrison, whose *Historicall Description of Britaine* with its Second Book, *The Description of England*, are printed at the beginning of both editions of Holinshed's *Chronicle*, that together with much particular detail he learned how important are the rivers as features in the topography of the island. No less than seven of Harrison's chapters are devoted to the rivers of Britain, great or small, which he takes in turn in the circuit of the island, tracing their several courses with a fulness not found even in *Poly-Olbion*. The astounding thing is that Harrison's account of them, though supplemented from Leland and from other sources, is largely written from notes made by himself in his travels in and about the island. Leland, Lambarde, Camden, Harrison, Saxton, Norden and Speed all show with what diligence those students of topography pursued their inquiries on the spot even in the remotest parts of Britain. A careful study of *Poly-Olbion* brings with it the conviction that for all the use Drayton made of the work of those and other writers and of the sources from which they drew, he too travelled widely in England and Wales and embodied in his poem much that he had seen and learned in the course of his journeyings and sojournings in different parts of the island.[1]

Even if we traced every name and every event which Drayton borrowed from printed books and manuscripts back to the passage from which it was taken, we should find that his chief source was his love for his native England alike in her soil, her history and her people. Although he took so much from the letter of the books, the spirit which selected and marshalled the material

---

[1] In his address 'To the Reader' of BW in 1603 D excuses himself for 'insufficient handling' of the argument of *Mortimeriados*, printed in 1596, as being due to his 'want of leasure and study competent, either of which travaile hardly affords.' By 'travaile,' however, he may mean 'labours.'

was his own. It is Drayton himself, and not Camden or Selden, who leads us

> forth into the *Tempe* and Feelds of the Muses, where through most delightfull Groves the Angellique harmony of Birds shall steale thee to the top of an easie hill, where in artificiall caves, cut out of the most naturall Rock, thou shalt see the ancient people of this Ile delivered thee in their lively images: from whose height thou mai'st behold both the old and later times, as in thy prospect, lying farre under thee; then convaying thee downe by a soule-pleasing Descent through delicate embrodered Meadowes, often veined with gentle gliding Brookes; in which thou maist fully view the dainty Nymphes in their simple naked bewties, bathing them in Crystalline streames; which shall lead thee, to most plesant Downes, where harmlesse Shepheards are, some exercising their pipes, some singing roundelaies, to their gazing flocks.[1]

If we go to the pains of collating *Poly-Olbion* passage by passage with the Latin text of *Britannia* or with Holland's translation, we shall note not only what Drayton took from Camden but also what he passed by as alien to his poetical purpose. The genealogies and family histories and the account of the manors and castles which fill so many passages in Camden have no place in *Poly-Olbion*. If Drayton ever pictured the life he would have led had he been free to choose, his fancy would have turned, perhaps, to that of his Hermit of Arden:

> a sweete retyred life,
> From villages repleate with ragg'd and sweating Clownes,
> And from the lothsome ayres of smoky cittied Townes.[2]

When towns are mentioned in the poem, it is generally as features of the rivers on which they stand, or sometimes for the part they played in some episode of

[1] Vol. IV, p. v*. [2] PO[13] 164-6.

legend or history. The towns and villages which are strewn so thickly on Saxton's maps are seldom shown in the fanciful plates, 'lively delineating . . . every Mountaine, Forrest, River, and Valley; expressing in their sundry postures, their loves, delights, and naturall situations,' which guide the pilgrim-reader through *Poly-Olbion*. But if the traveller through England or Wales will take Hebel's hint and make the Songs his companion, whatever river he may cross, and however small, the odds are that Drayton has it in the poem and shows it on the map.

The reader who studies the several Songs on the ground about which they were written will find evidence again and again that Drayton is describing country that he knew at first hand from his own lively observation. Warwickshire,

My native Country then, which so brave spirits hast bred,[1]

was doubtless known to him best of all. If he first learned to love rivers during his boyhood on the banks of the Anker, it is likely that his association with the ancient forest of Arden inspired him with the love of forests and woodlands which finds expression again and again in his poetry. In *Poly-Olbion* he repeatedly makes the forests lament the havoc they have suffered, chiefly from the felling of their trees to furnish fuel for the smelting furnaces. From other Songs we may note with certainty how well he knew and how much he loved Cotswold; Dovedale and the Peak of Derbyshire; Charnwood and Sherwood Forests; the Vale of Clwyd; the University towns of Oxford and Cambridge; the cities of Winchester and especially London. We find him at Nottingham about 1580 and again in 1613.[2] From his descriptions we may suspect also that whether on horseback or on foot he sometimes went into counties so far remote from one another as Kent and Cornwall, Westmorland and Dorset. Above all we know that dur-

[1] PO¹³ 8.   [2] See pp. 33, 206.

ing the years in which he was writing the poem he often sought retirement both at 'deere *Cliffords* seat' in Gloucestershire,[1] and at Tixall, the 'Astons *ancient seat*'[2] in Staffordshire.

For all his love of nature in solitude Drayton shows also his strong interest in country life and country pursuits. He writes about agriculture and grazing and especially sheep-farming (xiv, 235–278). He describes the sports of hawking in Norfolk (xx, 211–246); fishing, fowling, shooting and stilt walking in the Fens (xxv, 139–148); hunting in Arden (xiii, 93–161) and coursing at Kelmarsh (xxiii, 327–356); he writes of wrestling and hurling in Cornwall (i, 238–251) and of the Cotswold shepherds' game of nine-holes-on-the-heath (xiv, 21–24); of country dances and of merry-making in Lincolnshire and of the Lancashire wakes (xxv, 261–264; xxvii, 65–69, 248–254); of singing and music and musical instruments (iv, 349–368). He names the flowers and pot-herbs of the garden and describes the fruits of the Kentish orchards and their culture (xv, 174–204; xviii, 665–697). He shows a countryman's knowledge of the names and virtues of herbs and simples besides the detailed information about them which he has gathered out of Dodoens and Gerard (xiii, 199–234). On the other hand, he has little interest in the lives and pursuits of the rich, save that he deplores the draining of the country's wealth ever since

> idle Gentry up in such abundance sprong,
> Now pestring all this Ile . . . ;

especially their 'foolish foraine things,' 'the costly Coach, and silken Stock,'

> that . . . *Indian* weed . . .
> Where in such mighty summes we prodigally waste.[3]

---

[1] PO[14] 162.   [2] PO[12] 561.   [3] PO[16] 342–52.

He pours scorn upon sycophancy and social shams.[1] As
in so much more of his verse, he aims his bitter invective

at you,
(Of what degree soe'r) ye wretched worldly crue,
In all your brainlesse talke, that still direct your drifts
Against the Muses sonnes, and their most sacred gifts,
That hate a Poets name.[2]

Drayton shows his affection for 'my loved Wales' by
devoting the greater part of seven Songs to the antiquities and natural beauties of the principality. Moreover, he has a special dedication 'To my Friends, the
Cambro-Britans,' in which he confesses how 'the free
and gentle companie of that true lover of his Country
(as of all ancient and noble things) M. John Williams,
his Majesties Gold-smith, my deare and worthy friend,
hath made me the more seek into the antiquities of your
Country.'[3] His concern with Welsh legend and history,
however, is significant of more than any personal friendship or interest. The Welsh were the descendants of the
ancient inhabitants of the island; and when a prince of
Welsh descent assumed the crown of England as
Henry VII, the early history of Britain and the legends
with which it was confusedly mingled became of
political importance; for the Tudors traced their ancestry in a direct line back to King Arthur, and on it rested
their claim to the throne. Hence the large place which
the stories of Brute and King Arthur came to fill in
Tudor literature. The vision of the angel, from whom
Cadwallader, the last of the British kings, learned that
his line would not be restored until after successive
periods of dominion by the Saxons and Normans, was

[1] PO[13] 184–193.   [2] PO[21] 131–5.
[3] See above, p. 95. Cf. D's inscription of his Ballad of Agincourt 'To my frinds the Camber-britans and theyr harp' in Poemes
lyrick and Pastorall (1606). He seems to have thought the name
'Welsh' with its suggestion of 'strangers' derogatory to the descendants of the ancient inhabitants of Britain. His interest in
Welsh history is shown as early as 1597 in EHE[6b].

believed to have its fulfilment in the accession of the
first Tudor king. Already in the twelfth century
Geoffrey of Monmouth's *Historia Britonum*, which
sought to show that the Britons shared a common
ancestry with the Roman and Norman conquerors of
the island, had helped to unite the races. And now in
James Stuart, descended from Llewellyn, prince of
Wales, through Fleanch, the escaped son of the murdered Banqhuo, was 'commixt' the 'Kingly bloud' of
Tudor and Plantagenet.[1] Under the Tudors and especially under the last of the line the myths to which
Geoffrey gave currency, and which fill so many dreary
pages in Holinshed, were favourite matter both for
poetry and pageant. Popular interest in the accepted
story had been heightened by the fierce controversy
aroused by the hardihood of Polydore Vergil in denying
any historical truth to the legends.[2] Leland stoutly
maintained their genuineness; and the fight which
lasted through the sixteenth century endures in the
Welsh passages of *Poly-Olbion*. Drayton's muse argues
fiercely for their acceptance.[3] Camden, though he will
impeach no man's credit—'no, not Geoffrey of Monmouth, whose history (which I would gladly support) is
held suspected among the judicious,'—treats the
legends lightly and compares them with similar legends
current with other peoples. Selden, in the Illustrations
to *Poly-Olbion*, while humouring his friend's adherence
to them, values most of them merely for their poetical
worth. So far, however, from believing that Geoffrey
invented them, he is at one with Drayton in claiming
that the chronicler received them from earlier Welsh
sources: 'the name of *Brute* was long before him in
Welsh (out of which his storie was partly translated)'[4].
Drayton and Selden here anticipate the conclusion

---

[1] PO[5] 56 s.

[2] Cf. Edwin Greenlaw, *Studies in Spenser's Historical Allegory*,
1932.

[3] PO[10] 234–323.　　　　　[4] PO[10] 244 s.

reached by Geoffrey of Monmouth's latest editor that he was not the inventor of the story of Brute or of the other discredited episodes in his Chronicle, but that he did indeed take them (as he himself tells us) from an earlier Welsh source.[1] Drayton therefore seems to be justified in the protest which he puts into the speech of the river Dee,[2] that Geoffrey records what had been handed down by oral tradition through many centuries.

The controversy between those who on one side or the other maintained the relative superiority of the British or of the English is figured in the Fourth Song by the contest between the British and the English nymphs for the possession of Lundy. The issue is gracefully decided in the 'doom' pronounced by Severn, who, praising the valour and prowess of both races, declares that there is no more room for dispute, now that under King James

three sever'd Realmes in one shall firmly stand.[3]

The Faerie Queene has its 'chronicle of Briton kings,'[4] and the motive of *The Ruines of Time* runs through *Poly-Olbion* also: Verulam's complaint is substantially that of the river Ver in the Sixteenth Song. But Drayton's interest and studies in antiquity extend far beyond what he may have read in any of Spenser's writings. He may have found in *The Faerie Queene* a precedent for the inset narratives from legend or from history by which he so often relieves the descriptions and dialogues of the rivers, hills and forests personified in the Songs. Occasional topographical passages in Spenser, such as the wedding of the Thames and Medway[5] and the description of the river Dee,[6] furnished hints also for his poetical treatment of scenes and places in *Poly-Olbion*. But the poem as a whole shows in its construction only a little of that indebtedness to

[1] See A. Griscom, *The Historia Brit. of GM*, London, 1929.
[2] PO[10] 244–258.   [3] PO[5] 68.   [4] *FQ* II. 10.
[5] *FQ* IV, 11.   [6] *FQ* I, 9, 4.

Spenser which is so manifest in Drayton's early work. It owes nothing in its general conception or its treatment to any other writer. Unique in all literature, it is a monument both of Drayton's stubborn industry and of his passionate love for his country as well in her history, legends and traditions as for the natural beauty of her hills and vales, her forests and her rivers.

CHAPTER XIII

DRUMMOND OF HAWTHORNDEN

THE pleasant Bo-peep story told of William Drummond by Bishop Sage in the Life of the poet printed in the 1711 folio of his works—how 'being at London he . . . peep'd into the Room where Sir *William Alexander*, Sir *Robert Carr*, *Michael Drayton* and *Ben Johnson* were sitting,'[1] must be rejected on the evidence of Drummond himself, who at Drayton's death wrote to Alexander as one 'who never saw Drayton, save by his letters and poesy.'[2] It seems likely that Drayton first sought an introduction to the laird of Hawthornden in connection with *Poly-Olbion*, for which he was seeking a publisher for the Second Part and material as well for the Third Part, which was still to be written—that on Scotland. Whatever the occasion, it was a happy episode in the careers of both these predestined friends. Drayton was the leader of those who carried on the Spenserian tradition in English poetry. Drummond, a younger man by twenty-two years, was prominent in the group of Scoto-English poets who sought to regenerate Scottish verse by infusing into it the spirit of the Renaissance. Intended by his father for the law, he had been educated first at the Edinburgh High School and then at the University of the same city, 'in the common Metaphysical Learning, which then obtained in the Schools,' says his early biographer:[3]

> yet he did not take up all his time that way, but applied some of it to the reading of the Classick Authors and Mathematicks.
>
> Having past his Course at the University, he did not, according to the common Custom, give over Reading, or think that he had a full Stock of Learning, as a great many vainly imagine: . . . he contin-

[1] See pp. 139–40.   [2] See p. 189.   [3] Works, 1711, pp. i, ii.

ued close some Years reading the solid and unaffected Authors of Antiquity, which he not only retained in his Memory, but digested in his Judgment.

Then his father sent him to Bourges to study law. On his way there he stayed in London, whither his maternal uncle, William Fowler, himself a poet and secretary to Queen Anne, had followed her to the English Court. In a letter which is extant Drummond describes some of the Court pageantry held in honour of the visit of the King of Denmark, but he makes no mention of any literary acquaintance that he may have made there. He was already a diligent reader of English poetry and drama. Amongst the Hawthornden papers which are now preserved in the National Library of Scotland are lists of 'Bookes red by me' during the years spent abroad after he left the University and also later, as well as a list of the books which he owned in the year 1611. From these we are able to trace the trend and development of his studies and of his literary tastes. The list for 1606 opens with John Knox's *History of the Reformation in Scotland*. Drummond retained throughout his life an interest in the history of his country and in divinity, but the bent of his mind is shown better by the poetry and romances which make up the greater part of the list. It includes Sidney's *Arcadia*, Lyly's *Euphues*, Shakespeare's *Lucrece, Romeo and Juliet, Love's Labours Lost*, and *A Midsummer Night's Dream*, Robert Chester's *Loves Martyr*, Drayton's *The Owle*, William Alexander's *Aurora, The Paradise of Dainty Devices*, and the English translations of Ovid's *Metamorphoses, Orlando Furioso*, and *Amadis de Gaule*. By 1607 he was reading French romances and French translations of Tasso, Sannazaro and Montemayor. The list for 1608 includes many French works of controversy and history. In 1609 he read du Bartas and nearly the whole of Ronsard as well as others of the Pléiade; also Marston's *Parasitaster* and some other

English comedies. In 1610 he is reading a number of
Italian authors, including Sannazaro, Petrarch, Guarini,
and Tasso in the original 'et en Francais'—with a
French translation at his side. By 1611 the number of
Latin books in his library—both classical authors and
modern—had risen to 267. He had 120 French books,
61 Italian, and a few Spanish, but he only names 50
English. They include 'Draton's Workes,' *Ideas
Mirrour, Endimion and Phœbe*, and *The Owle*. In 1612
he read Drayton's *Heroicall Epistles, The Barons' Wars*
and the Legends; in 1613 *Poly-Olbion*, and in 1614
The Owle again.[1]
    In 1610, when his father died, Drummond re-
nounced the law for the Muses and settled down to a
life of literary dilettantism at his beloved Hawthornden,
on the river Esk, about seven miles south of Edinburgh,
'a sweet and solitary seat and very fit and proper for the
Muses. There in Obscurity and Retirement he fell
again to the studying the Greek and Latin Authors.'
    He also fell in love:

    Notwithstanding his close Retirement and serious
    Application to Studies, Love stole in upon him, and
    did intirely captivate his Heart: For he was on a
    sudden highly Enamour'd of a fine Beautiful young
    Lady, Daughter to *Cuninghame* of *Barns*, an Ancient
    and Honourable Family. He met with suitable
    Returns of chast Love from her, and fully gain'd her
    Affection: But when the Day for the Marriage was
    appointed, and all Things ready for the Solemniza-
    tion of it, she took a Fever, and was suddenly
    snatch'd away by it, to his great Grief and Sorrow.
    He express'd his Grief for her in several Letters and
    Poems; and with more Passion and Sincerity Cele-
    brated his dead Mistress, than others use to Praise
    their living Ones.[2]

[1] *Archaeologia Scotica*, IV, pp. 73–7.
[2] Works, 1711, p. iii.

He sang of her while yet living in the First Part of a sequence of Sonnets and Madrigals, and after her death in a Second Part. Both Parts were published together by Andro Hart, probably in 1614.[1]

In that year Drummond writes with discrimination but with some curious partialities about the *Character of several Authors*, printed by Bishop Sage and Ruddiman in their folio:[2]

> The Authors I have seen on the Subject of Love, are the Earl of *Surrey*, Sir *Thomas Wyat*, (whom, because of their Antiquity, I will not match with our better Times), *Sidney, Daniel, Drayton* and *Spencer.* . . . The last we have are Sir *William Alexander* and *Shakespear*, who have lately published their Works. . . .'

He compares these poets with Petrarch,

> the best and most exquisite Poet of this Subject, by Consent of the whole Senate of Poets. . . . Among our *English* Poets, *Petrarch* is imitated, nay surpast in some Things, in Matter and Manner: In Matter, none approach him to *Sidney*; . . . In Manner, the nearest I find to him, is *W. Alexander*; . . . After which Two, next (methinks) followeth *Daniel*, for Sweetness in Ryming Second to none. *Drayton* seemeth rather to have loved his Muse than his Mistress; by, I know not what artificial *Similes*, this sheweth well his Mind, but not the Passion.

Here Drummond seems to have in mind the Sonnets in Drayton's *Idea*, the miscellany, rather than *Ideas Mirrour*, the early sequence, which he also possessed. After discussing Donne, 'among the Anacreontick Lyricks, . . . Second to none, and far from all Second,' he describes Drayton's *Poly-Olbion* as

> one of the smoothest Poems I have seen in *English*, Poetical and well prosecuted; there are some Pieces

---

[1] Kastner, *Poems of W. Drummond*, pp. lii–lxi.
[2] Works, 1711, pp. 226–7.

in him, I dare compare with the best Transmarine
Poems. The 7th Song pleaseth me much. The 12th
is excellent. The 13th also: The *Discourse of Hunting*,
passeth with any Poet. And the 18th, which is his
Last in this Edition 1614. I find in him, which is in
most part of my Compatriots, too great an admiration of their Country: on the History of which, whilst
they muse, as wondering, they forget sometimes to
be good Poets.

A few years later Drayton began a correspondence
with the Scottish poet which continued till the end of
his life. The extant letters come to us from two sources.
Bishop Sage and Ruddiman printed some of them in
1711 in their folio edition of Drummond's Works, but
of those the originals are lost. For the others we have
Drummond's original drafts, which with one exception
are preserved in the Hawthornden collection at the
National Library of Scotland. Drummond was a careful
letter-writer, and he seems to have intended to keep a
letter-book or register of his correspondence, for the
first leaf of the volume containing them bears the title,
*Letters Amorous, Complimentall, Consolatorie, Militarie,
Historicall*. The correspondence with Drayton begins in
1618 and ends in July 1631, in which year Drayton
died. From the many cordial allusions made to Sir
William Alexander in letters written from either side
throughout that period it seems safe to judge that Drayton first wrote to Drummond at the suggestion of that
'general friend' to them both. When Prince Henry died
in 1612, Alexander continued to hold the office of
Gentleman of the Bedchamber to his brother, Prince
Charles. Perhaps Drayton owed to him the patronage
he enjoyed successively from the two Princes. In 1614
Alexander was appointed Master of Requests; and although he did not become Secretary for Scotland till
1620, he paid in the meantime frequent visits to Scotland, whether on the King's business or his own. In

N

1601 he had married Janet, daughter of Sir William Erskine, who was herself the bearer of one of Drayton's letters to Drummond. She or one of her three daughters may perhaps have been 'my Mistress, which I think is one of the fairest and worthiest living,' whom Drayton mentions in the second of the letters. She was the mother also of eight sons.

The first of the letters is undated, but it was written in 1618 in reply to one from Drayton conveyed by Joseph Davis, which has not survived. Nearly twenty years before, one Joseph Davis, 'who was reckoned a clever man,' had discussed religious questions with Anthony Greenway, and, although a 'schismatic,' was the means of 'finding some priest to come to my aid,' who received him into the Catholic Church.[1] Anthony Greenway had written the Latin prefatory verses to Drayton's *The Owle*; and it seems likely that the same Joseph Davis carried the earliest of the letters that passed between Drayton and Drummond. It is also likely that earlier he had been a spy set by Cecil on the Catholics.[2] It is possible that he was still in the service

[1] Foley, I, pp. 466–7. See below, p. 199.

[2] In 1604, the year in which *The Owle* was printed, the Government was already preparing the ground for the discovery and exploitation of the Powder Plot more than a year later. In April 1604 one Henry Wright wrote to Sir Thomas Chaloner, telling him that

Davies will not declare the treason, till his pardon under the seal, which is in great forwardness, is ready.

(Gunpowder Plot Book [*SP* 14/216], no. 236; Supplementary Patent Roll, c. 67, No. 71. *Cal SPD* Jas. I, 1603–10.)

What the 'treason' was is not disclosed; but the pardon of Joseph Davies, dated 25th April 1604, is at the Record Office. About the end of June Chaloner received intelligence that Blackwell, the Archpriest, Joseph Davies and others had received letters from Father Coffin, who was then at the English College, Rome, urging them to some action the nature of which is not stated.

About the same date Chaloner had another mysterious letter from one whose name has been carefully erased, desiring that Davies be sent privately to the Tower, and that the keeper of the

of the Government when he went to Scotland in 1618, taking with him Drayton's letter to Drummond, and brought back Drummond's reply, which is the first of the extant letters. If so, 'Mr. Davis's other Designs,' to which Drummond alludes in the third of the letters, may have been some business of the King's, which took him to the Northern kingdom.

To the Right Worshipful, Mr. Michael Drayton, *Esq*;
Sir,
     I Have understood by Mr. *Davis*, the Direction he received from you, to salute me here; which undeserved favour I value above the Commendations of the Greatest and Mightiest in this Isle: Tho' I have not had the Fortune to see you, (which Sight, is but like the near view of Pictures in Tapestry) yet, almost ever since I could know any, ye have been to me known and beloved. Long since, your amorous (and truly Heroical) Epistles, did ravish me; and lately your most happy *Albion*, put me into a new Trance. Works (most excellent Pourtraits of a rarely indued Mind) which (if one may conjecture of what is to come) shall be read, in Spite of Envy, so long as Men read Books. Of your great Love, Courtesy and generous Disposition. I have been informed by more than one, of the Worthiest of this Country; but what before was only known to me by Fame, I have now found by Experience: Your Goodness preventing me in that Duty, which a strange Bashfulness, or bashful

Gatehouse should be warned not to let Woodward the priest have access to him. In December 1605 Davies was suborned by the Council to give evidence against the Jesuit Thomas Strange, whom it was hoped to incriminate in the Gunpowder Plot. In the 'Interrogations to be ministered' to Strange Davies is noted as the source of information concerning the Jesuit's work in the Society to which he belonged and especially about a letter which he was said to have written to Davies in May 1604, advising him to get acquainted 'with all the best and stirring spirits he could.' (Foley, IV, pp. 11-4.)

Strangeness, hindred me to offer unto you. You have the first Advantage, the next should be mine; and hereafter you shall excuse my Boldness, if, when I write to your matchless Friend Sir *W. Alexander*, I now and then salute you; and in that claim, though unknown, to be

Your loving and assured Friend,

W. D.[1]

Doubtless William Alexander and David Murray were amongst 'the worthiest of this Country' from whom we, like Drummond, receive this charming glimpse at Drayton's kindly nature. The correspondence makes it clear that Drayton was in very close attendance on Sir William and his lady throughout its entire period. They seem to have been the principal channel through which the letters passed between Drayton and Hawthornden.

Drummond's letter gave him lively pleasure. He straightway took advantage of his newly made acquaintance to use him as an intermediary with Andro Hart in opening and carrying on negotiations for an edition of his poems and doubtless also for the projected Third Part of *Poly-Olbion*—that on Scotland. Hart was Alexander's and Drummond's publisher.

To My Honourable Friend Mr. William
Drummond, *in* Scotland.

My dear Noble Drummond,

Your Letters were as welcome to me, as if they had come from my Mistress, which I think is one of the fairest and worthiest Living. Little did you think how oft, that Noble Friend of yours, Sir *William Alexander*, (that Man of Men) and I, have remember'd you, before we traffick'd in Friendship. Love me as much as you can, and so I will you: I can never hear of you too oft, and I will ever mention you with much Respect of your deserved Worth. I enclosed

[1] Works, 1711, p. 233.

this Letter in a Letter of mine to Mr. *Andrew Hart* of *Edinburgh*, about some Business I have with him, which he may impart to you. Farewel, Noble Sir, and think me ever to be,

London, 9.   *Your Faithful Friend,*
Nov. 1618   Michael Drayton.
Joseph Davis *is in Love with you.*[1]

Drummond delivered the letter to Hart, with a commendation from himself:[2]

To the Right Worshipful, Mr. Michael Drayton *Esq*;
Sir,
    If my Letters were so welcome to you, what may you think yours were to me, which must be so much more welcome, in that the Conquest I make, is more than that of yours. They, who by some strange Means have had Conference with some of the old Heroes, can only judge that Delight I had in reading them; for they were to me, as if they had come from *Virgil, Ovid,* or the Father of our Sonnets, *Petrarch.* I must love this Year of my Life, more dearly than any that forwent it, because in it I was so happy to be acquainted with such Worth. Whatever were Mr. *Davis's* other Designs, methinks some secret Prudence directed him to those[3] Parts only: For this I will, in Love of you, surpass as far your Countrymen, as you go beyond them all in true worth; and shall strive to be second to none, save your fair and worthy Mistress. Your other Letters I delivered to *Andrew Hart,* and have been earnest with him in that particular. How would I be overjoy'd to see our North once honoured with your Works, as before it was with *Sidney's*; tho' it be barren of Excellency in it self, it can both love and admire the Excellency of others.
Decemb. 20. 1618.

[1] Ibid. p. 153.   [2] Ibid. p. 234.   [3] 'these'?

The two following letters from Drummond are both undated. It seems likely that they were written in the first quarter of 1619. They survive only in Drummond's drafts among the Hawthornden papers.

No. 14. *To* M. DRT.

Your great learning first bred in mee admiration, then love: which if not alwhere and allwayes I professe, testifie, I were not only an evill esteemer of you, but also of letters & all learning & poesie, which now being in the age of it beginneth to flowrish againe by you. When first I looked on your heroicall epistles, I was rapt from my selfe, & could not containe my selfe from blazing that of you, which both your worth merit and my love deserved required: although, what ever I can say of you is farre under your ingene and vertue. So farre as I can remember of our vulgare poesie none hath done better or can doe none hath done better and more, and from none can wee expect more. So have I persuaded my selfe, neither doth my opinion deceave mee. all that you have done delighte mee, your learning judgement, oration. Some of a greater judgment and wit will say more of you, as they ordinarly doe, but the chief of your praises non than I shall more willingly remember. Wee that have never shown yet any thing to the World but abortive births wee can doe no thing but follow your footsteps and which are by us unfortunately begun, leave to be by you perfected. Which the world rather carpeth than correctes, let your friendship continue w^t mee, to which the admiration of you convoyed us.

W D

No. 15.

To the right worshipfull
Michell Drayton Esquier

S^r

I have understood by Sr W. Alexanders letters yee have not receaved my last, if I could have thought of

their | *going wrong*[1] | losse or going so late I had pre-
vented them ere now by others. I am oft with S^r W
and you in my thoughts, and desire no thing more
than that by letters wee may ofte meet | *with their
Ladder* | and mingle our Soules.[2] Your workes make
you ever present | *with* | mee, than which their is not
anay booke I am more familiar with, nor anay by
which I estime my selfe more happy, by | *the* | famili-
aritie contracted w^t the author. I long to see the rest
of your polyalbion come forth (which is the onlye
epicke Poeme England (in my judgement) hath to be
prowd of: To be the author of which I had rather
have the praise, than (as Aquinas said of one of the
Fathers commentaries) to have the Signorie of Paris.
Thes our times now are so given to envenomed
Satyres and spitfull jeasts that | *like distempered tastes* |
they only taste | *nothing else but* | what is ranke &
smelling and hoarse. Out of what parte of the World
your late Prosaicke versers have their poesies it is
hard to find, it may be said of their new fits of Poetiz-
ing at Court

　　　et penitus toto divisos orbe Britannos.

Drayton's next letter[3] was written after he had received the foregoing from Drummond. He had just got
back to London after spending the winter in the country:

　　　　　To my Noble Friend Mr. William
　　　　　Drummond *of* Hawthornden.
My Noble Friend,
　　　I have at last received both your Letters, and the
Last in a Letter of Sir *William Alexander's* inclosed,
sent to me into the Country, where I have been all
this Winter, and came up to *London* not above Four

---

[1] These and other words so printed are scored through in the
MS.
[2] Cf. Donne, *To Sir Henry Wotton*, 'Sir, more then kisses, letters
mingle Soules.'
[3] Works, p. 153.

Days before the Date of these my Letters to you: I thank you, my dear sweet *Drummond*, for your good Opinion of *Poly-Olbyon*: I have done Twelve Books more, that is, from the Eighteenth Book, which was *Kent*, (if you note it) all the East Parts, and North to the River of *Tweed*; but it lyeth by me; for the Booksellers and I are in Terms: They are a Company of base Knaves, whom I both scorn and kick at. Your love, worthy Friend, I do heartily embrace and cherish, and the ofter your Letters come, the better they shall be welcome. And so, wishing you all Happiness I commit you to God's Tuition, and rest ever

London, 14.   *Your assured Friend*,
April 1619.   Michael Drayton.
I have written to Mr. Hart a
Letter, which comes with this.

Although two and a half years passed before the date of the next letter, its friendly and familiar language suggests that meanwhile the correspondence had not altogether lapsed. It was dated from London. In the summer Drayton had paid a long visit in the country. Alexander was at Newmarket, and Lady Alexander, who was about to travel to Scotland, undertook to convey the letter to Drummond in person. Andro Hart died in December 1621, and we hear no more of Drayton's negotiations with him or his heirs.

> *To my dear Noble Friend Mr.* William
> Drummond *of* Hawthornden, *in* Scotland.[1]

Noble Mr. Drummond,

I am oft thinking whether this long Silence proceeds from you or me, whether I know not; but I would have you take it upon you, and excuse me; and then I would have you lay it upon me, and excuse your self: But if you will, (if you think it our Fault, as I do) let us divide; and both, as we may, amend it. My long being in the Country this Summer, from

[1] Works, 1711, p. 154.

whence I had no Means to send my Letter, shall partly speak for me; for, believe me, worthy *William*, I am more than a Forthnight's Friend; where I love, I love for Years; which I hope you shall find. When I wrote this Letter, our general Friend, Sir *William Alexander*, was at Court at *Newmarket*; but my Lady promised me to have this Letter sent to you: Let me hear how you do, so soon as you can; and know that I am, and will be ever.

London, 22 *November*   *Your Faithful Friend*,
   1621. in haste   Michael Drayton.

In Lady Alexander's hands the letter took nearly five months to reach Hawthornden.

The draft of Drummond's reply is among the Hawthornden papers. It was sent under cover to John Bill, the King's printer in London.

No 16. *To* M.D.

Sir,—I receaved the twentye of Apryle a letter of yours which if it had beene an almanack, had long ere It came to mee expyred, bearing | *the* | dated the | 22 of november: it was well the yeere was | *not marked* | forgot | *afor* | of our long silence let us both excuse our selves, and (as our first Parents did) laye the fault on some thrid, I upon Sir W. who, notw^{th}standing my oft inquiring for you answered mee with silence, and you upon his Lady, | *who that shee might be assured*|to whom yee delivered this letter; who, that shee might be assured to have it | . . . | in my hands (perhaps for feare to violate her promise to you), durst not hazard it with anay bearer | *but* | till shee come with it her selfe. But because yee will not short-lye see her[,] if you please, revenge yee my querrelle against Sr W., and I shall take yours against his lady: neither for this shall her book[1] save her though it be

---

[1] An allusion to the legal fiction of 'benefit of clergy,' which one convicted of felony might plead if he showed himself able to read.

musicke. A whole yeere to have gone, paper being so cheape and never one letter. Let us blot this yeere in the calender as the Germane Astrologers have, with crueltye amongst them, with unkyndnesse heere.

I have directed these to Mr Bill, which I wish have no worse fortune than yours, which is to finde you at last; and testifye that neither yeeres nor fortune can ever so affect mee, but that I shall ever reverence your worth, and esteeme your freindship as one of the best |*pure*|conquests of my life. Which I would have extended (if possible) and enjoy even after Death that as this tyme, so the coming after might know what I am and shall be ever

Your loving

The draft of Drummond's next letter is undated. Its number in the correspondence, 17, shows that it must be of later date than the last, and that it was provoked by Drummond's disappointment when Sir William Alexander, visiting Scotland, had brought no letter from Drayton. The volume of 'Poemes' for the appearance of which its writer was impatiently waiting is more likely to have been the folio of 1627, containing *The Battaile of Agincourt* and the Elegies, than the Second Part of *Poly-Olbion*, printed in 1622. The letter is printed by David Laing with other draft letters from the Hawthornden MSS., but the original draft cannot now be found at the National Library of Scotland. It is here printed from Laing.[1]

17. To M. Drayton.

The Summer might [as well] come without flowers, as S^r W[illiam Alexander] without letters. Wonder have oft been inquisitive of, about your Poemes, wondering they are not come from the press. I long to heare the progresse of your Poemes printed. There is no verses I delight more to read than yours, 'Shine as the moone among the lesser

---

[1] *Archaeologia Scotica*, IV, 91.

starres.' If I heere of your byding at London, I will
repaire the long silence of tyme past of the last
yeere. Old Sr Wm Esken[1] chalenged me in your
name, of what I was most innocent: for witnesse all
that ever loved poesye | *all those powers that infuse or
love sweet poesye*|, that I did not answer your letter,
which a Tortoyse might have brought to Scotland in
such a period of tyme. Esteeme me among those that
love you, which can not have an end, being grounded on your owne worth.

The next letter was written by Drayton from Clifford
Manor in the last year of his life:

> *To my most Worthy and ever Honoured
> Friend Mr.* William Drummond
> *of* Hawthornden, *in* Scotland.[2]

Sir,

It was my Chance to meet with this Bearer, Mr.
Wilson, at a Knight's House in *Glocester-Shire*, to
which Place I Yearly use to come, in the Summer
Time, to recreate my self, and to spend some Two or
Three Months in the Country; and understanding
by him, that he was your Country-man, and after
some Enquiries of some few Things, I asked him, if
he had heard of such a Gentleman, (meaning your
self) who told me he was of your inward Acquaintance, and spake much Good to me of you: My Happiness of having so convenient a Messenger, gave
me the Means to write to you, and to assure you that
I am your perfect faithful Friend, in spight of
Destiny and Time. Not above Three Days before I
came from *London*, (and I had not been here above
Four Days) I was with your Noble Friend and mine,
Sir *William Alexander*,[3] when we talk'd of you; I left

---

[1] Sir William Erskine was Lady Alexander's father.
[2] Works, 1711, p. 154.
[3] Alexander, however, had been raised to the Scottish peerage
as Lord Alexander of Tullibody and Viscount Stirling in Septem-

him, his Lady and Family in good Health: This Messenger is going from hence, and I am call'd upon to do an earnest Business for a Friend of mine; and so I leave you to God's Protection, and rest ever

Your faithful Friend,

Michael Drayton.

Clifford, in Glocester-Shire,
14 *July* 1631. in haste

We may close the correspondence with two drafts, preserved with the Hawthornden papers, of a letter written by Drummond to Alexander on the occasion of Drayton's death.

[*The First Draft*]

My Lord
|*I would*| if my hand dared second my desires, there is scarce one weeke (I will not say moneth) in which |*I*|it would not write to your L. and in which I have not an aime to write unto you. But thus considering the great weight of bussinesses which your L. underlieth and knowing what a tedious progresse it is to your L. to read letters I voluntarlie abstaine from what I most desire to doe. I am greeved at the Death of your L. freind M. Drayton and more that hee should have left this world before hee had|*ended*| accomplished the northen part of his polyolbion. All wee can doe to preserve his Memorye, and if your L. can find any of the fragments which concerne this country they shall|*be printed suffer*|come to the presse heere, and be dedicated to your L. wᵗ the best remembrance of him which |*our*|freindship | *can* | did deserve.

[*Second Draft*]

My Lord
The Death of M.D. your great freind hath beene

ber 1630. It is possible that the letter is wrongly dated in the folio and that it was written when Alexander was still a commoner. More likely, Drayton continued to call him Sir William by force of habit.

verye grevous | much deplored | by all those which
love the Muses heere, | *especi*alye | cheflie that | *hee
should have* | in such sort left this world before hee
had perfected the northen | *part of his polyolbion* | that
it brake off that noble work of the northen part of the
poliolbion which had beene no litle honour to our
countrey. all wee can doo for him is to honour his
Memorye. If your L. can get those fragmentes
| *which* | remaines of his Worke which concerne
Scotland. wee shall endevour to put them in this
country to the presse w^t a dedication if | *your L.
thinke* | it shall be thought expedient to your L. w^t
the best remembrances his love to this countrey did
deserve. Of all the good race of poets who wrote
in the tyme of Queen Elizab your L. now alone
remaines.
Daniel Sylvester Kg James[1] Done and now Drayton
who besides his | *famili*aritye | love and kindlie
Observance of your L. hath made twice honorable
Mention in his works of your L. | *first in* | long since
in his odes and latlie in Elegies. 1627

So | *then* | Scotland sent us hithere for our owe'n
That man whose name I evere would have knowe'n
To stand by myne that most ingenious knight
My Alexander to whom in his right
| *I much am wanting* | I want extreamlye (yet in speak-
ing thus
I doe but shew the love that was twixt us
And not his numbers that wer brave & hie
So like his Mind was his cleare poesie)

If the date of a picture of his be | *right* | just Hee
heth lived three score and eight yeeres | *and* | but shall
live by all likeliehead so long as | *the english tongue* |
men speak English after his death. I who never saw
him | *but* | save by his letteres and poesie scarce be-

[1] King James is added between the lines.

leive hee is yet dead. | *he liveth so truelie in my Re'-* brance | and would faine misbeleive Veritye, if it were possible. The Town of Edenb: bussie themselves verye much for the erecting of pageantes for the Kings M: entrie notw^tstandinge some have writen to us from Court | *that* | notw^tstanding of his highnesse good intention to receave his crown in Scotland, it is impossible this yeere hee can see us considering the p'sent affaires of Germanye. Now I have continewed my letter too long considering the many other papers your L. hath to read. from your L.

Most affectionat Servant
W D.

Drayton's lines on 'My Alexander,' which Drummond has taken from the Elegy to Henry Reynolds, are followed there by these on Hawthornden himself:

And my deare *Drummond* to whom much I owe
For his much love, and proud I was to know,
His poesie, for which two worthy men,
I *Menstry* still shall love, and *Hauthorne-den*.[1]

[1] El[8] 163–74.

CHAPTER XIV

DRAYTON'S LITERARY CIRCLE 1603-31

THE evidence for Drayton's friendships in the latter part of his career continues to be found in his writings, especially in his pastoral poems, his *Elegies*, and his commendatory verses on the work of other men. It can be richly supplemented from poems addressed to him or allusions made to him by other writers. He speaks most clearly in the verse-letter to Henry Reynolds, *Of Poets and Poesie*,[1] so well-known to students for its critical appreciation of English poets from Chaucer down to the men of Drayton's own day. He there shows that the writers whom he regarded with most affection were Reynolds himself,[2] William Alexander,[3] Drummond of Hawthornden,[4] Sir John and Francis Beaumont and William Browne. George Chapman—the 'reverent Chapman' of the letter—was Drayton's senior by a few years. With Drayton he had served in Henslowe's team of playwrights. Like Drayton, too, he suffered the pinch of poverty. Drayton and Jonson are the writers of the two commendatory poems which preface his translations of Hesiod's *Georgicks*. (1618); and Drayton there bids his 'worthy friend,'

> In thy free labours . . . rest content,
> Feare not *Detraction*, neither fawne on *Praise*.[5]

'Dainty *Sands*' is the 'Master George Sandys, Treasurer for the English Colony in Virginia,' Drayton's Elegy to whom—printed earlier in the same folio of 1627—has already furnished us with evidence as to his relations with King James and his vain hope of advancement from the royal bounty. Sandys's translation of

---

[1] Many of the friends referred to in this chapter and others are considered more fully in the notes to the uncollected poems and Elegies in Vol. v.

[2] See notes to El⁸.   [3] See above, pp. 96-6, 189-90.
[4] See Chap. XIII.   [5] Unc¹².

Ovid's *Metamorphoses*, begun in England but continued while he held office in Virginia, is perhaps the earliest contribution of the New World to the *corpus* of English poetry. In the Elegy, with the frankness of a close friend, Michael lays bare his own splenetic attitude towards his contemporaries. His Elegy 'To My Noble Friend Master William Browne, of the evill time,'[1] carries the same note.

In the letter to Reynolds Drayton writes of Browne and of John and Francis Beaumont with a warmth of affection which he shows for no other poets of his day:

> Then the two *Beamounts* and my *Browne* arose,
> My deare companions whom I freely chose
> My bosome friends; and in their severall wayes,
> Rightly borne Poets, and in these last dayes,
> Men of much note, and no lesse nobler parts,
> Such as have freely tould to me their hearts,
> As I have mine to them.[2]

John Beaumont, who was born in 1583, had succeeded to the family estates in Nottinghamshire and Leicestershire on the death of his elder brother Henry without male issue in 1605. He was a devout Catholic, and suffered grievously from the laws against recusants. As early as 1602 he had dedicated *The Metamorphosis of Tabacco*

> To my loving Friend Master Michael Drayton.
>
> The tender labour of my wearie pen,
> And doubtfull triall of my first-borne rimes,
> Loaths to adorne the triumphs of those men,
> Which hold the raines of fortunes, and the times:
> Only to thee, which art with joy possest
> Of the faire hill, where troupes of Poets band,
> Where thou enthron'd with Laurel garlands blest,
> Maist lift me up with thy propitious hand;
> I send this poeme, which for nought doth care,
> But words for words, and love for love to share.

[1] El³. [2] El⁸ 175–181.

In apology for his presumption he quotes a passage from Catullus (i, 3–4) which suggests that the two were already well acquainted:

namque tu solebas
Meas esse aliquid putare nugas.

Beaumont wrote commendatory verses to Drayton's *Barrons Wars*[1] in 1603 and to *Moyses in a Map of His Miracles* in 1604.[2] In a tribute of affection which was first printed in the Eighth Eglog of 1606 Drayton joins with the two brothers their sister, Elizabeth Beaumont, later the wife of Thomas Seylyard, a Kentish squire:

. . . that deare Nymph that in the Muses joyes,
That in wild *Charnwood*[3] with her Flocks doth goe,
MIRTILLA, Sister to those hopefull Boyes,
My loved THIRSIS, and sweet PALMEO:
That oft to *Soar* the Southerne Shepheards bring,
Of whose cleere waters they divinely sing.[4]

Drayton's lines on the river Soar and Charnwood Forest in Song XXVI of *Poly-Olbion*[5] owe little to Camden. They are written from his own memories of days which he and other 'Southerne Shepheards' passed as guests of the Beaumonts at Gracedieu Priory. The ruins of that old nunnery, which the Beaumonts made their seat, are still standing, a few minutes walk from '*Sharpley* and *Cadmans* aged rocks' in Charnwood Forest. Francis Beaumont died in 1616. John, his elder brother, was created a Baronet in 1626 and died a year later. Ben Jonson wrote verses in commendation of Sir John Beaumont's poems which with his *Bosworth Field* his son, Sir John, brought out posthumously in 1629. The ageing Drayton offered as his own tribute 'To the deare Remembrance of his Noble Friend' the 'poore

[1] Vol. II, p. 6.   [2] Vol. III, p. 355.
[3] The version of 1606 has 'Cliffy Charnwood,' showing that D already knew the rocky character of Charnwood Forest.
[4] Pa[8] 139–44.   [5]PO[26] 107–48.

o

Branch of my withring Bayes' which is printed in the first volume of our edition.[1]

William Browne was known to Drayton by 1613, and the two poems[2] addressed by the elder poet to the younger reinforce the impression of intimacy and confidence conveyed in the lines in the Elegy to Reynolds. That the sympathy was reciprocated is evident from the repeated allusions which Browne makes to Drayton in his verse. In an Ode he invokes

> . . . honour'd Drayton, come and lend
> An ear to this sweet melody.[3]

In the First Book of his *Britannia's Pastorals*[1] he says of the lovers Aletheia and Amintas:

> [No] happyer names ere grac'd a golden tongue:
> O! they are better fitting his sweet-stripe,
> Who on the banckes of *Ancor* tun'd his Pype.[4]

And again he writes of Drayton:

> Our second *Ovid*, the most pleasing *Muse*
> That heav'n did e're in mortals braine infuse,
> All-loved *Draiton*, in soule-raping straines,
> A genuine noate, of all the *Nimphish* traines
> Began to tune; on it all eares were hung
> As sometimes *Dido*'s on *Æneas* tongue.[5]

In the lines which Browne wrote in *Poly-Olbion* in 1622, he seems to see Drayton as the admired survivor of an earlier golden age:

> Immortall *Sydney*, honoured *Colin Clout*,
> Presaging what wee feele, went timely out.
> Then why lives *Drayton*, when the *Times* refuse,
> Both *Meanes* to live, and *Matter* for a *Muse*?

Others shared this attitude. Henry Peacham, in an epigram to Drayton in 1620, asks pointedly,

---

[1] Unc[15].   [2] Unc[11] n, El[3] n; also introd. and notes to SS.
[3] BM MS. Lansd. 777.   [4] Bk I [1613], Song 5, p. 109.
[5] Bk II, 1616, Song 2.

What thinkst thou worthy *Michael* of our Times,
Where onely Almanack and ballad rimes
Are in request now. . .?[1]

The understanding and praise of such men as these
representatives of the younger generation must have
been as balm to Drayton's resentment at the poor recep-
tion accorded to his great poem. Browne's friend
George Wither also commended the Second Part of
Poly-Olbion, and calls Drayton his 'Noble Friend.' He
is nowhere mentioned by Drayton and may not have
known him so early as Browne. He first alludes to Drayton in *Abuses Stript and Whipt* (1613),[2] coupling his
name with those of Daniel, Jonson and Chapman, of
all of whom he knows as yet but 'your works and names.'
Eight years later, on 27 June 1621, when Wither was
charged at Whitehall with printing his *Withers Motto*,
for which licence had been refused on the ground that
it contained passages in breach of the Royal proclama-
tion that forbad licentious speaking or writing in
matters concerning the State, he said in examination
that before printing he 'did acquaint divers of his
friends with it, as namely Mr. Drayton, and some
other.'[3] That incident gives additional point to Drayton's wry comment, 'I feare, as I doe Stabbing; this
word State,' in a poem probably of the same year.[4]

If, as has been supposed, Wither is the author of *The
Great Assises Holden in Parnassus by Apollo and his
Assessours* (1645), we may judge that his early friendship for Drayton and his continued regard for his
memory inspired the powerful defence of the poet and
his work which he puts into the mouth of Apollo. The
defence of Drayton is warmer than that made on behalf

[1] *Thalias Banquet*, Epigram 38.
[2] The allusion may belong rather to 1611, the date of the lost
first edition of *Abuses*.
[3] *CSPD* 1619-23, p. 268.
[4] El[2] 9; see also El[11] 6 n and the case of John Reynolds, p. 201
below and Vol. v, p. 193.

of any of his fellow 'Jurours'—Wither, Carew, May, Davenant, Sylvester, Sandys, Beaumont, Fletcher, Heywood, Shakespeare and Massinger—who are challenged in turn by 'the traduceing *Spye*' and the other news-sheets that are brought to trial.

We do not know when Drayton first met Browne and Wither, but it is probable that his connection with Christopher Brooke, Edward Heyward and John Selden, all of whom he knew by 1610,[1] led to a wider circle of acquaintance amongst the young writers of the Inner Temple. If Drayton was already living near St Dunstan's Church, he was their near neighbour. The writing-master, John Davies of Hereford, who was Drayton's junior only by a few years, also lived by St Dunstan's Church, of which a few years later John Donne became vicar. He there taught writing in all the hands. In the lines which he wrote for Davies's *The Holy Roode* (1609), Drayton shows contempt for the log-rolling practised by writers who exchanged verses in commendation of each other's books. But he values Davies's own work:

> we rehearse
> Often (my good *John*, and I love) thy *Letters*
> Which lends me *Credit*, as I lend my *Verse*.[2]

In 1611, when Drayton must have been busy preparing the First Part of *Poly-Olbion* for his printer, Davies had the following Epigram:

> *To myne honest as loving friend* Mr. Michaell Drayton.
>
> *Michaell*, where are thou? what's become of thee?
> Have the nyne Wenches stolne thee from thy selfe?
> Or from their conversation dost thou flee,
> Sith they are rich in Science not in Pelfe?
> Bee not unconstant (*Michaell*) in thy love

---

[1] See below, pp. 200–1; and Vol. v, notes to BW, p. 60, notes to Cro, p. 170. For C. Brooke's lines on D's Cro see Vol. v, p. 173.
[2] Unc⁸.

To Girles so gracefull in the Hart, and Face;
Although thereby thou maist a Poet prove,
(That's poore as *Job*) yet ever those embrace
  By whome thou dost enjoy a Heav'n on Earth;
  And, in this vale of Teares, a Mount of mirth.[1]

Of Drayton's other commendatory verses at this period those to 'My kinde Friend Da: Murray,' written for his *Tragicall Death of Sophonisba* in 1611, also suggest personal friendship. Murray, as we have seen, was attached to the household of Prince Henry, and his accounts for 1612 include a grant of £10 from the prince to the poet. That Drayton should have addressed him with no handle to his name (he had been knighted in 1605) may be taken to show an unusually close bond of intimacy. But Murray himself suppresses his rank on his title-page, calling himself just 'David Murray, Scoto-Brittaine.' A manuscript note at the end of a copy of *Sophonisba* which once belonged to Heber suggests that Drayton helped Murray in some way when writing that poem: 'Daniell Brigges his Booke made and written by my Deare Kinsman Michael Drayton Esq. 1622.' Daniell Brigges must be the son of Daniell Brigges of Wedgenock Park in the county of Warwick, gent., who left him a legacy of £100 in his will, proved 9 May 1608.[2] It is not known how he was related to Drayton. Murray's *Cælia containing certaine Sonets*, printed in the same quarto with his *Sophonisba*, shows the influence of Drayton's *Idea* almost to imitation in subject and manner and even in its figures.

Tom Coryate was by no means a poet, but with Ben Jonson's help he unconscionably extorted a series of 'panegyrick verses' from more than fifty friendly wits—boon companions at the *Mermaid* and others —as makeweight for his *Crudities*, which the stationers judged too light a craft to sail without some such ballast. Like the rest Drayton's lines are written in the

[1] *The Scourge of Folly.* [2] 41 Windebancke.

burlesque spirit of the *Crudities* which they preface. Those 'To my Noble Friend Mr Robert Dover, on his brave annuall *Assemblies* upon *Cotswold*,' are upon a much more congenial theme. We cannot be sure, indeed, that Dover's famous Whitsun games are in any way related to the pastoral junketings at sheep-shearing on Cotswold of which Drayton sings in the Ninth Eglog of 1606 or those described in the Fourteenth Song of *Poly-Olbion* and shown on the map to that Song: sheep-shearing time is not at Whitsun. It is difficult to believe, however, that the fifty or so poets—Jonson, Randolph, Heywood, Basse, Shakerley Marmion and Trussell among them—who contribute to Matthew Walbancke's *Annalia Dubrensia: Upon the yeerely celebration of Mr Robert Dover's Olimpick Games upon Cotswold Hills*, did not have some kind of counterpart in the Cotswold Shepherds of whom Rowland himself 'for that yeare was the King.'[1] Jonson says of the games that they

Renew the glories of our blessed *Jeames*,

and it has been conjectured that Dover established them about the year 1604;[2] but he may have chosen for them some annual celebration of much older date. We know that Page's fallow greyhound was 'outrun on Cotsall'[3] at least as early as 1600.

Abraham Holland, to whose *Naumachia* Drayton wrote commendatory verses in 1622, was the son of Philemon Holland, 'the translator-general of his age.' He left a poem,[4] 'To my honest father Mr Michael Drayton and my new, yet loved freind, Mr Will. Browne,' which is preserved at the Bodleian. The following lines, from which we have already quoted for the evidence they offer that Drayton was at Coven-

---

[1] Pa⁹40.   [2] See note on Unc¹⁶.   [3] *Merry Wives of Windsor*, I, 1.
[4] MS. Ashmole 36, 37, no. 152, f. 151. Printed in part in *MLR*, 1930.

try school,[1] tell us what the disciple looked for and
found in his master's life and verse:

As for thee father, I'le no higher praise
Than say that thou art father of our bayes,
Heroick Ovid, Lucan, Juvenall,
Our still reviving Spencer, I'le thee call,
So long as thou still liv'st; and if I list
I will turne here a deepe Pythagorist
And sweare thou hast the soule of all the best
That ever yet have slept in Parnasse brest.
As I love thee, so let my truant muse
Grow up and impe her tender wings: and choose
To pen but good: and scorning to be mute
Yet shee may scorne to be a prostitute:
So may thy bays still grow upon thy head
So may the place wherin wee both were bred
Bring forth good poets: so may all the land
beholden to thee yet indebted stand,
So may wee both to each ingaged bee
Thou still my friend and I a freind to thee.

We may trace more of Drayton's friendships in the
commendatory lines which some of his fellow-writers
wrote for his books, as he for theirs. 'A. Grenewai,' who
in the Latin verses printed before *The Owle* in 1604
appraises Drayton's attack on the 'Graios proceres' in
that satire, is likely to be Anthony Greenway, of Leckhampstead, Bucks, where he was born in the year
1575. He matriculated as a demy at Magdalen College,
Oxford, in 1589. He won for himself 'a great name for
learning and the *belles lettres*.'[2] A convert to the Catholic faith about 1597, he lived partly in London, partly
in exile for religion in Belgium, until in 1606 he was
admitted to the English College at Rome. There he
was ordained priest in 1608. He became a Jesuit in
1611, and subsequently suffered arrest and imprison-

[1] See p. 19.
[2] H. Foley, *Records of the English Province S.J.*, II, p. 412.

ment in England. Beale Sapperton, whose verses in commendation of Drayton's *Moses*[1] were, like Greenway's, written in Latin, also lived at Leckhampstead. He is associated with Greenway's nephew, a younger Anthony Greenway, in a deed of conveyance relating to a portion of the Greenway estate at that place in 1624.[2]

Thomas Greene, whose sonnet 'To Master Michael Drayton'[3] was first printed in front of *The Barrons Wars* in 1603, is doubtless the author of that name who wrote *A Poets Vision and a Princes Glory* (1603) in the manner of *Endimion and Phæbe*. Like Drayton and Jonson, Greene hails the accession of a poet-king to the throne of England. He alludes also to Drayton's '*Sweete Idæa.*' The Catalogue of the British Museum and the late Edgar Fripp[4] identify him with Thomas Greene the younger of Warwick, who was educated at Staple Inn and the Middle Temple, where he became a Bencher, and afterwards a Reader and Treasurer. In August 1603 he was appointed Steward of Stratford-upon-Avon; and as Town Clerk in 1614–15 he withstood the Combes in the matter of the Welcombe enclosures, in which Shakespeare also was involved. In his Diary, preserved at Shakespeare's Birthplace, he thrice alludes to his 'Cousen Shakespeare,' and Mr Fripp conjectures a descent which would make him Shakespeare's second cousin once removed. Prior to 1611 he seems to have lived for a while at New Place.[5] He died at either Bristol or London in 1640.

John Selden's lines to Drayton[6] were first added to the edition of Poems dated 1610, with only an emphatic 'MICHAEL!' for a heading. He had entered the Inner

---

[1] Vol. III, p. 356.
[2] *Victoria County Hist. Bucks.*, IV, p. 183.   [3] Vol. II, p. 6.
[4] *Guide to Shakespeare's Stratford*, pp. 58–60; *Master Richard Quyney*, pp. 154–6.
[5] E. K. Chambers, *William Shakespeare*, II, p. 96.
[6] Vol. II, p. 8.

Temple in 1604, but was not called to the bar till 1612. In his *Analecton Anglo-Britannicon* (1607) and his *Janus Anglorum Facies Altera* (1610) he first revealed the vast store of historical and antiquarian information of which he was master, and on which he drew two years later for the Illustrations to *Poly-Olbion*. He shared chambers with Edward Heyward, a Norfolk gentleman, whose lines to Drayton accompany his own,[1] and he dedicated to him his *Titles of Honour* (1614).[2] In his Epistle to John Selden, there first printed, Ben Jonson writes of Heyward as 'thy learned Chamber-fellow,' who has 'wrought in the same Mines of knowledge':

> O how I doe count
> Among my commings in (and see it mount)
> The Gaine of your two friendships! *Heyward* and
> *Selden*! Two names that so much understand!

Ten years later Sir Simond D'Ewes[3] found Selden to be a man 'exceedingly puffed up with the apprehension of his own abilities.'

The 'J. Vaughan' who subscribes his name to the verses 'Upon the Battaile of *Agincourt* written by his Deare friend Michaell Drayton Esquire' in the folio of 1627 containing that poem is likely to be the 'amico longe charissimo Johanni Vaughan' to whom Selden dedicated his *Vindiciae Maris Clausi*, printed in 1653. The Sonnet that follows, 'To my worthy Friend Mr Michaell Drayton,' and the 'Acrosticke *Sonnet* upon his *Name*,' both signed 'John Reynolds,' are probably by the Exeter man of that name who wrote *The Triumphes of Gods Revenge against Murther* (1621), and was imprisoned for two years for his *Votivae Angliae; or the desires and wishes of England to perswade his majestie to drawe his sword for the restoring of the Pallatynate to*

---

[1] Vol. II, p. 7.
[2] See *The Poems of Ben Jonson*, Shakespeare Head Press, 1936, pp. 111–3, 401, 414.
[3] *Autobiography*, p. 254.

Prince Fredericke, printed at 'Utrecht' in 1624.[1] In 1622 he dedicated *A Treatise of the Court*, which he translated from the French of Eustache Du Refuge,[2] to 'Sʳ Edward Sackville ... My Honourable, and singular good Master,' who a few years later became Drayton's patron also.

Many more of Drayton's contemporaries profess themselves his friends or show their close acquaintance with his poetry in the allusions they make to it in their writings. William Burton's noble tribute to his 'neere contriman and olde acquaintance' in his *History of Leicestershire* (1622) is quoted in the first chapter of this book. In the second edition of *The Anatomy of Melancholy* (1624) his brother, Robert Burton, quotes from or alludes to *Englands Heroicall Epistles* seven times over.[3] About the year 1628 Robert Hayman in his *Quodlibets* makes the earliest reference to Drayton written in America. He alludes to Drayton's age:

> When I was young, I did *delight* your lines,
> I have *admyr'd* them since my judging times;
> Your *younger muse* plai'd many a dainty fit,
> And your *old muse* doth hold out stoutly yet.
> Though my *old muse* durst passe through frost and snow,
> In warres your *old muse* dares her Colours shew.

In 1629 a devout and apostolic young Oxford man, Samuel Austin, opens a poetical account of the fall and redemption of man, entitled *Austins Urania or The Heavenly Muse*, with an address

---

[1] Wrongly attributed (*STC* 22092) to Thomas Scott, but certainly by Reynolds. See BA notes on these commendatory verses for his identification and that of J. Vaughan.

[2] STC 7367.

[3] *Anat. of Melanch.*, 1624, e.g., pp. 85, 375, 396, 412, 418, 441–2. His copies of D's Maj, O, Poems 1605, Cro 1609, ME and BA are among the books bequeathed by Burton to the Bodleian (Malone Collection). They have been used by the editors of our edition.

To my ever honoured friends, those most refined Wits and favorers of most exquisite learning, Mr. *M. Drayton, Mr. Will. Browne,* and my ingenious Kinsman, *Mr. Andrew Pollexfen* (all knowne unto me) and to the rest (unknowne) the Poets of these times, *S.A.* wisheth the accomplishment of all true happinesse.

He appeals especially to Drayton to give up the writing of secular poetry and to write only sacred verse henceforth:

> *And thou, deare* Drayton! *let thy aged Muse*
> *Turne now divine; let her forget the use*
> *Of thy earst pleasing tunes of love, (which were*
> *But fruits of witty youth:) let her forbeare*
> *Those toyes, I say, and let her now breake forth*
> *Thy latest gaspe in heav'nly sighes, more worth*
> *Then is a world of all the rest; for this*
> *Will usher thee to heav'ns eternall blisse:*
> *And let thy strong-perswasive straines enforce*
> *These times into a penitent remorce*
> *For this their sinfull frowardnesse; and then*
> *Heav'n shall reward thee, never care for men.*

Aston Cokaine (1608–84) was still a young man when Drayton died. The chief seat of his ancient family was at Ashbourne in Derbyshire; but in Henry VII's reign the Sir Thomas Cokain of the day had built a manor-house and imparked the woods at Pooley in the parish of Polesworth in Warwickshire. In James's reign, and since, says Dugdale, writing about 1640, 'his Descendants have seldome dwelt at this place.' But after Cokaine had sold Ashbourne in 1671, he went to live at Pooley. Both Pooley and Polesworth come again and again into his rhymes. Dugdale's continuator, Thomas, has the following note about him: 'He was a Romanist, and suffered much for his Religion, and the King's cause in the Civil Wars. . . This Person mostly lived at *Pooley*, and sometimes in the great City, was esteemed by many an ingenious Gentleman, a good Poet, and a great lover of Learning; yet by others a perfect boon fellow, by which means he wasted all he had.'[1] Through Drayton he came to know '*my much honoured Cousin*, Sir Francis Burdet *Baronet*,' to whom he writes:

> The honest Poet, *Michael Drayton*, I
> Must ever honour for your Amity.
> He brought us first acquainted; which good turn
> Made me to fix an Elegie on's urn:
> Else I might well have spar'd my humble stuffe;
> His own sweet Muse renowning him enough.[2]

Sir Thomas Burdet, the first baronet and the father of Francis, had married Jane Franceis, a Derbyshire heiress; and he or his heir had left Bramcote and gone to live at Formark in that county. Aston Cokaine's mother was Anne, daughter to Sir John Stanhope of Elvaston, co. Derby, and so sister-in-law to Lady Olive Stanhope, at whose death Drayton wrote in his Elegy that, though

> I never knew thee:
> Me thou didst love unseene, so did I thee,
> It was our spirits lov'd then and not wee.[3]

About the year 1629 Olive's daughter Olivia, then under sixteen, eloped with and married Charles Cotton the elder. Olive herself was daughter and heir to Edward Beresford, of Beresford, Staffs, and of Bentley, co. Derby, and so Beresford came to the Cotton family. Cokaine wrote '*To my honoured Cousin* Mr. Charles Cotton *Junior*' how

> *Donne, Suckling, Randolph, Drayton, Massinger,*
> *Habbington, Sandy's, May,* my acquaintance were;

---

[1] Dugdale, *Warwickshire*, 1730, Index, s.v. Cokaine.
[2] *Small Poems of Divers Sorts*, 1658, p. 217.   [3] El[10] 18–20.

Johnson, Chapman, and *Holland* I have seen,
And with them too should have acquainted been.
What needs this Catalogue? Th'are dead and gone,
And to me you are all of them in one.[1]

The first of his Funeral Elegies in the same volume
is that 'On the Death of My very good Friend, Mr.
Michael Drayton.' He associates Drayton with Shakespeare and the Avon:

You *Swans* of *Avon*, change your fates, and all
Sing, and then die at *Drayton's* Funeral.
Sure shortly there will not a drop be seen,
And the smooth-pebbled Bottom be turn'd green,
When the *Nymphes* (that inhabit in it) have
(As they did *Shakespeere*) wept thee to thy grave.[2]

In this group of Drayton's Derbyshire and Staffordshire friends we must reckon also Izaak Walton, whose
bent, says his editor, Mr Geoffrey Keynes, was 'a
genius for friendship' and whom we know so intimately
and affectionately from Cotton's Second Part of *The
Compleat Angler*. It was natural that one who shared
Drayton's great love for the English countryside as
well as for books, should be a reader of his poetry.
We must believe Drayton to have been an angler too.
Showing how the salmon makes shift to go up river
from the sea, the author of *The Compleat Angler* takes
the description of the Salmon-leap in the river Tivy
'out of *Michael Draiton*, my honest old friend.'[3] In
another passage he quotes the first twelve lines of the
32nd Sonnet of *Idea*, in which 'my old deceased friend,
Michael Draiton,' writing of the Anker, comprehends
also the English rivers of 'principal note.'[4] In 1624,
living on the north side of Fleet Street two doors west
of Chancery Lane, Walton would have had Drayton for

---

[1] Ibid. p. 234.   [2] Ibid. p. 66.
[3] *Compleat Angler*, 3rd ed. 1661, p. 136; PO⁶39–55.
[4] *Compleat Angler*, 2nd ed. 1655, p. 330.

his near neighbour. He was his junior by some thirty years.

Another of Drayton's Derbyshire friends was Sir Henry Willoughby of Risley, 'the noble knyghte and my most honord ffrend . . . one of the selected Patrons of these my latest poems,' to whom Drayton presented the copy of *The Battaile of Agincourt* now in the Victoria and Albert Museum.[1] Willoughby had property in Warwickshire too, for by his marriage with Elizabeth, daughter and co-heir of Sir Henry Knolles, knight, of Greys, Oxon, he had come into possession of the manor of Nuneaton. Risley is only a few miles from Clifton, Notts, the seat of the ancient family of that name. A ballad concerning the tragic fate of a beautiful girl of humble station, who jilted James Bateman in order to marry Jerman Clifton, survives in chap-books of various dates. The story also furnishes the plot of a play called *The Vow-Breaker, or the Faire Maid of Clifton*, written by William Sampson, who in 1628 was in the service of Sir Henry Willoughby at Risley. He dedicated the play to Mrs Anne Willoughby. There is reason to believe that *The Vow-Breaker* is a recasting of the play called *Black Bateman of the North*, for the First Part of which Drayton, Chettle, Dekker and Wilson received payment from Henslowe in May 1598.[2] We know, at any rate that Drayton was acquainted with the place and the family of Clifton; for in his Elegy to Lady Penelope Clifton he tells how, when he heard of her death:

> With this ill newes amaz'd by chance I past,
> By that neere Grove, whereas both first and last,
> I saw her, not three moneths before shee di'd.[3]

She died in October 1613, and the context shows that it was early harvest-time when Drayton met her in the

[1] See facsimile.
[2] See above, p. 102; K. Tillotson,'William Sampson's *The Vow-Breaker*,' in *MLR*, July 1940.   [3] El[6] 33–5.

To the noble knight
my much honord frend
the worthy S.r Henry
willoughbye one of the speciall
Patrons of these my latest
Poems

from his Seruant

Mi: Drayton

Grove, which is still standing near the river Trent at Clifton. Full of extravagant flattery of the deceased lady, the Elegy seems to want the note of sincerity and true affection which marks those written for Drayton's more intimate friends. Lady Penelope was the daughter of Sidney's 'Stella,' Penelope Devereux, the wife of Robert Rich, Earl of Warwick. Thoroton gives the following account of Sir Gervase Clifton and his young wife:

> This Gervase was . . . generally the most noted person of his Time for Courtesy. He was very prosperous and beloved of all. He generously, hospitably, and charitably entertained all, from the King to the poorest Beggar. . . He was an extraordinary kind Landlord, and good Master, Husband to seven Wives. The first was the beautiful Penelope, Daughter of Robert Earl of Warwick and Penelope his Wife, (howbeit Ch. Blount Lord Mountjoy Earl of Devonshire paid her Portion). She was Mother of the wretched unfortunate Sir Gervas his father's greatest foil. She died Oct. 26, 1613, aged 23 Years.[1]

There is a passage in Aubrey's *Lives*[1] in which that assiduous antiquary notes incorrectly against Drayton's name:

> Natus in Warwickshire at Atherston upon Stower.
> *qu*. Th. Mariett. Sʳ J. Brawne was a gret Patron of his.

He means Sir Richard Brawne, of Alscot Park, near Stratford-upon-Avon, whose daughter Lucy married Thomas Mariett of Whitchurch and brought him the adjoining estate of Alscot on the death of her father in 1650. The Rawlinson-Bright copy of *The Muses Elizium* (1630), sold at Sotheby's in 1928, bears an inscription said not to be in Drayton's hand:

> To the Noble Knight and my heighly esteemed

[1] Thoroton, *Notts*, ed. Thoresby, 1, p. 108.

ffrend Sr Richard Brawne all health and happiness ffrom his servante and ffrend Michell Drayton.[1]

Sir Richard was the eldest son of Sir Hugh Brawne, a vintner and citizen of London, who was knighted in 1603 and died in 1616, possessed of several properties in several counties, particularly Alscot, Preston-upon-Stour, Saintbury, Meon and Admington in Gloucestershire.[2] All these places are in the near neighbourhood of Stratford-upon-Avon and Clifford Chambers.[3]

[1] See *Book Prices Current*, 1928, p. 331. See also George Hibbert Sale (1829), no. 2851; B. H. Bright Sale (1845), no. 1855.

[2] Thomas in Dugdale, p. 677.

[3] See Atkyns, *Gloucestershire*, 1712, ff. 608–9.

P

CHAPTER XV

DRAYTON'S LATER YEARS

HIS RELIGIOUS OUTLOOK

WE have seen how the folio of 1627, containing *The Battaile of Agincourt*, from which it takes its name, is a chief source for what we know of Drayton's friendships and of his life. The poems in it, all but two of which are printed there for the first time, show that although the manner and the expression have changed, the spirit in which most of his early work was written is still alive. There is, indeed, no allusion to his Idea, and only the Elegy 'Upon the Death of his Incomparable Friend Sir Henry Rainsford' to show how his early love had matured into a life-long friendship. But the Dedication of the volume and the long poem which gives it its title make it clear that there still glowed within him that intense love for England, fired by the glories of her past history, which is the motive of *Poly-Olbion*. *Agincourt*, and still more *The Miseries of Queen Margarite*, which follows it, seem a little old-fashioned when judged by the literary fashions of Charles's reign. When they were written, however, Buckingham was preparing his expedition for the relief of the Protestants of La Rochelle, whom Richelieu was determined to reduce. Although to us it seems a far cry indeed from the victories of Henry V to that disastrous venture, Drayton's epic and the lines in which Jonson and Vaughan greet it, suggest that it may have been inspired by the nation's enthusiasm for the cause and that the poet wished to rekindle and rally to its support the chivalry of a decadent age. The Dedication, too, like many of the new poems show him conscious as ever of the poet's high mission and sensitive as ever of the sad neglect from which poetry was suffering:

To you those Noblest of Gentlemen, of these Renowned Kingdoms of Great Britaine: who in these declining times, have yet in your brave bosomes the sparkes of that sprightly fire, of your couragious Ancestors; and to this houre retaine the seedes of their magnanimitie and Greatnesse, who out of the vertue of your mindes, love and cherish neglected Poesie, the delight of Blessed soules, & the language of Angels. To you are these my Poems dedicated.

In *Agincourt* and *Queene Margarite* Drayton drew upon the material which he had quarried in writing much of his earlier work. In other poems of the volume, however, there is freshness of outlook and manner. In his Introduction to it Professor Hebel writes of the 'lightness of mood and deftness of touch' which mark *Nimphidia, The Quest of Cynthia,* and *The Shepheards Sirena,* all of them printed for the first time in that folio. The first two of these were almost certainly written in Drayton's later period. In style and manner and subject they are very like the Nimphals of *The Muses Elizium,* which were printed in 1630. They have an air of contentment and of a happy playfulness which, we like to think, may have sprung from happier conditions in Drayton's life. Once more we must search his own writings for what scanty evidence they may offer concerning the closing years of his career.

The Muses Elizium is dedicated to Edward Sackville, the 4th Earl of Dorset, who after Aston went to Spain seems to have taken his place as Drayton's chief patron, and the 'divine Poemes' that follow it 'to your Religious Countesse, my most worthy Lady.' 'I have ever founde that constancie in your Favours,' he writes to Dorset, 'since your first acknowledging of mee, that their durablenesse have now made me one of your family, and I am become happy in the title to be called Yours.'[1] Edward Sackville, the younger son of Robert

[1] Vol. III, p. 246.

Sackville, the second Earl, and grandson of the author
of 'The Induction' to *The Mirrour of Magistrates*, was
born in 1590. In 1612 he married Mary, daughter and
heir of Sir George Curzon, of Croxall in Derbyshire.
The precise description of Sirena's birthplace in *The
Shepheards Sirena* leaves little room for doubt that
Croxall is the place indicated, and that Sirena is Mary
Curzon herself:

> Neare to the Silver *Trent*,
> *Sirena* dwelleth . . .

Dove and Derwent both flow into Trent; but

> My Love was higher borne
> tow'rds the full Fountaines,
> Yet she doth *Moorland* scorne,
> and the *Peake* Mountaines.[1]

She was born, then, on some 'humble . . . streame' flow-
ing into the Trent above the confluences of the Dove
and Derwent with the Trent, but her birthplace was
neither in the Staffordshire Moorland nor the Peak of
Derbyshire. Croxall fulfils all these indications. It stands
on the little river Mease, which, half-hidden among
the willows, glides gently towards its outlet in the Trent
just below:

> *Messe* a daintie Rill,
> Neere *Charnwood* rising first, where she begins to fill
> Her Banks, which all her course on both sides doe
>   abound
> With Heath and Finny olds, and often gleaby ground,
> Till *Croxals* fertill earth doth comfort her at last
> When shee is entring *Trent*.[2]

Neither Camden nor Saxton makes any mention of
Croxall. Here, as so often in *Poly-Olbion*, Drayton seems
to be describing country well-known to him at first

---

[1] SS 165–166, 302–305.   [2] PO[26] 153–8.

hand and in some way linked with his own life or that of his special friends.[1]

After their marriage in 1612 Edward Sackville and his bride lived at Croxall for a while. It was there that Sackville received the challenge from Bruce, 2nd Lord Kinloss, which ended with the fatal duel at Bergen-op-Zoom in August 1613. Kinloss attacked his opponent with great fury and wounded him severely; but he was himself slain by a thrust of Sackville's sword. Sackville was for some time in disgrace. If Mary Curzon is Sirena and if Sackville is the Dorilus of *The Shepheards Sirena*, it is possible that the quarrel with Kinloss or else some other episode of his unruly youth was the subject of the letter and the occasion of the dilemma into which Dorilus was betrayed. Sackville was a man of brilliant parts, and had a wide circle of friends both at Court and amongst the wits and poets. In 1612 he even won a wager of five pounds from the Princess Elizabeth.[2] Donne was his guest at Knole. Jonson bore witness to his generous nature and to his kindly liberality, and Herrick to his reputation as a literary critic. Howell writes of the power of his personality and of his oratory:

> Where ere he sate he sway'd, and Courts did awe,
> Gave *Bishops Gospel*, and the *Judges* Law
> With such exalted Reasons, which did flow
> So cleer and strong, that made *Astræa* bow
> To his Opinion, for where He did side
> Advantag'd more than half the *Bench* beside.[3]

At Dorset House off Fleet Street he had Drayton for a near neighbour. When he succeeded his spendthrift brother Richard as fourth Earl in 1624, he sometimes

[1] An avenue of elms leading to the Hall from the North is known as Dryden's Walk. (R. Ussher, *An Historical Sketch of . . . Croxall*, 1881, p. 14.) Can this be a corruption of 'Drayton's Walk'?

[2] E. K. Chambers, *Elizabethan Stage*, IV, p. 181.

[3] *Epp. Ho-Elianae*, IV, 1655, pp. 115–6.

lived at Knole, but only as tenant, for the manor had been sold to a wealthy and friendly neighbour, known as 'Dog' Smith, towards the liquidation of his brother's debts.

Drayton's tribute to the 'Right Noble Religious and truely vertuous Lady Mary, Countess of Dorset,' is fully supported by what we know of her subsequent history. At the birth of Prince Charles in 1630 she was put in charge of the royal nursery. She remained Governess of the King's children down to the eve of her death in 1645, on which she was granted a public funeral at Westminster Abbey: so great was the honour in which this Royalist lady was held by Parliament.

It is possible that *The Muses Elizium* is in some sort an idealized counterpart of Knole, and that the shepherds and nymphs who there disport themselves represent at however great a distance youths and maidens of the Sackvilles' circle. Mertilla in the Fourth Nimphall may be Elizabeth Beaumont, the Mirtilla of the Eighth Eglogue,[1] who had married Thomas Seylyard, and was living near Sevenoaks in the neighbourhood of Knole. Young as were the three children of the Dorsets— Richard, born at Dorset House in 1622, afterwards the fifth Earl; Edward, who fought at Newbury, was captured at Kidlington in 1645 and was brutally murdered by a soldier of the Parliamentary army; and Mary, born at Knole in July 1625,—it is just possible that they were cast for the parts of Doron, Dorilus and Dorida in the Nimphalls,[2] say at some children's pageant held in the gardens or the Great Hall at Knole.

Just as Drayton's published work begins with *The Harmonie of the Church* dedicated to Jane Devereux, so it ends with the Divine Poems dedicated to the Countess of Dorset. Of these the first and last, *Noahs Floud* and *David and Goliah*, were printed in 1630 for the first time. *Moses His Birth and Miracles* had been printed

[1] ME⁴, Pa⁸ 141.   [2] ME¹, ME³.

by itself under the title *Moyses in a Map of His Miracles* in 1604. These religious poems, written at the beginning, the middle and the end of his career, suggest that throughout his life he was a devout student of the Bible, and especially of the Old Testament. At each of these periods we find that friends who knew the bent of his mind and of his genius—Catholics like Thomas Lodge in 1595[1] and John Beaumont in 1604,[2] and Samuel Austin the evangelical in 1629[3]—urged Drayton to 'turn divine.'[3] If we seek further evidence of his religious beliefs, we shall find it difficult to attach him to any one of the creeds or sects into which England had become divided. There are passages in the First Eglog of *The Shepheards Garland* which suggest both the thought and the manner of Robert Southwell's *St Peters Complaynt*, which is written in the same metre and verse-form, and of other poems by that Jesuit martyr. Though not yet in print, Southwell's work was already circulating in manuscript. Drayton's 'contrition, for follies past,' may be no more than the self-reproach of a tender conscience stirred by the spirit of Southwell's verse. There are lines in the same Eglog which seem to have been inspired by hymns of the Roman Breviary.[4] The last line of the Song to Elizabeth in the Third Eglog, however,

> *And thou under thy feet mayst tread, that foule seven-headed beast,*

shows anti-Roman bias. In the new version of the Song, first printed *Englands Helicon* in 1600, it was changed to:

> *And* Albion *on the* Appenines *advance her conquering Crest.*

---

[1] See p. 89.

[2] Cf. his verses before *Moses* 1604, Vol. III, p. 355.

[3] See p. 202-3.

[4] Cf. SG[1] 26–31 with passages in the hymns, 'Creator alme siderum,' 'Audi benigne conditor,' and 'Lucis Creator optime.'

In *Mortimeriados*[1] we are safe in seeing an allusion to
the religious quarrels that disturbed England in Drayton's own day. There is no corresponding passage in
The Barons Warres. It is natural that *The Heroicall
Epistles* that passed between Lady Jane Grey and Gilford
Dudley should show sympathy for those on the side of
the Reformed faith. *The Legend of Cromwell* narrates
the intrigues of Wolsey, Cromwell and the King which
led to the dissolution of the religious houses and the
sapping of the ancient faith. The account there given by
Cromwell's ghost provoked an early owner of the copy
of the Legend now at Harvard to write the word
'Papist' against Drayton's name on the title-page. At
the same time it gives a balanced account of some of the
evil conditions within the Church which made the
Reformation possible. *The Owle* satirizes abuses which
prevailed in the English Church as well as in the State.
Drayton shows in it a measure of sympathy for the
Catholics who were exiles for their faith. In the First
Song of *Poly-Olbion* (86–94) he writes with reverent
appreciation of the British and Irish saints who gave
their names to so many places in Cornwall; and in the
XXIVth he makes note of some 300 saints who were
born or laboured in this island. He reproves the
'fayned' miracles, indeed, recorded in their legends;
but he pours scorn upon the Puritan—

> thou that art so pure,
> The name of such a Saint that no way canst endure.[2]

'Antiquitie I love,' he proclaims; and it was doubtless
his love for antiquity as well as his religious sense that
led him, like Camden and, later on, Sir William Dugdale, to deplore the destruction of the abbeys and all
the material havoc wrought by the Reformation.[3] Although he enjoyed the patronage of men and women
whose families had acquired wealth and social dignity
out of the spoiling of the Church, he writes with bitterness of '*the new Gentrie*':

[1] Mo 1499–1554.   [2] PO[24] 45–6.   [3] Cf. PO[3] 293–314.

> in some things they did erre,
> That put their helpe her braverie to deface,
> When as the Wealth, that taken was from her,
> Others soon raysed, that did them displace,
> Their Titles and their Offices confer
> On such before, as were obscure and base.[1]

Drayton, as we have seen, had for friends devout Catholics like John Beaumont and Davies of Hereford and strong Protestants like Selden and Izaak Walton. He was drawn to men of good will, whatever their religious profession. The miniature, by Peter Oliver, now in the possession of the Duke of Portland, which is shown as the frontispiece of this volume, was perhaps made for some devout lady of his circle—Lady Dorset, for instance; and the motto inscribed on the inner locket, which encloses the head of Christ, may have been written for it by Drayton himself:

> *Let Christ*
> *first thought on be*
> *Els never*
> *thinck on me*

His hold on Christian faith in the Redemption is shown when he is writing of his grief at the death of Sir Henry Rainsford. He there protests that he would be well pleased with those who in certain circumstances would allow suicide,

> But that I am a Christian, and am taught
> By him who with his precious blood me bought,
> Meekly like him my crosses to endure.[2]

That Drayton's life was as clean and his moral character as high as we should expect from the tone of his poetry with its freedom from obscenity and the complete absence of any pandering to vice is known to us from the testimony of his contemporaries quoted else-

---

[1] *Cro.* 761–68.   [2] El[9] 65–70.

where in these pages. In his *Worthies* Fuller sums up that aspect of his character:

> Michael Drayton . . . was a pious Poet, his conscience having always the command of his fancy, very temperate in his life, slow of speech, and inoffensive in company.[1]

[1] *The Worthies of England,* 1662, p. 126.

CHAPTER XVI

DRAYTON'S DEATH AND FUNERAL

WE have seen that in July 1631, if the date on the last of his letters to Drummond is correct, Drayton was paying his yearly visit to Clifford, then in the possession of Anne Goodere's eldest son, Sir Henry Rainsford the younger. Before the end of the year he was dead. The actual date is said by Laing[1]— we do not know on what authority—to have been 23rd December, and that date is shown on some almanacks.[2] William Fulman the antiquary (1632–1688) has the following note about his death and funeral:

> 1631.—He dyed at his lodging in Fleet Street below Saint Dunstans Church,[3] not rich; but so well beloved, that the Gentlemen of the Four Innes of Court and others of note about the Town, attended his body to Westminster, reaching in order by two and two, from his Lodging almost to Strandbridge. He was buryed [ends].[4]

The position of Drayton's grave in the Abbey is indicated by Peter Heylyn in his *Examen Historicum* (1659), in which he makes certain 'Necessary Animadversions' on Fuller's *Church History of Britain*,[5] published four years before. Fuller had stated that Chaucer 'lies buried in the South-Isle of *St. Peters, Westminster*, and since hath got the company of *Spencer* and *Drayton* (a

---

[1] *Archæol. Scot.*, IV, p. 93.   [2] Elton, p. 145.

[3] We do not know when he first went to lodge there. It is worth noting that John Busby, Nicholas Ling, and John Smethwick, the booksellers who published many of Drayton's books, all had their shops at St Dunstan's.

[4] Bodl. Corpus Christi Coll. MSS., Fulman Collection, B2, 15. 'Strand-bridge . . . crossed the street and received the water which ran from the high grounds, through the present Catherine-street, and delivered it into the Thames.' (Pennant, *Some Account of London*, p. 95.)

[5] P. 152.

pair-royal of Poets) enough (almost) to make passengers feet to move metrically, who go over the place, where so much *Poetical dust* is interred.' Heylyn corrects him:

> Not *Draytons* company I am sure, whose body was not buryed in the South-Isle of that Church, but under the North wall thereof in the main body of it, not far from a little dore which openeth into one of the Prebends houses. This I can say on certain knowledge, being casually invited to his Funeral, when I thought not of it; though since his *Statua* hath been set up in the other place which our Author speaks of.[1]

In *The Appeal of Injured Innocence* (1659)[2] Fuller, in answering Heylyn's 'animadversion,' quotes the verses on Drayton's monument, and asks: 'Have *Stones* learnt to *Lye*, and abuse posterity? Must there needs be a *Fiction* in the Epitaph of a *Poet?*' The monument, shown on p. 244 of our third volume, is of black marble, and is surmounted by the bust of Drayton also in marble. It bears the following inscription:

> Michael Draiton Esq[r] a memorable Poet of this Age,
> Exchanged his Lawrell for a Crowne of Glorye
> A° 1631:
> Doe pious Marble: Let thy Readers Knowe
> What they, and what their children owe
> To DRAITONS name; whose sacred dust
> Wee recommend unto thy TRUST:
> Protect his Mem'ry, and Preserve his Storye:
> Remaine a lastinge Monument of his Glorye;
> And when thy Ruines shall disclame
> To be the Treas'rer of his NAME;
> His NAME, that canot fade, shall be
> An everlasting MONUMENT to thee.

On a scutcheon on the left is Drayton's crest, On a sun

---

[1] Heylyn, *Examen Historicum*, 1659, p. 69.
[2] Pt. II, p. 42.

in glory a cap of Mercury, and on the right his arms,
A winged horse.

'He lived at the bay-window house next the Eastend
of St Dunstans ch in Fleetstreet,' says Aubrey. 'Sepult.
in N + of W. Abbey and the Countess of Dorset
(Clifford) gave his monument. This Mr Marshall (the
stonecutter) who made it, told me so.'[1] Aubrey has here
confused Mary Countess of Dorset with her redoubtable sister-in-law, Anne Clifford, wife of Richard, the
3rd Earl of Dorset, and later Countess of Pembroke
and Montgomery. He described her correctly to
Anthony Wood in a letter dated 17 May 1673:[2] 'The
Countess of Dorset, that was governess to Prince
Charles, now our King, was at the cost of erecting his
monument.' In his *Brief Lives* he records the inscription on the monument 'in Westm. Abby near Spencer';
and he has the following note:

> Mr Marshall the Stone-cutter of Fetter Lane, also
> told me, that these verses were made by Mr Francis
> Quarles, who was his great Freind: and whose head
> he wrought curiously in playster, and valued for his
> sake. 'Tis pitty it should be lost. Mr Quarles was a
> very good man. Here is his bust in Alabaster.

The lines have also been attributed to Ben Jonson[3]
and Thomas Randolph.[4]

Drayton died poor as he had lived. Henry Peacham,
writing of the small remuneration which men of letters
received in return for their dedications,[5] says that

> Honest Mr. *Michael Drayton* had about some five
> pound lying by him at his death, which was *Satis*

---

[1] Bodl. MS. Aubrey 8, f. 8^v.
[2] MS. Wood F.39 fo. 208.
[3] See W. D. Briggs, 'Studies on Jonson,' in *Anglia* XXXIX, 1916,
p. 211. He doubts Jonson's authorship. It was attributed to
Jonson by Winstanley, *Lives of the Poets*, 1687, p. 107.
[4] Bodl. MS. Ash. 38, f. 184.
[5] *The Truth of our Times*, 1638, p. 38.

viatici ad cælum, as *William Warham*, Bishop of *Canterbury*, answered his Steward, (when lying upon his
death-bed, he had asked him how much money hee
had in the house, hee told his Grace Thirty pounds).

The sum of Drayton's fortune was just about that. He
left no will; and his brother Edmund, to whom was
granted the administration of his little estate, returned
the inventory of his goods at £24 8s. 2d.[1]

[1] The document, preserved at Somerset House, is printed as
follows:

Mense Januarii, 1631 /1632 N.S./

Michael Drayton. Decimo septimo die p[er] m[agist]rum Will-
mum James legum D[o]c[t]orem Surrogatum &c. Em[an]avi[t]
Com[m]issio Edmundo Drayton fr[atr]i natural[i] et l[egi]timo
Michael Drayton nup[er] p[ar]o[chia]e S[anct]i Dunstan in
occiden[te] London ab intestato Defunct[o] Ad administrand[a]
bona, &c., de bene, &c., ac de pleno, &c., necnon de vero, &c.,
Jurat., &c., Salvo jure, &c.

Civit London.

Ascen[sione] In[ventorium] ex[peditum]. 24^{li} 8^s 2^d.

(Elton, p. 147.)

HE died, not rich indeed, 'but so well beloved.' And though he made no testamentary bequest, he left a memorial of his devotion to his mistress which is unique in all literature. It is said that there sometimes flashes across the consciousness of a drowning man a review of his whole life: so, in the verses which Drayton made 'the night before he dyed,' there seems to pass before his mind his lifelong service of Anne Goodere from the time when her 'eyes taught mee the alphabet of love' down to that last day of his life:

So well I love thee, as without thee I
Love nothing. If I might choose, I'd rather die
Than be one day debar'd thy company.

Since beasts, and plants do grow, and live and move,
Beasts are those men, that such a life approve.
He only lives, that deadly is in love.

The corn that in the ground is sown, first dies,
And of one seed do many ears arise.
Love, this world's corn, by dying multiplies.

The seeds of Love first by thy eyes were thrown
Into a ground untill'd, a heart unknown
To bear such fruit, till by thy hands t'was sown.

Look as your looking-glass by chance may fall,
Divide and break in many pieces small,
And yet shews forth the selfsame face in all,

Proportions, features, graces just the same;
And in the smallest piece as well the name
Of fairest one deserves, as in the richest frame.

So all my thoughts are pieces but of you,
Which put together makes a Glass so true
As I therein no other's face but yours can view.[1]

[1] Bodl. MS. Ash. 38, f. 77; Unc[17] n. The spelling is modernized here.

ADDENDA ET CORRIGENDA

PAGE 13, line 8 from the bottom, for Guy's Cliff read Guy's Cliffe.

Page 30. For Sir Henry Goodere's supposed kinship with Sir Philip Sidney see the Goodere pedigree on p. 227.

Page 31, lines 10–11. For Sir James Harington read Sir Henry Harington. Thomas West was the future Lord de la Warr, first Governor of Virginia.

Page 37, line 16. Thomas Goodiere of Newgate Street, Herts., was probably the grandson of William Goodere, brother of John Goodere (d. 1513–4), from whom the Gooderes of Polesworth were descended. See pedigree, p. 227.

Page 83, line 26. Sir Henry Rainsford died in January 1621–2. The Clifford Register records his burial on 30 January 1621(–2), but his monument (see p. 53) gives the date of his death as '27th of January 1622.'

Page 91. Hassel's verses in *Englands Heroicall Epistles* were first printed in the edition of 1598.

Page 103, l. 3 from the bottom, for 9 Nov. read 12 Nov. In the footnote for Mundy read Munday.

Page 134. Add to Note 3: In *Polyolbion*, XIII, 187–88 Drayton seems to be alluding to the rebuffs he had encountered at Court and to his changed relations with the Countess of Bedford:

'nor of a pin he wayes
'What fooles, abused kings, and humorous ladies raise.'

Page 153. Drayton was presumably at Tixall 31 May 1609, when he signed his name in full, 'Michaell Drayton,' as witness to Aston's signature on a tripartite indenture of lease between Sir Thomas Gresley of Drakelow, Co. Derby, his son and wife; Symon Jasson of Drakelow, and Thomas Sanders of Lullington, Co. Derby; and Sir Walter Aston of Tyxall, concerning the manor of Coulton, Staffs., and other estates. (BM, MS. Facs. Supp. VI t.)

CONJECTURAL FAMILY TREE OF MICHAEL DRAYTON

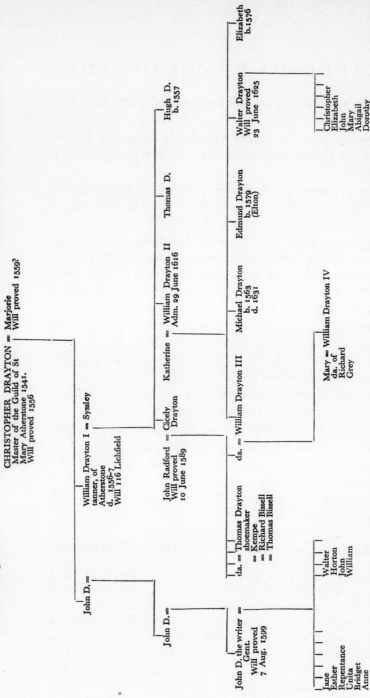

CHRISTOPHER DRAYTON = Marjorie
Master of the Guild of St   Will proved 1559?
Mary Atherstone 1541.
Will proved 1556

John D. =

William Drayton I = Syssley
tanner, of
Atherstone
d. 1556-7
Will 116 Lichfield

John Radford = Cicely
Will proved   Drayton
10 June 1589

Katherine = William Drayton II   Thomas D.   Hugh D.   Elizabeth
             Adm. 29 June 1616   b. 1557   b. 1576

da. = William Drayton III

Michael Drayton   Edmund Drayton   Walter Drayton
b. 1563   b. 1579   Will proved
d. 1631   (Elton)   23 June 1625

John D. =

da. = Thomas Drayton
      shoemaker
      = Kempe
      = Richard Bissell
      = Thomas Bissell

Mary = William Drayton IV
da. of
Richard
Grey

John D., the writer
Gent.
Will proved
7 Aug. 1599

Walter
Horton
John
William

Jane
Esther
Repentance
Unita
Bridget
Anne

Christopher
Elizabeth
John
Mary
Abigail
Dorothy

*I have notes of other children of William Drayton (III?, IV?), bapt. at Mancetter,
but owing to the War I have not been able to confirm them by the Mancetter Register.
They are: Elinor (9 Oct. 1577); Samuel (15 Feb. 1580); Edward (30 Mar.
1580); Richard (28 Sept. 1580).*

*According to the Register of St Gregory's near St Paul's, London, John Drayton
married Anne Goodyeare at that Church 4 March 1572-3. I have not been able to
trace the connection (if any) of John with the Draytons of Atherstone or of Anne
with the Gooderes of Polesworth.*

B.H.N.

PEDIGREE OF GOODERE OF POLESWORTH

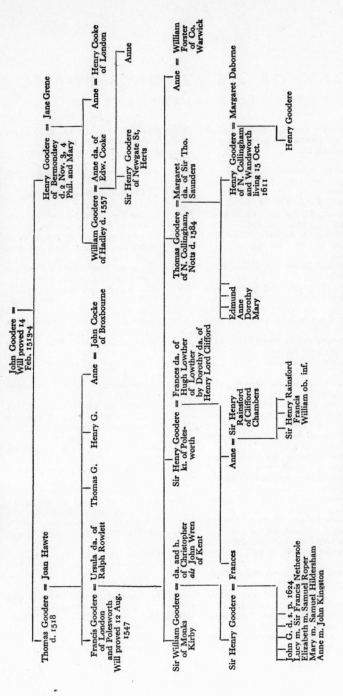

John Goodere =
Will proved 14
Feb. 1513-4

Thomas Goodere = Joan Hawte
d. 1518

Francis Goodere = Ursula da. of
of London   Ralph Rowlett
and Polesworth
Will proved 12 Aug.
1547

Thomas G.   Henry G.

Anne = John Cocke
       of Broxbourne

Henry Goodere = Jane Grene
of Bermondsey
d. 2 Nov. 3, 4
Phil. and Mary

Anne = Henry Cooke
       of London

William Goodere = Anne da. of
of Hadley d. 1557   Edw. Cooke

Sir Henry Goodere
of Newgate St,
Herts

Anne

Sir Henry Goodere = Frances da. of
kt. of Poles-   Hugh Lowther
worth   of Lowther
                     by Dorothy da. of
                     Henry Lord Clifford

Thomas Goodere = Margaret
of N. Collingham,   da. of Sir Tho.
Notts d. 1584   Saunders

Anne = William
       Forster
       of Co.
       Warwick

Edmund
Anne
Dorothy
Mary

Henry Goodere = Margaret Daborne
of N. Collingham
and Wandsworth
living 15 Oct.
1611

Henry Goodere

Sir William Goodere = da. and h.
of Monks   of Christopher
Kirby   als John Wren
                      of Kent

Anne = Sir Henry
       Rainsford
       of Clifford
       Chambers

Sir Henry Rainsford
Francis
William ob. inf.

Sir Henry Goodere = Frances

John G. d. s. p. 1624
Lucy m. Sir Francis Nethersole
Elizabeth m. Samuel Roper
Mary m. Samuel Hildersham
Anne m. John Kingston

FITZWILLIAMS—COOKE—BACON—CECIL—ROWLETT—GOODERE—SIDNEY

Ursula Rowlett's* mother, Sir Henry Goodere's* grandmother, was Margaret, daughter of Sir Anthony Cooke,* of Gidea Hall, Essex, by Anne, daughter of Sir William Fitzwilliams. (See page 25.) Sir Anthony Cooke's* daughter, Mildred, was married to Sir William Cecil,* Lord Burghley, and his daughter Anne to Sir Nicholas Bacon.* Sir Henry therefore was first cousin once removed to Sir Robert Cecil,* Earl of Salisbury, and also to

Anthony and Francis Bacon.* He was great-nephew to William Cooke* of St Martin's-in-the-Fields, and first cousin once removed to the younger Sir Anthony Cooke.* Sir William Fitzwilliams's grandson, Sir William,* (d. 1599) married Anne, daughter of Sir William Sidney* and aunt to Sir Philip Sidney.*

*Refer to the index and text for these names.

INDEX OF DRAYTON'S POEMS

WITH THEIR ABBREVIATIONS

Unless otherwise stated, superior figures refer to the number of the Canto, Eclogue, Song, Nimphall, etc.

References in ( ) are to pages in Vols. I–V of the Shakespeare Head edition. See also the Bibliography in Vol. V.

BA   *Battle of Agincourt, The* (III, 9; V, 192), 23, 136, 186, 201–2, 206, 210–1

BW   *Barons' Wars, The* (II, 9; V, 63), 12, 23, 47, 59, 97, 111, 129–30, 149, 175, 193, 200, 216

Cro   *Cromwell, The Legend of Great*, (II, 451; V, 167), 14, 84, 99, 152, 202, 216–7

DG   *David and Goliah* (III, 418; V, 228), 214

DP   *Divine Poems* (III, 324; V, 224), 214

EHE   *England's Heroical Epistles* (II, 129; V, 97), 57, 71, 85, 88, 91, 94–5, 97, 99, 104, 111, 124, 132, 175, 202, 216

EHE¹ –*Rosamond and K. Henry II* (II, 133; V, 102), 57, 69, 72

EHE² –*K. John and Matilda* (II, 147; V, 104), 72

EHE³ –*Queen Isabel and Mortimer* (II, 160; V, 106), 73

EHE⁴ –*The Black Prince and the Countess of Salisbury* (II, 175; V, 108), 17, 56, 86, 110, 148

EHE⁵ –*Queen Isabel and Richard II* (II, 188; V, 113), 56–7, 62, 74

EHE⁶ –*Queen Katharine and Owen Tudor* (II, 201; V, 116), 75–6, 169

EHE⁷ –*Elinor Cobham and Duke Humphrey* (II, 215; V, 119), 85, 110

EHE⁸ –*William De-La-Poole and Queen Margaret* (II, 230; V, 122), 77

EHE⁹ –*Edward IV and Mistress Shore* (II, 247; V, 126), 20, 78, 94

EHE¹⁰ –*Mary the French Queen and Charles Brandon* (II, 261; V, 128), 13, 17, 79

EHE¹¹ –*Henry Earl of Surrey and the Lady Geraldine* (II, 277; V, 130), 84

EHE¹² –*The Lady Jane Gray and Gilford Dudley* (II, 295; V, 133), 32

El   *Elegies upon Sundry Occasions* (III, 203; V, 213), 186

El¹   –*Of his Lady's not Coming to London* (III, 203; V, 214)

El²   –*To Master George Sandys* (III, 206; V, 214), 125, 195

El³   –*To William Browne* (III, 209; V, 215), 192, 194

El⁴   –*Upon the Three Sons of the Lord Sheffield* (III, 213; V, 215), 70

El⁵   –*To the Lady I.S.* (III, 216; V, 215)

El⁶   –*Upon the . . . Lady Penelope Clifton* (III, 219; V, 216), 206

El⁷   –*Upon the Lady Aston's Departure for Spain* (III, 223; V, 216), 155

El⁸   –*To Henry Reynolds* (III, 226; V, 216), 16–7, 87, 90, 109, 137–8, 189–90, 190

El⁹   –*Upon . . . Sir Henry Raynsford* (III, 232; V, 217), 52, 217

El¹⁰ –*Upon . . . the Lady Olive Stanhope* 236; V, 217), 204

El¹¹ –*To William Jeffreys* (III, 238; V, (III, 217), 155, 195

El¹² –*Upon Mistress Eleanor Fallowfield* (III, 242)

EP   *Endimion and Phœbe* (I, 125; V, 19), 46, 57, 69, 87–90, 124, 175, 200

HC   *Harmony of the Church, The* (I, 1; V, 1), 14, 23, 36, 163, 214

Id   *Idea* (II, 309; V, 137), 44, 47, 96, 100, 111, 144–5, 176, 197

Idᵃ   Sonnets not in *Idea's Mirror* 1594 or *Idea* 1619 (I, 485 V, 56), *Idea the Shepherds' Garland*, see SG

IM   *Idea's Mirror* (I, 95; V, 13), 11, 12, 40–3, 45, 47, 71, 87–90, 97, 109, 143–4, 175–6

JO   *Sir John Oldcastle* (I, 393; V, 44), 103–4, 110.

Maᵃ   *Matilda* (1594) (I, 209; V, 32), 46, 56–7, 82, 88, 90, 97, 99, 111, 144

Maᵇ   *Matilda* (1619) (II, 411; V, 156)

Maj   *Majesty of K. James, To the* (I, 469; V, 33), 126–8, 130, 133, 202

MBM   *Moses in a Map of his Miracles* (1604) (III, 355; V, 225), 35, 150, 152, 200, 214–5
      –*his Birth and Miracles* (1630)

MC   *Moon-Calf, The* (III, 166; V, 209)

ME   *Muses' Elizium, The* (III, 245; V, 220), 35–6, 163, 193, 202, 208, 211, 214

MM   *Man in the Moon, The* (II, 574; V, 190), 23

MMa   *Miseries of Queen Margaret, The,* (III, 73; V, 197), 210–1

Mo   *Mortimeriados* (I, 305; V, 41), 36, 57, 59, 87, 94, 107–8, 111, 137, 149, 163, 216

N   *Nimphidia* (III, 125; V, 202), 211

NF   *Noah's Flood* (III, 327; V, 224), 214

O   *Owl, The* (II, 477; V, 174), 20, 62, 97, 130–3, 138, 150, 175–6, 178, 199, 202, 216

Od   *Odes. With other Lyric Poesies* (II, 343; V, 144)

Od¹   *–To . . . Sir Henry Goodere* (II, 344; V, 146)

Od²   *–To Himself, and the Harp* (II, 347; V, 146), 8–12

Od³   *–To the New Year* (II, 350; V, 146)

Od⁴   *–To His Valentine* (II, 352; V, 146)

Od⁵   *–The Heart* (II, 355)

Od⁶   *–The Sacrifice to Apollo* (II, 357; V, 146), 138

Od⁷   *–To Cupid* (II, 359; V, 147)

Od⁸   *–Amouret Anacreontic, An* (II, 360; V, 147)

Od⁹   *–Love's Conquest* (II, 362)

Od¹⁰   *–To the Virginian Voyage* (II, 363; V, 147), 82

Od¹¹   *–An Ode Written in the Peak,* (II, 365; V, 147)

Od¹²   *–His Defence against the Idle Critic* (II, 366; V, 147)

Od¹³   *–To His Rival* (II, 368)

Od¹⁴   *–A Skeltoniad* (II, 370; V, 147)

Od¹⁵   *–The Cryer* (II, 371; V, 147)

Od¹⁶   *–To His Coy Love* (II, 372; V, 147)

Od¹⁷   *–Hymn to His Lady's Birth-Place* (II, 373; V, 147), 41, 51–2

Od¹⁸   *–To the Cambro-Britons* (II, 375; V, 147)

Odᵃ   *Odes not reprinted in 1619* (I, 489; V, 57)

Pa¹⁻¹⁰   *Pastorals* I–X (II, 515; V, 183), 41, 48, 83, 87, 91–2, 95, 98, 133–4, 193, 198

PGᵃ   *Peirs Gaveston* (1593–4) (I, 157; V, 23), 23, 36–7, 46, 57, 70, 90, 92, 97, 99, 111, 144

PGᵇ   *Pierce Gaveston* (1619) (II, 431; V, 161)

PO   *Poly-Olbion* (IV, V, 230) 2, 11, 14, 21, 23, 50–1, 70, 82, 92, 94–5, 97, 99,

PO *cont.*—127, 135, 137, 152–3, 159–73, 175–6, 179–80, 183–4, 188–9, 193, 201, 205, 210, 212, 216

Poems Lyric and Pastoral 59, 91–2, 97, 152

Plays written for the Admiral's Company, 101–7, 206

PT   *Pæan Triumphal, A* (I, 479; V, 55), 127

QC   *Quest of Cynthia, The* (III, 147; V, 206), 211

Redemption of Time, For D.P.'s The 135

Roᵃ   *Robert D. of Normandy* (1596) (I, 247; V, 38), 37, 57, 74, 97, 99–100, 111, 144

Roᵇ   *Robert D. of Normandy* (1619) (II, 383; V, 149), 134, 175

SG   *Shepherds' Garland, Idea the* (I, 45; V, 4), 24, 40–5, 48–9, 59, 70, 87–9, 92, 97, 99, 109, 133, 212–3, 215

SS   *Shepherds' Sirena, The* (III, 155; V, 206), 134, 211

Unc   Uncollected Poems (V, 57)

Unc¹   –To Thomas Morley (I, 493; V, 58), 99

Unc²   –For Anthony Munday (I, 493; V, 58), 99

Unc³   –For Nicholas Ling's *Politeuphuia*, (I, 494; V, 58), 97, 99

Unc⁴   –To Christopher Middleton (I, 494, V, 58), 98–9

Unc⁵   –*Rowland's Madrigal* (I, 495; V, 59), 98–9

Unc⁶   –For Thomas Palmer (I, 497; V, 59)

Unc⁷   –To Nicholas Geffe (I, 498; V, 59)

Unc⁸   –To John Davies (I, 499; V, 59), 99, 196

Unc⁹   –To Sir David Murray (I, 499; V, 59), 197

Unc¹⁰   –To Thomas Coryate (I, 500; V, 59), 197–8

Unc¹¹   –To William Browne (I, 502; V, 60), 194

Unc¹²   –To George Chapman (I, 503; V, 60), 66, 191

Unc¹³   –To Abraham Holland (I, 504; V, 60)

Unc¹⁴   –To Thomas Vicars (I, 504; V, 60)

Unc¹⁵   –To Sir John Beaumont (I, 505; V, 60), 193

Unc¹⁶   –To Mr Robert Dover (I, 506; V, 61), 198

Unc¹⁷   –Verses made by D the night before he died (I, 507; V, 61), 54–5, 223

Weever, To John, 99

INDEX OF NAMES

A Bell, Richard, 8
Adams, J. Quincy, 82, 121, 135
Admington, 209
Agrippa, Cornelius, 23
Alexander, Sir William, 95, 96, 124, 137, 140, 142, 161, 173, 174, 176, 177, 180, 182–91
— Janet (Erskine), Lady, 178, 180, 184, 185, 187
Allen, P. S., *Erasmus*, 20
Alleyn, Edward, 101
Allot, Robert, 97, 98
Alscot, 208, 209
Althorpe, 127
Amadas, Capt., 82
Amwell, Herts, 90
Anacreon, 22
Androwes, George, 112, 114, 116, 118–21
Anker, r., 2, 3, 11, 12, 40, 41, 42, 46, 47, 48, 51, 83, 87, 167, 194, 205
Anne of Denmark, Queen, 64, 174
Aquinas, St Thomas, 183
Archelaus, 22
Arden, Osbert, 13
Arden, forest of, 11, 12, 48, 83, 166
Ariosto, 22
Armada, Spanish, 30, 35
Armin, Robert, 112, 113
Arnhem, 30
Ashbourne, 203
Ashley, Sir Anthony, 115, 116
Ashton, Thomas, 21
Astley Castle, 13
Aston, Anne (Lucy), Lady, 146
— Constantia, w. of Walter Fowler, 156
— Sir Edward, 146, 147
— Gertrude (Sadleir), Lady, 147, 157
— Herbert, 156
— James, 5th Lord, 157
— Joyce, 146
— Roger, 125
— Sir Walter, 1st Lord, 59, 86, 125, 130, 141, 145–58, 211
— Walter, 3rd Lord, 146
Atherstone, 2, 4, 5, 6, 7, 8, 9, 10, 14, 15, 16, 41, 208
Atkyns, Sir John, 18,
— Sir Robert, 209
Aubrey, John, 2, 208, 221
Augustine, St, 42
Austin Friars, 14, 15, 77
Austin, Samuel, 202, 215
Avon, r., 46, 205

B Acon, Francis, 12, 61, 66, 82, 131
— Sir Nicholas, 25, 30
Baginton, 25, 38
Bagot, Richard, 146
Bandello, *Novelle*, 22
Banester, the Duke of Norfolk's servant, 28
Banquho, 170
Barclay, Alexander, 22
Barlowe, Arthur, voyager, 82
Barnfield, Richard, 88
Barry, Anne (Lording), 122
— 'David,' 'Lord,' 122
— Lording, 112–22
— Nicholas, 122
Bartlett, Benjamin, *Hist. of Manceter*, 4, 8, 10, 12, 42
Baskerville, Edward, 120
Basse, William, 198
Bastard, Thomas, 108
Bateman, James, 206
Baxter, Nathaniel, 131
Beaumont, Elizabeth, 193, 214, 215
— Francis, 138, 142, 191, 192, 193
— Henry, 192
— Sir John, 95, 136, 138, 142, 191–93, 196, 214
— Sir John, the younger, 193, 217
Bedford, Edward Russell, 3rd Earl of, 24, 56, 58, 61, 63, 64, 69, 74, 158
— Dowager Countess of, 61
— Lucy (Harington), Countess of, 33, 42, 56–69, 72, 74, 82, 84, 87, 88, 89, 94, 108, 126, 128, 133, 138, 141, 149, 158; death of her child, 66
Belvoir Castle, 103
Beresford, Edward, 204
— Olive (Lady Stanhope), 204
Bergen-op-Zoom, 213
Bess of Hardwick, *see* Cavendish, Lady, 71
Bevis of Hampton, 22, 91
Bill, John, King's printer, 185, 186
Birde, William, 120
Bissell, Richard, 6
— Thomas, 6
Black, Richard, 114
Blacklow Hill, 13
Blackwell, George, the Archpriest, 178
Blithfield, 146
Blount, Charles, Earl of Devonshire, Baron Mountjoy, 208
Bodenham, John, 97
Boethius, 23

Bolton, Edmund, 94
Boswell, Robert, 53
Bourges, 174
Bramcote, 18, 93, 204
Brandon, Charles, 1st Duke of Suffolk, 13
Bratyswast, 5
Brawne, Sir Hugh, 209
— Lucy, wife of Thomas Mariett, 208
— Sir Richard, 208, 209
Brigges, Daniell, 197
— Daniell, the younger, 197
Briggs, W. D., 221
Brogden, Richard, 114
Brooke, Christopher, 196
Brown, F. Howard, *Elizabethan School-
days*, 20
Browne, Elizabeth, 114
— John, 161
— William, 95, 134, 136, 142, 164, 191,
192, 194–5, 198, 202
Broxbourne, 37
Bryan, Sir Francis, 22
Buckhurst, Robert Sackville, Lord, 117
Buchanan, George, 23
Buckingham, George Villiers, 1st Duke
of, 81, 95, 210
Burdet, Sir Francis, 204
— Jane (Franceis), Lady, 204
— Thomas, 18, 93
Burford, 78
Burgoine, Robert, 37
Burleigh, Lord, *see* Cecil, William
Burley, 56, 60, 65, 127
Burton, Robert, 202
— William, 1, 202
Busbie, John, 161, 219
Buttevant, David Barry, 9th Viscount, 121
Byrd, William, 40

CAdiz, 71
Cadwallader, 169
Caesar, Julius, 23
Cambridge, 21, 98, 139, 167
Camden, William, 23, 24, 31, 93, 94, 150,
159, 162, 164, 166, 170, 212, 216
Canterbury, John Whitgift, Archbp of,
129
Caradoc of Llancarvan, *Historie of Cam-
bria*, 92
Carew, Sir George, 71,
— Thomas, 196
Carleton, Dudley, 65, 138
Carlisle, 27
Carpenter, Frederick Ives, 20
Carr, Sir Robert, 140, 173
Cato's *Distichs*, 20
Catullus, 192

Cary, Elizabeth (Tanfield), Viscountess
Falkland, 77–8
— Henry, 1st Viscount Falkland, 78
— Lucius, 2nd Viscount Falkland, 78
— Patrick, 78
Cavendish, Caundish, Henry, 70
— Elizabeth, Lady, 'Bess of Hardwick,' 71
— Sir William, 70
Cecil, Robert, Viscount Cranborne, 1st
Earl of Salisbury, 12, 27, 29, 68, 71, 81,
121, 125, 130, 131, 178
— William, Lord Burleigh, 25, 29, 30, 62
Chaloner, Sir Thomas, 178
Chamberlain, John, 138
Chambers, Sir E. K., 67, 110, 122, 142,
200, 213
Chapman, George, 35, 64, 66, 95, 136,
191, 195, 204, 205
Charing Cross, 120
Charlecote, 37, 142
Charles I, King, 95, 160, 177, 210, 214,
221
Charlwood, Surrey, 33
Charnwood forest, 167, 193, 212
Chatsworth, 70
Chaucer, Geoffrey, 22, 107, 219
Chester, Robert, *Loves Martyr*, 63, 174
Chettle, Henry, 102, 103, 105, 125, 158, 206
Cicero, 21, 23
Clifford, Anne, Countess of Pembroke and
Montgomery, 221
— Arthur, 157
— Dorothy, wife of Hugh Lowther, 26
— Florence (Pudsey), Lady, 26, 27
— Henry, 14th Lord, 26
— Rosamond, *see* Rosamond
Clifford Chambers, 46, 48, 50, 52–5, 83,
141, 168, 187, 188, 209, 219
Clifton, Sir Gervase, 208
— Jerman, 206
— Penelope (Rich), Lady, 206, 208
Clifton, Notts, 206, 208
Cnut, King, 105
Cobham, Elinor, 85
Cocke, Sir Henry, 37, 39
Coffey, Charles, 124
Coffin, Edward, S.J., 178
Coggeshall, Ralph of, 92
Cokaine, Anne (Stanhope), Lady, 204
— Sir Aston, 21, 203, 204
— Sir William, 203
Coke, Sir Edward, 95, 146, 147
Collingham, 33, 34, 35
Colvile, F. L., *The Worthies of Warwick-
shire*, 19
Combe Abbey, Warwickshire, 30, 37, 42,
56, 60

Combe, Hants, 53
Commines, Philip de, 23
Connan, Prince of Cornwall, 105
Cooke, Sir Anthony, 12, 26, 42, 71, 87, 120
— Sir Anthony, the younger, 12, 120
— James, 50, 51
— Margaret, 26
— Richard, 12
— William, 12, 114, 117, 118, 120
Cope, Rafe, 38, 39
Coryate, Tom, 136, 196
Corin, Corineus, 105
Cotswolds, 40, 48, 50, 167, 198
Cotton, Charles, the elder, 204
— Charles, the younger, 204, 205
— Olivia (Stanhope) 204
— Robert, 24
Courthope, Prof. W. J., 42
Covell, William, 21
Coventry, 5, 13, 26, 27, 30, 41, 51, 80
— Grammar School, 4, 13, 18–21, 27, 51, 91, 198
Cox, Captain, 91
— Leonard, 19, 20, 91
Coxeter, Thomas, 110
Cracow University, 19
Cromwell, Oliver, 17, 84, 216
Croxall, 212, 213
Crundell, H. W., 110
Culpeper family, 12
Cuninghame of Barns, 175 ; his daughter, 175
Cunningham, Peter, 160
Curdworth, 13
Curzon, Sir George, 212
— Mary, later Countess of Dorset, 212, 213

DAbridgecourt, Thomas, 36
Daniel, Samuel, 40, 64–6, 95, 96, 116, 127, 130, 139, 140, 142, 144, 149, 176, 189, 195
Dante, 22
Darnley, Henry Stewart, Earl of, 126
Davenant, Sir William, 196
Davies, (Sir) John, 21, 67, 137, 196
— John, of Hereford, 99, 217
Davis, Joseph, 178, 179, 181
Day, John, 112, 113
Dee, r., 171
Degge, Sir Simon, 146, 148
Dekker, Thomas, 67, 77, 102–3, 107, 206
Democritus, 23
Denmark, King of, 174
Derwent, r., 212
Desainliens (Holyband), Claude, 56

Desportes, Philippe, 22
Devereux, Jane, Lady, 14, 36, 214
— Penelope, Lady, 208
— Robert, *see* Essex
— Sir William, 14, 15
Dethick, Sir William, 150
Devonshire, Charles Blount, Earl of, 208
Dewe, Thomas, 161
D'Ewes, Sir Simonds, 201
Dickson, M. J., 123
Digbie, Sir George, 31
Don Quixote, 22, 43
Diodati, Theodore, 61
Dodoens, 168
Dodsley, James, 110
Donne, John, 40, 64, 65, 66–8, 81–2, 83, 87, 128, 157, 176, 183, 189, 196, 204, 213
Dorset, 3rd Marquis of, *see* Grey, Henry, Duke of Suffolk
— Thomas Grey, 1st Marquis of, 26
— Edward Sackville, 4th Earl of, 202, 211, 213–4
— Mary (Curzon), Countess of, 212, 214, 217, 221
— Richard Sackville, 1st Earl of, 116
— Richard Sackville, 3rd Earl of, 213
— Robert Sackville, 2nd Earl of, 214
Douza, Jan, 93
Dove, r., 95, 96, 212
Dovedale, 167
Dover, Robert, 198
Dowling, Margaret, 123, 129
Downton, Thomas, 120
Drew, F. W., 14
Drayton family : Abigail, 8; Bridget, 10; Christopher, 5, 7; Christopher, son of Walter, 8; Christopher, 9; Cicely, 6; Daniel, 8; Dorothy, 8; Edmund, 7, 222; Edward, 9; Esther, 10; Elizabeth, 9; Elizabeth (More), Walter's dau., 8; Harrington, 10; Hester, 10; Horton, 10; Hugh, 5, 6; Jane, 10; John, 5–7; John, Walter's son, 7; John, John's son, 10; Katherine, 6, 7; Mary, 8; Ralph, 9; Repentance, 10; Richard, 9; Robert, 5; Samuel, 9; Syssley, 5; Thomas, 5–7; Thomas, 6; Unita, 10; Walter, 7–9; William I, 5–7; William II, 5–9; 140; William III, 5, 8, 9, 10; William IV, 9; pedigree, 225
Drayton, Michael: date and place of birth, 1–4; the Draytons of Atherstone, 4–10; D's education and reading, 16–24; with the Gooderes of Polesworth, 32, 35–6, 37; with the Gooderes of Collingham, 33–5; in London, 35–6; relations with Anne Goodere, 41–54, 83; with Lucy

Harington, Countess of Bedford, 56–60, 63, 66–9, 72–5, 108, 128; early friends and patrons, 70–85; relations with Henry Goodere the younger, 79–80, 82; with Walter Aston, 86, 146–55; literary friends 1591–1603, 87–100; friendship with Stow, 92; with Camden, 93; with William Alexander, 95, 177–8, 180, 183, 185–90; testimony of Francis Meres, 96–7; friendship with Nicholas Ling, 97–8; relations with Weever, Hall, Marston, 99–100; writes plays for Henslowe, 101–7; his ambition as a playwright, 109–10; plays falsely attributed to him, 110; the Whitefriars playhouse, 112–23; sonnet to James VI of Scotland, 124; death of Elizabeth and accession of James, 126; disappointed hopes of preferment 127; relations with King James, 127–35; supposed friendship with Jonson and Shakespeare, 136–45; Jonson's criticism, 146–7; was D the 'rival poet' of Shakespeare's Sonnets? 141–5; correspondence with Drummond of Hawthornden, 173, 177–90; D's literary circle 1603–31, 191–209; friendship with Sir Edward and Lady Sackville (Earl and Countess of Dorset), 210–4; D's religious outlook, 214–8; his death, 218; his burial at Westminster Abbey, 218–21; Verses made 'the night before he dyed,' 223
— Works: see Index of Poems, 228
Drummond, William, of Hawthornden, 50, 54, 76, 95, 136, 139, 140, 142, 161, 164, 173–91, 219
Dudley, Ambrose, E. of Warwick, 70
— Douglas (Lady Sheffield), Countess of Leicester, 70
— Lord Guildford, 13, 32, 79, 216
— (Sir) Robert, 70
— Robert, Earl of Leicester, see Leicester
Dugdale, Sir William, 2, 10, 11, 12, 18, 26, 27, 29, 30, 31, 203, 204, 209, 216
Dulwich College, 101
Duperron, Cardinal, 78
Du Refuge, Eustache, 202
Dyce, Alexander, 36

EDge Hill, 25, 90
Edinburgh, 190
Editha, St, of Polesworth, 26
Edstone Hall, 30
Edward the Confessor, St, 105
— II, King, 129
— IV, King, 78
— the Black Prince, 85, 86, 148
Egbert, King, 26

Elderton, William, 17
Elizabeth, Queen, 15, 16, 20, 27, 28, 29, 30, 52, 61, 70, 71, 125, 126, 127, 128, 130, 135, 158, 189, 215
— Princess, Queen of Bohemia, 84, 213
Elphin, see Sidney, Sir P., 41
Elton, Oliver, 5, 42, 153, 219
Elvaston, 204
England's Helicon, 97, 215
Englebert, Lawrence, 3, 33, 35
'E.P.' (Edward Purefoy?), 57
Epicurus, 23
Erasmus, 19, 20, 23
Erskine, Sir William, 178, 187
— Janet, 178, see Alexander, Lady
Esk, r., 175
Essex, Robert, 2nd Earl of, 62, 63, 69, 71, 73, 129
Essex House, 62
Euripides, 22
Euphues, 61, 174
Eversden, John of, 92
Evesham, vale of, 48, 50
Exton, 56, 60, 74
Exton, Sir Piers, 102

FAlkland, Viscount, see Cary, 78
Feldon, the, 5
Fenny Drayton, 1, 7, 57
Fens, the, 168
Ferrers, John, 26
Ferrour, John, 124
Fisher, G. W., Annals of Shrewsbury School, 21
Fitzwalter, Lord Robert, 13
— Amabil, 13, 14
— Matilda, 13, 46, 111, 144
FitzWilliams, Sir William, 31
Fleanch, 170
Fleay, F. C., 90, 110
Fletcher, John, 153, 154, 196
Florence of Worcester, 92
Florio, John, 61, 67–8, 128
Foley, H., Records of the English Province S.J., 178, 179, 199
Formark, 204
Fowler, Constantia (Aston), 156, 157
— Walter, 156
— William, 174
Foxe, John, martyrologist, 76
Frederick, Elector Palatine, 202
Fripp, Edgar, 200
Froissart, 23, 164
Fuller, Thomas, 19, 140, 218–20
Fulman, William, 219
Fulmer, Thomas, 15
Furnivall, F. J., 47

Fitzgerald, Elizabeth, see Geraldine, 84

Gascoigne, George, 22
Gaveston, Piers, 13, 23, 45, 111, 144
Geoffrey of Monmouth, 23, 105, 162, 163, 164, 170, 171
George, Thomas, of Grendon, 6
Geraldine, Lady (Elizabeth Fitzgerald), 84
Gerard, John, Herball, 168
Gidea Hall, Essex, 25, 120
Gildas, 23
Gildas Sapiens (Nennius), 92
Giraldus Cambrensis, 23, 135, 159, 164
Gloucester, Humphrey Duke of, 85, 95
Gloucester, monks of, 46
Godiva, Lady, 51
Goodere, Anne (Lady Rainsford), 11, 26–7, 33, 37–55, 57, 219, 223
— Frances (Lady Goodere), 12, 18, 32, 33–4, 38, 42, 48, 79, 80, 83, 158
— Francis, 25
— Sir Henry, the elder, 12, 17–8, 22, 25–40, 46, 52–3, 56, 66–7, 74, 79–81, 91, 124, 141–2, 158
— Sir Henry, the younger, 17–8, 29, 30, 33, 37, 41, 48, 52, 78, 79, 80, 82–4
— Henry, s. of Thomas G. of Collingham, 33–5, 37
— Thomas, of Collingham, 33–5, 37, 39, 41
— Thomas, of Newgate St, 37
— Ursula (Rowlett), 25
— Sir William, 32–4, 37–8
— Margaret (Saunders; mar. Mering, Price, Englebert), 33–5
— Lucy (mar. Nethersole), 84
Goodere pedigree, 225
G[oodere?] H[enry?], The Vision of Matilda, 82
Goodier, Goodiere, Goodyere, see Goodere
Goodman, Gabriel, 121
Goodwin, Earl, 102, 105
Goodyear, T. Edw., 26, 35
Gosse, Edmund, 66, 82
Gower, John, 22, 107
Gracedieu Priory, 193
Gray, Arthur, 17, 88
Gray's Inn, 25
Greene, Thomas, 200
Greenstreet, James, 117, 120
Greenway, Anthony, 178, 199
— Anthony, his nephew, 200
Greenwich, 56
Greg, Dr W. W., 101–3, 105, 106, 122
Greville, Sir Fulke, 26
Grey, Henry, 3rd Marquis of Dorset, 1st Duke of Suffolk, 4, 13, 19, 121

Grey, Lady Elizabeth, 61
— Elizabeth (mar. Martin), 9
— Frances, 13, 121
— Lady Jane, 4, 12, 13, 32, 79, 216
— Lord John, 13, 121
— Lord Richard, 26
— Mary, 9
— Richard, 9
— Thomas, 1st Marquis of Dorset, 26
Greys, Oxon, 206
Grierson, Sir Herbert J. C., 157
Griscom, A., 171
Grismand, John, 161
Guarini, 175
Gunpowder Plot, 73, 178, 179
Guy of Warwick, 22
Guy's Cliffe, 13
Gwynn, Matthew, 61

Habington, William, 204
Hakluyt, Richard, 82, 164
Hales, John, 19; his Grammar, 21
Hall, John, 41, 50, 51, 54
— Joseph, 67, 99, 100
Halliwell-Phillipps, J. O., 106
Hampton Court, 64
Hampton-in-Arden, 11
Hardredeshull, Hugh de, 12
Harington, Anne (Kelway), Lady, 56–7, 61, 64, 68, 73–4
— Frances, 61
— Sir James, 31, 58
— Sir John, 1st Lord Harington of Exton, 30, 37, 56, 58, 60–1, 64–5, 68–9, 73
— Sir John, 2nd Lord, 61, 69
— Lucy, 33; see Bedford, Countess of
— Sir John, of Kelston, 60, 65, 67
Harold, 105
Harrison, William, 165
Hart, Andro, 161, 176, 180, 181, 184
— Thomas, 141
Hartshill, 2, 3, 7, 10–3, 14, 71, 120, 141
Haslewood, Joseph, 95
Hassall, Thomas, 91
Hathway, Richard, 103
Hauteville (Altavilla), John de 23
Hawthornden, 175; see also Drummond, William
Hayman, Robert, 202
Hayward, Sir John, 129
Hebel, Prof. J. William, 36, 68, 158, 167, 211
Heber, Richard, 197
Helme, John, 161
Henley-in-Arden, 11
Henry I, King, 101
— II, 58, 72

Henry IV, 129
— V, 210
— VII, 126, 169, 170
— VIII, 14, 25, 216
— Prince of Wales, 96, 147, 152, 154, 169, 177, 196, 197
Henslowe, Philip, 101-7, 111, 116, 120, 124, 158, 191, 206
Herbert, Sir Edward, 128
— Sir Henry, 106
— William, 3rd Earl of Pembroke, 149
Herrick, Robert, 213
Hesiod, *Georgics*, 191
Hewes, John, 82
Heylin, Peter, 219, 220
Heyward, Edward, 196, 201
Heywood, Thomas, 110, 198
Hibbert, George, 209
Higden, Ranulf, 23, 162
Hill, Amias, 14, 15
Hillebrand, H. N., 113, 115
Hole, William, 2
Holinshed, Raphael, 18, 23, 93, 105, 164, 170
Holland, Abraham, 18, 19, 198
— Henry, 19
— Hugh, 95, 205
— Philemon, 19, 163, 166, 198
Holyband, Claude (Desainliens), 56
Homer, 22
Honterus, Joannes, 97
Horace, 23
Hoveden, Roger of, 23, 92
Howard of Effingham, Lord, 101
— Henry, Earl of Surrey, 22, 76, 84, 176
— Henry, Earl of Northampton, 75-6, 85
Howell, James, 213
Huish, James, 85
Humber, r., 70
Hunter, Richard, 114
Huntingdon, Henry of, 92
Hurley, 13

Isabella, Queen of Richard II, 24, 58
— Queen of Edward II, 58, 73-4
Inns of Court, etc., 21; Inner Temple, 196, 200; Lincoln's Inn, 21; Middle Temple, 200; Staple Inn, 200
Islington, 35

James I, King, 3, 29, 52, 64-5, 68, 76, 78-9, 81, 95, 115, 124-35, 149-50, 154-5, 170-1, 189, 190, 201
James, William, 222
Jeffreys, William, 155
Jobber, Richard, 114
John, King, 69, 72

Jonson, Ben, 35, 40, 63-8, 76, 82, 87, 95, 127, 130, 136-9, 141, 164, 173, 191, 193, 195-6, 198, 200-1, 204, 210, 213, 221
Juvenal, 23, 199

Kastner, L. E., 176
Katherine, Queen of Henry V, 75, 105
Kelmarsh, 168
Kelway, Anne, 56; *see* Harington, Lady
Kempe, —, 6
Kenilworth Castle, 13, 29, 70, 91
Keynes, Geoffrey, 205
Kidd, —, 10
Kingsbury, 14
Kinloss, Bruce, 2nd Lord, 213
Kirkman, Francis, 121
Knole, 213-4,
Knolles, Sir Henry, 206
Knox, John, 174
Kysse, Robert, 5, 6

Laing, David, 186, 219
Lambarde, William, 94
Laneham, Robert, 91
Langbaine, Gerard, 121
Langland, William, 22
Lant, Thomas, 31
La Rochelle, 210
Lawrence, W. J., 121
Lee, Richard, 34
— Richard, 37
Leicester, Robert Dudley, Earl of, 29, 31, 38, 91
Leland, John, 170
L'Estrange Ewen, C., 122
Lily, William, 20
Lincoln's Inn, 21
Lindley, 1
Ling, Nicholas, 97-9, 219
Llewellyn, Prince of Wales, 170
Llwyd, Humphrey, 92, 164
Lodge, Thomas, 87-8, 106, 115, 214-5
London, 35, 54, 76-7, 79, 92, 108, 113, 120, 136, 139, 167, 183
— plague at, 36, 118
Low Countries, 30, 36, 38
Lownes, Humphrey, 161
— Mathew, 161-2
Lowther, 36
Lowther, Hugh, 26, 36
— Dorothy (Clifford), 26
— Frances, Lady Goodere, 26, 27
— Gerard, 27, 29
— Richard, 27
Lucan, 23, 199
Lucas, Edward, 84
— Henry, 84-5

Russell, Anne (Cooke), Lady, 71
— Edward, see Bedford
— Lucy, see Bedford
Rutland, Roger, 5th Earl of, 61
— Elizabeth (Sidney), Countess of, 61, 65

SAckville, see Dorset
Sadlier, Anne (Coke), Mrs, 147
— Gertrude, see Aston, Gertrude
— Ralph, 147, 150
— Sir Thomas, 147
Sage, Bishop, 139, 173, 176-7
St Dunstan's, 98, 108, 196, 219, 221, 222
St John's Hospital, Coventry, 19
St Martin's-in-the-Fields, 12
St Paul's, 31, 98
Saintbury, 209
Salisbury, Alice, Countess of, 85, 148
— William, 3rd Earl of, 106
Saluste du Bartas, Guillaume de, 22, 174
Sampson, William, 206
Sandys, George, 54, 124, 191, 196, 204
Sannazaro, 174, 175
Sapperton, Beale, 152
Saunders, Margaret, 33-5, see Goodere, Margaret
— Sir Thomas, 33
Savage, John, 18
— John, of the Inner Temple, 18
Saxton, Christopher, 162, 167, 212
Schelling, F. E., 102
Scory, Sir Edmund, 95
Segar, Sir William, 150
Selden, John, 24, 95, 159, 162-3, 166, 170, 196, 201, 217
Seneca, 23, 138
Severn, r., 11, 171
Seylyard, Elizabeth (Beaumont), 193, 214
— Sir Thomas, 193
Shad, Robert, 104
Shakerley, Marmion, 198
Shakespeare, John, 140, 141
— Judith, 141
— William, 4, 17, 20, 22, 63, 64, 66, 91-2, 96, 111, 136, 140-1, 149, 150, 153, 174, 176, 196, 200, 205
Sharpham, Edward, 112
Shaw, Weston, 12
Sheffield, Edmund, 3rd Baron, afterwards 1st Earl of Mulcaster, 70
— Lady, see Dudley, Douglas
Sherwood Forest, 167
Shore, Jane, 78, 123
Shoreditch, 101
Short, Dr R. W., 65, 68
Shrewsbury School, 21

Sibthorpe, Sybthorpe, Edward, 113, 117, 118
Sidney, Mary, Countess of Pembroke, 41, 65, 87
— Sir Philip, 30-1, 40, 58, 61, 65, 68, 87, 90, 96, 98, 132-3, 174, 176, 181, 194
— Lucy (Lady Harington), 58
— Sir Robert, afterwards 1st Earl of Leicester, 31
— Thomas, 31
— Sir William, 58
Simeon of Durham, 92
Simpson, Percy, 65, 68, 78, 136, 138
Silius Italicus, 23
Skelton, John, 22
Skiddaw, 36
Slatier, Slatyer, Martin, 112,-4, 116-9, 120-2
Sluys, 31
Smethwicke, John, 97, 219
Smith, Wentworth, 103
Somervile, John, 30
Sophocles, 22
Southampton, Henry Wriothesley, 3rd Earl of, 57, 61, 62, 142
Southern, John, 22
Southwark, 101
Southwell, Robert, 215
Spagnuoli, Baptista, Mantuan, 20, 40
Spain, 155
Spanish Armada, 36
Sparkenhoe Hundred, 1
Spenser, Edmund, 48, 68, 88, 96, 142, 171, 172, 176, 199, 219, 221
— Gabriel, 120
Standon, 147
Stanhope, Anne (Lady Cokaine), 204
— Sir John, 204
— Lady Olive (Beresford), 204
— Olivia (w. of Charles Cotton), 204
— Sir Thomas, 27
Stanmore, 150
Staple Inn, 200
Stepney, 56, 60
Stopes, Charlotte C., 57, 62
Stour, r., 46, 47, 208
Stow, John, 23, 36, 92, 93
Strachey, Sir Charles, 144
Strand, The, 36, 62, 120
Strange, Thomas, 179
Stratford-upon-Avon, 11, 26, 30, 41, 46, 141-2, 208-9
Suckling, Sir John, 204
Suffolk, Duke of, see Grey, Henry
Surrey, Earl of, see Howard, Henry
Sutton, Mr, Hartshill, 4
Swega, 105
Swinerton, Sir John, 76
Sylvester, Joshua, 9, 139-40, 189, 196

TAlbot, Thomas, 26
Tacitus, 23
Tamworth, 7
— Castle, 26
Tanfield, Elizabeth, 77, 78
— Lawrence, 77, 78
Tasso, 22, 174, 175
Taverns:—Devil and St Dunstan, 137–9;
Mermaid, 138; Naked Boy, 120; Tun, 138
Tayler, N., 9
Terence, 21
Thame, 19
Thames, the, 135, 171, 219
Theatres:—Fortune, 101; Globe, 63; Rose,
101; Whitefriars, 112–123
Theddingworth, 25
Theocritus, 22, 40
Thimelby, Catherine, 155
— Gertrude (Aston), 157
— Henry, 157
Thomas, John, 122
Thorn-Drury, G., 139
Thoroton, Robert, 208
Throckmorton, Clement, 26
Tibullus, 23
Tillotson, Kathleen, 68, 88, 102, 110, 129,
134, 206
Tilney, Edmund, 106
Tixall, 94, 153, 168
Tixall Letters, 154, 156
Tixall Poetry, 157
Tostig, 105
Tower of London, 27, 29, 94, 129, 179
Trent, r., 11, 40, 152, 208, 212
Trevill, William, 113–23, 120
Trinidad, 70
Trivet, Nicholas, 92
Trussell, John, 198
Tübingen, University of, 19
Tudor, Owen, 75, 109
— Mary, dau. of King Henry VII, Queen
of Louis XII, 13, 79
Tutbury, 71
Tweed, r., 184
Twickenham, 66, 82

UDall, Nicholas, 21
Upton, Nicholas, 23
Ussher, R., 213
Utrecht, 202

VAle of Clwyd, 167
Vaughan, J., 201, 202, 210
Ver, r., 171
Vergil, Polydore, 23, 170
Verulam, 171
Virgil, 20, 23, 181
Virginia, 82

WAlbancke, Matthew, 198
Walton, Izaak, 205, 217
Ward, John, 141
Warham, William, 222
Warner, William, 90
Warwick, 13, 14
— College of St Mary, 25
Warwick, Ambrose Dudley, Earl of, 70
— Lady (Penelope), 208
— Robert Dudley, Earl of, see Leicester
— Robert Rich, Earl of, 208
Watling Street, 1, 3, 5, 7
Watson, Foster, 21
Webster, John, 104
Weever, John, 90, 98–9, 144
Welcombe enclosures, 200
Westminster Abbey, 150, 214, 219, 221
Wetherley, 5, 7
Whitaker, Lemuel, 111
Whitehall, 76
William Longsword, 103, 106
Williams, F. B., 98
— John, 95, 127, 169
Willington, Thomas, 13
Willoughby, Anne, 206
— Sir Henry, 206
Wilson, Elkin C., 135
— Felix, 114
— John, 164
— Robert, 102–3, 206
— Mr, 187
Wilton, 90
Winchester, 167
Winchester, 4th Marquis of, 77
Winstanley, William, 139, 221
Wither, George, 76, 134, 160, 195–6
Wolsey, Cardinal, 103–5, 216
Wood, Anthony, 21, 121, 221
Woodforde, Thomas, 113–7, 119, 120
Woodland, the Warwickshire, 5
Woodward, priest, 179
Wotton, Sir Henry, 183
Wright, Henry, 178
Wroxall, 37
Wyatt, Sir Thomas, 22, 176
Wyatt's (Sir Thomas, the Younger) rebel-
lion, 13
Wycliffe, 23
Wylles, — 35
Wyndham, George, 142

YOung, Bartholomew, 108

ZEno, 23
Zutphen, battle of, 30, 41